BLOOD CROWN

ELIZABETH BROWN
TORRI HEAT

Chapter Art by Jeanne Bradley

Edited By: Elemental Editing & Proofreading

Cover by Fantastical Ink.

❀ Created with Vellum

ACKNOWLEDGMENTS

Acknowledgements: Elizabeth

First and foremost, I need to thank Torri for being an *amazing* writing partner. This whole thing started on a crazy whim and I couldn't be more thrilled with how it ended. I'm so glad we're friends and that we're going to keep working together. Love you lady!

Julia—I'm sorry I drive you nuts. You are literally the *best* PA a girl could ever ask for. I love you. Seriously.

Jamie—Thank you for telling me you needed more steam in your life. You are the reason I felt the need to put spice in every single chapter. I also just love the shit out of you.

My husband and son—You two are my rocks. I honestly couldn't have even started this insane journey without you guys. You gave me the courage and support I needed to make all of this possible.

And, as always, to my readers, ladies I love you all so freakin' much. I've seen comments about how you wanted more dick... so I decided to give you *all of the dick*. No joke.

To the people who know me IRL—I'm a romance writer... There are going to be books that are a bit more smut-filled than others. This is one of those books that, if you don't like sex in your book, you should *not* read the book. While I appreciate the support, I don't need you making shit weird. Mmkay?

Acknowledgements: Torri

For every strong woman who's been looking for themself in the wrong places.

For my mother, who raised me to be a strong woman.

For my daughter, who I'm raising to be a strong woman.

And for Beth, Petty, and the Ricers -- some of the strongest women I know.

TRIGGER WARNINGS

Please note that the authors are not responsible for any children begot as a result of reading this book.

If you are triggered by:

- Kidnapping
- Torture
- Discussions of Rape (no actual rape takes place! All sex in this book is consensual)
- Explicit Sex
- Gore

Turn back now

Pronunciation Guide

ASHERA: A·SHEER·A

MALACHI: MA·LUH·KAI

JACOBI: JA·CO·BI

DUNYA: DOON·YAH

SHAYTAN: SHAY·TAN

MASAS: MAH·SAS

MALAK: MAL·LAC

JUNIYA: JU·NEE·YAH

QAMAR: KAH·MAR

SAHIRA: SA·HERE·A

Shaytan

Qamar

Malak

Juniya

Sahira

Masas

Dunya

1

ASHERA

Bathing in the blood of one's enemies was an invigorating way to start the day. Unfortunately, this morning required me to forgo my morning ritual of having the former oppressors of Shaytan fill my tub. Today was the day the envoys would arrive from the other five kingdoms that were still as backward as mine had once been. Needless to say, I was not overjoyed to meet them.

I stood in front of the floor-to-ceiling mirror and carefully inspected myself. I needed to dress the part for my visitors' arrival. As a succubus queen, I intended to portray power and lust—two things no man could ignore. My dress was constructed from sheer, golden fabric that was held together at my shoulders by a series of small black pearls. It cascaded down my body in two small panels just big enough to cover most of my breasts while still allowing the shadows of my nipples to show. An intricately beaded belt was slung low on my hips, below which the dress fell to the floor in a single sweep of fabric. I looked very much like the succubus I was. The pearls at my shoulders formed small caps that clinked lightly when I walked. It felt like armor, all the while looking like a trick.

My biceps were adorned with three blood-red bands, a clear display of my skill on the battlefield. Most of the other royals had never seen action in real life. They had been handed a crown because they had been born to the right parents, while I had earned my place spilling the blood of men like them.

The most important item on my body was the small golden circlet that graced my brow. I refused to wear something so ostentatious as the crown worn by Shaytan's previous ruler. His head now swayed on a pike on the main bridge leading to the palace, along with other members of the nobility who refused to free their slaves. The monstrosity he wore had already been melted down to create my circlet. That didn't mean I wasn't one for spectacles though. My thighs were encircled with diamond garters that held two forearm-length daggers, and my plaited hair had gold, diamond, and ruby beads woven into it. I appeared much like any other deadly creature—stunning enough to draw you in without realizing the danger.

I knew the envoys would be comprised mostly of princes or the kings themselves. Whether they openly presented themselves as such was another matter entirely. I'd learned much about their kingdoms during my preparation to seize control of the demon's territory. Going into a coup for a kingdom as extensive as Shaytan would have been a suicide mission without having adequate knowledge of everything that went into keeping the people inside the borders alive, and more importantly, free. Besides, I had ample time to prepare.

From whispers in the castle, I'd gleaned that the other rulers weren't pleased a woman now sat on the throne, and they certainly weren't happy I'd freed all the slaves in Shaytan. They knew that single act could cause rebellion in their own kingdoms. I hoped it did. And maybe one day, if their people didn't do it on their own, I'd give them a hand. Honestly, I wasn't sure what bothered the kings more, but I had a sneaking suspicion it was the lack of cock between my legs that was most unsettling.

Heavy footsteps echoed in the chamber, and I knew who it was without having to look—Malachi, my top general and closest friend. He'd been with me since the beginning. As an elite assassin in the former king's army, he'd surprised me when he had drunkenly confessed that he didn't agree with the slave trade either. Many in the king's army didn't. In fact, it appeared that only Shaytan's nobility had wanted the practice to continue. I'd needed help, and he'd needed a push.

I glanced over as he moved into the room. He walked with the grace of a man who knew the best ways to kill you, and it had always stirred my succubus. It didn't hurt that he was gorgeous. At a little over seven feet, he was the tallest male I knew. He had muscles for days and large, bat-like wings topped with wickedly sharp talons. His dark olive skin always made me think of summer days and that one time we'd gone skinny dipping before we'd started our army. His honey-colored eyes warmed as he looked me over, and I licked my lips, watching his gaze track the motion like a predator stalking its prey. Large horns flowed seamlessly from his hairline and curved down toward his ears before arching back up into deadly points. His hair was tied back in a messy bun, making my fingers itch to pull the strands loose. He always looked better when he was a little messy.

"Ashera." His low timbre had heat pooling between my legs. "Not covered in blood, I see."

"Mal," I responded with a smile. He grinned at me as he took me in again, arching a dark brow as he examined my outfit. "I didn't have time this morning."

"So you're going to try to kill them?"

I laughed, smoothing out my dress. "What makes you say that?" I glanced at myself in the mirror. "This is perfectly acceptable for a succubus queen."

I didn't miss the eye roll. "For a succubus, I swear..." Mal chuckled and shook his head. "Don't let them rattle you."

I searched his gaze before I nodded. "I won't."

"Good. I'll be monitoring who is coming and going." Mal bowed and turned to leave, stopping at the doorway. "Are you keeping your glamor up?"

I shrugged. "For now. What they don't know won't hurt them." The glamor he was referring to hid my wings and horns —signs of a truly powerful succubus. I preferred to keep any signs of my differences under wraps and use that to my advantage.

Mal pressed his lips together tightly and walked out the door, muttering about blood flow to different body parts regardless of the glamor. He was older than me, although not by much—450 years to my 325—but sometimes he acted as though it was a millennium.

I sighed. Mal had always kept our relationship distant and friendly, much to my annoyance, but it was reassuring to know he had my back today. I knew, without a doubt, that he would kill anyone who dared to hurt me. He certainly wouldn't allow any of the envoys to try anything stupid while they were here.

"Your Highness." A servant entered my bedchamber, pulling me from my thoughts. She held her head high, and her eyes met mine. A flash of pride surged through me at the sight. Before me, before my rule, a servant would have been killed for merely lifting their gaze off the floor. "The first envoy is here."

"I'll be down shortly. Have them shown to the throne room." She bowed her head in acknowledgment and left.

She was one of the many slaves I'd freed immediately upon gaining control of the kingdom. They had been given the choice to either work under better conditions in the same job they'd had, paid of course, or find a new position that suited them better. Grateful, most of them remained in the castle. Thank the gods for that. Even growing up working at one of the small manor houses, I would have never known where to begin in taking care of an entire castle. I was better at delegating, divvying up jobs, and making sure people were in the roles they were most successful at. In fewer words, I was born to be a queen.

The kingdom still needed individuals to work, but I refused to allow any more slaves to wither away in chains all because they were mortal. Dunya, our realm, functioned based on the separation of the two factions. On one side were beings like me, the immortals—fae, shifters, vampires, angels, witches, and demons. We all lived in our own separate kingdoms, and we all used different kinds of the same magic. We could perform basic magic as well as our own unique magic based on our species. On the other side of our realm were the mortals—humans. They were the beings the immortals enslaved to do the dirty work they didn't want to do themselves.

I was disgusted by the thought. Just because my kind, and those of the nobility and royalty of the other kingdoms, could live for centuries without aging and humans could not, that did not mean mortals' lives held less value. If anything, they lived life with far more passion than our kind ever could. Less time to live meant more desire to make each moment count. One day, when I had a moment or two to breathe, I hoped to experience that kind of passion in my own life.

I looked at myself one last time in the mirror, a pleased grin spreading across my face. The envoys, all men, would see a partially naked woman on the throne. It was a big part of why I was keeping the glamor in place—I *wanted* them to underestimate me. I wanted them to assume I'd merely slept my way to the front of the rebellion despite the bands on my arm. I would relish the looks on their faces when I proved just how wrong they were.

I walked through my palace, the usual contradiction of feelings rushing through me. The palace of Shaytan was beautiful, decorated in the styles of the old world, but the memories of who built it, maintained it, were ones I'd like to forget.

The floors were white marble, reflecting the smooth golden walls on their gleaming surfaces. All the doors were a rich wood, cut from the Forest of the Void that bordered our kingdom, and ornately carved with the history of Shaytan—in other words, they were made from wood hewn by slaves which had then been sculpted by slaves and depicted the history of slavery as something to be celebrated. They were next on my list to burn. Unlike most palaces, we had no ornaments on display. When our coup was successful, I had given those pieces of gold and silver to my men to do with as they pleased. Some brought them home to their mates as trophies. Others used them as target practice.

My footsteps were silent as I made my way to the throne room, my bare feet allowing me to move around the palace like a ghost. Demons typically needed skin-to-skin contact to receive or give power, which meant most of us walked around fully clothed. Succubi and incubi in particular used touch to feed off of sexual energy and to restore our magical stores. We didn't want anyone siphoning our power without permission. My outfit had a dual purpose—seduction and a blatant invitation to attempt to take my power. I'd like to see them fucking try.

I stopped in front of the throne room—this door depicted one of the old lords on the throne as a young slave placed a crown atop his head. Another servant stood just outside, proud and at attention. I turned to face the young man. "Do you know which envoy has arrived?" I inquired.

"Masas, Your Highness." He gave me a soft smile. *Masas.* I thought back to my research. From what I could remember, Masas was ruled by an ancient vampire—one of the first. Tomas, I believed his name was. I would expect him to go for the power rather than the seduction. I straightened my shoulders. *Let's see this old vamp try to touch me.*

My back was straight, and my head was held high as my

name was announced and the doors were slowly opened. The new nobility I'd handpicked to help me lead this kingdom into a new era were stationed around the room. They bowed their heads as I entered. I tried telling them it wasn't necessary, but it was of no use. Today, however, it worked to my advantage. My people respected me. I walked toward my throne, which was elegant and simple in the ornate room. I had burned the original throne, not wanting to sit in the same place as slaveholders. In front of my throne, with his back to me, stood Tomas. His black cloak was long and oddly unpretentious. I had thought the vampires were lavish in their clothing.

I kept my eyes forward and sat on my throne, draping the pieces of my dress around me. I wouldn't greet him before I was ready. I needed Masas on my side because they ruled with both money and an iron fist. I forced a sensual smile on my face and finally looked at the vampire waiting for my acknowledgment.

I nearly choked. In front of me was not the decrepit, wrinkly creature I was expecting. Instead, one of the most beautiful creatures I had ever seen stood before me. His skin was the purest ivory, like the first snowfall of winter. His black hair was thick and lush, curling softly around his neck and ears. He was easily over six feet tall, but his frame was heavily muscled. While not nearly as tall as Malachi, the vampire had just as many delicious muscles. I wanted to drool, and a familiar ache crept between my legs. *Focus, Ashera, focus.* And then my gaze met his.

A pair of blood-red, cold eyes stared back at me. There was no warmth in his gaze. I wasn't sure if he wanted to kill me or eat me. *Maybe both...* The image of him feasting between my thighs as blood trickled out of the corner of his mouth sharpened the ache between my legs.

I forced myself to remain in control. I hadn't taken over a whole godsdamn kingdom of demons to be shaken by a vamp. "Where is Tomas?"

The vampire's expression didn't shift. "Tomas is too sickly to travel. He sent me in his stead."

I sighed, trying not to let my annoyance show on my face. Was a straight answer really too much to ask for? "And you are?" My mask of cool, detached sensuality slipped with my desperation to know who this handsome stranger—staring at me with such hatred—was. The succubus in me was already stirring. That cold, hate-filled gaze made me want to fuck the hate right out of him.

"Ambrose." His voice was a low rumble, each syllable sending a shockwave of desire to my core. The Crown Prince of Masas. Obviously, it had been too long since my last fling. With the war going on, my desires had taken a backseat, which was difficult for a succubus since we thrived on touch and connection—sex. My mouth watered as I imagined the rush of power that would flood my body with another's release. *What would a vampire feel like?* I mused. I *needed* to know...

I allowed my power to fill me, releasing pheromones into the room. All the unmated males leaned in. I knew the moment Ambrose felt my energy, the pupils of his red eyes dilating, but he didn't move or allow himself to give in to the feelings that had to be coursing through his body. *What the hell?* He had shaken me, and while I wanted nothing more than to ride him on this very throne, I needed to regain some control.

I slid my hands down my body as I leaned forward, maintaining eye contact with the arrogant vampire. His gaze flicked from my hands back to my eyes almost faster than I could track. A slow, seductive smile curled my lips, and I flicked my tongue out to drag it along my full bottom lip.

"Ambrose." My voice was a husky purr. Everything about me was meant to seduce. Tempt. Torture. I stood, making my way over to him with rolling hips and swaying limbs. "It's certainly a pleasure to have you in my kingdom, and I'm so glad you provided your name." I trailed my fingers down his chest as I stepped close. "It would be a terrible shame if a nameless vampire were to go missing in my kingdom."

∽

Ambrose

WHEN I'D HEARD a woman had staged a successful coup against Shaytan's king, I'd laughed. I was sure the other princes and kings laughed as well. In my 400 plus years, a woman had never ruled—they'd never been powerful enough. Whoever was spreading rumors like that was bored out of their mind.

But then, to my shock and horror, the rumors turned out to be true. I needed to see her for myself. Surely she had been a concubine who had gotten lucky enough to murder the former ruler in his sleep. She'd be weak and easily manipulated or overthrown. Either way, it would be a significant gain for Masas when I returned with the queen under my thumb.

My father was nearing the end of his exceptionally long life, thank the gods, and wanted nothing to do with the typical diplomatic envoy that was sent after a transfer of power. I could have sent trusted men in my place, but I was too curious. I needed to go myself. It was possible I'd be able to drain the new queen dry while I fucked her—not to kill though, as it would be easier to rule through the queen—get a mild power boost from her blood, and then be on my way home.

I was sure the other kingdoms would be sending their kings or princes hidden within their envoys as well. I wasn't the only one who would want to put an end to the queen's rule before she'd even really begun. I would need to connect with Masas' allies, because it would be easier to kill her if one of us could get between her thighs—preferably me.

I'd already been on the road when word reached me that the new queen, Ashera, had freed all the slaves in Shaytan. My gaze had bounced to all the slaves traveling with me and my men. They were blood slaves, and we needed them for power. We could feed off each other, or even other species—if we wanted a more powerful boost—but the act of giving and taking blood was something only done between trusted individuals or on the battlefield.

Disgust filled me at the thought of freeing our blood slaves —or *any* of our slaves, for that matter. How this *queen* thought she could keep an entire country running without the labor they provided baffled me. Not only could this cause a widespread economic collapse, but if word spread about her freed slaves, it could prove ruinous for the other kingdoms. There would be countless rebellions to quell.

We were shown to a large suite of rooms when we finally arrived at the Shaytan palace. I was surprised to see people still running the place. Had she really not freed her slaves? Upon closer examination, I discovered that they no longer wore the collar that symbolized their status. My eyes narrowed in thought. *How the fuck had she gotten them to stay?*

Not bothering to dress in accordance with my station to confuse the little queen, I donned a simple black cloak over my black slacks and shirt. I instructed my men to stay in the suite while I went to meet with the monarch—no need for us all to suffer.

I was shown to the throne room and made to wait with the new nobility of Shaytan. While I'd never been particularly friendly with anyone from this kingdom, I knew a few faces from court. Most now lined the bridge into the palace, along with the former king and his consorts. Such a waste of blood. There were still a few here I recognized, so it seemed she hadn't cleaned house entirely.

When her presence was finally announced, I turned my back in a clear display of disrespect. I made her wait for my full attention. Curiosity, however, won the day. When I saw her sitting upon her throne, my breath stilled in my lungs, my cock hardened, and I felt a savage urge to *mark* that unblemished flesh with my fangs. I immediately hated her for the response she ripped out of my body.

And yet... I couldn't tear my eyes away. She was a goddess in gold. Her garment—if you could even call it that—played to her succubus heritage, showing off her supple curves, generous breasts, and smooth golden skin that seemed to shimmer against the fabric she wore. Her bright green eyes betrayed her surprise as she looked at me before they heated to reveal her hunger.

Gods be damned... My cock hardened further as we continued to gaze at one another.

"Where is Tomas?" she purred.

Even her voice was seductive. Just hearing it made me want to see those lush, full lips wrapped around me as she sucked me dry.

I remained outwardly stoic, even as my mind rebelled and desire weighed heavily in my veins. "Tomas is too sickly to travel. He sent me in his stead."

The sigh that left her lips had me biting back a smirk. She didn't like that I hadn't told her who I was, nor did she like that Tomas wasn't in attendance. Best of all, she had no idea who she was dealing with.

"And you are?"

Your fucking master, little queen. She just didn't know it yet. "Ambrose." I inhaled, and the scent of her blood and arousal had my fangs dropping in my mouth. I wanted to sink my fangs into one of those lush thighs before I buried my tongue in her sweet pussy. I'd make her beg for release.

Suddenly, her power washed over me as she released pheromones into the room. *Fuck me sideways.* I forced myself to remain still as every instinct screamed for me to wrap my hand around her slender throat as I buried myself inside her, pinning her to the wall. Better yet, I'd take her in front of all these other assholes. It would certainly show them that she belonged to me.

Something fierce and feral rose within me, snarling and snapping to be unleashed. I'd never had this strong of a reaction to a woman before. It was possible I'd gone too long between fucks. Even other succubi had never had this sort of impact on me, but this little queen... I wanted to own her.

She drifted her hands down her body, bringing my attention to her full breasts and erect nipples before I dragged my gaze back to her face. That feral beast within me fought to surface, needing to bend her over my knee and redden her ass for teasing me.

"Ambrose." Her voice was low and husky, making my cock twitch. She stood and made her way to me, her every step causing her hips and breasts to sway enticingly. "It's certainly a pleasure to have you in my kingdom. I'm so glad you provided your name." Her fingers trailed down my chest as light as a whisper. "It would be a terrible shame if a nameless vampire were to go missing in my kingdom."

A dark chuckle rumbled through my chest. In a flash, I had my hand wrapped around the back of her neck, and I pulled her flush against me. I tightened my fingers possessively around her. I could feel everyone around us stiffen in shock, but it didn't faze me. "It's not wise to threaten me."

The little queen's eyes darkened with desire, but she didn't pull away or fight my hold. She also didn't attempt to siphon any of my power where our skin touched. She was either too weak to do so, or too cocky. Either was a mistake. "And it's not wise to underestimate me," she replied.

I could have been mistaken, but the little queen almost sounded amused. It was adorable, really. She stood before me in little more than scraps of cloth, and yet, despite the possessiveness of my grip, she wasn't trying to break my hold on her, nor was she attempting to pull any power from me. But I was underestimating her? I scoffed at the thought. No. I could read her far better than she realized, and what I saw made me hungry for the taste of her surrender as her luscious body writhed beneath me, my thick cock demanding nothing less than her absolute submission.

I was thinking too much with the wrong brain. I wanted this *queen*—as she called herself—too much. I would have to keep my desires tightly in check to accomplish what I needed during my time here. I released my grip on her smooth, glowing skin, and once again turned my back on her. I was in control here, and I needed to make sure no one forgot that. I faced her ragtag court of what were once slaves. Now what were they? Free? Disgusting. Such a thing would never come to fruition in Masas. I would make sure of that. "Ashera."

"Queen Ashera," she corrected. The voice behind me was quiet but sure. She was bolder than she let on. Strength rippled through the air between us.

So the little queen's come out to play.

I stole a quick glance over my shoulder. Ashera hadn't moved, but her entire court seemed to hang on her every word. She had either actually earned their respect, or she was a bit of a loose cannon. I was going to assume the latter.

"Queen Ashera. Masas has sent me here as a delegate to meet the new ruler, and to also create a new treaty between our two great kingdoms." I paused, and a few of her servants peeked up at me. I couldn't believe her humans had the nerve to meet the gaze of a creature better than them. I sneered, letting my fangs drop into view, and those few brave souls quickly looked back at the floor.

"I, too, am hoping to continue the relationship between our territories," Ashera began. "But I have a request in order to build this treaty."

A request? This new queen, this *woman* with no royal blood, had a request? Did she not understand how these things worked? Annoyance flooded my veins, followed by a singular thought. *I need to teach her some respect.* I could see her now, tied up to my headboard with those luscious curves on display as I showed her what it meant to truly respect a prince. But I would humor her for the time being. "And your request would be?"

~

Ashera

IT WAS OFFICIAL. Ambrose was a prick. My traitorous body wanted to do unspeakable things to him, but he was still a prick. His visit was going to be hell, and my demands were not going to make it any easier on either of us, but they were not up for discussion. And Prince Ambrose of the Pricks still had his back to me.

That wouldn't last long. I knew who was really in control here—even as something ancient and long since forgotten inside me called to him. I needed Masas on my side. They worked the mines, providing resources for our buildings and money for our banks. That didn't mean I was going to make it simple for him, however.

"Free the slaves of Masas. Allow them to work for you for a fair wage. Give them the opportunity to build their own lives."

Ambrose whipped back around to face me. "Absolutely not. Who will work the mines if not for the slaves?" If his gaze had been cold and unfeeling before, it was absolutely murderous now. Another man who's frightened of change and a woman in power. Typical.

"You *will* free the slaves of Masas, or we will have no relationship to form a treaty around." I should have zapped his power when I had the chance. Not because I needed it, but just to make him suffer. Prick.

Ambrose ran a large hand through his hair, making the carefully arranged curls stand up in awkward places. I liked him better this way. *Messy.* "Ashera. Queen Ashera. That will not happen. In fact, if you want to have a lasting relationship with Masas, then I recommend you reinstate the practice of human slavery. Immediately."

A collective gasp sounded throughout the throne room, and people immediately began to whisper nervously to each other. I held my hand up for silence, and the chatter quieted down. "Shaytan will never again own another human. Not now. Not ever."

"Then you will fall and your people will be forced back into slavery whether you like it or not." Ambrose's tone was frigid, and for a brief moment, I imagined it thawing as he slid inside me. He wouldn't sound so cold and distant when I fed off of him.

I lashed out with my fingers and wrapped them around the vampire prince's cool wrist. "Clearly we need to have this discussion in private. I won't have you upsetting my entire court." My tone was harsh and reprimanding, as though I were talking to a child.

I dragged him out of the throne room to a small study nearby. He was still and seemed surprised that I could force him to move. *Idiot. I'm stronger than I look.* I quickly closed and locked the door behind us before whirling on him, not bothering to hide my wrath.

"If you so much as *think* to threaten my people again—"

"You'll what?" Ambrose challenged in a low, mocking tone as he herded me against the door, bracing both arms on either side of my body to box me in. "What will you do, *little queen?*"

My fury rose, and I needed to take a deep breath before I could answer him. "Don't think I won't fight with everything Shaytan has, everything I have, to keep my people safe."

"And what is it, exactly, that you have?"

I wanted to rip the condescending smirk off his beautiful, annoying face. Instead, I pushed him away from me and relished the look of surprise that quickly flitted across his features before he stalked me over to the table in the center of the room. His low growl was like a flick to my clit, and I clenched my thighs in response.

"Answer me, little queen," he snarled.

I curved my lips in a condescending smile as I spoke two words that would always make men lose their godsdamn minds. "Make me."

In a flash, he was behind me, slamming my front to the top of the table as his hand fisted in my hair. I stiffened, but the air around him didn't feel hostile. It throbbed with heat. Besides, I knew that if I didn't want this, hadn't planned this, I would have him on his back before he could blink. I bit back a smirk, knowing I'd snapped the prick's control.

"Wrong answer," Ambrose growled against my ear before pulling back.

The sound of his hand meeting my ass registered mere seconds before I felt the hot sting of the slap, and pleasure flooded my veins. With the way my dress fell, he didn't even need to shift the back panel to gain access to the flesh there.

He struck again, this time on the other side, and I bit back a moan, trying to force my hips to remain still as he continued his assault. Ambrose tightened his fist in my hair as he moved the rear panel of my dress and widened my legs. I shivered as my hips lifted with a mind of their own.

"Now you're going to be a good little queen and tell me that you want my cock buried deep in this wet little pussy of yours." His hand roughly massaged the flesh of my ass before his fingers skimmed the seam of my core. A small, breathy gasp forced its way past my lips.

I didn't need to feed directly from him with all the sexual energy in the air, so I started pulling from that. I planned to save feasting on him for later. I wanted him to think he'd bested me, that he'd made the Queen of Shaytan his slut. I knew how to play a man and his body to get what I wanted. Just because I'd slaughtered all those who'd stood in my way in the past didn't mean I had to. I planned to take a more... delicate approach to the other kingdoms. At least for the time being.

Ambrose pulled me up, so my back was flush against his chest. His magic swirled around my nipples, and I bit my lip at the sensation. He licked my neck before whispering in my ear. "Tell me, Ashera. You know you want me to own your pussy. I can smell how aroused you are." He nibbled on my ear, and I shivered.

"Do it," I bit out. My chest was once more slammed against the table, and Ambrose's hand returned to my core. I widened my stance and thrust my hips back against him.

He worked two fingers inside me and started to circle my clit with his thumb. I moaned at the pleasure building deep inside my core and moved in time with the thrusts of his fingers.

"Good girl, ride my fingers." I did as he demanded, working my hips against his slender digits as a third slipped in to join the others. "You're so damn tight and wet, little queen. My cock might just ruin you."

"Promise, promises," I taunted.

A low snarl met my ears as he ripped his fingers away from me. The sound of rustling fabric followed before the blunt tip of his cock nudged against my opening. His magic never once left my nipples, continuing to tease me as he readied himself. The hand not buried in my hair roughly gripped my hips. We stayed that way, pausing as both of us sucked in deep lungfuls of air before he slammed to the hilt inside me.

Gods. The sting was so good, and it had been too long. I cried out, long and loud, as he started to set a relentless pace, not giving my body time to adjust. Every few strokes, his hand would slap my ass, and he'd release a feral sounding snarl when my pussy clamped around his cock in response.

Once again, he yanked me up by my hair, but this time he abandoned my golden locks. Sliding his hand down my body, Ambrose began pinching my nipples. He used his other hand to lift one of my legs and prop it on the table before attacking my clit. I rested my head against his shoulder as pleasure rushed through every nerve ending in my body.

"Who is your fucking master?"

My eyes snapped open. *Did he just...*

"Who?" he ground out against my ear as his pace became more frantic.

Absolutely not. In a blink, I turned on him, and his eyes flared with shock as I tackled him to the ground. I pinned his arms down on either side of his head as I slammed my hips down against his, forcing his cock deeper with this new angle.

"I don't think you realize who is actually in charge here, *Prince* Ambrose." Instead of setting a similar brutal pace, I rocked my hips slowly against his, dragging his cock out so he felt every inch of my pussy clenching around him.

He gritted his jaw as he glared up at me, his hips arching beneath me in an attempt to urge me to move faster. I kept my pace tortuously slow and rejoiced when his eyes practically rolled into the back of his head as I purposely clamped around him.

I stopped moving my hips, leaving us flush against one another as I lowered my chest to his. I kept pulsing around his cock, and he let out a low groan. Nibbling lightly on his ear, I breathed, "Who is *your* master?"

He pushed me off him, the two of us panting and staring at one another before he pounced again. Ambrose closed his hand around my throat as he slammed my back into the wall. I distantly heard something—more than one something—smash against the floor. I lifted my legs and locked them around his hips as he plunged back into me.

"I'm going to fuck that attitude right out of you," he snarled against my cheek. He kept his hand around my throat as he once again set a brutal pace.

"I'd love to see you try." I turned my head and nipped his ear. That only served to make him piston his hips faster, harder. "Is this the best you have?" I laughed quietly.

We were moving again, and my back was pressed against the table as Ambrose stood above me. He tightened his hand around my throat as the sound of slick flesh slapping together filled the room. His gaze blazed with hunger, and the succubus in me rose at the sight. I was still feeding off the energy in the room, waiting for the right time to feed directly from him.

Ambrose moved his other hand back to my clit, and I felt my orgasm build inside me. "You're going to drench my cock, little queen. We aren't leaving here until you can't walk for at least a week. The only thought on your mind will be how to get me to fuck you all over again, and then you'll know exactly whom you belong to."

My pussy fluttered around him even though I chafed at his words. "I belong to no one."

He chuckled, the sound a caress against my aching nipples. "That's where you're wrong. You belong to *me*."

Despite my ruffled feathers at his blatant possessiveness, I shattered. My scream as I came echoed around the room. Ambrose groaned as he continued to thrust deep inside me, moving my legs so they were up on his shoulders. The angle allowed his cock to slide even deeper inside me, prolonging my orgasm.

"Now let's see if we can get you to scream my name, little queen," he growled as he gripped my legs and continued to pound into me.

I bit my lip until I tasted the metallic tang of my blood. He was relentless, but two could play at this game. I released more pheromones into the air.

With a viciously feral snarl, Ambrose crawled onto the table above me, and his red gaze seemed to glow as the new angle allowed him to thrust harder. He slammed his hands down on the table on either side of my head, the wood groaning loudly on impact. I gripped his hair as I pulled him down for our lips to clash.

He was just as aggressive when he kissed. We battled for dominance with our mouths, sucking, licking, and nipping. He became more frenzied at the taste of my blood from when I'd bit my lip a moment ago. The table beneath us creaked loudly with each thrust.

"What the fuck is going on?" Malachi's snarl broke us apart, but Ambrose didn't bother to stop his thrusts as we both turned our heads to look at the two males now standing just inside the door. One was Malachi, and the other was a man I had never seen before. He was tall, between Ambrose's and Malachi's heights, and blond, with thick white wings and stunning sapphire blue eyes. My hips tilted on their own, causing both of us to groan, and Malachi snarled violently while the male at his side merely watched us with wide eyes.

"Would you care for a turn?" Ambrose taunted, his hips never missing a beat. "It seems that fucking the royal cunt is the best way to get what you want."

My vision turned red. *Fucking the royal cunt is the best way to get what he wants, huh?* I watched with a sense of sick joy as both Malachi and the other male stiffened, instantly knowing that Ambrose had said the wrong thing. Malachi's growl increased in volume, while the other male's wings fluttered and a savage look marred his extremely handsome face.

I moved my hands from Ambrose's hair to his throat as I spun us so fast he didn't have a chance to react. Since we were plastered together, I started to hungrily and aggressively drain him. His eyes went wide as he felt me pull the magic and power from him at every point our bodies touched. I leaned down to lick his ear, feeling his cock jerk inside me.

"The royal cunt is hungry," I whispered against him. "And you're damn lucky there are witnesses here to prevent me from draining you dry." With that, I extracted myself, readjusted my dress, and walked over to Malachi and the other male.

With a stunning smile that had the male blinking down at me, I asked, "And who is this?"

"Jacobi, King of Malak," Malachi murmured, his eyes glued to Ambrose who remained on the table behind me. "If you'll take him to the throne room, my queen, I'll take care of the trash."

When Malachi's gaze met mine, I was surprised by just how much rage there was in their depths. I studied him for a moment before turning back to Jacobi. "Of course." I smiled again and led the angel king out of the room. The sound of flesh beating flesh rang out after us.

2

JACOBI

I knew I was meeting the first queen our realm had ever seen. I had heard the stories of how she overthrew the demon rulers who came before her, doing away with the practice of human slavery that was overly prevalent in most regions. I knew that to throw a coup of that magnitude, she would have to be bold, strong, and probably ridiculously powerful.

What I wasn't expecting, however, was Ashera. I hadn't anticipated how beautiful she would be or how strongly her body would call to mine. I hadn't realized I would be walking into her... making love with another male. If you could call it that. I think "fucking" was what people called it these days. And with a vamp, of all creatures. Yet I couldn't tear my eyes away from the scene and the way her golden hair was splayed around her in a halo as the vampire thrust away inside her.

Gods. Years of practicing celibacy allowed me to perfect my control over my wants and desires. It was expected of me as King of Malak. Not all kings did so, but I had taken a vow when I ascended to the throne. I wanted to be pure, a shining beacon of what ultimate control looked like. But when I saw him, his hard cock diving deep into her soaked folds, and heard the moans slipping between her full pink lips... *gods*. I now had a raging hard-on and no way to get rid of it, not with Queen Ashera herself sashaying down the golden hallways to the throne room. Her dress left little to the imagination, all curves and sinewy muscles. Yes, she was strong—of that I was certain —but damn. She was the most beautiful woman I had ever seen. She looked like the mermaids our sailors brought back tales of. I subtly rearranged myself behind my pale linen trousers—the standard in Malak, but not the wisest of clothing choices to hide the boner of an overexcited twelve-year-old. I was pure. What was wrong with me? Was I jealous of the vampire fucking her, or did I want to join in?

"Sorry, what was that?" Ashera's voice was a golden melody filled with humor.

Shit. Had I spoken aloud? Fuck, now I was swearing. Double shit. Ugh. An hour in Shaytan, and all my morals were already out the window. Next thing I knew, I would be screwing the queen on her throne while her entire court watched.

Where the hell had that come from? Purity, Jacobi. Purity. Strength. Morals. I had survived hundreds of years by focusing on that motto, so surely I could handle a few days in the presence of a succubus.

"Nothing, Your Highness. Just trying to remember the words to a song." *Gods.* What was happening to me? That was the best response I could come up with?

Ashera glanced back at me, tossing her golden hair over her shoulder. She gave me a sly smirk as if she knew what I was thinking. "Well, hopefully you remember it. The throne room is right up here."

At the mention of the throne room, my cock instantly stood at attention again. I wouldn't even need to strip that dress off her to have my way. She could keep it on, that and those bands of jewels around her arms designating her as a warrior. She could keep it all on, and I would worship every inch of her smooth skin. First with my hands, then with my mouth, and those sounds she had made for the vamp... she would make them for me tenfold. *What kind of sounds would she make if we had our way together? Fuck.* Morals. Morals needed to be front and center, not visualizing the vamp tweaking Ashera's perfectly pink nipples while I feasted on what I imagined to be a flawless pussy between her legs. Not that I had ever seen one, celibacy and all that, but I was certain it would be perfect.

I just needed to focus on the meeting. We made our way through the throne room, empty except for a few servants—no longer slaves—prepping the room for the formal dinner we'd be having later this evening. Ashera took her seat, and I kneeled before her.

"Your Highness. The kingdom of Malak has come to offer you its gratitude for the liberation of your slaves," I began, keeping my head low out of respect.

"Please, Jacobi, there's no need for formality between friends. And I expect we'll be friends. Ashera is fine." She gave me another bright smile, and I felt a spark of electricity shoot right to my cock. Purity. Purity, morals, and... What was the last one again? But then her smile fell, and her voice grew cold. "They were never my slaves. I simply gave them back what was theirs in the first place."

"I apologize, Your High—Ashera." I rolled the name around on my tongue. It flowed, curved, and filled my mouth the way I imagined her full breasts would as well. I groaned, shaking my head to rid my mind of the image. "I apologize. Regardless, you have our respect. Malak would be honored to continue a trade relationship with Shaytan."

Ashera stood, walking toward me with careful steps. Her bright green eyes sparkled boldly at me. "That's wonderful news, because I need all the grain Malak can spare. I have a lot more free people who need food this season." Was it just me, or had her voice dropped an octave? She could have all the wheat in Malaks's fields and all the fish in our waters for all I cared. The energy in the room was suddenly palpable. I should use some of my own power and adjust the room to a more neutral atmosphere, but I found myself curious, wondering where this was going. The same way succubi fed off sexual energy, and vampires fed off blood, angels restored our magic through strong emotions. Ashera was close enough for me to reach out and touch. As much as I wanted to touch that smooth, glowing skin, I wouldn't. Couldn't. It wouldn't be right. Would it?

Ashera made the decision for me, dragging one long fingernail down my forearm. The connection between our bodies sent a shiver down my spine before I could control it, and she offered me another smirk. "I saw you watching us, Jacobi. I wonder, do you wish it was you instead of Ambrose? Or were you imagining joining in?"

I sucked in a quiet breath, certain that she was able to read my mind. I had been imagining joining in. The darkness of the vamp captivated me just as much as Ashera's bold beauty. *Ambrose*. Ambrose was his name. Realization dawned—the Prince of Masas. "I'm sure I don't know what you mean, Your High—Ashera."

She withdrew her hand from my arm, tapping a finely boned finger against her lip. "Malakian... Malakian..." Her green eyes widened. "You're celibate!"

I was taught not to be embarrassed of my purity. It was something to be proud of, and for others to strive for in their journey to enlightenment. But when Ashera looked at me, desire blowing her pupils wide, I found myself wishing I was anyone other than myself. If ruling Malak required my purity, I no longer wanted the throne. I'd rather take control of Ashera, body and mind. "Yes, I am."

She raised an eyebrow, and I felt the moment she released an ounce of her power. She was designed for seduction, every part of her built to lead a man down the path of temptation. I was supposed to be above temptation, but I was quickly learning I was no better than any other man. Ashera leaned into my space again, trailing her hand up my neck and into my hair. Gods, her touch was like nothing I'd ever felt. "So you've never felt a woman do this then," she whispered, pressing her lips against my ear.

"No," I murmured. I forced myself to stay still, even though every cell in my body was screaming for me to reach out and touch her, to press her body against mine as I consumed her lips with my own. My cock was so hard, I was sure I would implode from a single touch of her body.

"Or this?" Ashera licked the sensitive skin beneath my neck, and I closed my eyes, focusing on my breath. "Have you ever touched a woman?" She grasped one of my hands, bringing it to cup her full breast. I couldn't stop the groan from exploding out of my chest. It was like something possessed me, and I growled, desperately kneading her breast with my hand. When had I learned to do this?

"Fuck, Ashera. You're too much of a temptation." I bent my head so my lips rested on hers, but I couldn't cross that line. Not yet. I still had my purity. Purity and... Fuck it. I was fairly certain the only thing pure in this world was the feeling of Ashera's body pressed against mine, and I was sure that being inside her would be the closest to heaven I'd ever get.

She smiled against my lips. "Temptation is my middle name. But really, I just know how to get what I want."

I sighed softly, breathing in her delicious, honeyed scent. "You have the kingdom. The throne. The power. What more do you want?"

Ashera opened her mouth to respond, but we were interrupted by a cool voice.

"Ashera, I have an urgent matter I need to speak with you about." Malachi. Her bodyguard.

I wanted to punch him in the face for interrupting us, but I stepped back with a polite smile. Maybe it was for the best. I had maintained most of my purity. Maybe I could keep it that way. "Your Highness, we can hash out the details of the trade negotiations later."

Ashera winked, straightening the folds of her dress as she turned to Malachi. I sighed again, trying to ignore my disappointment. "Oh, and Jacobi?"

"Yes?"

"What I want is you."

Fuck. I was going to hell.

~

Ashera

FEELING the pull toward two men back-to-back like that wasn't something I was used to, especially now that I was standing in front of Malachi, fighting the urge to climb him like a damn tree. To be fair, this wasn't a new feeling with Mal, but he wanted to keep things businesslike, so that was what I did. That didn't mean I wasn't struggling to get my brain back on matters of state. My succubus was demanding that I hunt down Ambrose and Jacobi, lock them in here with Mal and me, and have them fuck me within an inch of my life. My skin was so sensitive that even the brush of the light fabric against my nipples had me battling the urge to moan.

Malachi led me to my bedchamber, a fierce scowl on his face. "I've just received word that there's a potential threat to your rule."

I raised my brow at him, cocking a hip and crossing my arms. "That's what you interrupted me for?"

He bristled, flaring his wings for a moment. His eyes darkened, and he moved to stand chest to chest with me. "A threat to your life is more important than dick, Sher." His tone was a low growl, and since we were so close, I could feel the rumble of that sound against my nipples. I fought the urge to moan again.

I glared up at him. I wanted to argue with him. Though he did have a point, my succubus didn't give a fuck. She was aching and empty, and he'd denied her the chance to ride an angel all the way to heaven. Or hell. I really wasn't picky. "What do you care about me getting dicked?" If he was going to cockblock me, I was going to call him on it.

He snarled and leaned down so close our lips were almost touching. "I can smell how turned on you are."

"Your point?" I so badly wanted to close the distance between our mouths.

"You're allowing those two to distract you," he rumbled. "You have a kingdom to run. You can't get sloppy."

"I couldn't be sloppy if I tried. So, I'll repeat, why do you care?" I knew I was pushing him, but I didn't care. Desire surged through every cell in my body and demanded that I sate it in any way possible.

"Because," he snarled, his gaze now so dark and heated my breath caught, "you're mine." He wrapped my braid around his hand and jerked me against his body. "If you're going to get any dick, it's going to be mine."

It was mildly embarrassing that I whimpered as his mouth crashed against mine. I'd wanted Mal for years. Was my inner hussy making me hallucinate? He traced my lips with his tongue and a shiver raced down my spine. Our tongues started to battle for dominance as he backed me to my bed. Definitely not a hallucination.

He ripped my dress away with his free hand, and then he pulled his mouth from mine. We panted as our lips brushed together. Mal pushed me back on the bed and dropped to his knees, then he slid his large hands up my legs, spreading them wide.

"Smelling your need and not doing anything to ease it has

been driving me mad." Malachi's hot breath teased my core, and my hips bucked in invitation. He skimmed my inner thigh with his lips, forcing a low moan out of my throat.

A commotion from my doorway had me turning my head to see what the problem was. I had no intention of making Mal stop, and it seemed he agreed. My breath hitched when I saw Jacobi and Ambrose flanked by two guards, their backs to me as they stood in front of the royals so they couldn't approach. *What the—*

A loud moan escaped me, and my hips arched as Malachi started to devour me. I wanted to let go of the hold I had on my glamor, just for a moment, but I wasn't ready to share that part of me with everyone. I tangled my hands in his hair, but I couldn't rip my gaze from the two other males by the door. Jacobi seemed uncomfortable at first until I moaned. Now, his heated gaze traveled over my body, stopping with interest at the sight of Mal feasting between my thighs. Ambrose, on the other hand, looked like he was ready to slaughter my guards to get back inside me. A low snarl from Malachi—which caused me to gasp and dig my fingers harder into his hair—stopped Ambrose cold.

He slid two fingers into my core as my assassin licked my clit. My breath hitched when he crooked his digits to hit my G-spot. "Mal." My voice was low and breathy, but I had no doubt the two men by the door heard me. "Don't stop."

A low rumble vibrated against my clit when he growled, and that catapulted me over the edge. I came screaming Mal's name. But he didn't stop. I had a sneaking suspicion Malachi wanted to prove to the two men by the door that he was the alpha male here. His power washed over me, and my back bowed off the bed as my grip on my own power slipped and my arousal flooded the air.

Jacobi's low moan, followed by a feral snarl from Ambrose,

had me coming again, clenching tightly around Malachi's fingers.

Malachi pulled away from my pussy, slowly dragging his fingers out of me before licking them clean. My chest heaved as my gaze bounced from him to the others. Before I could say anything, Malachi had me on my hands and knees facing the door. He gripped my hips tightly as his cock nudged my slick opening.

"Don't you dare close your eyes, Sher." He rubbed himself against me, and I fisted the sheets as I tried to push back against him. "You two are going to watch me fuck her. You're going to watch as she comes on my cock. And then I'm going to show you how I filled her pussy." His command was met with silence, and two sets of eyes remained pinned on me as Malachi eased himself inside me.

He started to thrust shallowly, just the tip of his cock moving back and forth. My pussy clenched around it, and I tried to push back to take more of him, but he wouldn't let me. I whimpered, desperately needing him to thrust to the hilt.

"Tell them, Sher," he ground out as he continued his torture. "Tell them whose cock is inside you right now."

"Yours," I moaned out. A squeak escaped me as his palm slapped my ass before his hand tangled in my hair, pulling back just enough so my throat was bared to the two men at the door.

"My *name*, Sher."

I was having a hard time focusing. He continued his shallow thrusts as my eyes remained locked on Ambrose and Jacobi. Jacobi had his hands clenched tightly at his sides, his cock heavy against his linen pants. I licked my lips in a blatant invitation, and he groaned. Ambrose was stroking himself through his pants as he watched Malachi tease me, and his red eyes almost glowed with heat.

"Sher." Malachi's tone was threatening, and he pulled out

until his tip was rubbing against my opening. I whimpered louder than before.

"Please," I cried. "Malachi."

"That's it, Sher." He slammed home, and my cry of ecstasy filled the room. My eyes were drawn back to Jacobi, our gazes locking as Malachi started to thrust with hard, deep movements. He kept his hand in my hair so my gaze would stay fastened on Jacobi's as his other hand wrapped around my waist. He started to circle my clit with his fingers, and I couldn't stop the moan that burst from my lips.

"Come for me again, Ashera."

Jacobi's almost imperceptible nod had me crying out his name as I came around Malachi. I heard a dark chuckle behind me as the incubus shifted our position, his movements smooth and quick. I was still facing away from him and toward the door, but he was under me. I didn't stop to think about it as I moved my body along his cock.

Mal gripped my hips, and he set the pace. Both Ambrose and Jacobi stood entranced by the sight of my bouncing breasts as I took all of that delicious incubus cock.

"Play with your nipples." Ambrose's harsh demand had me flicking my gaze to him. Malachi snarled but didn't dispute the command. I moved my fingers to my aching peaks and started to pinch them in time with my descent on Malachi's cock.

My pussy fluttered around him as I approached the edge yet again. His silence broke as he groaned beneath me.

"One more time, Sher." He used his hands to help me pick up my pace, and soon the sound of skin slapping against skin filled the room, punctuated with my breathy moans and Mal's grunts as we both neared our release. "That's it."

I tossed my head and arched my back as I came again, screaming Malachi's name to the heavens. His own roar of release had my hips jerking against his as I tried to prolong my orgasm for as long as possible. I collapsed back against Malachi, and he lifted my hips before rolling us both so he was on top of me.

My chest heaved as I glanced up at him. His lips curved in a typical satisfied male grin before he rolled off me. "I'll be back in a minute." I watched as he strode over to Jacobi and Ambrose, ushering them and the guards out of my bedroom. He hadn't bothered to put any clothes on.

I was too spent to go after them, and before I knew it, my eyes drifted close.

3

AMBROSE

I fought the urge to rip Malachi apart. Our fight in the small room where I'd been balls deep in Ashera had only heightened my bloodlust. Watching him empty himself inside her tight little pussy—when I'd been denied my own release—had me feeling exceptionally hostile.

The angel king seemed perplexed by his body's response to the show we just witnessed. I almost felt bad for the feathered fuck. *Almost.*

In an instant, I was pinned against the hallway wall with Malachi's arm against my throat. "Listen here you fanged asshole," he growled. "Ashera is my *mate*."

I smirked. "And does the little queen know this?"

Malachi was silent, glowering at me inches from my face, and I knew I had my answer. He hadn't told her this important fact yet. A secret... How delicious. I opened my mouth to inform him of my plan with my newfound information, but he cut me off before I could. "Regardless, I have no issue sharing Ashera with any of her other mates, but I highly doubt you're one of them."

How dare he assume what I was or wasn't? I snarled but didn't get the chance to respond as he continued his assault.

"I know why you're here, and I won't let you hurt her."

At this, Jacobi stiffened and moved to stand beside Malachi, his own glare firmly fixed on me.

"I know you want to bring her down," Malachi continued, "but that's not going to happen. And I know you brought a merry little band with you to do just that."

"He *what?*" Jacobi snarled. I hadn't even known angels could snarl. My gaze narrowed as it bounced between the two men. *Why the fuck isn't the feathered asshole getting his dick handed to him?* For a pure shmuck, I hadn't missed the way he had been eye-fucking Ashera.

"He threatened Ashera in the throne room." We both knew he was withholding information from the angel king.

I wasn't expecting the fist that slammed into my face, knocking my head back against the wall with a sickening thud, nor was I expecting it to come from the fucking angel.

Masas and Malak had an uneasy truce. We tended to avoid most dealings with one another, and we had little interest in fighting. I was surprised the king would risk that truce for a woman.

"I merely stated she needed to reinstate slavery or Shaytan would fall." It was like I was explaining simple facts to idiots. Which I was, and they were.

"Malak has no slaves, and we have never fallen. It is entirely possible to run a kingdom without them." Jacobi looked as though he wanted to punch me again. "Queen Ashera should be commended for what she has done for her people."

Malachi hummed his agreement.

I scoffed.

"You cannot possibly compare the two kingdoms," I argued. "Malak has always been without slaves. Shaytan has not. Ashera has not only painted a target on her back for those who wish to return to the old ways and those who seek her territory, but she's also created a massive economic problem Shaytan isn't equipped to handle. What the fuck are they going to do without the slave trade to sustain them? She's a child and nothing more than a weak female seeking to play with the grown-ups."

At this, Malachi threw his head back and laughed. The sound boomed down the hallway. "Ashera is well over three hundred years old, hardly a child. As for the economic problem, you insult your own intelligence if you think she doesn't already have multiple plans in place to ensure this kingdom doesn't crumble around her." He tipped his head as he glared at me. "She only toyed with you in that room when she drained you. Make no mistake—she's a savage warrior and has power I've never seen before."

That caught me off guard. The little queen who succumbed so easily to my advances was a warrior? Powerful? When I had felt her energy in the throne room, I had assumed it was merely sexual in nature and meant to seduce and tempt, but for Malachi to speak of her this way, she had to be more.

I wasn't ready to admit I was wrong just yet, but it was entirely possible I had misjudged the intelligence of the woman I had just fucked like it was going out of style. Some kind of feeling was building inside me, something I had never felt before. Something more than just my dick standing at attention. A voice deep inside whispered things I couldn't understand. *Is she my mate?* No. Impossible. But my doubts about who the little queen was to me didn't stop me from glaring at Malachi. "I didn't know. And you insult your intelligence if you think I would stoop so low as to use a small rebellion to take Ashera off the throne. What benefit would that serve me?"

Malachi searched my gaze before turning to Jacobi with a brow raised in question. Right. The fucking angel could tell if I was lying or some shit. Birdbrain nodded, which seemed to satisfy the homicidal incubus. Really. If I was going to over-throw a queen, it would have to be much more public than the rumors of an underground coup. A beheading maybe. Or perhaps I wouldn't even have to kill her. Maybe I could just get her on her knees in front of me, sucking my dick while her kingdom of "freed" people watched. That could be rather enjoyable... I pictured Ashera's full lips wrapped around my cock, her blazing green eyes bright behind dark lashes as she looked up at me. *Fuck.* And now I was as hard as a rock again. *Gods.* This little queen would be the death of me.

Jacobi still looked like he wanted to kill me, or maybe convert me, but Malachi was eyeing me with newfound interest. I had value to him now. "Do you have any idea who could be planning something like this?" he asked.

I cocked my head at him. "Your queen didn't make any friends in Masas when she freed her slaves. Any number of people would want her head on a platter."

"Including you," the angel king rumbled.

I shot my hand out to grab his throat, but Jacobi caught me before I could touch him, leaving us in an awkward kind of stalemate. Anger raced through my veins, and I knew that if Ashera hadn't drained me, I would have had him on his back. "I do not wish to harm Ashera, and regardless, Masas has enough funds that I wouldn't need to dirty my own hands if I desired to."

Malachi stepped between the two of us. "Until you prove that, you won't be pleasuring her either."

I snarled, "Why the fuck aren't you threatening the feath-ered douche here?"

Jacobi narrowed his murderous gaze on me.

Malachi glared, but answered, "He has no intention of hurting my mate." There was that fucking word again. "She said she wanted him. If he's amenable, then she'll have him. She hasn't said the same for you, blood sucker."

The look on the angel king's face told us he was more than amenable to Ashera having him. I opened my mouth to argue that she'd said she wanted me but paused. Those words had never actually left her mouth during our encounter. *Fuck.* If I wanted to gain any ground, I would have to contend with these two cockblocks to get her to openly admit she wanted me.

Was that even what I wanted? That dark feral part of me roared its answer. *Fuck. Yes.*

I was escorted to my suite by several guards after that. My thoughts raced the entire way there. I had a strange urge to hunt down the faction Malachi had mentioned, but that would be detrimental to my end goal... Wouldn't it? What exactly was my end goal?

An image of Ashera naked above me with Malachi thrusting away behind her as she sucked the angel king's cock entered my mind. That couldn't be what I wanted. No.

I wouldn't allow it.

~

Ashera

THE METALLIC SCENT *of blood bloomed in the air, screams echoed around me, and the fog of smoke from burning buildings stung my eyes. A small sob ravaged my tiny body as I frantically searched for Mommy and Daddy. Where were they?*

My tiny hands struggled to reach the doorknob as coughs racked my body. More smoke was drifting in through the windows of our small hut.

"Mama?" I tugged on the door. "Papa?" My tugging grew more frantic as my coughing continued. I feared the fire was inside the house, not outside.

The pounding of hooves against the ground had me whimpering and cowering against the door. Nothing good ever came from the sound of horses. I'd always had to hide when we heard that sound.

"Mama!" I screamed when the searing heat started to lick its way closer. "Mama! Help!"

I was finally able to turn the knob enough to open the front door, and I toppled out with a cry. Why couldn't I find my parents?

"We've heard there is a demon child here in this village," a dark voice roared over the screams. "Hand her to us now."

I couldn't see who had spoken, but I knew they were talking about me. I was the demon child. I was only seven summers, but I knew I wasn't like my parents. I was one of them. I was a monster.

I shuddered against the fear that swamped my mind. My parents had found me abandoned in the woods outside our village when I was just a baby, wrapped in an ivory blanket. They'd known instantly what I was, but they'd taken me in anyway. Loved me. Taught me.

And now I was what brought death to those who had only shown me love.

A scream pierced the air. Mama!

I scrambled to my feet and ran as fast as my tiny legs could carry me to the sound. What I saw would forever be imprinted on my mind.

My father's lifeless body was mounted on a pike, his head on the ground beneath him. Demon soldiers were jabbing him with their swords, laughing and taunting the dead man.

But my mother... My sobs rushed out of me at the sight. My poor, sweet mother was being brutalized by these men, passed around and impaled not just with their bodies but their weapons too.

"Mama!" My scream echoed so loudly the noise stopped. I hadn't yet reached my coming of age, but the rage that built inside me coaxed what little magic I had to life. The fires raged higher, the ground trembled, and the sky darkened. They'd hurt my mama and my papa because of me.

I would hurt them in return.

"Now, now, little demon. We can't have you doing that." I didn't have time to see who was talking to me before my world went dark.

≈

I WAS STANDING *naked in front of Lord Pyper, one of the most influential incubi lords in the kingdom. "It's possible the king will make an offer for her. But she's still too young, too volatile for that. She'll stay here with me until she learns a woman's place is beneath the man she's servicing."*

My rage bubbled up, and I bit my lip to keep my control. I would be no man's whore. I'd learned over the last several decades how to use my body to make a man do what I wanted, but I desired power of my own, so I'd let the lord assume I was a good little consort. I'd manage his house, and when the time was right, I'd rip his head from his body—the same way he'd ripped my father's head off.

"Now, come." He gestured to his lap. The man next to him, a messenger from the king, laughed. I allowed my succubus to rise and released a heavy dose of pheromones into the air. If I riled him up enough, he only lasted mere moments when I touched him. Pathetic.

≈

MALACHI ROARED BESIDE ME, *his fury palpable as he hacked at the soldiers around us. It was always a surprise how efficient he was at killing. He was so gentle and kind with me that I sometimes forgot he was a skilled assassin—one of the many teachers I'd had over the past few centuries.*

My eyes narrowed on the king, who stood in front of a row of severed heads. It didn't take a genius to see whose head was directly in the middle—Visa's, my mate. The sick son of a bitch had had it magically frozen. My heart pounded in my ears as I moved without thought, slicing down bodies without actually looking at them. The king had a sadistic smirk on his face as he watched me cut through his men. He knew I was coming for him, yet he foolishly thought I wouldn't be able to kill him myself.

I'd been tortured for decades before Malachi had finally been able to free me. During that time, I'd learned how to manage my pain. There was nothing stopping me, not even the wounds I received as I continued to slaughter the men around me.

Finally, I was standing in front of the man who had ordered the death of my parents, the death of the only people I'd ever loved. The sovereign who had enslaved an entire people. The male who used my mate's severed head as decoration.

I was going to kill him. Slowly.

We traded blows, and my body was soon covered in blood as he landed just as many as I did. I couldn't hold back my screams when I realized his blade was poisoned, the fire raging through my body. Each movement was torture all over again, yet we continued to hack at one another.

I hadn't come this far to fail. I hadn't lost almost everything to give up now.

"Ashera!" Malachi's frantic cry woke me, and I blinked away the last vestiges of the nightmare. I was still naked from his earlier display of dominance, and he was nude as well, wrapped tightly around me as he pressed his lips against my forehead.

"Thank the gods," he mumbled as he ran soothing hands down my back. "I couldn't fucking wake you."

I took several deep breaths as the pain I'd felt, physical and emotional, began to fade. My gaze locked with Malachi's as my trembling ceased.

"Why are you in my bed?" I questioned in confusion.

He narrowed his eyes, and a frown appeared on his face. "I escorted the two royals out of the door before coming right back to you. You were already asleep."

I searched his gaze as his eyes lowered to my lips. "Sher." That one word, my name, spoken like that had my heart pounding in my chest. He said it with such longing and so much heat. "My mate."

Mate. My heart continued to pound as we inched our faces closer. I should have fucking known from the first moment we met, from that voice calling inside me, crying out to be closer to him. It made so much sense. Most females had more than one mate, and even though I'd had a mate many years ago, she was dead. Malachi wasn't. He was here. And he was mine.

"I should have acted sooner, Sher." He brushed his lips against mine, and I whimpered against his mouth. *This is finally happening!*

"Malachi," I murmured before launching myself at him. Our lips clashed as we licked and nipped each other, running our hands over any skin we could reach. I doubted either of us could slow down. Despite having each other hours ago, we hadn't acknowledged what was really between us.

I was suddenly pinned beneath him, my hands magically restrained above my head as Mal's heated gaze roamed across my body.

"I need to taste you again," he murmured, and my hips bucked, "but first I want you to let your glamor down."

We stared at each other for a moment, and then I loosened the power keeping my glamor in check. Golden wings sprouted from my shoulders, and a set of delicately curved horns appeared near my hairline. Not all succubi had wings and horns, so I tended to keep them hidden. Mal looked over me, reaching out to touch the edge of one delicate golden wing. I shuddered at his light touch.

"Fuck, you're beautiful, Sher. I don't want you to ever hide from me."

He started nibbling down my body, beginning at my neck. I tilted my head to give him better access. He used his fingers to circle my nipples as those delicious lips made their way lower. My back bowed off the bed, begging him to touch me, taste me.

His dark chuckle against my collarbone had me fighting the urge to scream at him to move faster. I didn't want to go slow. I wanted him inside me, around me, everywhere. I needed him everywhere.

"Easy, my queen." He sank his teeth into my collarbone, and I moaned. "I'll give us what we both need, but first, I get to taste every inch of you. I've waited too long."

When he puts it like that...

He closed his lips around an aching nipple and used his fingers to twist the other. Pleasure sparked through my veins, and I tangled my legs with his. I needed to touch every inch of him. Our demon powers flooded the room as we fed off each other. I'd never had this happen with another demon before, and I hadn't realized it was possible to feed off someone while they fed from you. It felt as though our souls were touching. Merging. A searing heat spread from my heart to my shoulder, and I knew instantly our mating marks were appearing as we accepted and recognized our bond.

Malachi didn't acknowledge the mark, too intent on tasting me to realize that his would be emerging at the same time. His lips traveled lower, swirling around my navel before he crouched between my thighs. I wanted a portrait of him there, with that look of acute hunger on his face. I shivered.

My legs opened wider, and he let out a dark chuckle before leaning his head down to swirl his tongue around my clit. I flung my head back against the pillows, and a sharp cry slipped between my lips when he slid two fingers inside me. I was hurtled so close to the edge so quickly, I didn't have any warning before I came with a shout of his name, my legs shaking.

The urge to taste him flooded me. I broke his hold on my hands and had our positions reversed before he could comprehend what had happened. With a sly grin, I immediately wrapped my lips around his cock. His loud groan of approval spurred me on. The gods had seen fit to bless me without a gag reflex, so I was able to take all of him down my throat. His body shuddered as I moved against him, and he tangled his hands roughly in my hair to keep me in place.

"That's it, my little slut," he praised. "Take all of my cock."

I hummed around him, causing him to bark out a curse.

"Fuck, just like that."

His breathing picked up, and I could tell he was close. I wanted him to spill down my throat, but he had other plans. With surprising strength, he pulled me off his cock, flipped us, and linked our hands next to my head. I wrapped my legs around him as he slowly sank to the hilt.

"Keep your eyes on me, Sher," he rumbled as he started to move. His thrusts were slow, gentle, and hit so deep my eyes wanted to roll into the back of my head. "I want to see the look on your face when you come for me."

"Malachi," I cried out when he adjusted our position just a bit so his pelvis rubbed against my clit each time he thrust deep. Our gazes locked and something intimate, deep... *loving*... passed between us. My heart lurched, and I came with a strangled scream. He roared my name as his own release claimed him moments later.

We stayed locked like that for a moment, our chests heaving against each other. We'd mated. My eyes found his mate mark, a bold crown that wrapped around his bicep, and my lips tugged into a satisfied grin. This male was mine. His gentle hands turned me so he could inspect his mark on my shoulder.

"Wings." His voice was rough and filled with emotion. "You've got my wings."

I turned back to him, a giant smile spreading across my face. There would be no mistaking whom we belonged to. Malachi's head dipped as he dragged his nose along my neck, taking in my scent.

"You're finally *mine*," he growled.

4

ASHERA

I lay awake in my bed after we'd spent several moments snuggling and basking in the feel of the newly formed mate bond. I watched the moonlight filter in through the sheer curtains, the light illuminating my mate's gorgeous dark skin against my own golden tone. Mal was a light sleeper, but tonight he was snoring heavily beside me while sleep seemed to evade me.

Mate. Was it truly possible that the gods had blessed me with another mate? I didn't think it would ever happen for me again despite knowing that most females took multiple mates. My hands were stained with too much blood, and my soul... I couldn't even imagine how black my soul must be. I told myself it was all worth it, that paying my dues meant that others like me wouldn't have to live a life of pain. Of torture. No. I would dirty my hands to save my people. I had no regrets about that, but I didn't expect another mate.

I must have done something right somewhere along the way. I glanced down at Mal, his brow creased as he dreamed. I bent to kiss his forehead. He relaxed into a deeper sleep, and a soft smile lifted his lips. Mal didn't smile often, so I was glad that I could be something pleasant in his life.

Mal. It felt surreal. I had wanted him for so long, and now I had him. Yet... something was clawing inside my soul. I was unsettled. I should have been fast asleep, dreaming of the future we would build, but a voice long since locked away was calling me, dragging me out of bed and toward the door. The moonlight dappled floors were cool beneath my bare feet as I draped a light chiffon robe over my shoulders. I turned back once more to check on my slumbering mate, who was still sleeping soundly, and then quietly closed my door behind me. I willed my glamor back into place, not needing any unnecessary questions from any of my guests should I run into them wandering the halls.

I didn't know where I was going. I simply followed the voice inside me as it called me closer, directing me as I walked the corridors. I didn't pass any guards, but I wasn't afraid. I could take most of the men in the kingdom with my sheer strength alone, but it didn't matter. The soft voice calling me told me not to be afraid. I clutched my robe tighter around my body, my nipples hardening in the chill of the night. I was in the west wing now, far from my bedroom, where the envoys had been given rooms. After my altercation turned into a sexual domi-nance display earlier today, I wasn't sure I wanted to see Ambrose quite yet.

The sex was good, but we had some major moral differences to work out before I got back on that dick again—namely the fact that he liked to own people and I stole his power. Oops.

I made my way to one of the wooden doors, not surprised to find it unlocked. I had servants make sure that all the best guest rooms were properly prepared, which included leaving them unlocked for easy access.

I entered one of the rooms without knocking. The balcony

doors were open, allowing the fresh spring breeze to flutter through the light curtains. The smell of rejuvenation was in the air. Hope. It was a new era in Shaytan, and I was honored to be a small part of that.

"Why are you in my room?" The softly spoken question had me whirling around, my robe dropping open as I spun.

Jacobi. I'm in Jacobi's room. The incredibly handsome angel king was sitting up in his bed, the sheets pooling at his hips. His chest was bare, providing a sinful view of his large, broad shoulders that narrowed down to his hips, and I couldn't stop myself from drinking him in. His honey blond hair, cropped close on the sides and longer on top, was sexily mussed from sleep.

Why was I not surprised? I'd felt drawn to him earlier, so it made sense that I was pulled here.

"I couldn't sleep." It wasn't really an answer, but I was a queen, dammit. I could go where I wanted, and right now, I wanted Jacobi just as badly as I wanted Malachi. My desire was all I could focus on as a damp heat spread eagerly between my legs. Was I really going to lead the pure angel king down the path of temptation?

Jacobi opened his mouth to speak and then closed it. His gaze drifted out the window before turning back to me and running hungrily over my body. It was then that I noticed he was wide awake. There didn't appear to be even a hint of sleep in his eyes. They were clear and aware.

"Why are you awake?" I inquired quietly.

I knew what his answer was going to be before he spoke with adorable confusion written all over his perfect face. "A voice... A voice called to me." He met my gaze, his bright blue eyes searing into my soul. "I think it was your voice."

Two mates. Two fucking mates. Could it even be possible?

Fuck it. I took a step closer.

~

Jacobi

SHE ASKED why I was awake. I wasn't sure. I thought the voice might have been part of a dream, but as soon as I saw Ashera step into my bedroom, moonlight illuminating her golden skin, I knew. I was awake because something called us together, something bigger than either of us or possibly anything else in this world.

Was it wrong to want her? To fantasize about her perfect lips calling my name as I thrust into her, watching her slender hands touching my body? *Technically.* But whatever it was that kept me awake and called her into my room told me this could only ever be right.

Ashera took another step toward me, and her light robe blew in the breeze. The smooth curve of her hip made my mouth water, and I needed to know if she tasted as sweet as she smelled. I wasn't going to wait another moment to find out. I pushed the covers off me, standing to meet her where she stood.

Her bright green gaze met mine for a moment, and for the first time, I saw uncertainty flickering there. "Jacobi, are you sure you want this? Want me?"

"Ashera," I whispered, cupping the back of her head with my hands. "Ashera, I think it's always been you."

Was I willing to share her? I wasn't sure if it was technically sharing when our souls were aligned. All I knew was I wanted Ashera in any way she'd let me have her.

She stood on her tiptoes to press her lips to mine, gently at first as if not to scare me away, but I didn't scare easily, and I'd made my decision. I had been rock-hard since I saw that vamp asshole taking her in the study, and I wasn't sure how long I would be able to hold out. I deepened the kiss, crushing her body to mine. *Gods.* Is this what I had been missing out on? Somehow, I doubted it. I instinctively knew that only she could make me feel like this. I needed to feel more of her and hear her cry my name like she did with Malachi earlier today, so I parted her legs with my knee, desperate to get closer.

"Ashera," I moaned. "I want to taste you. Let me taste you."

She gave me an easy smile and nodded, slipping the robe off her shoulders. A growl rumbled deep inside my chest, something I never knew I was capable of. I wanted to own her and consume every last inch of her. Something primal, bestial, roared inside me. Before the night was out, she'd wear my mark. Fuck purity. I wanted everyone to know that this queen was *mine*. She'd chosen me. I pushed her onto the bed, and her laugh as she fell was nearly enough to make me come on its own. I needed to focus.

She had been with Malachi and Ambrose, and I doubted either man had abstained as I had. I was the celibate king from the gentle kingdom of wheat and fish. Would I be able to live up to her standards? She parted her legs for me, and I stared at the slick, pink folds waiting for me to taste them. I couldn't stop myself from pumping my hand around my cock a few times just to relieve some of the tension.

"It's okay, Jacobi. We don't have to do anything you don't want to," Ashera murmured. Her eyes were heated and fixed on my cock, and she licked her lips as she watched me move my hand over my shaft, her actions betraying her words.

It was too late for that. I had a taste of temptation when I kissed her lips, and now I needed to see what full corruption would feel like when I sunk inside of her. I needed to hear her scream my name in passion. I needed to fill her up as Malachi had. Mark her. Claim her. Nothing else would satisfy me.

I shook my head and kissed the soft skin on the inside of

her thigh. It wasn't enough. I nipped her leg then licked the spot to soothe the sting. I nearly missed the hitch in her breath, the soft pant of need that left her. *Control, Jacobi.* I needed to stay in control, which was impossible once I caught the scent of her pheromones saturating the air.

"Fuck, Ashera. You don't play fair," I growled, but when desire fogged my brain, there was no more room for talking. No room for thinking. I licked her soaked pussy, finally getting a taste of the most delicious honey. Ashera sucked in a breath and moaned lightly as I licked again and again, swirling my tongue around her clit. It was like something had been awoken in me, some other Jacobi that knew where to put his hands and mouth. A Jacobi that could make Ashera writhe and cry out as he pleasured her. One that freely unleashed his hunger.

Not that I was complaining, especially not with the knowledge that I was making her moan and cry out, not another male. I trailed my fingertips down her legs, moving to suck gently on her clit as I teased her opening with my fingers. My confidence grew, so I didn't filter my words. "I want all of you, Ashera. I want you to come on my tongue, just like this. And then I want your tight little pussy to come around my cock. Show me what I've been missing out on all my life."

Ashera's hips bucked into my mouth, needing release. Who was I to deny her what she wanted? She was my queen. My mate. I slipped one finger inside of her, and then two, curving them as I moved my mouth along her sweet flesh.

"Oh, Jacobi. Oh!" That part of me that knew how to make her arch her back, how to make her moan, how to make her come, roared with triumph at the urgency in her voice. Any doubts fled as I glanced up at her body to see her head flung back in pleasure, her hands gripping the sheets as her stomach quivered with her impending release.

"Just like that, my love. Just like that. Show me how good I make you feel." Who would have thought I would know how to do any of this? My cock pulsed with need, so I worked my tongue faster, harder, feeling Ashera's pussy clench and tremble around my fingers. She came with a soft cry as I lapped her up. She was the most delicious thing I'd ever tasted, and I knew I never wanted to go a day without the taste of her on my tongue.

Ashera sat up, her eyes dazed with pleasure. "Well, angel king. Who knew?"

I laughed. "We're not done yet."

I pulled her out of bed and led her out to the balcony, which was bright even at night. The moon was full, and the spring festival was just around the corner, a celebration of new life.

I focused on the desire and feelings I had never experienced before as they flooded my body. Ashera leaned against the stone railing, and I kissed her lightly. "I'm going to make sure the world knows you're mine."

She shivered at my words, her breath hitching at the heat she saw in my eyes. I made no attempt to hide my body's reaction to her.

My wrist began to burn as I spun Ashera around so that her waist rested on the balustrade. Her ass was toward me, perfect and round. The image of my cock sinking into that tight hole seared into my mind. One day. Maybe. I slipped my hand between her legs, spreading her wetness. She released a low moan, and her hips bucked against my hand. I nudged my cock against her pussy, sinking in as her walls clenched around me. The small sounds she made as I filled her spurred me on until I was fully seated inside her.

My eyes fluttered closed as I took in all the sensations. *Fuck.* Ashera was perfect. I could say that with complete awareness now. Every single inch of her was made for me, and I felt certain I had been made for her. What other explanation was there? I started to pump in and out of her, her cries and moans of desire fueling me. The waves of pleasure were overwhelming, and I was building up to crest a wave of gratification I had never experienced before. I slid my fingers around to Ashera's clit, feeling her ride the edge of her release as her pussy pulsed erratically around my cock. Her pleasure drove me to take my own, keeping my momentum as I roared and shattered within her.

Fuck. I couldn't stop myself from laughing as I caught my breath and sat on the balcony before dragging Ashera down to sit on my lap. She joined in my laughter, stroking my face as we looked at each other with wonder.

I caught her hand in my palm. "Feed off me, love."

"Are you sure?"

I nodded. "Please."

She was gentle, and I watched her eyes as they closed in satisfaction. I didn't feel any weaker. Instead, I felt full, satisfied, for the first time in my life. I realized my wrist was still tingling from the burning sensation, and I glanced down to see a small, perfect crown appearing on the skin there.

"Is this your mark?" I asked.

"It must be," she replied. "Malachi has the same one on his arm now." She settled back against my chest when I noticed my own mark on her skin—a large feather taking up most of her forearm. I tapped lightly, pointing it out to her. "Oh shit. That's massive!"

A grin tugged at my lips. She seemed surprised, which pleased me. She dragged her lips across mine as her fingers laced behind my neck. I could feel her desire spiking again, and I was instantly hard and ready for her. A muffled murmur of surprise against my lips had me chuckling.

I gripped her hips as I slid her down over my cock, both of us breaking away from our kiss to moan.

"Are you sure you've never done this before?" Her breathy voice had me clutching her hips harder as I rocked her against me, dragging her clit against me with each pull.

Pride burst within me. I was making this stunningly beautiful succubus queen breathless with my cock. I slowed our pace, which had her head falling forward against my shoulder as she whimpered with need. My lips trailed down her neck, and she leaned back so I could take her nipple into my mouth as I continued my slow pace. Her nails dug into my shoulders as her head fell back and a long, loud moan ripped from her throat.

"Jacobi," she cried. "Gods. You keep hitting just the right spot. Please, don't stop."

I sucked harder on her nipple, and she screamed my name as she came. *Fuck.* She felt so damn good clenching around me like that, but I wanted her to come completely undone. I stood, not letting her slip off my cock as I braced her against the wall next to the balcony doors. My arms moved to take her legs up over my shoulders, and I slid deeper into her. She whispered my name like a prayer.

I could feel more than her lust as I opened to her. Our mate bond flared, her love and affection flowed with it, and my hips jerked in response. I could also feel Malachi, who was now awake and fisting himself in Ashera's room as our pleasure flowed to him through the bond. Ashera was nearly mindless with her desire for me, and a sense of pure male satisfaction had me preening.

"More. Gods, Jacobi. More."

I gave her more, but I kept my pace slow, ensuring to angle my hips just right so I brushed both her clit and G-spot with each thrust. She came twice more before I finally started thrusting harder, faster. Her moans of pleasure rang out in the night around us.

"Do you like how I fill you, love?"

"Yes!" she screamed. "Gods, I love it."

She came one last time, sobbing out my name with her release. I shouted out my own release moments later, my hips jerking against hers as she clenched so tightly around me, I was sure we'd never be parted.

We stayed like that, spent and connected, staring into each other's eyes. Her hands tangled in my hair as she dragged me down for another searing kiss. Ashera pulled away only slightly to murmur, "Come back to my bed."

"Of course."

~

Ashera

BACK IN MY CHAMBERS, I was plastered between two hard male bodies as the sun started to crest the horizon. Jacobi had brought me back to my room, where Malachi had greeted us with heated, hungry eyes. Unfortunately, I was too exhausted to engage in a round with both of them. I'd fallen asleep almost instantly when Jacobi had delicately laid me on the bed.

Malachi was on his back, sound asleep, and I had one leg up and over his hips. His hand rested possessively on my thigh, and our faces were so close, I wouldn't be surprised if we had been kissing in our sleep. One of my hands rested low on his stomach, while the other was clutching Jacobi's wrist.

My head rested on Jacobi's bicep as he spooned behind me. He had his arm curled up and around my shoulder, clutching me tightly to his chest. It was his other hand, however, that had me fighting the urge to move against them. He had two of his fingers buried in my pussy, as though the thought of not being inside me, even to sleep, offended him.

I could tell by their breathing that they were still asleep, but Jacobi's fingers had me drenched in seconds. I bit my lip as my core fluttered around the digits. *Oh gods.* My mind flooded with images from last night. For a man who had never touched a woman before, Jacobi had amazing stamina, and he knew instinctively where to touch me to make me melt into a puddle at his feet.

Both men were hard against me, and I couldn't be sure if they were now awake and waiting to see what I would do, or if the scent of my arousal affected them in slumber. I released a low moan at the thought of both of them filling me. My heart rate picked up, and I knew I was getting wetter at the thought.

Jacobi started to move his fingers inside me, rubbing his thumb lightly against my clit. My breath hitched in my lungs, and I started to grind my hips against his fingers. Malachi trailed his fingers down my leg.

Shit, they're awake.

"Jacobi is going to make you come on his fingers before we fill you, because you're a greedy slut, aren't you, Sher?" Malachi's sleepy voice had me shuddering against them. The thought of them both inside me at the same time was almost too much, and all I could do was nod.

Jacobi trailed his lips down my neck, and Malachi found my nipple with his fingers. I clenched around the angel king's digits in response, causing him to groan. "She's so damn wet." He pressed his smirk against my neck and started to move his fingers faster. They crooked at just the right angle to rub against my G-spot.

I wasn't entirely sure what I screamed as I came around those thick digits. Neither male stopped touching me, and my orgasm dragged out longer than normal. Malachi released a dark chuckle as they both moved to position our bodies in a manner that would allow them to take me at the same time.

"I'm going to let Jacobi take your pert little ass, Sher," Malachi rumbled as he reached into my nightstand. "I think the good king has earned the right to claim that first, considering he wasn't a complete fucking moron who ignored the bond."

I could feel the excitement radiating off Jacobi as Malachi leaned back against the pillows and pulled me on top of him.

He handed Jacobi the small bottle he had found in my nightstand, and instructed, "Lube up, champ. If you think her pussy is tight, you haven't felt anything yet."

I slapped his chest. "How the hell would you know what my ass feels like?" A rogue grin spread across Mal's face, and he simply pulled me down for a searing kiss.

Malachi didn't bother answering me, instead, he moved me into position and slid into me to the hilt. He kept my hips trapped against his as he looked over my shoulder at my angel. Jacobi moved closer, toying with my ass, preparing me for that heavenly cock of his before he started to work his way inside me.

"Gods," we both moaned out in unison. I felt so full. Jacobi leaned down until I was pressed between both of them. Every breath I took had me shuddering. It was too much.

"Now, Your Majesty," Malachi addressed Jacobi, "we're going to fuck our queen senseless. Don't hold back."

They moved in unison as though they'd been fucking me together for centuries. I whimpered as they picked up the pace, both of them thrusting hard and fast. Jacobi eased back slightly, just enough so my nipples dragged against Malachi's chest with each plunge. My clit bumped against the incubus's pelvis as they continued their assault.

"You were right." Jacobi's low growl rumbled against my back. "But while her ass is damn tight, I much prefer her pink little pussy gripping my cock. But gods, she feels amazing no matter how I'm inside her."

"Do you hear that, my queen?" Malachi sounded so damn pleased. "You have the King of Malak claiming your ass while I fuck your perfect wet pussy. A king and an assassin. Do you feel worshipped?"

My head fell against Mal's chest as I sighed out my answer. I felt worshipped, full, and so overwhelmed with pleasure. Our bonds shimmered brightly between us, and I could feel their pleasure as well. It was too much.

I shattered. My scream echoed in the chamber around us as both men roared their releases at the same time. Jacobi collapsed on top of me, squeezing me in the best possible way between my two mates. I felt loved, protected, and safe.

"You're ours, my queen," Mal rumbled.

"Yours," I agreed. "Always."

5

AMBROSE

It was bad enough that I had to eat breakfast with the winged Rambo and the feathered douche, but the fact that I had to watch Ashera sit on King Birdbrain's lap was going to send me into a murderous tailspin.

What was worse was that she was smiling up at him like he was the only thing that mattered in the world. I picked at my toast, fuming. Why the hell did we have to eat together anyway? It wasn't like we were going to suddenly be friends. If anything, I was waiting for my opportunity to drain the virgin king dry.

Although, I was beginning to doubt the virgin status as I watched the way Jacobi's hand curved possessively over Ashera's full breast before he flicked his thumb over her raised nipple. She giggled, actually fucking giggled, and fed Jacobi a bite of toast.

That was *my* fucking nipple. A warning growl built in my chest, and I glowered at Jacobi and what I deemed as *my* woman.

Jacobi raised an eyebrow at me, swallowing his mouthful.

He didn't remove his hand from Ashera's breast. "Problem, Prince Ambrose?"

"Get your fucking hands off of her," I growled. Fuck, I was pissed. Or was I jealous? I wasn't sure anymore. All I knew was the rage that surged through me. But I wanted to be the one touching her. How fucking dare he touch her like that in front of me?

"I don't think that's your call, vamp." Malachi had been silent through our meal, but he decided now was the time to speak up? Asshole.

"And it's yours?" I countered. Ashera was watching the interaction with a sly smile on her face, probably waiting for me to bite someone's head off—which was going to happen if the feathered fuckface didn't take his godsdamn hands off her.

Malachi shrugged, dropping his napkin over his demolished plate of food. He leaned back in his chair and watched me with a smirk. "Considering she bears my mark, yeah, I'd say it's my call."

My vision turned red with my anger. *He marked her?* They'd all fucking die. She was mine to mark.

Malachi continued, "But I'd never make Sher's decisions for her. It's her call."

Malachi and I both turned to face Ashera. Her smile turned into a full-blown grin, and I knew I wasn't going to like whatever she was going to say next. "I mean, he's already had my ass. Is a hand on my nipple at breakfast really that scandalous?"

Death. Death for all of them. The fucking virgin king had taken *my* little queen in the ass before I had? I snarled angrily, clenching the wooden table hard enough for it to splinter. Malachi slapped his arm against me, holding me back from slaughtering the feathered fuck where he sat. Ashera might be covered in blood at the end of it, but honestly, it would probably be even more of a turn-on as I took her, her pussy slick with their blood and my release.

"Easy there, vamp," Malachi warned. "We need to pool our knowledge and figure out who has it in for Ashera."

Jacobi leered at me, looking awfully devilish for such a holy being. Asshole. He slid his hand down Ashera's waist before slipping below the gauzy material covering her thighs. I couldn't see what he was doing, but her face contorted into an expression of sheer bliss as he pleasured her. *Right. The. Fuck. In. Front. Of. Me. Fuck!* I shot a quick glance at Malachi, who wore a similar mask of enjoyment. What the fuck? "You're seriously okay with this winged asshole fingering your mate right in front of you?"

Malachi glared at me. "First of all, he's not the only winged asshole here. Second, Jacobi is also Ashera's mate. He can do whatever he pleases as long as Ashera is happy."

I whipped my head around to observe the lust-filled scene in front of me. Ashera's head rested against Birdbrain's broad shoulder as she moaned and made small cries of pleasure, and Malachi wore a dazed expression as he watched them. I was rock-hard and struggling to remain in control of my dick, who was currently ready to punch out Jacobi and take my rightful place underneath Ashera. "Are you fucking kidding me?"

Jacobi, who was fingering Ashera like he was born to do it, nodded toward her wrist. Her entire fucking forearm was covered by a feather tattoo-like mark. That did it for me. Just as Ashera cried out in release, I flipped the long table we had been dining at and stood, fury controlling my every thought and move. I glared back and forth between Malachi and Jacobi, pointing a finger between them. As much as I wanted to, I couldn't kill them, because if I killed them, I'd never get to fuck Ashera again. That didn't mean I was happy though. "That was my fucking asshole to take. You'll both pay." I stormed off, slamming the door behind me, but not before I heard Ashera laugh loudly.

"Should we call him back?" she asked.

Malachi's voice was quiet behind the door. "Nah. Let him cool off. We'll bring the discussion to him in a bit."

Assholes. Every single one of them. I should have never left Masas.

Ashera

I TURNED my head toward the door that Ambrose just stormed out of, pissed beyond belief. The breakfast dishes and the table were in disarray at our feet. Something deep inside me felt connected to the vampire prince, and for some insane reason, I was worried about his feelings.

"You're upset. Did he bother you, love?" Jacobi murmured against my ear, and I leaned back against his firm body.

Mal looked over at us with concern. "Sher, are you okay?"

I shook my head. "I'm fine. Annoyed, but okay."

Mal pressed his lips together, tapping his fingers on his legs. "I have an idea." He walked toward us, avoiding the mess on the floor, and pressed a quick kiss to my head. "Let me go figure some things out, and I'll be back." He strode out the door.

Jacobi rubbed his nose against my neck, and I shivered from the gentle touch. "Now that we're alone..." He trailed off as he licked the bare skin of my shoulder.

His cock was hard beneath my ass, and I laughed. "I swear, you're insatiable."

In a flash, Jacobi had me turned around in his lap, my knees splayed on either side of his trim hips as he grinned at me. His brilliant blue eyes darkened ever so slightly with his desire. "So says the succubus queen who corrupted the innocent angel king."

I smirked, running my fingers through his soft hair. "I'm not so sure about the innocent part after last night. And this morning."

"Oh, definitely innocent. In fact, I think I could use more practice." His teasing fingers throughout breakfast had left me needy, aching, and he knew it.

I lowered my head to kiss him. "Good thing I'm a willing teacher." The sexual energy was already thick in the room, and I had to force myself not to feed off it. Not yet.

Jacobi shifted underneath me, releasing his heavy erection from his pants and positioning himself at my slick entrance beneath my gauzy skirt. "Thank the gods for that." His smile was gentle but teasing.

I ran my hands down his broad shoulders as I sank onto his cock. "Gods, Jacobi!" I cried, feeling stretched in the most delicious way possible. I rolled my hips against him, and he arched up into me. Jacobi thrust inside of me, and I clung to his strong biceps as we moved together. The wooden chair beneath us creaked and groaned, echoing our moans of pleasure. The pressure that told me I was close kept building, and my eyes shut, but not before seeing Jacobi staring at me like I had hung the sun and moon myself.

"Feed, love." Jacobi's harsh whisper interrupted the grind of my hips.

"Are you sure? I just fed off your energy this morning. I don't want to drain you." I wasn't sure of Jacobi's limits, and I didn't want to hurt him.

Jacobi pulled me farther down onto his cock, causing me to cry out in pleasure. "Love, I'm 700 years old. I'll be fine. Now, feed."

I arched my back, feeling the delicious swell of the sexual energy as it absorbed into my body, and it tipped me over the edge. I called out Jacobi's name as my pussy clenched and trembled around him. My angel king roared out his own release, pumping furiously inside me. Somewhere else in the castle, I could feel Mal's desire rushing through the bond between us.

Jacobi rested his head against my chest. "When's our next lesson?" he whispered against my skin.

I smiled down at his fair head. "You get a five-minute recess. Don't be late."

A FEW HOURS AFTER BREAKFAST, I had a guard escort Ambrose out to the courtyard. I was dressed head to toe in fighting leathers. My eyes were covered with a silk ribbon, my hands were bound behind my back, and my feet were tied together. My glamor was still in place—I hadn't dropped it since last night with Mal. I could tell when he'd been moved into place by his angry energy. The fact that I was so aware of him, just as I was of Malachi and Jacobi, unsettled me. Could someone like Ambrose really be one of my mates?

Turns out, Malachi's idea, which he'd rushed off to prepare, had been this little demonstration. Ambrose believed I was a weak female, and Malachi wanted to dispel some of that. I wouldn't be showing off the full extent of my magic today. I'd only be demonstrating my fighting abilities. Malachi and Jacobi would be standing on either side of Ambrose for this, just in case the dramatic vamp got any ideas.

Ten nobles, all seasoned fighters, all males, stood in front of me. They were armed. I was not. These ten nobles were part of the prior king's court and had fought for him and refused to free their slaves once I'd taken the crown. Today, they'd get the chance to earn their freedom... if they could best me.

"Queen Ashera has decided that she will allow the men before her a chance to fight for their freedom. They have all committed crimes against the kingdom of Shaytan." Malachi's voice boomed around the courtyard. "This is a fight to the death. Any of the surviving nobles will be free to do as they please." A deadly quiet met his words, but I could feel Ambrose tense. "You may begin."

"What the fuck are you playing at?" That was the only thing Ambrose could get out before I sensed the nobles rushing me.

When the first one reached me, I dropped into a crouch before jumping high into the air. I swung my arms under my feet so that they were now in front of me, then I landed with my thighs on either side of the noble's head. I threw myself back, my hands arching above my head and my thighs clenching tightly as I flipped the two of us, slamming the noble's skull into the ground with enough force that I broke his neck on impact. I quickly took his sword and cut the ropes binding my ankles.

That was all the time I had before the second man was upon me. I planned to kill the first five before draining the others dry. I also had no intention of removing my blindfold. Moving with a sword in my hand even while they were bound was like dancing. My body swayed with each movement, each thrust, and each dodge.

"Stop playing with them!" The shout came from the crowd and was followed by a round of laughter. Fine then.

In a blink, the remaining four were dead, and there wasn't a drop of blood on me. I stood in the center of the other five and dropped my sword on the ground. What I was about to do was something no other succubus or incubus could, and I'd relish the shock on Ambrose's face once this was all over.

I took several deep inhales as I felt the former nobles circle me. They all knew how dangerous I was. They'd seen me on the battlefield. I tilted my head back, a showing which, for the vampires in the audience, would be a display of submission, weakness, but for those of my kingdom, it signaled the coming of the end.

Without having to touch the men around me, I drained

them of their energy in a flash. One by one, I heard their bodies collapse to the ground, and their screams of agony rang out as I continued the onslaught. When the silence finally returned, I lifted my blindfold and made direct eye contact with Ambrose.

Ambrose

W*HAT THE FUCK had I just watched?*

I was furious and aroused as my gaze locked with Ashera's. When several guards had come to my suite and told me that Ashera had requested my presence, I'd still been pretty angry—and eager to remind her that her pussy was *mine*—but when I'd been led out to the courtyard to see Ashera blindfolded and bound, I'd been instantly wary.

Rage flooded me when Malachi explained what was about to happen. He'd nearly ripped me to fucking pieces based on a rumor, but now he was letting her get slaughtered? I bristled. I wouldn't allow her to get hurt. *Some fucking mates she has if they would allow this to happen.*

They'd held me back, barely, as the fight commenced, and now that it was over, their grips tightened as I continued to stare at Ashera.

She was far stronger than I'd given her credit for.

She could drain people without touching them? I thought that was what aroused me the most—knowing what a deadly predator she was. I blatantly reached down to adjust myself and grinned when her eyes dropped to follow the movement. I didn't think I had ever heard of a succubus able to feed without touching. A light touch? Sure. But no skin-to-skin contact? That was something else entirely.

"Now I suggest the four of us sit down and discuss several

matters." Her voice was husky with her own arousal. *So the little queen liked to fuck after she fought. Perfect.*

Jacobi, Malachi, and I followed Ashera into a room similar to the one she and I had destroyed yesterday. She had removed the ropes that bound her hands on the walk into the palace. I was tempted to lean down and grab them so I could tie her down and own her ass, but the two cockblocks behind me wouldn't let me get within an inch of her bare flesh. I'd need to find a way to corner her alone.

We settled around the table, and Ashera's eyes went to Malachi. "I believe you'd mentioned there was a threat to my rule?"

If they weren't as hard as I was, they didn't deserve to be her mates. I released a low growl, and their eyes darted to me. "Just remember that I fucked you first, little queen." Her gaze heated at my words, and the beast within me roared to the surface. I wanted to claim her in front of these other two. Malachi thought he was the alpha in the room, but he was fucking wrong.

"Be that as it may, Prince Ambrose," Ashera replied, "we have other business to attend to. More important business."

I was going to slap her ass raw for that. There was *nothing* more important than my cock claiming her pussy and then her ass.

"Word of an underground faction has been spreading, Sher," Malachi began, bringing our attention back to him. "And it seems that there are vampires in the mix." I bristled at that. "We aren't sure when they will strike, but the threat is legitimate."

Jacobi let loose a growl that was actually impressive. "They won't be able to touch her."

"No," Malachi agreed. "But that doesn't mean we shouldn't take precautions. With the fae delegation arriving today, and the Beltane celebration in three days, there are several security concerns."

"Then one of us should be with her at all times," I snarled.

"I accepted that you weren't a part of this threat, but I haven't accepted that you don't wish to harm her," Malachi growled back.

"*She* is right here in the room." She spoke like a queen, and it turned me on even more. "And I refuse to be babysat like a child."

"This isn't about thinking you're a child," Jacobi soothed. "It's about keeping you safe." I still wanted to drain the feathered fuck dry, but he had a very calming energy about him, and I could understand the logic behind his words. It was almost as if...

"Jacobi, are you fucking controlling the room's atmosphere?" I grimaced. The less touchy-feely shit the birdbrained idiot and I had to go through while I won over Ashera, the better. I definitely didn't need his feelings in my mind.

He held up his hands, not one ounce of apology visible on his face. "Sorry."

"Boys, please," Ashera interrupted. Jacobi and I were still locked in an intense staring match. I was not going to be the first to back down. She placed a hand on Malachi's shoulder. "I will allow one of you to stay with me as backup, not as protection. I can handle myself."

Malachi nodded, barely relaxing his stance.

"But," she continued, "Ambrose will be the first to stay while you and Jacobi go out and canvass the kingdom for any details."

"What?" Malachi and I spoke at the same time, glaring at each other and then giving our full attention to Ashera. A small part of me wanted to taunt the winged asshole. She'd chosen me.

She nodded, no room for debate in her steely green gaze. "You know the region, Malachi. And Jacobi can help... convince people to talk. Ambrose will just get people worked up if they aren't a part of the faction, or nervous if they are."

"You've got that right," Jacobi muttered. He did not look impressed either. But from the size of his hard-on beneath his linen pants, he was probably just pissed he wouldn't get a chance to fuck my little queen again. I wanted to make it clear that I'd own her ass as soon as we were alone, but I knew Ashera would most likely take offense to that.

"Fuck off, both of you. I told you I'm not a danger to Ashera, and I meant it."

Ashera turned her steady gaze on me. "Besides, Ambrose and I have important things to discuss."

Things to discuss? I perked up. I'd like to discuss how great her ass would look while I fucked her from behind on this table in a repeat of previous events. My blood heated, and my dick stood at attention, ready to discuss things immediately and for several hours.

"Yes," Ashera continued. "We have the ongoing matter of ending the slave trade in Masas to discuss."

Fuck. It wasn't the discussion I was hoping for, but maybe it wasn't too late to sway matters my way. Malachi laughed at my obvious displeasure. *Fucker.* Why was I putting up with him again?

That was right. My little queen and her perfect, tight pussy. I sneered at Malachi. "Don't you have people to harass while I stay and guard your mate for you?"

"You're not guarding me." Ashera's tone was unimpressed as she got up to kiss both men goodbye. I was going to fucking kill both of them. Those were *my* lips.

Malachi shot me a sharp look as they walked out the door together. "You fuck her, and I'll chop your dick off."

The door closed softly behind them, and I dropped into one of the comfier chairs strewn around the room. Ashera sat across from me, still dressed in her fighting leathers. Fuck, they were hot. Of course, she'd probably look even hotter after I ripped them off with my teeth.

"Ambrose."

I looked up to see Ashera staring at me with a smirk. "Yes, little queen?"

"You were drooling."

I rolled my eyes. "Are you sure about that? To me, it seems like you sent away the two men you fucked after me because you couldn't stop thinking about how good it felt when I pounded your pussy on that table."

Ashera smiled, but it was laced with acid. "Seems to me like I bear the marks of both of those men, while yours is nowhere to be found."

"Yet." *Yet? Where the hell had that come from?* Did I really want to be stuck with Lord Featherfuck and Batdude for the rest of my life? Then again, the thought of being able to bury myself in either her pussy or her ass every day had merit. Owning her had merit. Drinking from her. Marking her. *Fuck.*

She arched a brow at me. "You seem awfully sure of yourself. What makes you think we even have a mate bond, let alone that I would accept it?"

I leaned forward, resting my elbows on my thighs as I smiled at her. "You seemed to have a pretty hard time saying no yesterday."

"And you seemed to have a hard time finishing. Or maybe that was because I drained you of all your power after using your body as my own personal plaything?" She tipped her head with the taunt. If I'd thought I was going to slap her ass raw before, she wouldn't be able to sit for a week now.

The air was thick between us, heavy with sexual tension and the energy of something more than either of us wanted to acknowledge. The whispers were back, calling to me.

Ashera pursed her full lips, considering. "You know, I could never accept a mate bond with someone who supports the human slave trade."

"I'm willing to take that into account."

Ashera leaned closer so that our lips were a mere whisper apart. Her eyes dilated as I felt her release her pheromones into the air. Now that I knew she could drain energy without even touching another's skin, I would have to be more careful around her.

"Play fair, little queen," I whispered.

Ashera ran her hands through my hair, and her touch shocked me to my core. I could scent her desire, and if I wasn't careful it was going to drive me mad. "Would you free your slaves for me?"

"I would go to hell and back if it meant I got to fuck you raw again." So much for the upper hand and playing it cool.

She pressed her lips to mine, the connection flooding my veins with something powerful and addictive. "Good." Ashera bridged the small space between us, swinging over to sit on my lap. The pressure of her tight ass against my erection was fucking delicious. How could she have let that asshole king fuck her there first? That was supposed to be mine.

She was supposed to be mine. I kissed her deeply, sliding my hands down the leathers that covered her, frustrated it wasn't her silky smooth skin, while fucking her mouth with my tongue. She made a moan of approval, and I knew she wanted it as badly as I did. She wanted me. Gods, I needed to touch her everywhere. I needed to be inside her. *Fuck that asshole Malachi.*

I needed to keep my dick.

I pushed her back so there was space between our bodies. "Little queen, I'm desperate, and I mean fucking desperate, to be inside of you again. But I don't trust that mates one and two won't castrate me if I fuck you."

Ashera glared at me. "Don't tell me you're growing a conscience now."

I huffed. "More like I'm attached to my dick and I'd like it to stay attached."

Her voice dropped, and I felt her flood the room with more power. *Fuck.* It was taking everything in me to stay upright, let alone not to succumb to my feral instincts and take her over the chair. "No one has to know, Ambrose. It's just you and me."

I shook my head. "No, they'll know. I don't know how, but they'll know, and then I'll be dickless, watching them screwing you every chance they get."

She pouted. "You're no fun."

"Take that up with them."

Ashera opened her mouth to protest, but a knock sounded on the door, interrupting us.

A servant poked their head into the study, bowing quickly to Ashera. "Your Highness, the representative from Juniya has arrived. They're waiting for you in the throne room."

I groaned loudly, and Ashera stood with a quick glare my way. "Thank you. Tell him I'll be there momentarily." Ashera made her way toward the door.

"Excuse me, where do you think you're going?" I was out of my chair in a flash, holding the door closed with one hand.

"To my chambers to dress for our new guest." She was annoyed, but I knew there was more than one way to lose my dick, and I didn't like any of them. I moved my hand but followed her out the door and into the hallway as she walked. "There's no need to follow me, Ambrose. I allowed you to stay so Malachi would get off my back, but I think I can handle myself in my own castle."

I shrugged. "All the same, I think I'll walk with you." We strolled toward her bedchamber in silence, both of us lost in thought.

When we arrived at her suite, Ashera stepped inside and slammed the door before I could squeeze inside. I pounded the ornately carved wooden door. "Ashera! Godsdammit, woman!

Open this door." For fuck's sake. The little queen was going to be the death of me and my dick.

Ashera's voice was muffled when she spoke. "Seriously, Ambrose, I can get dressed on my own. Just wait out there. I wouldn't want to put you in a precarious position by getting undressed in front of you anyway."

How had my life come to this, waiting outside the door for a woman who refused to own slaves? I slid down the door and sat on the floor. Now I was hard again, imagining her pulling her leathers off her lithe body. "You can be a right tease when you want to be, little queen. Someone needs to teach you some respect."

"Good thing I have two mates to help me with that then." I rolled my eyes. I couldn't imagine either of those two love-struck idiots disciplining her the way she needed to be. The way she wanted to be.

She was quiet for a moment. "Ashera? You okay in there?" I called. No response.

Glass shattered behind the door, and still nothing from Ashera. "Ashera? Ashera!" Something was wrong. I felt it in the very marrow of my bones. Of course it had to be on my watch. I was on my feet in an instant, banging the door with every ounce of power I had. "Ashera! Open the fucking door!"

I started ramming my shoulder into the wood, and then stood back to take a running kick at it. The strong wooden door swung open to display an empty room with the balcony doors wide open. A wine glass was shattered in front of Ashera's dressing table, but Ashera was nowhere to be found.

I ran out to the balcony, feeling the sense of loss so keenly I was surprised I hadn't collapsed. She was gone, and it was my fucking fault. If we never got her back, I would never forgive myself. I fell to my knees on the balcony, praying to every god and goddess I had never believed in.

"Ashera! I'm coming for you!" I buried my head in my hands.

I wasn't looking forward to what came next, because now I needed to explain what had happened to Malachi and Jacobi. I just hoped my dick would still be intact by the time we found her.

Make no mistake, the little queen was mine, and I was going to find her and claim her if it meant I had to slaughter every single person in my path.

6

ASHERA

I awoke with a groan. Everything fucking hurt. My eyes were gritty as I blinked them open, and I was disoriented when I discovered I wasn't in my chambers. I glanced around, my head oddly fuzzy, and took in the large, dark empty room around me. Where was I?

A chill settled in my bones, and that was when I realized I was naked. A collar was wrapped around my neck, connecting me to the floor. I brought my hands up to feel the collar and fear flooded me. If I was right, the metal around my neck wouldn't allow me to use any of my abilities, even if I was able to touch someone.

What the hell happened? The last thing I remembered was walking with Ambrose to my chambers. I'd had some wine, I think... It was all so blurry.

I looked down at myself and noticed I was covered in bite marks and blood. *Fuck, vampires.* The collar was even impacting my ability to heal.

Bright light flooded the room, and I slammed my eyes shut against the assault. I slowly opened them again as they adjusted.

The room appeared empty and cavernous. It didn't provide any clues as to where I might be.

"Hello, Queen Ashera." I turned my head toward the voice. "Don't be shy. All of the kingdoms are watching you, even the delegates in Shaytan." The speaker, a male, gestured above me. I turned my head and noticed the magical sphere that would allow for this all to be broadcast to everyone the caster wished.

I slowly rose to my feet, the chain attached to my collar only allowing for that and not much else. "Who the fuck are you?"

"Is that any way for a royal to talk?" the man taunted. I snarled. "Your blood was delicious by the way. I could see why my prince was so enamored with you."

Ice raced down my spine. *Ambrose?* I immediately dismissed the notion. I wasn't sure why, but I knew without a doubt he had nothing to do with this. "We plan to test out the other part of you he seems so addicted to as well before we take your head."

I didn't respond. Let the idiot continue to talk about his grand plans. My eyes darted around the room, and my heart rate picked up when I noticed far more men in the room with each passing minute.

"You'll all notice the collar around our beautiful queen's throat," the man continued. "It's a special blend of magicked metal that ensures she can't use her powers or any other magic. She's essentially just like the slaves she loves so much." Chuckles rang out around the room as the circle closed in on me. "Which means the time we have with her is going to be a lot more fun."

Crack!

The snap of a whip behind me had me jerking my head toward the sound. "Boys." Two vampires rushed forward and grabbed my arms, forcing me to my knees.

"We took the liberty of draining Her Highness before

bringing her here. We wanted to make sure she had an authentic experience." More chuckles broke through the silence.

I heard the crack of the whip before the pain seared across my back. I bit my lip to stop myself from screaming as my body jerked. I wasn't given time to brace for a second hit before it came, repeatedly. The motherfucker was damn near hitting the same spot every time.

The heat of my blood burned as it poured down my back. The vampires around me shuffled closer, their low growls of hunger and arousal now laced with the crack of the whip. I refused to scream. I wouldn't give them the pleasure. Instead, I stared into the eyes of the man who continued to provide commentary for those watching. I noticed several other orbs now taking in the spectacle from different angles. I was going to kill every single one of them. My stash of blood for my bath had been running low lately, and I would be happy to refill it.

I was so busy focusing on not screaming and staring into the eyes of a dead man that I failed to notice the foot that swung toward my face from the side. Stars burst behind my eyes as my head snapped sideways, followed quickly by the lash of the whip against my neck and shoulder.

This time I screamed.

"Now, I'd heard you'd been tortured for decades before you started your little army." The vampire tutted as he knelt in front of me. "I doubt you'll last that long since we won't be allowing you to feed, but I'm still interested to see how long we can keep you alive."

I spat in his face. He punched me in mine.

"Bring them in."

Two small cries had me fighting against the hold of the two vampires who still clutched my arms—children. Dread coiled low in my stomach. No. Not children. A young boy and girl were dragged before me, their hands bound in front of them. I surged to my feet, surprising the vampires restraining me.

I took one of them out with my leg and then punched the other square in the face. I reached out to attack the vampire holding the children when the whip wrapped around my neck and dragged me backward.

"Now, now..." The vampire orchestrating all of this clicked his tongue. "We didn't say you could get up, and a woman must always know her place." I glared up at him. "What will you do to keep these children untouched?" He laughed. "Would you get on your knees and blow me? Open those lovely thighs and let all my men take turns fucking you? Give up your own life for theirs?"

I got back up to my knees without answering. I wouldn't fucking break. I knew Malachi and Jacobi were looking for me. I needed to hold out until they found me or I escaped. These vampires were sloppy, and there was bound to be a moment I would be able to take advantage of. And then they'd all be fucking sorry.

The vampire snapped his fingers, and the children were taken away. Confused, I returned my gaze to his. "We'll get to them in a few days once we've reinforced a woman's place." Someone rushed over with a red-hot brand. "Starting with this."

∿

Malachi

BEING FORCED to watch your mate, the woman you loved more than anything else, getting tortured in front of you was worse than death itself.

The first time Ashera screamed, Jacobi, Ambrose, and I had shattered the table we'd been strategizing at.

That fanged douche-canoe is a walking dead man. He'd found us shortly after Ashera had been taken and explained everything. We hadn't ripped his dick off yet, but his usefulness would run out as soon as she was safe.

When the vampires brought out those children, my stomach sank. I knew, without a doubt, she would do anything to keep them from harm. My gaze floated to Jacobi for a split second, and I could see he had realized this as well. Ambrose didn't warrant a fucking look. If I looked at him right now, I'd fucking kill him.

I knew Ashera wouldn't sit back and take this quietly. She would already be planning her escape and her revenge. But that didn't make watching it any easier. Jacobi started pacing when they brought out the brand. I stood stiffly, every muscle in my body aching to fly to her and fuck those vampires up.

Her agonized scream as the main kidnapper pressed the brand to the side of her neck almost had me lunging to wrap my hands around another vampire's throat.

"Do any of them look familiar? Does the room look familiar?" Jacobi was sending out those calming waves of his again, and I was surprisingly grateful for it.

Ambrose's tortured gaze was riveted on Ashera. Now that they'd branded her, they were beating her mercilessly. Even with Jacobi's influence, the vamp grew more and more tense with each blow they landed.

I was offended that he felt this upset. "Don't you fucking get it?" Ambrose's gaze whipped to me. "You're the reason they're doing this. You and that fae fuck in our dungeon. The two of you wanted to take her down a peg and show her her place as a woman. Reinstate slavery. You. Did. This."

He bristled and looked lost for a minute before he steeled himself. "I told you she'd painted a target on her back—"

I slammed my fist into his face. "That is not an excuse for what they are doing to her," I roared.

He pushed me away from him and rubbed his face. Ashera's

next scream had him turning paler than usual. "No. It isn't a fucking excuse. They'll all have me to deal with when we figure out where she is."

"The only reason you're up here and not locked away with the fae is because those are your people who have her. Your ass will be rotting away in our dungeon once we have her back, and then the full might of Shaytan will wage war against Masas."

"Thank fuck you can't make those calls," he snapped.

"He can't." Jacobi's voice was deadly calm. "But I can. You need to watch yourself. Our mate is being tortured, and it seems as though it's by your order."

"She's my mate too!" he roared. Jacobi and I froze in shock. "Ashera is mine! And don't you fuckers think for one second I sanctioned this. I may be a sadistic bastard, but I'm not nearly this terrible, and when I find out where she is, blood will rain down, and not one of those assholes will be left alive."

We stared at him, studying him closely. "His emotions suggest he's telling the truth," Jacobi confirmed, reading him.

Color me surprised. I'd known Ambrose had felt some sort of draw for Ashera, but it hadn't seemed as though it was a mate bond. He was better at hiding his feelings than Jacobi or me— or he was just a spoiled asshole who didn't like having a toy taken away from him.

"I'll take your word for it... for now." Ambrose seemed to sag a bit with relief. "But if you so much as put one fucking toe out of place, I will make sure that Ashera wipes Masas from the map, am I clear?"

He glared at me before giving me a tight nod.

"Where the fuck would they have taken her?" I asked. Ambrose bounced his gaze between Jacobi and me before he realized I expected him to answer the question.

"While they could have stayed here in Shaytan, it would make finding her far too easy. It's more likely they took her to another kingdom." He ran his fingers through his hair as he started to pace. "I'd say Masas, but that would also be too easy. Though, given that they took her from the damn palace, they're just a bunch of fucking idiots." He was rambling now, but I let him continue, hoping something useful would come out of this. "My father and I weren't pleased when we'd heard a woman had taken the Shaytan throne and then freed all their slaves, but I didn't come here with the intention of killing her. Manipulate her into doing what would be in the best interest of Masas, yes. Fuck her, undoubtedly, especially once I saw her, but not kill her."

I growled, and Ambrose stopped pacing to look at me, almost shocked that he'd been saying any of that out loud. I gestured for him to get to the point.

"I doubt Caspian and the fae are in on this," he admitted. "While Juniya is a very close ally of Masas, this isn't Caspian's style. He's very... flashy."

"Flashy?" Jacobi snorted. "That's a mild way of putting it."

I'd never had the pleasure of meeting Prince Caspian, so I wasn't sure what his "style" was, but I knew of King Judah, the witch king of Sahira, and this stank of his ilk. However, I wouldn't put it past any of these assholes aside from Jacobi. Malak had always been slave free, and now their king was Ashera's mate. I trusted Jacobi implicitly and had before he'd mated with my queen.

Actually, out of all the royalty, Ashera aside, he was the only one I could really see myself getting along with, which was probably why I hadn't bristled at the thought of him touching Ashera before I'd realized they were mates. Unlike the fanged asshole in front of me, I hadn't once doubted that Jacobi would respect Ashera.

I suspected Ambrose, on the other hand, really just wanted to fuck Ashera senseless and that was it, even if she was really his mate. It made me want to punch him again.

"Caspian is very over the top," Jacobi commented, breaking

me out of my musings. "Subtly isn't exactly in his vocabulary. Then again, given how close the fae and vampires are, I wouldn't be surprised if he knew or had some idea this was going to happen. What does surprise me is that you would be left out of the loop." He gestured to Ambrose.

Ashera's cry of outrage pulled our heads out of our asses faster than anything else could have. We all swiveled to look at the magical projection in front of us.

She'd been brutally beaten, and one arm hung limply by her side, but she was back on her feet. I knew they'd stripped her in an attempt to humiliate her, but something like that wouldn't bother Sher. It bothered me only because of the sheer number of wounds that littered her body. She wouldn't be able to stay up for much longer without feeding. I could already see the signs of fatigue around her eyes and the slight trembling in her hands. I was weak myself, not having fed since Ashera was taken, so I could only imagine how she would be feeling.

Her eyes weren't focused on her captor anymore, instead, they were narrowed on a naked young woman who was being dragged in front of her. *How many fucking humans do these assholes have to taunt her with?*

"You realize that she'll do whatever she can to keep any of the humans from harm, right?" I stated. Jacobi looked horrified by what he was witnessing, but Ambrose appeared as though he was seeing Ashera, truly seeing her, for the first time.

"We're going to play a little game," her captor said as they forced the young woman to her knees in front of Ashera. "This is one of my blood slaves, Kora. Not only does she provide me with blood, she also knows that her place is to provide for my every need." Ambrose let loose a feral snarl. "Moreover, she knows what the punishment is for disobeying her master."

Kora's sobs carried loudly at the mention of punishment, and my stomach sank.

"We're going to have her decide your punishment."

Ashera's eyes cut suspiciously to the vampire. Her lips tightened with the understanding that what had already come before was going to be nothing compared to what was ahead.

"Kora, what is the punishment if a female denies her master her body?" Ambrose's snarl increased in volume, and my entire body clenched. This asshole knew what was going to happen.

"She is to be passed to whomever her master decides for as long as he decides." Kora's voice was barely above a whisper.

"And what is the punishment if a female were to ever raise her hand or her voice against her master?"

"She would have her hand or her tongue removed. She would then be required to service her master in any way he deemed appropriate." *Gods.*

"Very good, Kora," the vampire praised. "What would happen to the female if she were to pretend to be above her station?"

Kora shuddered before answering. "She would no longer be a woman."

"That's correct, Kora." The vampire smiled at Ashera. "You have committed all of these grave sins against your masters, Queen Ashera." Ashera actually paled. The vampire came closer, grabbed her chin, and brought her face close to his. Now all three of us were snarling. "We're going to go through every sin you've committed and have Kora tell you your fate. Then the citizens of Shaytan will be able to watch their queen be put in her proper place."

"We don't have fucking time to dick around. Ambrose, we need to find her now!" I roared. My wings spread out as rage tore through my veins, and I stormed out of the room, slamming the heavy door behind me. It felt as though stones were crushing my lungs as I struggled to catch my breath. I needed to find Ashera.

The door opened behind me, and Ambrose joined me in the

hall. "I'm going to go question my men." He stalked down the corridor.

I slumped back against the wall. All the stress and fear since finding out about Ashera's disappearance had drained my energy. I knew I was going to need to fight to get my mate back, but without being able to feed... What I needed was sexual energy to feed off of, and seducing the maids was completely out of the question. I doubted I'd even be able to get a hard-on since they weren't my mate, and the thought of touching someone who wasn't my mate or part of our mate bond sickened me. I would have to take care of this myself. It wouldn't give me as much power as feeding off someone else, but it was better than nothing.

Ashera. My cock grew hard as I imagined her full lips giving me a teasing smile. Her luscious curves would be on display as she reached her hand into my pants and stroked me, softly at first, and then gaining speed with the intensity of her kisses.

I undid my pants and wrapped my hand around my cock. It was a poor substitute for Ashera's soft skin, but it would have to do. I groaned, pumping my aching cock, my hips thrusting against the air as I visualized sinking into her delicious pussy. She was always so wet for me, so ready. She wrapped around me as though she'd been made to take every godsdamn inch of my cock. I'd never fucked anything more delicious.

And the way my sweet little slut would beg as I teased her. "Mal, please."

The intensity was building under my skin, rushing through my veins as I moved my hand faster, harder, imagining I was driving in and out of her slick heat. *Fuck.* As I edged closer toward my release, I fed off the energy in the air, holding onto the vision of her ripe breasts bouncing with each hard, demanding thrust of my hips, and how her pussy would squeeze my cock as she got closer and closer to screaming my name. I kept the image of her fresh in my mind as I fucked my hand. I practically felt the scrape of her nails down my back as she urged me to fuck her as hard as I could, giving her my all.

My release hit me hard and fast, leaving me whispering Ashera's name. I punched my hand into the wall behind me, cursing the gods that she wasn't here herself.

"What the hell are you doing?" Ambrose had snuck up on me, obviously back from questioning his men. Clearly, I'd been too caught up in my fantasy of my delicious little war queen wrapped around my cock to notice anyone coming down the hall. I was losing my edge.

I pulled up my pants, glaring at the vamp. "What the fuck does it matter to you?"

"Maybe because our mate is being tortured to death, and you're sitting out here getting yourself off."

I sneered and used my significant height to tower over the fanged fucker. "I'm a fucking incubus, moron. How the fuck do you think I feed my magic?" I used my most condescending tone with the fucker. "Ashera isn't your mate yet. Hell, we don't even know for sure that she is."

Ambrose growled.

"What's going on out here?" Jacobi stuck his head out of the study. Surely, he had to have heard what was happening. The angel king needed to stop being so damn polite if he was going to survive being mated to Ashera.

Ambrose just rolled his eyes. "It doesn't fucking matter. I know where she is."

7

AMBROSE

We stood in front of a nondescript door inside the basement of an old, abandoned mineral processing factory in Masas. Knowing what was happening behind it turned my stomach. Ashera was in there being tortured to within an inch of her life. My little queen. My *mate*. If I had wings, I would have fucking flown into the dungeon where she was being held. But I didn't, so I would have to settle for dramatics, especially after being *carried* here by Malachi. Not only did I have to save my mate, but I also needed to assert some dominance.

My subjects didn't have a healthy dose of fear for the royal family—me in particular—for nothing. I didn't glance back at Malachi or the feathered fuck—I was apparently stuck with both of them now. Instead, I kept my gaze forward, focused on getting my little queen and killing every single asshole who stood in between us. With all the power and rage in my body, I kicked the door open, roaring as I did so.

Mine. And they would fucking regret ever taking her.

My vision blurred as I raced inside, but the shocked faces of my supposed people would remain with me—especially since that expression stayed frozen on their faces as I ripped their heads off their bodies. Men, women, it made no difference to me. They had dared to touch what was mine. It was an instant death sentence.

I was born into a world of violence, a kingdom where human flesh was worth less than a sack of produce. I was the prince of blood, the king of night. The slick blood that coated the floor as I ripped the limbs off Ashera's captors was merely a price to pay, and I'd pay it gladly. But the memories of Ashera's injuries as she stood up for what she believed in, for protecting innocent children... that was spilled blood I refused to accept, so I made my way toward her, snapping bones and ripping skin with my teeth. None of these vampires deserved to live. Even becoming slaves was too good for them. Death was the only justice for what had been done here today.

I stood at the far end of the room, in front of a door that was locked with a heavy chain, trying to catch my breath. I cracked my neck and ran my bloody fingers through my hair to achieve some semblance of decorum before I turned around to admire my handiwork.

I had painted the room a mix of bright and dark red, and the bodies of ten or so vamps lay strewn in various positions. Some had all their limbs attached. Some didn't. And back at the entrance stood Malachi and Jacobi. The feathered fuck looked taken aback, but Malachi actually appeared impressed.

"Well, princess, looks like you might actually care more than you let on." Malachi grinned at me, and I wanted to punch that smirk right off his fucking face. I would fuck his face up later for calling me princess.

A low, tortured moan drifted through the door in front of me, and all three of us froze before slowly turning our heads in that direction. *Ashera*. The beast within me roared at the sound of our wounded mate. My bloodlust rose even higher.

I grabbed hold of the chain, and with a quick yank, pulled it free. I slammed my foot against the door, and it flew off its hinges, revealing the dimly lit room. My head tilted as I took in the scene before me—a predator watching its prey.

Ashera lay in the middle of a large group of vampires. Even though we'd gotten here as quickly as possible once I realized where these morons were holding her, they'd still been able to do quite a bit more damage. She was bruised, bleeding, and desperately in need of power. I could see the tremble in her limbs from here as she struggled to remain conscious. A low rumble rose in my chest, and every vampire in the room froze in fear. They knew the better, stronger predator had arrived. I was the alpha male, and they were going to be sorry they ever fucked with what was mine.

I sauntered into the room, allowing my rage to build to savage levels within me, and then I took a deep breath. When I spoke, my voice was surprisingly calm. "Imagine my surprise when I saw that *vampires* had taken a royal."

The vampires shifted uneasily as I continued forward.

"Imagine my further surprise that these vampires suggested to the world that *I* was somehow responsible for the kidnapping and torture of a royal."

"M-My lord," the vampire who'd been orchestrating this whole thing whimpered. "She is a w-woman. She—she f-freed her slaves. She m-must be d-dealt with."

"And who are you to deal with her?" My roar had all the vampires falling to their knees.

I finally stood in front of Ashera. *My mate.* She had propped herself up on her arm and was now tilting her head up to look at me. I clenched my hands at my sides. She was covered almost entirely in her own blood. She'd been whipped, stabbed, burned, and beaten, and yet the fire that had always been present in her eyes still burned bright.

I knelt in front of her and lightly placed a hand on her cheek. To my amazement, she turned her head into my hand. I could feel the connection running between us as what had always been there flared vividly.

"Ambrose," she murmured.

My heart clenched, and I could no longer contain my rage. I no longer *wanted* to contain my rage. "Malachi. Jacobi." My voice was a low snarl, but I knew they heard me. "Remove her collar and feed her."

The vampire who'd been torturing my mate protested. I shot to my feet in a blink and watched as he collapsed to the ground, clenching his still beating heart in my hand. I sank my fangs into it, quickly draining it of all the blood it possessed. That was all it took to unleash my beast.

I closed my eyes, feeling the power rush to every cell in my body. Everything in the small, dank room was very clear to me. Vampires didn't typically drink the blood of one of their own. The aftermath usually wasn't pretty. Bloodlust could easily take hold and never release its grip on the vampire in question. I had to stay in control though. For her.

Ashera's sigh of relief woke me from my trance, and my eyes sprang open to size up the remaining vampires in the room. Elites. Friends of my father's. Noblemen. And not one of them deserved a quick death for what they had done to my little queen.

"Did you really think this would end well for you?" I growled, stalking closer to the vampires. They shrank away in fear. The bravado they had demonstrated while torturing Ashera was gone. They knew this was the end for them, and there was no changing my mind.

I approached the first—an older vamp I had known since I was a child. I stroked his cheek with my blood-soaked hand, leaving a bright red streak behind. "Did you think I would praise you for this?"

"Please—please, my lord. My family," he begged, looking anywhere except at me.

"Look at me when I am speaking to you!" I roared, and his nervous gaze locked onto mine. My voice dropped to a deadly whisper. "The woman you have been torturing is *my* family." I snapped my hand out, ripping his arm clean off and throwing it to the ground with a sickening, squelching thunk.

He screamed, and the other vampires looked away as he clutched the wound with his remaining arm to try and staunch the bleeding.

"I told you to look at me!" His eyes wouldn't meet mine. I growled and gave his neck a quick snap, leaving him slumped in a pool of his own blood. I had killed him far too quickly, but there were so many more who needed to be punished.

The next vamp in line had never been a favorite of mine, a piddly bootlicker of my father's. I slit his throat efficiently with the obsidian blade I kept in my boot. I couldn't deny it, my cock hardened eagerly as I listened to the sounds of him choking on his own blood. I'd always been a sick son of a bitch who needed a rough fucking after a good killing spree.

I could feel Ashera behind me, stronger after feeding, but the remaining vampires in this room still needed to pay. The spilling of blood demanded a high price be paid in return. Three more remained, and fury was still blazing hot within my soul. I wanted to tear them limb from limb and burn the bodies, but I also needed answers. I needed to stay in control of the beast inside me until I had them. I paced in front of them, lazily twirling my knife on my finger. "One of you will tell me who you work for, and the one who does gets to go home at the end of this."

The oldest spit at my boots. "If you think I'll ever bow down before that human loving whore, you're sorely mistaken. King Tomas would be disgus—" With a quick flick of my wrist, I flung the knife to pierce one of the old vampire's blood-red eyes. He screeched and fell to the ground.

I kneeled over him. "You will not speak of my queen that

way." Slowly, I dug the knife in deeper until the tip had reached his brain. It wasn't deep enough to instantly kill him, but the wound was certainly fatal. He could suffer with the other asshole.

I stood up, dusting off my pants. "Which one of you will tell me who you work for?" A dark-haired idiot kept nervously glancing at his dying comrades as they rolled on the floor in agony next to him. "Pay them no mind, it's no different than what you did to Ashera," I commanded, but he couldn't keep his eyes off them. I sighed and stepped forward to snap his neck.

I turned to the final man, the youngest of the group. His name was Ramon, and he was one of the noblemen I had grown up and trained with. "Ramon, tell me who you work for, and you can go home."

Ramon boldly met my gaze. "Shaytan will fall. If you aren't careful, you'll fall with it."

Control. I needed to stay in control. A growl rumbled deep in my chest. "Ramon, I'll give you one more chance." I stepped closer, pressing my knife against the delicate skin of his neck.

Ramon didn't look away and narrowed his eyes on me. "Humans are a disgrace and shouldn't walk our great land. And your *queen*" —he glanced behind me at Ashera as he spat the word— "deserves everything that's coming for her."

I wanted to kill him. I *really* wanted to kill him. I could hear the blood pumping in my veins as every cell in my body screamed for me to slay him where he stood. But I stepped back and turned to Ashera. I crouched in front of her, offering her the knife. "Ramon is right about one thing, little queen. You deserve everything coming to you, including killing him in whichever way you see fit."

Ashera met my gaze, weakened and bruised, but a fire still burned in her green eyes. She gave me a knowing smile, a simple twist of her full lips, and got to her feet. I stood as well, brushing off my pants. "You can make it last as long as you want, Ashera." I wanted Ramon to suffer for the disgusting things he had said about her. I wanted to hear him scream for mercy.

Ashera stepped up to Ramon, still unwavering and defiant. He didn't attempt to beg for his life. He knew this was the end for him. I wondered how long she would draw it out for. Ashera turned my knife in her hand, feeling the sharpness along her finger, and then she swiftly and efficiently severed his head from his body.

She turned around to look at the three of us, giving us a casual shrug. "He didn't deserve to live a moment longer."

I was certain my jaw hit the floor as surprise and lust warred within me. Behind me, Jacobi was also silent. Malachi, however, was laughing. "That's my girl," he praised. Ashera rewarded him with a blinding smile.

Now that the immediate threat was over, exhaustion weighed heavily on my bones. The knowledge that my people weren't who I thought they were ate at me. I sank to my knees. For the first time since Ashera had been kidnapped, I felt like I could breathe. A gentle hand rested on my shoulder, and I leaned into the touch, away from the bodies strewn around us.

"It's okay, Ambrose," Ashera whispered, her spirit bright even through her bruised body. "It's okay."

~

Ashera

"It's okay," I whispered again, resting my hand on his face like he had done to me as I lay in chains. "I'm okay."

Ambrose looked up at me, and for once I didn't see the cocky, self-assured vampire. I saw a broken man, one who had gone to hell and back just as he'd promised. I leaned in and kissed him softly.

He groaned, deepening the kiss as he wrapped his hands around me, still slick with the blood of the vampires he had slaughtered. He had killed his own people for me.

If I had doubted the mate bond before, I no longer had those doubts. Everything he had done for me today, everything he had sacrificed...

Ambrose moaned, and the hard length of his erection pressed against my naked thigh. I could feel his desperation in his kiss, his desire, his need to possess. I could feel it all because I felt it too. I could feel Jacobi's and Mal's emotions flooding my veins as well, igniting all my senses. These vampires had battered my body, but they hadn't shattered my mind. These men—*my* men—their minds had been tortured as they imagined the worst. We needed to heal before we took on the resistance, and we needed to do that together.

I opened my mouth, letting my vampire's tongue dart in and swirl around my own. A gasp escaped me, and Ambrose broke our embrace. When he glanced at me, his eyes were dark with lust. "Oh, my little queen," he breathed. "You're in so much trouble. If you had just let me into your room, none of this would have happened. You won't be able to walk by the time I'm done with you. Your feathered king will have to carry you home."

Jacobi made a noise of discontent behind me, and I heard him mutter, "Are you seriously going to let the vampire prick do this right now?" to Malachi under his breath.

Malachi chuckled, a dark sound that sent a shock of desire straight to my core. "I think Princess Ambrose has earned it at this point."

Ambrose growled, biting and licking his way down my neck. He slid his fingers between my legs. "I'll show you fucking Princess Ambrose. You two watch while I demonstrate how a real man fucks a succubus queen."

He tweaked my nipple with his fingers, stroking my wet folds with his other hand. I wasn't surprised to find myself already soaked with desire for him. As much as I wanted to, I couldn't deny the attraction I had to my dark prince, and seeing him kill ruthlessly like that to save me... it was the biggest turn-on. His lips and fingers made me a panting mess in no time at all.

"More," I begged.

"On your hands and knees for me, little queen," Ambrose demanded.

I sank to the floor eagerly, not paying any mind to the blood pooling around us. It was a real disappointment that the blood was wasted and I couldn't use it for a bath. Most of it was probably mine anyway. No matter. We'd all make them pay, and I was sure there'd be more blood for my store before this was finished.

Ambrose dropped to his knees behind me and slid his finger into my wet pussy. I moaned at the sudden intrusion, but it wasn't enough.

"Spread your legs wider."

I did what he asked without question, my knee slipping in the blood I was resting on. He took his finger away, and I whipped my head back to look at him. "Are you going to fuck me, or are you going to tease me?"

Ambrose laughed, unbuttoned his pants, and stripped off his shirt to display his impressively carved stomach. He leisurely stroked his cock before slipping it between my legs. "I never said I was going to make it easy."

He slapped my ass as hard as he could, the smack echoing in the small room. I cried out, but before I had time to register the pain, he slammed his dick inside of me. My cry of pain turned into one of pleasure as I felt whole once more. Ambrose started a punishing pace, only slowing occasionally to smack my ass *hard*. The room slipped away and the punishments disappeared as I focused on Ambrose and the way he moved inside me. The connection we had was real, and the sexual energy between us gave me enough energy to help me heal. I could feel Malachi and Jacobi's desire as they watched Ambrose fuck me, and it only added to the overwhelming sensation building within me.

I needed a release, I was so close to orgasm, but Ambrose suddenly pulled out, leaning over my back to whisper in my ear. "I asked you once before, little queen, and I'll ask you again. Who is your master? Who can make you come like no other?"

I moaned, arching my back, and pressed against him as my need soared.

"Not until I have my answer, Ashera. You've made me ache, made me wait for you. Now, who owns you body and soul?"

I wouldn't cave. *Couldn't* cave. Before I could protest, he dragged a finger down my back, and I curved my spine to meet his touch.

"Because I'll tell you a secret, *mate*. You've been my master since that first moment I saw you in the throne room."

I felt the bond sink into place with the confession, both of us acknowledging what had always been there. "Ambrose. Fuck me. Please," I begged, craving to feel him inside me.

"Say it, Ashera. Say the words," he hissed, and I felt his cock ease into me, but not nearly enough to satisfy me. "Say it, and I'll give you what you need."

"I'm yours!" I screamed, and he sank to the hilt. It was all I needed, and I shattered around his cock, calling out his name. The back of my neck burned, and I knew the mate bond was solidifying between all four of us as my vampire joined our group. Ambrose stroked my back, brushing my hair over my shoulder as he continued to thrust, prolonging my orgasm. When he slowed to a stop, I sighed, my hands and knees trembling as my body came back down.

"Fuck, that's beautiful." Ambrose pushed my hair over my shoulder before running his finger over the mark.

"What is it?" I whispered, knowing he was admiring his mate mark as he once again moved inside of me.

"An ankh."

I smiled. It was the perfect representation for my vampire mate—life. I relaxed into his touch, comfortable in the knowledge that we were one.

"Feathered fuck," Ambrose called softly.

"I have a name," Jacobi responded with annoyance.

"Whatever. I can feel how badly you want her. Get over here and fuck her mouth. Show her what happens when she doesn't listen to her mates." His tone was filled with wicked amusement. I shuddered, suddenly far more alert and aroused than I'd been moments ago despite having had a mind-numbing orgasm.

Jacobi mumbled something I couldn't hear before he was down on his knees in front of me, his cock already out and deliciously hard. Malachi's footsteps drifted closer, but he didn't come down to play just yet. It seemed he was willing to let Ambrose lead for the time being. Something had definitely shifted between them while I was gone.

Jacobi fisted his hands tightly in my hair, and a low growl rumbled up his chest. "Don't you *ever* do something like that again." The emotional strain in his voice had tears welling in my eyes. "Now suck my cock and show me how sorry you are."

My gaze darted up to meet his. Where did *that* come from? Wherever it came from, it was fucking *hot*. I clenched around Ambrose, who let out a soft groan, before I leaned in to lick the tip of Jacobi's cock. I moaned at the taste of him, salty and sweet and oh so heavenly. I lapped at him, wanting to tease him the way Ambrose had teased me.

Ambrose brought his hand down on my ass. "He said suck his cock, little queen." His voice was low and deadly, and I clenched around him again. "Don't squeeze my cock, suck the feathered king."

Jacobi tightened his hands in my hair, pulling my face closer. My gaze dropped to his cock as I wrapped my lips around the tip, sucking hard.

"Gods!" Jacobi shuddered. Ambrose rewarded me with a hard thrust, which forced my mouth farther down on Jacobi's length. My angel used his hands to guide his shaft deeper until he was fully seated in my mouth. I swallowed around him, and he cried out his pleasure as he tilted his head back.

I wanted a portrait of this moment. His wings spread wide, his head arched back in ecstasy. He was stunning. *And mine.*

"Let me show you." Malachi's voice was suddenly right in my ear as he placed his hands over Jacobi's. He slid me off the king's cock, keeping just the tip in my mouth before saying, "Now fuck it like you would her delicious little pussy."

Jacobi's head snapped up, and our eyes locked as he thrust against my face. I moaned low in the back of my throat, and he bit off a curse, never once stopping. Ambrose started moving at a leisurely pace behind me, every now and then thrusting hard enough to slide me down Jacobi's cock as he thrust into my mouth.

"Princess." Malachi's deep tenor sent shivers down my spine. "I believe you threw an epic tantrum once you'd learned the angel king here had fucked that tight little ass before you. Since you did all the work tonight, I'm willing to let you claim it right now without a fight. So I'll ask you, do you want to remain buried in her dripping pussy? Or do you want to fuck her ass?"

Jacobi stopped thrusting, holding me against his cock, and Ambrose pulled out immediately and instructed Malachi to get on his back under me.

Almost as though they'd been doing this for ages, Jacobi and Malachi moved my body in a way so my mouth never once left the throbbing cock it was wrapped around as my assassin settled beneath me. As they lowered my body back down, Mal viciously thrust up into me, causing me to cry out around Jacobi.

Gods, all three of them. I was fully healed by the time Ambrose and I completed our mate bond, so all of this extra sexual energy had me humming with power and flooded me with a savage, primal need.

Ambrose's slick hand spread the cheeks of my ass as he inserted one finger, and then a second, working me in time with Malachi's and Jacobi's thrusts into my body. I could feel my eyes start to roll into the back of my head when the vampire replaced his fingers with his cock. He slid in with one smooth thrust, and I shattered again.

And then again when Jacobi opened his gift to all of us, causing my other two mates to bite back curses as we were inundated with the pleasure the others were feeling. It was like I couldn't stop coming. I might actually pass out.

Malachi played with my nipples as all three of them started thrusting, and Ambrose trailed his fingers down to play with my clit.

I am absolutely going to pass out.

With Jacobi's gift open, I hadn't had the chance to come down from the high of one orgasm before being thrown into the next. The sensations didn't stop as they continued to use my body to find their own releases.

"Holy fuck," Malachi cursed. "I think she's trying to strangle my cock."

"I'm never letting either of you have her ass," Ambrose growled. "I will literally kill you both first."

"Gods, her mouth. It's almost like she wants to suck my very soul from my body." Jacobi shuddered, and his release set off the other two.

Three sets of roars had my ears ringing as their hips all jerked against me, emptying themselves into my body. I couldn't hold myself up, my bones turned to jelly from the continuous orgasm I just experienced. We collapsed into a sated heap, our limbs tangled as our hearts pounded wildly.

"My chest hurts," Ambrose complained.

"Shut the fuck up," Malachi grumbled. Seriously. Couldn't they get along for two fucking seconds?

"No, I'm fucking serious. It's burning."

I rolled my eyes. "Come here, princess. I'll kiss it better." Ambrose rolled over to glare at me, and as soon as I saw his chest, I couldn't control my laughter.

Malachi saw what I was laughing at and quickly joined in.

"What the *fuck* is so funny?" Ambrose looked absolutely livid. I really shouldn't push him, not after the day he'd had, but I couldn't help myself.

"Your chest," I gasped between bouts of laughter. "My mark." I couldn't get the words out without collapsing again.

Ambrose's gaze darted down to his chest—broad and deliciously muscular—which was now covered in a large tattoo of a crown. His eyes narrowed, and he glared at me again. "You've got to be fucking kidding me. It's covering my entire fucking chest!"

I stopped laughing for a moment as a sense of possessive pride filled me. "I know. Isn't it great?"

Ambrose huffed. "You'll pay for this one, Ashera. And don't you fucking start, you feathered fuck!" He turned to point at Jacobi, who was trying to hide his smirk behind his hand.

"Come on," I purred, allowing my hungry gaze to slide over every inch of his chest, making it damn clear what I thought of the mark. "Don't you think it's kind of sexy? I mean, now everyone will know you're my mate."

Ambrose stopped for a moment, considering my words. "Everyone will know you're mine..." He leaned over me again, kissing me hard enough to take my breath away. He pulled back, looking at me seriously. "You're *mine*. And don't you fucking forget it."

I pushed him off me, rising to my feet. "Time to stop thinking with your dick. We need to start tracking down whoever is running this resistance. Please tell me one of you thought to bring me clothes?"

The three of them glanced at each other and then back at me. "Why am I not fucking surprised?" I muttered. "Get dressed. I'll deal with this."

I made my way back into the front room, grimacing at the mess Ambrose had left behind. I scoured through the bodies before I found a woman about the same size as me and stripped her of her dress. She wouldn't need it anymore. I pulled the loose-fitting garment over my head. It wasn't my style, but it would do to get me home at least. "Are you guys ready, or are you in there jerking each other off?" I called, crossing my arms impatiently.

Malachi exited first, his dark energy making me smile. My incubus was all snarls and fighting leathers, but so loving—toward me at least. Jacobi followed close behind him, offering me a sweet smile as he shook out his bright wings. Last but not least, Ambrose sauntered out of the door, his glare firmly in place. He had pants and shoes on, but no shirt as he proudly showed off the giant crown he was so pissed about only moments before.

I shook my head at them, my heart swelling with love for these wonderful creatures who hadn't given up on me. My men. My mates.

8

JACOBI

We'd gotten Ashera back to her palace, washed, dressed, and fed when it occurred to me that we still had the fae delegation locked in the dungeon. Shit. I scrubbed my hand down my face as I looked at Ashera with a grimace.

"Prince Caspian and his delegation are locked in the dungeon."

Her eyes snapped to me before narrowing on Malachi. "Why?"

I was actually happy I wasn't the incubus right now. If looks could kill, Malachi would have been a pile of ash on the floor.

"It was too much of a coincidence that they arrived at the same moment you'd been taken." Malachi shrugged, not at all sorry. "We can go down and free them now."

Ashera groaned and put her head in her hands. "If he's anything like the princess here, this is going to suck." She jerked her thumb at Ambrose, who instantly bristled at her words.

"Caspian and I are close allies—"

Ashera cut Ambrose off. "That's what I'm afraid of." He

leveled her with a steely glare, but she paid him no mind. "You're a pain in the ass!"

Malachi and I chuckled. Ambrose looked extremely offended.

"Excuse you? *I'm* a pain in the ass? Really? Me?" He waved a hand toward Ashera's body. "Have you met yourself?"

Malachi choked back a laugh, and I fought to keep my lips from twitching. Apparently, life with these two was never going to be dull. I rather liked it. This was definitely more pleasurable than droning on about the wonders of chastity to my people.

"Because you just saved my life, I'm going to ignore that comment." Ashera huffed, switching her attention back to Malachi. "Let's go get them out of their cells and into the best suites we have."

"I should come with you, love." I stood. "While Ambrose and Caspian might be close allies, I may be able to help with any ill feelings."

Ambrose stiffened, bouncing his gaze between Ashera and me. "I'm coming too. If he even puts one toe out of line, I'm going to punch him in the throat."

Ashera shot me a look as if to say, *Can you believe him right now?* I couldn't fight the chuckle that rumbled in my chest.

Malachi held up his hand when it became apparent Ambrose wanted to argue more with Ashera. "We'll all go." That seemed to settle everyone.

"Since Caspian was in the dungeons this whole time, we know that he wasn't part of what happened today. Is it possible he's part of the resistance?" Ashera asked, looking at Ambrose for an answer.

"I doubt it," he replied honestly. "Look, I won't lie. We're very alike, little queen. I'm sure he had a similar reaction when he'd heard that a woman had taken the throne and freed all her slaves. Though, if he thought to fuck you into submission like I did, I'm going to cut off his dick."

Surprisingly, neither I nor Malachi growled at the thought of Ambrose fucking Ashera into submission. In fact, images started to play through my mind of our queen tied up to her bed, taking us one after the other over and over again. I reached down to adjust myself, not missing the knowing smirk on the vamp's face.

"I think we all agree that if Caspian has any designs on Ashera, his dick will be swiftly removed from his body," Malachi grumbled. Ambrose and I nodded in agreement, while Ashera rolled her eyes.

"Can we get back on topic please?" She sounded mildly annoyed. "Jacobi, you'll be able to tell if he's lying, right?"

I shrugged. "My powers don't necessarily work that way. If he believes something to be true, I won't be able to tell if he's lying. But if he is knowingly stating something that is false, I'll be able to pick that up."

She looked thoughtful, but our conversation was cut short as we arrived in the dungeons. Malachi led us right to the cell that held Caspian and his men. The fae prince hadn't aged a day since I'd last seen him. Almost as tall as I was, his icy white hair was carefully coiffed—not surprising despite having spent time in the dungeons. The shimmering white tattoos declaring his elemental control twisted across his face and down his neck. Both his hair and tattoos were a stark contrast to his skin, which was as black as the night sky, and his narrowed hazel eyes held startling hints of gold around the pupil.

The fae all looked slightly disheveled, but no worse for wear. Caspian wore a deep scowl that turned murderous at the sight of Ambrose.

Ashera pushed in front of us, despite our growls of protest, and magically unlocked the door. "I would like to personally apologize, Prince Caspian." He moved so fast none of us could track him, and a second later, he had Ashera pinned to the wall by her throat.

Ambrose let out a snarl as Malachi and I growled low. How dare he touch our mate that way?

"Is this how you treat all royals? Or am I just lucky?" Caspian's gaze was locked on Ashera. We moved to pull him from her, but she held up her hand to stay us.

"I do apologize, Prince Caspian. If you would allow me to explain." Ashera's tone was surprisingly calm and soothing. His eyes searched hers before he leaned in to run his nose along her neck. Her eyes fluttered, and every muscle in my body stiffened.

"Un-fucking-believable," Ambrose raged, grabbing Caspian by the shoulder and ripping him away from our mate. "You don't fucking touch her. Are we clear?"

Caspian merely raised a brow at Ambrose before taking me in. "Since when does the king of celibacy get worked up over a female? And you, Ambrose." He returned his attention to the vampire. "You're defending a *woman*? I never thought I'd see the day," he mused.

If we thought Ambrose was a prick, he was nothing compared to this jackass. I was kind of glad we had kept him trapped in the cell for as long as we had. I kept my mouth shut, glaring at him. Ashera had said she wanted to handle it, and I didn't want to step on any toes. It wasn't like she couldn't handle herself.

Ashera shot Ambrose a warning glance. "I've got this." She turned back to Caspian. "As I was saying —"

Caspian smirked at Ambrose. "That's right. Listen to what your queen tells you to do. Wouldn't want you to get in trouble, now would we?" He ran an appreciative glance over Ashera's body. "Although I have to say, I understand the interest. A succubus, right?"

Ashera tipped her head as she studied the fae prince. She took a deep breath and shimmered before our eyes. Glittering golden wings sprouted from her back, and delicate black horns arched gracefully from her hairline. In this state, she was even more stunning. I hadn't even realized she'd been using a glamor. As far as I was aware, not all incubi or succubi had horns and wings.

Ambrose reached down to blatantly adjust himself, and Malachi's wings flared. I didn't bother adjusting myself again, instead I merely widened my stance.

Caspian practically purred at the sight of our queen. "A delicious succubus." A wicked grin spread across his face. He moved into her personal space, and all three of us took a step closer to him. "Have you fucked her yet, Ambrose? What am I saying? Of course you have." He chuckled. "Care to give me a spin, pretty demon?"

The fae wants us to rip his dick off. Our collective growls filled the air. Ashera glanced over at each of us before returning her gaze to Caspian.

"My mate has certainly fucked me." Ambrose puffed up a bit at that. "So have my other two mates. I'm not sure I have room in my bed for your dick, no matter how tiny it may be."

Caspian grabbed her hand and placed it over the growing bulge in his pants. "There's nothing small about me."

I choked back a laugh. Did this fae actually think Ashera was going to fall for this bullshit? Ambrose looked like he was ready to slaughter Caspian where he stood, and I could feel anger bubbling beneath the surface of Malachi's icy demeanor.

Something else was lacing the emotions I was siphoning in the air though, something that was more than lust, and it floated between Ashera and Caspian... It couldn't be, could it?

~

Caspian

I had hoped to arrive in Shaytan before Ambrose did, wanting to see this queen for myself. I knew he would do everything in his power to fuck her, and I wanted to take that pleasure away from him, maybe even set up an accidental meeting where he caught me fucking her. Yes, that would have been delicious.

Technically, Ambrose and I were allies. We had grown up together as princes, and we were close in age. I was only five years older than Ambrose's 410. That didn't mean we liked each other. It just meant we tolerated the other long enough to get what we wanted—used would be the more accurate term—but if the vampire got in the way of what I coveted, all fucking bets were off.

Like now, for example. I wanted to fuck the pretty succubus senseless until she forgot all about her supposed mates and came only for my dick. But these cockblocks, Ambrose included, were standing in my way. That wouldn't fucking do. It didn't help that my magic was weakened from my time in the cells. Fae fed off the elements they used, and the dank dungeons they had held us in were barren of anything we could use for energy.

I just needed to get them far enough away from her so I could sway her to my side. She'd see reason soon enough. After all, she needed me and my resources. Juniya was the largest provider of produce in Dunya, and Ashera suddenly had a lot more mouths to feed. Obviously, Ambrose had lost his head to a pretty pussy and was willing to go along with whatever ridiculous ideas Ashera had dreamed up. Slaves were an important economic component to all our regions, and they needed to be reinstated immediately. No other outcome would be acceptable.

A plan slowly fell into place in my mind. Step one, getting out of this godsforsaken dungeon.

I took a step away from Ashera and her shimmering wings, giving her my most charming smile. "Apology accepted. Now, if you wouldn't mind, my men are exhausted and could use a real bed to sleep in."

Ambrose narrowed his eyes over his mate's shoulder, and the other two winged fuckwads growled, but Ashera silenced them all with a single look. That pussy was either something else, or she was using massive amounts of her power to keep them in line.

She gave me a bright smile. "Wonderful, Prince Caspian. I've prepared our best rooms, please, come."

I kept my mouth shut as Ashera led us through the castle, the three men making sure I kept my distance from their queen. My men were safely dropped off in rooms much more finely furnished than our dungeon quarters, and then we finally arrived at the last room at the end of the hall.

Ashera turned to me. "These will be your quarters while you are here in Shaytan. Again, I apologize."

I waved away her apologies. "No apologies necessary—*if you'll come inside and have a drink with me and explain the whole story.*" *Step two, get her away from these idiots.*

Ambrose slammed me against the wall before I could think, his fangs a breath away from my face. "If you think we would ever leave you alone with her..."

I raised an eyebrow at Ambrose. "Are you afraid, blood sucker? Nervous that your little mate might actually want to take a ride on my cock?" His grip on my shoulders tightened, but I just laughed. "Hell, maybe you're jealous. Do you want to watch? If you're really good, maybe I'll even let you take a turn."

His arm swung back to punch me in the face, but before he could, Ashera covered his fist with her hand. "Enough, Ambrose. Caspian is our guest." She turned to me. "I'll have a drink with you, but they come with me, and if you step out of line, I can't guarantee your safety."

I sneered at Ambrose and brushed off the velvet shoulders of my coat. Guess I would just have to figure out how to seduce the queen with the pricks in the room. Although I wouldn't put it past them to enjoy it, especially with the way they all seemed to move in sync with each other. *Mates*. I rolled my eyes internally. Thankfully I hadn't been subjected to that hell yet. Ashera opened the door, gesturing for me to enter.

I took a seat on the couch, watching Ashera as she poured glasses of amber liquid for all of us. She was talking to me, but I wasn't listening. She was rather elegant in her actions, her body moving as fluidly as the swell of her curves. Was this truly the fearless warrior I had heard so much about? The one who bathed in the blood of her enemies? Noticing me watching, she peeked up at me, giving me a sensual smile. *Right*. Succubus. I needed to be careful with this one. Seduce without being seduced—easier said than done with this winged beauty sitting in front of me. The deep red silk of her gown emphasized the outline of her hips, draping low on her chest, and a trio of blood-red war bands wrapped her trim bicep. An ancient need began to grow deep within me, a whisper of something I couldn't quite decipher, and when she passed me my drink, a shock of desire passed through our touching hands. I couldn't control myself and shot my free hand out to grab her wrist, dragging her closer to me so I could kiss her deeply.

Ashera was frozen at first, unyielding, but then she softened and began to move her lips against mine. Her lips parted, and that was when I was thrown across the room. My head smacked loudly on the windowsill, and I looked up to glare at Ambrose, who still sat next to Ashera. The bat fuck stood behind the winged queen with his hand on the hilt of his blade. And in the middle of the room, next to where I had been sitting on the couch, stood the angel king breathing heavily.

"She's ours. You will not touch her." *Interesting*. I wasn't expecting him to be the one to snap.

Ashera jumped to her feet, coming over to soothe him with a hand. "I had it handled."

He glanced down at her, stroking her cheek. I would bet it was soft to the touch. "We told him not to touch you."

She looked over at me. "I did warn you, Prince Caspian."

I rubbed the back of my neck, getting to my feet. "I didn't realize you meant that literally."

Bat Fuck was at my side in a flash, holding his blade to my chest to keep me from moving any closer to the queen.

Ambrose stood, leering at me with a snide grin. "Jacobi, I feel like our guest needs a clear demonstration on whom Ashera belongs to."

I stiffened, my cock growing hard in my pants. The image of the golden queen on her knees in front of me flashed through my mind. She belonged to me. "I think you've made that quite clear," I snapped.

Ambrose walked toward Ashera and Jacobi. He gripped Ashera's neck, bringing her face to his for a deep kiss, and slid his hand down her chest to caress her full breast. She moaned, the sound sending waves of desire through my body. I took an unintentional step toward her, but Bat Fuck pressed his sword harder against my chest, and my skin split open. He growled in warning, and I clenched my teeth.

Ambrose trailed his hand down her hip, slipping it inside the ruby fabric of Ashera's dress. The scent of need was thick in the room, and I was desperate to be the one pleasuring her. A small gasp escaped Ashera's lips, and Jacobi took a step closer. "How wet is she?" he murmured.

Ambrose locked his gaze onto mine. "She's perfect." He took his fingers out of Ashera and walked over to me before holding them up. "Taste what you'll never get to have."

I sneered at him, and Bat Fuck dug his blade in deeper. "You heard him. Taste our queen," he commanded.

Ambrose shoved his fingers—slick with Ashera's desire—into my mouth, and I internally groaned as the most delicious taste overwhelmed my senses. *Fuck.* I couldn't let them know how badly I wanted her, even as my pants tented with my erection, so I lied. "I've had better."

The angel king spoke up from behind Ambrose. "He's lying."

I knew I didn't like him.

I pushed Ambrose away, only to be confronted with the sight of Ashera's naked body winding around Jacobi's solid frame. "Make sure he's watching," he rumbled.

Ashera met my gaze with lust gleaming in her bright green eyes as Jacobi pulled her down to the floor. He settled her on top of him, facing the three of us. "Ride me, love. Show him what he's missing out on." Ashera lowered herself onto his thick cock, her back arching as she took him in. Who would have expected that from the celibate king?

Bat Fuck groaned as he watched his mate circle her hips to take Jacobi in even deeper. Ambrose was unashamedly stroking himself through his pants, shooting me a knowing glance as I leashed my own primal urges to fight my way over there and take the queen myself.

Ashera moaned and rolled her hips, fucking herself to release on the angel king's cock. Fuck, it was a turn-on. Jacobi met my gaze, trailing his hand down Ashera's back as she rode him. "See how beautiful she is? And she's all ours."

Jacobi lifted his hips, meeting Ashera's movements, and she cried out. "Come for me, my love." I couldn't stop myself from moaning at the delicious sight, watching the stunning queen shatter as she brought herself to orgasm. She panted heavily and offered me a small smile.

Ambrose leaned toward me. "Remember your place, fae fuck." I bristled.

The angel king, meanwhile, gripped Ashera's hips and started moving her faster and harder over his cock. Her breasts bounced enticingly, and I couldn't take my gaze away from the sight. Her hands wrapped around Jacobi's neck, which only served to arch her back farther, thrusting up her clearly aching nipples. My hands twitched at the urge to flick them before sucking them into my mouth.

"Come one more time, little queen," Ambrose encouraged. Ashera dropped her head back as Jacobi continued to move at a harsh pace, and his groans now echoed her cries of passion.

"When she comes around you, it's like her body never wants to let your cock go," Bat Fuck murmured in a husky whisper. *Dammit.*

"Touch yourself, my love," Jacobi growled into Ashera's ear. She whimpered and complied, moving one hand to her stiff nipples and the other to her clit. My hips jerked at the view.

"Jacobi," she cried. "I'm close."

Fuck, so am I.

"Let go, little queen," Ambrose rumbled.

That seemed to be all she needed. She came screaming the angel king's name as he finished with her, both of their hips jerking in the aftermath of their release. I could feel wetness spreading across my pants as I came with them, but I refused to draw attention to myself in the hopes that none of them noticed.

I was more desperate than ever to get inside this stunning succubus queen. If she had the ability to make me come without ever touching me... *Shit.*

9

ASHERA

The morning after we released Prince Caspian from my dungeons, I soaked in a bath. No blood this morning, just bubbles. I'd kept my glamor down, feeling more relaxed and at peace around my mates now that they'd seen the real me. Malachi had kissed me awake a while ago to tell me that he had meetings to attend to, especially now that they had additional information on the resistance. Ambrose and Jacobi had insisted on going with him.

I wanted a moment to myself.

Well... I wasn't really alone. There were two servants in the room with me and three guards stationed outside my bathroom door. My mates weren't taking any risks where my safety was concerned. It was oddly touching.

I needed time to decompress and process what had transpired yesterday. I had been tortured mentally and physically for centuries while I was Lord Pyper's ward, so being physically beaten didn't bother me nearly as much as the emotional component. The faces of those children, that human slave, all of them... Gods, we hadn't seen any other occupied rooms before leaving, which meant that we hadn't killed all the vampires involved. They took those innocent humans. I shuddered at the thought of what was being done to them—if they were even still alive.

I felt as though I'd failed them. I hadn't been able to get them out of those assholes' hands. I had barely been able to stand by the time my mates found me. Running my hands down my face, I knew that I was being unfair to myself, but I couldn't help it. I made a promise years ago. Realistically, I knew that I couldn't change everything for every human overnight, but that didn't stop me from yearning to do the right thing.

My mates would undoubtedly be angry at me for my train of thought.

My eyes drifted to the small dragon mark on my bicep that was usually hidden by my war bands. I'd been exceptionally lucky to have a mate before my rebellion, and I never considered that I might find another mate, let alone three. Visa had been beautiful, and I'd loved her far too much. When she'd been killed at the start of the rebellion by several incubus lords, I'd nearly lost my mind with grief, but I had to stay focused. For her. For Shaytan.

I scrubbed my face before I sank beneath the water. When it happened, I'd been meeting with Malachi to discuss our military strategy. I'd thought it had been safe to leave her at home.

I burst from the surface of the water and leaned back against the tub. I knew better than to focus on the past. I couldn't change Visa's fate, but I could appreciate the mates I had now.

And what mates they were. Malachi, the rock, steadfast and loyal to a fault. Ambrose, a volatile mix of deep love and violence. Jacobi, my sweet angel and secret sexual deviant. I loved them all. I wouldn't let the resistance take away what I'd found, what I'd fought for. Not after I'd already lost so much.

The door flew open, and all three of my mates sauntered into the room. Ambrose still refused to don a shirt, which had me smiling like an idiot every time I caught sight of his chest. Malachi had taken to wearing shirts without sleeves so he, too, could show off his mark. Jacobi always rolled his sleeves up and typically sat with his wrist up so his mark was fully visible.

I had decided to start wearing backless dresses so I could show off Malachi's mark on my shoulder—Jacobi's was hard to miss—and now I wanted to wear my hair pulled away from my neck so Ambrose's mark was also visible. I wore their marks with pride, just as they did mine.

I studied all three of them for a moment before speaking. "You know, you can't just fuck me in front of every male that expresses sexual interest in me." They all scoffed. "I'm a succubus. Even without putting my pheromones into the air or using my powers, men and women are going to want to fuck me."

"Then we're just going to have to clearly demonstrate that you belong to us." Ambrose sounded as though it were that simple. The other two nodded eagerly in agreement.

I rolled my eyes at them. "I'm serious."

"As are we." Jacobi looked and sounded quite serious. "You're ours."

"Of course I am," I soothed. "And you're all mine, but—"

"Save it, Sher," Mal interrupted with a chuckle. "You're not going to talk us out of this."

I glared at them. "You're all lucky I like having sex with you, or else I'd tell you it's off the table until you reconsider."

That had all of them grinning like the smug bastards they were. I rolled my eyes again before standing to get out of the tub. All three of them became unnaturally still, their gazes completely focused on the trails of water that ran down my body. I felt stalked in the best possible way.

I stepped out of the tub and bent down to grab the towel on the floor. I wrapped it around myself as they continued to stare at me, and then I shot them a smug grin of my own. "Not right now. We have a lot to go over. And we need to meet with Caspian again."

Ambrose growled, and Jacobi and Malachi folded their large arms across their chests. "Just send him home, little queen," Ambrose said.

I tilted my head as I studied him. "I'm sure the same could have been said about you, princess. We all still need to sit down and discuss the original reasons you're all here. Not to mention how each kingdom plans to deal with the resistance. I'm slightly worried that we haven't seen the delegates from Qamar or Sahira yet."

Ambrose scoffed.

"Love, I feel that Sahira will leave you waiting for a while yet." My gaze flicked to Jacobi. "King Judah is... temperamental. I've only met him once in the centuries we've been kings. He doesn't often leave his palace. He may not actually come."

"And the Qamar king is an old shitface who probably doesn't know what day it is," Ambrose grumbled. "I don't think you need to worry about those two just yet, little queen."

I nodded. I would trust them on this since I didn't know the other rulers personally. "Very well. That still leaves our treaties, Caspian, and the resistance."

"Given that we're mates, our kingdoms and societies should merge together." My heart stuttered at Jacobi's comment. We'd rule both kingdoms jointly. My eyes flew to Ambrose, would that mean that we would also rule over Masas?

My heart rate sped up at the thought. Would the other kings see our mating as a threat? Were we painting an even larger target on our backs? It was one thing to have trade agreements and alliances in place, but it was something else entirely to join three kingdoms together under mated rulers.

To my knowledge, something like this had never happened in our history. Royals mated with other royals, but never heirs or current rulers.

Sensing my rising panic, Jacobi moved over to wrap his arms around me, rubbing my back in a soothing manner. Ambrose and Mal soon followed, all three of them touching me in some way.

"Don't worry, my love. We won't rush joining the kingdoms. Our priority will be to settle temporary treaties until we can deal with the resistance, then we can deal with any issues that arise as they come." My king kept his tone low and soothing.

"Despite the fact that my father is older than dirt, I doubt I'll be king any time soon. We have plenty of time to figure out how all of this is going to work, Ashera. We'll run things as usual." At my sharp look, Ambrose amended, "With the exception of slavery, of course."

"Are you really going to return to Masas to free your slaves?"

He looked offended that I even bothered to ask. "Of course I am, little queen. I gave you my word. I knew I would need to do this if we mated. You're worth more to me than any of the nobles who want to hold onto slave labor." He lightly bumped his nose against mine and I giggled.

"I love you," I blurted. "All of you."

They once again went unnaturally still.

"We don't have time to fuck her until she can't walk," Mal groused with a groan.

"Which is bullshit," Ambrose grumbled.

"Indeed," Jacobi agreed.

They all pulled back, looking conflicted. "I need to get dressed," I told them. "Mal, will you go fetch Caspian? We can sit in the library."

He pulled me flush against him before claiming my mouth in a soul searing kiss. I felt his love through our bond and tasted it in his kiss. Before I could get too caught up in him, he pulled away. "I'm going to have you later." He looked at the other two. "We each get alone time with her. Starting today." They didn't bother to argue, and neither did I.

Ambrose

I LOVE YOU, all of you. Ashera's words rang in my head before winding around my heart and burrowing into my soul. My little queen, my mate, loved me. I wasn't a fool. I was well aware I was a very difficult man to love, especially after the start we'd had.

I knew my more primal instincts, my urge to violently protect her, my need to own and claim her, and my almost feral need to always be buried in her would get me into trouble.

She loves me.

Jacobi and I escorted Ashera to her library. I was surprised yesterday when she dropped her glamor, revealing her wings and horns. Why had she even bothered to conceal them? They made her all the more stunning. She was dressed in an emerald green dress of a similar design to the one she'd worn when we met, and the blood-red war bands were proudly displayed on her arm. Her hair was coiled high on her head, and she was displaying all our mating marks.

Pride and lust warred for dominance within me. At first, I'd been pissed that my mark wasn't larger or in a more visible spot on her body, but she'd taken great pains to ensure that all our marks were clearly visible. I sure as fuck wouldn't bother to cover mine.

I watched as her hips swayed enticingly as she moved to her desk. Images of bending her over that desk, riding me in the chair, or fucking all of us before the fire filled my mind. I adjusted myself before sitting on a plush chair that faced her desk. She leaned her hip against the edge of it, looking down at the papers that were scattered there. Jacobi took up position by the fire, leaning on the mantel.

"Should I be worried that Caspian is potentially involved in all of this?" she asked quietly.

Even though we had talked about this earlier, doubt nagged me. I wanted to tell her no, but after seeing so many familiar faces in that dank room, I couldn't be sure of anything right now. The fact that there were nobles present, men and women I'd grown up with who were close to my father, meant that something was going on in Masas I wasn't aware of. It pricked my pride to admit it.

"We can ask him when he gets here," Jacobi offered. "Though I doubt he had anything to do with your abduction. He was telling the truth about that."

I ran a hand through my hair. I'd wait until Malachi was back before telling them everything I knew about Ashera's captors. We needed to make a game plan.

"Can you bring Malakian soldiers here to help beef up security?" I inquired, my gaze falling on the angel king.

When did I stop thinking of him strictly as the feathered fuck?

"If Ashera is okay with that." We glanced over at her.

She sighed and started to twist the war bands on her arm. "Why don't we wait until Mal is here with Caspian before we make any decisions?"

Like he'd been summoned from hell, Caspian opened the door and waltzed in ahead of Malachi. The latter closed the door behind him. Caspian took the seat by my side, and Malachi took up position right next to our little queen.

Caspian studied me intently before shifting his gaze to Jacobi. "I realize that Ashera mating with the king of birds means that Shaytan has an automatic alliance with Malak, but where does Masas sit?"

"We're here to discuss that," I said, drawing his attention to me again. "We've got a lot to fill you in on."

And so we did. I added the details about the nobles at the end of our tale, and everyone in the room tensed. My father wasn't stable enough to have given orders to the nobles, which meant that one of them was calling the shots and making it seem like I'd sanctioned everything. I needed to find out who and quickly.

"I think it's safe to say," Caspian commented, his gaze now riveted to Ashera, "that there will most likely be a faction in every kingdom aside from Malak. Although, once they hear that their pure and holy king has fallen to sins of the flesh, that might change."

Jacobi growled low in his throat. "I can handle my people. A mate bond is even more sacred than chastity."

It was true. A mate bond was the one thing all kingdoms and their people held most sacred above anything else—once we got our heads out of our asses long enough to admit we had a mate. I raked my gaze over Ashera's body, basking in the feel of our bond. She was worth everything.

"The first order of business is to secure trade agreements between our kingdoms in the short term," Ashera said, every inch a queen. How I'd doubted it, doubted her, was a mystery to me now. "Then we need to form a plan to weed out the head of the resistance. I agree with Caspian—there are most likely factions in each kingdom."

Caspian raised a brow. "I can agree to hold off negotiations regarding slaves until the issue of the resistance has been dealt with, since they are the most pressing threat, but we will return to it." Caspian, ever the fae prick.

I tried to hide my smirk. I'd been that arrogant prick only a few short days ago. Ashera was going to wipe the floor with him.

"We can continue with a temporary trade agreement," Ashera agreed. "But if you insist on Shaytan reinstating slavery, the agreement will end after we have taken care of the resistance. This is not negotiable."

Caspian growled and glared at her but gave her a stiff nod.

He knew it wasn't worth the fight right now. Not with more pressing matters at hand.

"Beltane is tomorrow." Ashera's statement had us all confused. "We can use me as bait."

My roar mirrored that of Jacobi, Malachi, and surprisingly, Caspian.

"Absolutely not, Sher."

"Malachi—"

"Bat Fuck's name is *Malachi*?" All of us turned to Caspian in shock.

"Bat... Fuck?" Malachi's hand went to his sword. I leaned forward, eagerly awaiting Caspian's beheading.

Ashera killed that dream by placing a hand on Malachi's arm. "I'm sure he meant nothing by it, Mal."

"Back to using you as bait." Thank fuck Jacobi was the adult in the room. "There's no way that will happen, Ashera."

"Perhaps we can glamor someone to look like you," I suggested.

"No." Her tone was firm. "I will not risk someone else for this. I'm what they want. Beltane is the perfect time to try for me again. Surely they know that the vampire group that took me failed to kill me. They'll want to strike again."

"But trying so soon after Ambrose's vengeance wouldn't make sense." Malachi had a valid point. "They'll know we're watching you closely. If they don't know that you're mates with Jacobi and Ambrose by now, they will by Beltane."

"We need to lure them out," she argued. I wanted to strangle her. Or fuck her. *Both*. I wanted to do both at the same time.

"They'll know it's a trap." I grumbled. She was insane.

"That may be, but if they're desperate enough, they'll want to take the bait." I hated that she was right.

None of us said anything. We didn't want to go through

with this, but if we could make it work... No. I refused to even entertain the thought.

"It's not enough time to prepare," Malachi finally said.

Ashera contemplated this while Jacobi and I remained silent.

Caspian exploded.

"Are you fucking kidding me right now?" He burst from his seat and started pacing. "You want to put her directly in the reach of the group that's already publicly tortured her? What sort of mates are you?" That had all of us, including Ashera, growling. "No. There's no fucking way."

"I think we've found ourselves a new princess," Jacobi deadpanned.

"Hush," Ashera scolded him, clearly trying to fight a grin. "Caspian..."

"No, Dick Slayer. Just. No."

I blinked. "Did you just call her... *Dick Slayer?*"

"Don't fucking question me right now, blood sucker." I'd never seen Caspian like this. What the fuck was going on? I glanced over at Jacobi. He was studying Caspian intently, no doubt reading the irritating fae. I was curious about what he was picking up. He looked torn between amusement and anger. I'd have to corner the feathered fuck later and have him tell me what the hell was going on.

"Caspian." Ashera's tone left no room for interruption. "I'm sorry you don't agree, but frankly, you don't get a say."

That was my queen, putting the bitch fae in his place. Fuck, I needed to get inside her sweet pussy. I had to adjust myself again.

Caspian stormed out of the room.

"Well, that went well." Malachi slid his hands into his pockets. "Jacobi, let's go talk to him. Ambrose, watch our queen."

I nodded, and they left the room.

"Are the other two kings going to be as annoying as you and Caspian?"

I frowned. I wasn't nearly as bad as Caspian. "Watch your mouth, little queen." I stood and moved until we were inches apart. "I'm your mate. The whiny little bitch isn't."

"You're both far too over the top and dramatic."

I lashed out and wrapped my hand around the back of her neck, dragging her against me. I crushed my mouth to hers as I ground my erection against her hip. Ashera's breath hitched as our tongues fought and our teeth nipped. I pulled back a bit, both of us panting, to search her eyes.

"Little queen." My growl was huskier than I would have liked.

She cupped my face with her hands as she studied me. "Ambrose..." I didn't let her continue as I dragged her to the floor in front of the fire.

I pulled away the wisp of a dress and tore at my own clothes. "I can't go slow, little queen."

"Don't need slow. Don't want slow," she purred.

Then, I was on her. I slid one of my arms under her back so my hand clutched her shoulder, anchoring her to me. The other hand tilted her head so our eyes met and held as I slowly pressed into her. Once I was fully seated inside her, I leaned down to nip her lips. She was the most decadent dessert, the sweetest wine. I always wanted to have the taste of her on my tongue.

I slid out, dragging my cock along her slick folds. Despite my earlier statement, I didn't want to rush this. I wanted to feel every inch of her against me.

"Feed, little queen." My thrusts remained unhurried, but they grew in force, and each time I bottomed out our skin slapped together.

She moaned, and I felt the sweet pull of her power around me. "You need to feed too."

My fangs dropped as my gaze homed in on her neck. I wasn't sure I'd be able to restrain myself if I fed off her, but fuck if I wasn't willing to try. My teeth pierced the soft skin of her neck, and her blood rushed into my mouth. The burst of flavor and the flare of power had me picking up my pace and slamming into her with abandon.

She was everywhere. She was everything.

Mate.

Her soft cries soon gained volume as she neared her release. She wrapped her legs around my waist, crying out my name and her love for me.

I lapped at the wound on her neck, sealing it. I was so damn close, but I needed her to come with me, so I angled my hips just enough so I was rubbing her clit with each thrust into her now dripping pussy. She fluttered and clenched around me, her nails digging into my shoulders as her head flew back.

"Right there, Ambrose. Please."

"Let go, little queen." I pressed a kiss to her lips before I murmured, "I love you."

She screamed my name as she pulsed around me, and I didn't bother to fight my own release as it flooded me. I'd come to realize that she owned me just as much as I owned her, body and soul.

10

CASPIAN

I stormed down the hall, not caring where I was headed. I couldn't believe Ashera, the fucking queen, wanted to offer herself up as bait to the resistance and that her supposed mates were just going to stand by and let it happen. Weren't they supposed to protect her?

Why do I care so much? Ashera was a trophy on my wall, another notch on my bedpost. She was something to lord over the other kingdoms, that I, the prince of Juniya, had gotten the Queen of Shaytan to submit to me.

But something was nagging at me, a feeling I couldn't quite shake. It left me unsettled, anxious as I roamed the great hallways of the castle. I didn't know when my disgust for the little queen had shifted into something more—respect. I was beginning to respect the hold Ashera had over her kingdom and her people, and for some unknown reason, she had sway over the men too. Maybe the whisper called out to them as well. The angel king, Jacobi, idiotic Ambrose, and Bat Fuck... Malachi. *Fuck.* I had a sour taste in my mouth imagining the way they fawned over her, eye-fucking her like no one else was in the room. But picturing Ashera as she rode Jacobi's cock, making eye contact with her other mates—with me—had me growing hard. She was elegant and beautiful, wild and untamed. She was a woman full of contradictions, and one I wanted to stuff with my dick.

"Prince Caspian!" Heavy footsteps caught up to me, and I turned around to see King Jacobi and Malachi.

I sneered at my company. "What the hell do you want? If you're here to convince me that sending your little mate in as bait is a good idea, there's no point. Luckily for you, I don't give a shit."

"He's lying," Jacobi murmured to Malachi.

I shot him a deadly glare. "Would you please stop fucking doing that?" I turned to Malachi, who seemed like the more levelheaded one at the moment. "Seriously, how do you even stand him?"

Malachi shrugged, clapping Jacobi on the shoulder. "He grows on you."

I snorted. "Sure. And I often invite my slaves to share my dinner table when there's too much food."

Jacobi frowned. "You do?"

I looked at the angel king in disgust. "You're kidding, right? Anyway, this little trip has been swell, and I'm glad I got to see all Shaytan has to offer, but seeing as you're about to sacrifice your queen, I've got to get home to Juniya to prepare for war."

I turned on my heel, hoping I was walking in the direction of my room. Honestly, I had no idea. But before I could take a step, Malachi clasped my shoulder. "Look. I know what you must think of us, sending our mate into a situation like this."

I scoffed. "Really? You know that I think you're all sorry excuses for mates? She'll die, you know. That's not a possibility, that's a fact. From what you told me, she only survived the last round with the resistance by the skin of her teeth." A pang hit my heart, imagining the beautiful, golden queen with the glittering wings bound and broken. Alone. What the hell was wrong with me?

Malachi didn't release my shoulder, and I turned around to face him. His expression was grim, and Jacobi had his arms crossed over his chest. It seemed that neither of them liked to be reminded of their mate's time in captivity.

Probably because they had failed. It didn't matter, because Ashera was no longer my problem. I didn't need to speak with her again to know that. I would never hear that soul piercing laugh, or the soft moans she made as she called out for her mates in the throes of release. I shook my head, giving Malachi the dirtiest sneer I could. "Look, it's not my call. You made that quite clear. Let me go home."

Malachi tipped his head to the side. "I don't like you, Caspian. Even Ambrose was more amenable to me. But Ashera is right, and we need as many people on our side as possible if we're going to take down the resistance."

I rolled my eyes. "That's what I'm saying. There's not going to be a resistance, because Ashera is going to offer herself up on a silver platter, and then bang! No more Ashera, no more freedom, end of problem. You don't need me."

Jacobi took a step forward. "You don't know Ashera. She can handle herself."

I laughed loudly, the sound echoing in the empty hall. "I'm sure. The dick slayer will take down an entire resistance faction with her pretty wings and a sexy smile or two, maybe she'll flash that pussy you're all so obsessed with. That's how it usually works, right?"

Jacobi had his arm at my throat, pressing me against a pillar. "I'm really fucking sick of you insulting my queen. When I say she can handle herself, I mean it." He released me, and I dropped to the floor, rubbing the tender skin of my throat.

Maybe it wouldn't be such a bad thing to see this for myself, even if it was sure to be a failure. My magic pooled inside of me, eager for a challenge. I could picture the little queen on her knees in front of me, my magic swirling and shifting around her to keep her in place. Ultimate submission. I looked into the angel's wary gaze. "Prove it."

~

Ashera

AMBROSE and I were tangled up on the floor, enjoying the bliss of the feeding we had just shared, when Malachi and Jacobi walked back in the room followed by an irritated-looking Caspian. I was beginning to wonder if that was just his default expression.

Ambrose groaned. "What the hell is the fae fuck doing back here?"

Caspian huffed. "This fae fuck is here to save your sorry ass."

I placed a hand on Ambrose's chest, feeling him still against my touch. "It's okay, Ambrose." I stood, pulling my dress back over my shoulders. I felt four sets of eyes run appreciatively over my body, Caspian's included. "Caspian, what do you need from me to earn your trust?"

"Reinstate slavery." His smile was cruel, a mere twist of his lips.

"Anything but that."

He shrugged easily. "Worth a shot." Shoving his hands in his pockets, he walked closer to me, and I could feel elemental magic flooding the room. "Your mates tell me you're quite the warrior."

I tipped my head to the side, taking stock of the fae in front of me. The magic had reached Ambrose where he still lay on the floor, and he growled in warning. "One could say that."

"Well then, Dick Slayer, I want proof," he whispered. His

bold gaze locked on mine. I could feel the tendrils of air magic stroking my legs.

If Caspian wanted a fight, then I was going to give it to him. I wasn't dressed for battle, but a warrior was always prepared. I smiled at him, feeling full from the energy I had just absorbed from Ambrose, and there was enough sexual tension in the room that I could easily feed again if I needed to. I wasn't worried. "Then what are you waiting for?" I smiled at my prey.

Caspian tried to wrap his air whips around my ankles, but I easily jumped out of their reach. He tried, again and again, to tangle me in his snares, not realizing I could read the energy in the room. I knew when he was going to strike before it happened.

I grinned at him, and my men chuckled behind me. Did he really think it was going to be that easy? "Is that all you've got?"

His eyes flashed with annoyance, and with a snap of his fingers, the large wooden coffee table soared toward me. I put my hand on the edge as it came near, flipping myself easily over to the other side of it. "More than just an air fae, eh?" His persistence was kind of cute.

Caspian pressed his lips together, his gaze darkening. "You have no idea." A flick of his wrist brought the thick vines just outside the window crashing through the glass. I leaped over the back of the couch, but the end of my dress caught on the edge of the sharp vines and ripped. I stood chest to chest with Caspian, glaring. "This was one of my favorite dresses."

Caspian traced the outline of my lips with a soft finger. "So sorry."

Ambrose groaned and heaved himself off the floor, which now looked more like a war zone at this point. "Are you seriously going to let this continue?" he muttered to one of the others.

Malachi chuckled. "Looks like she's got it under control. Besides, she's hot when she's fighting."

Caspian turned back to me. "This has been fun and all, but I want to see some real power now."

"Oh, believe me," I whispered, leaning in as if I was going to kiss him. He moved closer, our lips almost touching. I could hear the annoyed growls of my mates behind me, but I couldn't stop myself from teasing Caspian. It just felt so good. *Too good.* "You couldn't handle that."

I pushed myself away from him, ripping off the torn part of my dress so it wouldn't get caught on anything else. "Now what else do you have in store for me?"

Caspian's eyes darkened, and his breathing grew heavy. He tipped his head, and the roaring fire shot toward me in the form of a fireball. I easily dodged the flames, and the fireball hit my desk. I gaped in shock at my desk, blazing away, and then turned toward a shelf of books, snatching the small knife I had stashed there. I stalked over to Caspian, who hurriedly started shooting books my way. I stabbed and slashed at various pages, narrowing my eyes on the fae. I was angry now, and I wanted to show him who he was dealing with.

Ambrose whistled. "He's in for it now, boys."

I whipped my head toward him. "Shut up and get some water to put out the fire." Ambrose hurried out of the room. I turned my attention back to Caspian, and he shot me a heated look. "You break my coffee table. Fine. You smash my window, whatever." I paused to knock another book out of the way. "Rip my dress? Great. But you fucking thought you could set my desk on fire and get away with it?"

Caspian narrowed his eyes on me. "The desk? That's what did it for you?"

"I really fucking liked that desk!" I roared, staring up into his dark gaze. I pressed my small blade into his neck. "You wanted to feel my power? You'll feel my fucking power." I began to absorb Caspian's energy, both from where we touched and where we weren't. His eyes widened as he felt me consuming his magic. I wouldn't take all of it—I needed him, after all—just enough for him to understand who I was. The desk fire roared behind us as we stood locked in a stalemate of wills.

I stared at Caspian, waiting for him to acknowledge me and my power, but something shifted in his gaze, something dark and primal. Possessive. I was about to call him out on being weak when I felt it snap into place.

I dropped my knife to the floor, taking a step back. "No. This isn't happening. Not with you."

Caspian snarled, "You think I want this?"

I huffed. "You'd be fucking lucky to have me."

He stepped closer, the air between us rushing out as the fire crawled closer. Where was Ambrose with the water? "You'd be lucky to have *me*, Dick Slayer."

"Watch your mouth," I snapped. *Caspian. Really?* What were the gods thinking? But I couldn't deny my soul, and the succubus inside me was clawing for Caspian, desperate to be close. To be whole.

I sighed. "Alright. This is how this is going to go."

Caspian shook his head. "No. I'll be the one to decide how this is going to go." He took another step closer and brushed his lips against mine. He slid his hand down my neck like I was made of glass.

I sighed into his mouth, clutching him closer to me as he ground his erection against my stomach. *Is this seriously happening?*

"You've been torturing me since that night in my room, Ashera."

The door swung open, and I heard Ambrose's angry voice. "Are you fucking kidding me? I just went out to get some fucking water." The fire hissed as he put it out. Then, his heavy footsteps came up behind me. "I told you not to fucking touch her." Ambrose pulled me away from Caspian, and it was like a trance had been broken.

Caspian sneered at me, and I glared back even as my succubus called to him. This was not what I needed right now, not when I had the resistance to worry about. Ambrose clutched me to him as if I would run away, and Caspian straightened his shirt.

"You don't need to worry about me," Caspian stated. "I'll help you take down the resistance and then I'm leaving. Now, if you'll excuse me."

He pushed past Ambrose and me, walking around Malachi and Jacobi who stood guard at the door. Malachi raised an eyebrow at me, and when I gave him a quick nod, he let Caspian walk out of the room, slamming the door behind him.

I sighed heavily, picking up the remains of the trashed room and righting the coffee table. My mates watched me with concern. The desk was another matter entirely. Caspian was another matter entirely. I wasn't sure if I wanted to accept the mate bond, but I knew the consequences of rejecting it. I flopped down onto the couch, and Jacobi sat down next to me, rubbing my shoulders reassuringly. "What's wrong, love?"

I groaned. "Caspian. Caspian is wrong."

Ambrose knelt in front of me, placing his hands on my bare thighs. "Don't worry about Caspian. You heard him. He's going to help us, and then he'll fuck off back to Juniya and his stupid tomato plants."

"Well, that's the problem." I stroked Ambrose's dark hair reassuringly, knowing he wasn't going to like what I had to say next. "I don't think Caspian should leave."

Malachi joined our small group, sitting on the arm of the sofa so our bodies touched. "He's leaving."

I turned to Malachi and grimaced. "That's going to be a bit of a problem considering he's my mate."

Malachi and Jacobi exploded into a symphony of denials. "Absolutely not," Malachi shouted.

I rolled my neck, waiting for them to calm down. Surprisingly, the only silent one was Ambrose. I tipped Ambrose's face up to look at me, his serious, blood-red gaze meeting my own. "What are you thinking?" I asked him.

He was silent for a moment. "I don't like Caspian any more than any of you. In fact, I might like him the least. He's a self-ish, spoiled, good-for-nothing prick. But I'm also aware that these two dickwads might have thought that about me not too long ago."

Jacobi groaned, and Malachi muttered under his breath.

"Look," Ambrose continued. "I'm not saying we have to like the guy. I'm just saying that maybe... and I can't believe I'm fucking saying this, but maybe it's not something we can fight."

I pushed them all off of me, suddenly feeling smothered. "It's not something that needs to be dealt with right now, so let's focus on the important stuff, like planning for Beltane, but right now, I'm hungry. Can we eat?"

I trailed behind them, lost in my thoughts as we made our way out to the hallway. A hand snaked out and grabbed my wrist, and I turned as Malachi pulled me against his chest. "Mal," I breathed, giving him a smile. My heart always stuttered when I saw him, his dark horns so striking against his hand-some face. I don't know why I ever bothered to glamor my own horns, because I found them so attractive on Mal.

He pressed a soft kiss to my forehead. "I don't like it, Sher. I don't like him." He sighed, pressing his nose into my neck and breathing deeply. I could feel his body trembling with repressed emotion, and I knew my assassin was struggling not to take out the issue himself.

"This doesn't change what I feel for you, Mal," I whispered against his hair.

He huffed quietly, stroking my back with gentle fingers. "I know that, but that doesn't alter the fact that I don't trust him. What if he hurts you?"

"He won't. He'd have to be able to catch me first," I teased, but Malachi just gave me a solemn look. "Oh, Mal. How did you survive the war without worrying yourself to death?"

"I nearly didn't," he responded darkly. "I was terrified I was going to lose you every second of every day. But who was I to tell you to back down, Sher? You were born for this. You were destined to lead."

My heart swelled with his praise and the emotions behind it. I had loved this man for longer than I could remember. I raised his face so I could kiss him, and he eagerly kissed me back. With no hesitation, he began to slip his hand under my dress, and I laughed. "Really? Won't the others be wondering where we are?"

"No," he murmured against my lips. "They'll know exactly where we are. They'll just be jealous that they didn't think of it first." Sure enough, I could feel Ambrose's and Jacobi's desire barreling down our bond. No matter. They, too, would have their time. My incubus slid his fingers through my already soaked folds, groaning when he realized how wet I was for him. "I need you, Sher."

He dipped one finger inside my pussy, and I pushed against him, arching my hips into his hand. Mal groaned, adding an extra finger. "That's right, my queen. Show me how much you love me. Give yourself over to me. Every breath..." He swirled his thumb around my clit, adding to the delicious, building pressure. "Every moan..." A third finger slipped into me, and I cried out, trying to force him to move faster, harder. With a grin, he complied. "Every single part of you... is mine." I shattered around his hand, screaming out his name with my release.

Malachi slipped his fingers out of me, undid his pants, and turned me so I was pressed against the wall. "One more time, Sher. Only this time, we'll do it together." He eased his thick cock inside of me, and I shuddered at the incredible fullness as I took him in. Mal began to thrust, his pace desperate and hard. I clung to him, riding the waves of pleasure and pain—the contradiction that was Mal himself. Nothing else mattered in this moment, not the threats on my life, Caspian, or any other problems. The only thing in my world was Malachi, and the way he was arching his hips to bring me crashing into another orgasm. He called out my name as he reached his release, resting his head against my neck.

He pressed a kiss to my skin. "Let's see the fae fuck do that."

11

ASHERA

W hen I awoke the next morning, completely surrounded by hard, warm, male bodies, I realized that I'd fucked up with Caspian. He was just so... annoying. He drove me insane, and I was constantly torn between wanting to strip him nude and wanting to throat punch him. But he was my mate, and I couldn't hide from that. I just had to accept that it would be torture for both of us.

I snuggled into Ambrose, who was underneath me, with Jacobi and Malachi crammed in on either side. We were all naked, and I had been mildly surprised that none of the men minded touching one another without clothes. It had my mind spinning with all sorts of delicious scenarios... Malachi fucking Jacobi as Jacobi fucked me, Ambrose sucking Jacobi's cock while I was tied to the bed, forced to watch as Malachi teased me mercilessly. There were just so many endless possibilities.

A hand slid down my back to cup my ass. "I can feel how aroused you are, mate." Jacobi leaned in to nibble on my ear, and I shuddered.

The teeth at my neck had me groaning softly. "What has you so worked up, little queen?" Ambrose murmured.

"Mmm. Must be something good, Sher." Malachi slid his hand down to play between my legs.

They flipped me so my back was on Ambrose, and he held my arms as Jacobi and Malachi began to tease the rest of my body.

"Tell us," Jacobi coaxed.

Malachi drifted down my body before he settled between my thighs. He blew against my slick folds, leaning in to lick my clit. I tried to arch against his mouth, but Jacobi held me down with a low chuckle.

"Come on, little queen." Ambrose's husky whisper in my ear had me whimpering.

"I... I was thinking about you three."

"Doing what?" Ambrose pressed.

"Malachi was fucking Jacobi, who was fucking me, and I was sucking Ambrose's cock." The intensity in the room instantly rose. I could feel their eyes on me, and Malachi's tongue had stopped flicking my clit.

"Well, boys," Malachi purred from his spot between my thighs, "it looks as though our queen has a need that must be met." The other two chuckled darkly.

There was suddenly an explosion of movement as they began to arrange me in a position they liked. They placed me on my back with my head hanging off the edge of the bed. Ambrose stood directly in front of me, his hard, thick cock staring me right in the face.

The sound of a fist landing on flesh had me wrenching up to see that Malachi and Jacobi were wrestling. Ambrose moved to kneel behind me, draping his arms over my shoulders so he could play with my nipples as we watched my other two mates.

"Even though you want Malachi to fuck the angel king, we're all alphas here, little queen. Malachi needs to get Jacobi to submit." My pussy clenched at the idea. "None of us have any issues fucking the others, or being fucked for that matter, but that doesn't mean we're going to make it easy." He glided his hand lower, and I slid my legs open wider so his fingers could caress my clit.

For a moment, the two wrestling males paused, their nostrils flaring as they turned to focus on the display before them. Jacobi made a lunge for me, but Malachi placed him in a headlock. He kicked the winged king's legs out and forced his top half onto the mattress between my legs.

"Now, Your Majesty," Malachi growled in Jacobi's ear, "you're going to feast on our queen. Make her come on your tongue before I fuck you."

Jacobi surged between my legs, moving Ambrose's fingers away from my clit before he devoured me, and pleasure enveloped me in no time. Ambrose tossed Malachi the bottle of lube I kept in my nightstand before going back to playing with my nipples, then Malachi adjusted both himself and Jacobi without removing the angel's mouth from between my legs.

The angel king slid two fingers into my pussy, groaning against me when I clenched around them. He crooked his fingers to hit my G-spot, and my back bowed, which only served to thrust my breasts farther into Ambrose's hands and my clit closer to Jacobi's face.

Ambrose leaned down to kiss me deeply, his tongue stroking mine. He pinched my nipples hard, and I saw stars. I ripped my lips from his to scream to the heavens as I came, my hips twitching against Jacobi's face.

"You did well, Your Majesty," Malachi praised, chuckling. "Now slide your cock into our queen's tight little pussy." When he'd done as Mal demanded, he was prevented from thrusting as Mal's hands gripped his hips.

Ambrose stood and gently pulled my head back so it was hanging off the edge of the bed again, the tip of his cock bumping my mouth playfully. "I'm going to tell you everything they're doing, little queen. We don't want you to miss out." I whimpered and slid my tongue along the head of his cock.

"Malachi is about to slide into your king, little queen. Now wrap your mouth around my cock before I make you do it." He leaned down to tightly grip my hair in both of his hands. I slid my mouth around the tip of his cock and sucked, waiting for the other two to move.

Jacobi's low moan, followed by the touch of his head against my shoulder as his hips jerked, told me that Malachi had started to work himself inside the angel. My pussy clenched around Jacobi as I thought about it.

"Suck her tits, you feathered fuck," Ambrose growled.

Jacobi snarled slightly but complied. Suddenly, he was grinding into me. I moaned and Ambrose slid deeper down my throat. With that, Ambrose started to roll his hips in time with the light grinding thrusts caused by Jacobi and Malachi.

"Malachi is controlling Jacobi's thrusts, little queen. He's fucking you using a king." The pace started to increase. "I can see how much Jacobi likes having a cock up his ass. It's similar to the look you had when you were eagerly sucking his cock while covered in blood."

Jacobi moaned and sucked harder on my nipples, bringing one of his hands between us to start playing with my clit. Ambrose kept fucking my mouth like it was my pussy, occasionally snarling quietly.

Every nerve ending was on fire, and pleasure flooded my system until all I could think about was just how good they felt.

"Fuck me," Ambrose snarled. "Make her come already. She's sucking me dry here."

Jacobi pressed his fingers down harder and started to move them faster. Ambrose's hips lost their rhythm as he got closer to his release.

"Make her fucking come, Jacobi." Malachi's dark order had me screaming around Ambrose's cock as I came. Ambrose cursed as he came down my throat, and Jacobi and Malachi both roared as they, too, found their releases.

Mal pulled Jacobi away, and Ambrose fell on the bed next to me. We were all panting. I shivered from the loss of body heat until all three of my mates moved as one, and we were once again wrapped together.

∼

Malachi

IT TOOK us a while to get out of bed, and another one or two orgasms. Ashera had gone with Jacobi to check on preparations for Beltane, and Ambrose was off doing whatever the fuck Ambrose did—probably sucking his own cock or admiring himself in the mirror.

I hadn't lied to Ashera in the hallway. I *was* worried about her, possibly more than was healthy, but there were a lot of moving parts that had the opportunity to go wrong, and while I felt confident that my queen could handle herself in any situation, it didn't stop me from thinking of every little possibility. Like the idea that there could be more members of the resistance than we had anticipated, or that they would hurt Ashera before we had the chance to figure out who was behind it all.

Last time was close, too close, and we had almost lost our mate. I wasn't sure any of us would have been able to survive that. I don't know why it had taken me so long to admit that Ashera was my mate. This woman was my entire world, and I would do anything for her, whether that was taking down an entire resistance to protect her or fucking another one of her mates while he fucked her.

Although truthfully, I hadn't really minded that bit. Getting Jacobi to submit, fucking his tight little asshole, controlling the way he fucked Ashera... yeah, it was good. But next time, I'd be the one claiming Ashera's ass. At this point, I deserved a fucking reward for putting up with these jerkoffs she kept inviting into our lives, and slipping inside her ass while she screamed my name seemed like a pretty good place to start. Hell, I'd even be generous and let Princess Ambrose fuck her pussy while I did it. In Ashera's point of view, the more dicks, the better. My queen definitely loved to be stretched and filled in the most delicious ways, and who was I to deny her pleasure?

She had been through so much. We both had. I knew Ashera had a mate before me—I had even met Visa a time or two—and she had watched her die. How she had managed to find the strength to carry on after losing half her soul, let alone lead an entire rebellion, was beyond me. The previous rulers of Shaytan had taken a lot out of us, sapping our souls. We were stripped down, defined by nothing more than our blood and the location of our birth. Slaves would always be slaves, and royalty begot royalty. Until Ashera.

I sighed heavily, rubbing my hand against my forehead. In truth, I was no better than the dictators that ruled before me when it came to Caspian. I was judging him by his blood, who his father was, and what his kingdom stood for, as well as his fussy clothes and the way he looked down his nose at me. But that was beside the point. Ashera wanted him and felt a connection to him, so I was going to have to do my best to set aside any assumptions and at least give the fae fuck a chance. I groaned. *Fucking hell, Ashera.* Why did it have to be him? This was going to suck.

I got dressed in my usual fighting leathers. The only thing that had changed in the way I wore my clothes was that I now preferred to wear sleeveless leathers to show off the bold crown on my bicep. I wanted everyone to know whom I belonged to. I wanted them to be shaken with jealousy and uncontrollable envy as they realized that the assassin incubus was mated to the golden queen. Caspian would be no different.

I left the suite on a mission to find Caspian. We had all begun to share Ashera's bedchambers since the mate bonds had taken hold. There was no point in pretending that we all didn't want to be with her every moment of every day, and this morning was proof enough that the mate bond was stretching to include all of us. I wasn't sure how we would find room in our small bubble for the fae fuck—whom I should probably stop calling "fae fuck" if I ever hoped to build any kind of a relationship with him. But his sneering, pompous little face made that rather difficult. The derogatory moniker just suited him so much better than Caspian. I stood outside his room, my hand poised to knock, when the door swung open.

Caspian stood before me in all his glory, dressed in his velvet and furs, with his trademark sneer on display and his piercing blue eyes glaring at me. I was taken aback. "Um..."

He rolled his eyes. "For an assassin, you're not overly quiet. It sounded like an entire herd of elephants was storming toward my room. What do you want?"

I threw my shoulders back, finding my purpose once more. "I want to talk."

Caspian opened the door wider but turned his back on me. "If you're here to talk about Beltane, there's nothing more to discuss. I agreed to help, and unlike your kind, my word means something."

I frowned, annoyance flooding my veins. "My kind?" Actually, I didn't want to know the answer to that. I held my hand up to stop Caspian from responding. "It doesn't matter. I'm not here to discuss Beltane. I'm here to talk about Ashera."

At the mention of Ashera's name, Caspian's face softened—barely, just for a moment, but I caught it. "What about the dick slayer?" His tone was indifferent, a schooled veneer of boredom masking any emotions he might feel.

I sat on the edge of the chair facing the fae prince, ready to make a quick getaway if need be. "Ashera told us that you're mates." I cringed at the mention of the sacred bond and the idea that this prick in front of me could share that with my queen.

Caspian tensed, immediately defensive. "Your queen has misinterpreted the situation. I would never accept a mate bond with a non-royal."

I glared at him, touching the hilt of my sword at my side. "Ashera is royalty."

He tipped his head to the side, the expression of careful boredom returning. "She's not *true* royalty, Malachi. Surely you know that, as uneducated as you might be." I opened my mouth to protest, but Caspian cut me off with a wave of his hand as he stood. He wandered silently over to the window. "I meant no disrespect. I was merely trying to explain that you may not fully understand the situation. Ashera, as beautiful and strong as she may be, was not born to royal blood." He turned back to me, his gaze serious. "Even if she hadn't freed her slaves, there would have been a target on her back. Freeing the humans just made it easier for those people to hate her, but the other royals will not accept a queen who was not born to the crown. Ashera took her crown with force and paid a heavy price in blood to wear it upon her pretty blonde head, however, there will be other prices to pay."

I couldn't be certain, but I could have sworn there was awe lacing his words. I was pretty sure the fae fuck was impressed with how Ashera had taken her crown, royal blood or no. "Why are you fighting the mate bond?" I didn't want this asshole to permanently be a part of our lives, but I wanted Ashera to be happy, and if that meant convincing Caspian to give her a chance, then that was what I was going to do.

Caspian raised a perfectly groomed eyebrow. "I'm not fighting anything. There is no mate bond."

I stood, joining him at the window. "I fought the mate bond longer than I should have. It's not good for us, for our abilities.

Your magic will soon begin to weaken, and your strength will lessen as time goes on. Everyday moments will lose their impact. It's like the world is zapped of emotion, of color, and then when you're around her... magic." I thought about Ashera's bold beauty, the gentle way she smiled at me, and her ability to captivate me with a single word. *Magic*.

Caspian smirked at me. "Who would have taken the incubus assassin for a poet?"

"Fuck off," I muttered.

He was quiet for a moment, taking in the truth of what I said. Likely, he had already begun to feel some of the effects. "My people will never accept a war queen."

"You're royalty. Make them accept her." The answer seemed pretty straightforward to me.

"You just won't give up, will you?" Caspian huffed. "Fine! Fine. If it'll get you off my back, I'll give her a chance to prove the mate bond. Is that what you wanted to hear?"

"Yes." A smirk spread across my face before I could stop it.

"What is it now?" He looked entirely unimpressed with the situation.

I shrugged, leading him out the door to find Ashera and the others. "Ashera thinks you two are mates. I'll go along with whatever she tells me, but you still have to convince the other two that you're worthy, and I can't wait to see what Ambrose's reaction is going to be."

Caspian groaned, and my laughter echoed around us. I didn't know for certain what Ambrose would do when I arrived with the fae prince, but I knew it was going to be fucking dramatic.

12

AMBROSE

A shera, Jacobi, and I were in the throne room, trying to decide on the best location for the little queen to be kidnapped.

"But if I'm up on the throne, it'll be much more public," Ashera mused, tapping a finger against her full bottom lip. Those magical lips had been wrapped around my cock only a few hours ago, sucking on me like I was the cure to everything wrong in the world. How long until I could get her on her knees again? I adjusted myself, and Jacobi rolled his eyes. *Like he wasn't thinking of it...*

Jacobi turned his attention to Ashera. "Too public. We need something that will make them think they've gotten away with grabbing you, but also someplace where we'll be able to see where they're going."

Ashera nodded, turning around the throne room in a graceful circle. Her dress was a rich forest green, accentuating her bright eyes. She wore the silk and chiffon with the same boldness that she had donned the fighting leathers that day in the courtyard, and always with the bright red war bands. She hadn't put the glamor back up after she had taken it off, her horns and wings proudly on display, glittering in the soft daylight. Yes, my little queen was not someone to be messed with, whether the crown was on her head or not.

Behind us, the door slammed open, and Malachi stormed in with Caspian close on his heels. "I thought assassins were supposed to be quiet," I quipped.

Malachi glared at me. "Not you too." *What the hell?* He turned toward Ashera. "Prince Caspian has something he'd like to talk to you about."

Hopefully, it was that he was taking his pitiful little army and his tiny little cock and fucking off back to Juniya. Ashera shot me a look as if she could hear what I was thinking, smiling as she made her way over to Caspian. To anyone else, the smile would look like the sweetest of honey, the welcoming grin of a succubus designed to seduce, but I knew my little queen now, and I was well aware that sickly sweet smile was laced with poison.

Caspian looked at all of us. "Alone."

Jacobi's wings fluttered in irritation, and I growled, "That's not going to happen."

Ashera turned to give us a look, but we didn't back down. "Why don't you three go to the other end of the room then? Caspian and I can talk over here."

I huffed, but at least we'd be able to keep an eye on the fae. If he was going to push to finalize the mate bond, we sure as shit weren't going to make it easy for him. The three of us moved to the far end of the room to watch, not that the distance did much. We could still see them well enough and hear them without any difficulty.

Caspian sighed. "Dick Slayer..."

Ashera's laugh caused all four of us to stare at her as if she was the brightest star in the sky. Caspian looked as though he'd been given the most precious gift before his face settled into its usual scowl. He wasn't going to make this easier on himself with an attitude like that.

"I like that nickname." Ashera's husky voice told us just how much she truly did enjoy the nickname. If Caspian wasn't as hard as the rest of us, then he was a fucking idiot. He appeared to be at a loss for what to say in response before he coughed in an attempt to recover.

"It's come to my attention that you believe we're mates, despite the fact that you already have three annoying ones."

My lips twitched.

Ashera threw a death glare over her shoulder at Malachi and mouthed, "Traitor" before turning back to Caspian. "I don't believe it, Caspian. I know it. And as for already having three, you know full well the females of all species typically take multiple mates. Royals are the exception, but only because the men keep consorts—typically against their will, I might add." Caspian glowered, not liking her response. "Men outnumber females in all species, not only that, but it also ensures the survival of offspring since there are multiple males to guard the children. It's a natural way of life."

Caspian opened his mouth to argue, closed it, and then tried again. "I am well aware of how those of you who are not born of a superior lineage do things." Malachi coughed loudly, which caused Caspian to glare at him.

Ashera's entire body stiffened at the remark, and her hands clenched at her sides. We could all sense how angry and upset his comment made her. It had the three of us growling.

"Caspian." Her voice was quiet. "I understand I'm not royal by blood, and I'm well aware that being a woman on the throne causes... issues. But denying the mate bond will cause pain for both of us. We'll both suffer from it. Is that what you want?"

His face softened, and he let out a heavy sigh. "No. But how can you truly be sure that we're mates?"

Ashera

HE WANTED to know how I was sure? How could he even doubt it? He was a dick, but I could still feel the pull toward him. I slid my hands up his chest. He stiffened, but I was undeterred. I clasped my fingers behind his neck and leaned into him. Everywhere our skin touched felt as though it had caught on fire. Judging by his now ragged breathing, he felt it too.

"Kiss me," I murmured, pulling his face down to mine. "That's how you'll know."

I could feel the indecision in his rigid body as he fought against the pull of the bond. I licked my lips, and his gaze tracked the movement like I'd dangled a steak in front of a starving man. The groan he released when he finally met my lips would echo in the hall forever.

A single taste was all it took. He wrapped his hands around me, one hand angling my head, the other grabbing my ass and pulling me flush against his erection. Our mouths battled just as our wills did, neither of us giving in.

His hands weren't content to stay in one place for long and were soon moving hungrily over my body. Each touch seared into my skin, causing need to pulse through every nerve ending. I buried my hands in his hair as I tried to pull him even closer to me. His dark chuckle had my thighs rubbing together to try to ease the painful ache building there.

A cleared throat had us slowly pulling away from one another. Caspian's eyes were dark with possessive hunger, and his hands refused to let me pull too far away from him. He growled loudly at the interruption, and his gaze swung to my mates.

"What?" The lash of his voice had the other three males chuckling.

"Do you believe her?" Malachi asked as he crossed his arms over his broad, delicious chest. They had come to stand closer to us as we kissed. Gods, I hadn't even noticed.

"If you don't, we can just take her from you." Ambrose's tone was teasing and wicked.

Caspian released a feral, violent snarl. "You take her, and I'll fucking rip you all the shreds." That answer had my three mates grinning broadly. They may not be pleased that Caspian was my mate, but they didn't want me to suffer. "She's mine."

"Not yet, you fucker." Ambrose gently tugged me from Caspian's arms despite the savage growl he was emitting. "You need to earn your place with us."

Caspian stiffened. "What the fuck are you talking about?"

"You heard him," Jacobi responded. "You need to earn your place here. We won't deny Ashera a mate, but you sure as fuck better believe that after the way you acted, we aren't going to just allow you to waltz into our pack."

"Your pack?" Caspian lifted a brow. "So am I going to have to fight you assholes or something?"

Ambrose chuckled, and the other two just grinned. Gods, what did they have planned? In a flash, Ambrose had grabbed the fae by the throat, and he pulled him closer. "We'll certainly kick your ass at a later time, but right now, if you want Ashera, you're going to have to prove it."

Caspian's eyes narrowed on the vampire prince.

"You're going to suck my cock, fae fuck."

Caspian stiffened, but not in disgust as I would have thought. He stiffened in resolve. "Drop your damn pants, blood sucker." My breath caught at the demand.

Ambrose released Caspian's throat with a smug smirk on his arrogant face. I still wanted to punch him sometimes, especially when he had that damn look on his face. His pants fell to his knees, and he braced his hands on his hips as his cock jutted proudly toward Caspian.

The fae prince knelt, and his gaze flicked to mine. He moved slowly so I wouldn't miss anything as his lips wrapped around the head of the vampire's cock. Ambrose let out a soft groan. As he stared intently at me, Caspian started to work the other man's cock into his mouth and partially down his throat.

Ambrose's knuckles whitened, and he let out a low growl filled with heat. Caspian picked up the pace, and my hands drifted down my body. I flicked my nipples before moving the skirt of my dress out of the way and sliding my fingers through my damp folds. Malachi and Jacobi instantly jumped into action. Jacobi stood behind me, kneading my breasts with his hands, while Malachi tore the skirt of my dress clean off before he replaced my fingers with his own.

My moan had Caspian groaning around Ambrose's cock, which only served to force the vampire to release a moan of his own. Caspian worked the cock in his mouth harder, faster, like a damn cock sucking champion. It had me panting and crying out. Malachi slid a finger deep into my pussy, rubbing solidly on my G-spot. We were both feeding off the sexual energy in the room, and it was delicious.

Ambrose fisted his hands in the fae prince's hair and started to fuck his face with abandon, all of us groaning when it caused my pussy to pulse around Malachi's finger.

"I'm going to come, little queen. Come with me." I made a helpless sound in the back of my throat in agreement. "Come. Now!"

We both cried out as we came. Caspian, much to my shock, swallowed every drop Ambrose gave him, his lust-filled eyes never leaving me. I was still so aroused I couldn't move, couldn't breathe without the need to feel Caspian inside me burning painfully through my body.

～

Caspian

I HAD NEVER WANTED another as badly as I wanted to possess Ashera at this moment. Every fiber of my being was alive with desire for this little queen, and from the way her gaze had locked onto mine while I sucked Ambrose's cock... *fuck*. Her bright green eyes were so dark with lust, I could have come in my pants again just watching her moan and writhe in the arms of the other two assholes.

Mates. I was going to have to get used to that idea. But to feel Ashera's creamy skin underneath my hands, and to hear her cry out my name as she came around my cock... yeah. It'd be worth the trouble.

I got up from the floor, ready to claim my prize—Ashera, who was stripped bare and panting heavily as I stalked closer. If needed, I would fight off Malachi and Jacobi to get to her, but to my surprise, they took a step back, their thick erections visible in their pants. Unfortunately for them, it was my turn with our queen, and I wasn't quite ready to share just yet.

"Caspian," Ashera breathed, and my cock hardened painfully with the sound of my name on her lips. I wanted her to beg.

I dropped to my knees in front of her, a reflection of the position I'd been in in front of the blood sucker only moments before, and then I pushed her legs apart, pressing my face closer to her perfect pussy. "I'm going to taste you, Dick Slayer. I want you coming apart on my tongue exactly like your vamp mate just did. I want you begging to feel me inside of you, stretching you with my thick cock."

She whimpered, staring down at me with her thickly lashed gaze. I kept my eyes locked on her as I licked her wet folds, groaning at the taste of the most delicious honey. Ashera was decadent, addictive, and if I wasn't careful, she was going to be downright dangerous to my carefully leashed control.

Her fingers tangled in my hair and tugged me closer as I swirled my tongue around her throbbing bundle of nerves, sucking on her clit hard enough to elicit a deep moan. The other men were still in the room, watching, but I couldn't see them. The only thing I was focused on was this stunning creature in front of me and making her come in a way she never had before. I tugged gently on her clit with my teeth, and Ashera cried out above me in response. I slid my hand between her legs, slipping a finger inside of her and curling it in a way I knew would make her scream. I didn't want her falling apart just yet though. I wanted to drag this out.

"Beg, Ashera. Beg for me to fuck you," I commanded, letting my fingers take over where my mouth had left off. She was close, I could feel her body straining for release, feel the energy she was radiating into the air.

She laughed hoarsely, tossing her golden locks over her shoulder. "I don't beg."

"You will." I brought my mouth back to her clit, working my hand and tongue in time together until she was rolling her hips against my mouth.

"Caspian, please." Her legs were beginning to tremble with the effort it was taking to hold herself up.

"Not good enough, Dick Slayer," I murmured. I wasn't planning on entering her until she was an absolute mess. The tight walls of her pussy clamped around my fingers, desperate for friction, so I slowed my strokes, licking and teasing with my tongue instead. The scent of Ashera's desire was thick in the air, and I could hear her other mates growling with need around us.

Slow. Gentle. Tease. I ignored my own achingly hard cock, wanting to take the little queen right to the brink of ecstasy.

"Caspian. Caspian, please... oh, fuck." Ashera's breath was coming in quiet pants, and I knew I had her where I wanted her.

"Please, what? Tell me what you need." I knew what she needed. She needed me. *Her mate.*

She twisted her fingers in my hair, pulling my face up to look at her, desperate with need. "Fuck me. Please."

I licked my lips clean of her sweet juices. "Anything for you." I tugged her down to her knees in front of me, turning her so she faced her other mates. Ashera groaned as I ran my fingers through her soaked pussy, ready and waiting for me. "Such a good girl," I crooned. "So eager for my cock."

I looked up, meeting the hungry gazes of the other men for the first time since I had dropped to my knees in front of the blood sucker. None of this was for them. It was for her. I was put on this earth to pleasure Ashera, and my gods, I was going to make sure I did that to the best of my abilities.

I fisted my heavy cock in my hand before sliding it through the little queen's folds, then I addressed the others, a reflection of how they had tormented me that day in my chambers. "Pay attention. This is how true royalty fucks a queen."

The moment I started easing myself inside her molten heat, I nearly lost control altogether. A fierce growl overtook me, and I was frantic to lay claim to this wonderful creature beneath me. Ashera fit me like no other had, and my soul felt complete for the first time in my life. Desire washed over my body, flooding my veins as I set a desperate pace, pushing deeper, harder. I needed more. Ashera arched her back, meeting me thrust for thrust. She was perfect. How could I have ever denied the craving between us? I ran my hand down her taut stomach, coming to swirl lazy circles around her clit. I leaned forward, whispering in her ear. "I know you're desperate for release, Dick Slayer. I know you're imagining what it would feel like to come all over my cock."

Ashera moaned in response, and I knew I had her where I wanted her. I thrust harder, pressing my finger against her throbbing clit.

"Come for me. Look your other mates in the eye and come for me." I drove into her, watching her head rise to meet the gazes of her other mates as she screamed my name. Her pussy tightened around me like sheer perfection, and I continued the pace to draw out every bit of her orgasm before I caved to my own release, calling her name as I fell forward.

I pulled her down onto my lap, stroking her golden hair off her damp neck. She laughed, the sound reverberating through my chest, and I looked down at my little mate. "What's so funny, Dick Slayer?" I murmured against her neck.

"I just never took you for the cuddling type." Ashera gave me a sly grin, knowing she was pushing my buttons.

I scowled, glaring at the guys smirking down at us before they could join in with any funny remarks. "Yeah, well, first time for everything." I nipped her neck before soothing my bite with a kiss. "Huh."

Behind the curve of Ashera's ear, nestled at the base of her hairline, was a tiny, delicate star—my mark, a reflection of the elemental magic I used as a fae. It wasn't bold, and it wasn't upfront, but it was perfect. She snatched my hand away, trying to see what I was admiring. "It's my mark, Dick Slayer." I trailed my finger across the mark, watching her body react to my touch with a gentle shiver.

"Mine's appearing too," Ashera replied. I took my hand back from her, examining the skin she had been looking at. Across the back of my hand, sprawling across my knuckles, was the crown mark I had noticed on the men, most obviously across Ambrose's chest. The prick insisted on being shirtless to show it off. Asshole. He was going to be pissed, because I wouldn't even need to try to show mine off, it was just there. Ashera was mine. I growled low, the feral need to possess her growing within me again, along with my hardening cock.

Ashera laughed, easing into my touch. "I think you'll find you're not the only one."

I glanced up to look at the other three, all hard as rocks, eyeing Ashera with lust. *Fuck.*

This was going to take some getting used to.

13

ASHERA

The celebration of Beltane had always been my favorite. It was a time to revel in rebirth, new life, and hope. That last one had always been the main point for me. *Hope.* Something humans had had in short supply, something my parents never even imagined, but now...

Hope ripened the air, rang through the halls, and filled every soul in Shaytan. Hope allowed all my people a chance to finally live.

I was dressed in a gown that was fairly modest compared to what I typically wore. It was made entirely of a light lilac lace. The halter neckline framed my chest, and the fabric dipped low on my back. The delicate lace was sheer, and heavier beading kept all the important bits covered. From there, the clinging fabric flowed gracefully to the floor. My hair was done in a half up style that was then swept over the front of my shoulder so I could proudly display my mate marks.

My golden circlet felt both lighter and heavier tonight. My mates and I would be able to see the palace decorated in bold and vibrant colors, celebrate with my people, and touch each other until we passed out, but I was also responsible for all these lives now. I needed to ensure everyone had enough food to eat, water to drink, and sturdy homes to live in. I needed to battle against the resistance that wanted to once again subjugate my people and force them to live through horrible torture and a lifetime of servitude.

My fae prince came up behind me, wrapping a possessive arm around my waist so his hand rested low on my stomach. He brushed his lips against my neck, causing me to shiver. His dark chuckle told me he appreciated my response to him. Caspian had settled a little since formalizing the bond. He was still an asshole—he was my asshole now—but he was just as fiercely loyal and protective as the others, which meant getting him to leave me alone tonight would be difficult.

"You know you can't be with me all night." I turned my head so I could look up at Caspian. He gave me a mutinous look, almost daring me to fight him on the issue, no matter that we had all already settled this yesterday. "I know you don't like this plan, Caspian, and I know that because our bond is so new you're a little... ruffled. There's no way to tell for sure if they'll try anything tonight, but we need to give them the chance."

"No, we fucking don't," he growled. He looked as though he was tempted to tie me to the bed and lock us away in my room. Which, admittedly, didn't sound horrible. "There are so many different ways we could be handling this."

"How?" My tone was sharp. "How the hell can we do this differently? I'm all ears." By that point, my other three mates had joined us. I wrenched myself away from Caspian and started to pace, and all four of my mates tensed. "Because let's be really fucking clear here, we all know that Ambrose and Caspian came here to see if the rumors were true, fuck me into submission, get what they wanted, and possibly—assuming I didn't play nice—have me taken off the throne." The two men in question turned sheepish. "Jacobi, while well-intentioned in his coming here, had no idea what the hell he was getting himself into. And you!" I whirled on Malachi, who flinched at my pointed finger. "You ignored the mate bond for-fucking-ever.

"I have literally had to do all of this mostly on my own without mates in the way. I am the one who formed the rebellion. I am the one who almost died from poison during the battle with the king. I am the one who took his fucking head. I am the one who reformed all of Shaytan. I am the one who got kidnapped for it. And *I* am the fucking queen."

My breathing was labored, rushing in and searing my lungs with each panting breath I took. My rage scorched my veins. While I might be offloading some of this on them when it didn't need to be, I was tired of this bullshit. I was under no delusions when it came to Ambrose's or Caspian's original motives for coming to Shaytan. I knew I'd been a toy, someone to fuck into submission, maybe even a pawn to play against the other, just as I knew Malachi might have continued to fight the mate bond had he not seen me with both Ambrose and Jacobi. And Jacobi, my sweet, well-meaning angel, he'd come here with an offer of friendship and peace, and he'd always stayed true to that. He was my rock, I realized. While he could have moments of possessiveness, it wasn't unexpected with new mates, especially males, but he had always been steadfast in his devotion to me.

"I acknowledge we are mates," I continued, "but you all need to understand that Shaytan is my kingdom. I will gladly accept any guidance you wish to give, but you need to respect that the end decision is ultimately mine and mine alone. I am not some pretty figurehead to plop on the throne while men scheme behind my back. I fought for this throne, for these people, and I will not be pushed aside."

I locked eyes with all of them. They were deadly silent, and their expressions ranged from shocked to ashamed, but I wasn't quite finished.

"We want to keep each other safe. It's what mates do. It's ingrained in us. I appreciate and understand how difficult this is for all of you to allow me to put myself in danger. But I need you to trust me." Stupid tears started to well in my eyes, and at the sight, they all seemed to panic. I wasn't entirely sure if these were angry, frustrated, or sad tears, and I hated shedding them regardless of why they'd formed. I also didn't want them to assume that I was attempting to manipulate them into giving me what I wanted because I'd started crying, so I did my best to prevent even a single, tiny drop from falling.

"Love." Jacobi was the first to speak, the first to approach, and he did so as if I was a wounded animal. "This is hard," he admitted, "but we all know just how strong and powerful you truly are. When those vampires took you, it rattled us. We're still rattled, even the asshole who hadn't been mated with you." Caspian huffed at the insult.

"Sher." Malachi didn't approach me, leaving the physical soothing to Jacobi for the time being. "I know I should have done something about the bond sooner, and I know the reason you didn't act on it is because of what happened with Visa. But I swear to you, I won't let anything like that happen again. I do trust you. I've followed you into battle, I've watched you kill without mercy, and I've watched you show incredible compassion. I am so honored and proud to have you as my mate. I will follow you into battle again, Sher. And you're right, none of us have a different plan that would effectively lead us where we need to go."

"Unbelievable," Caspian raged. "I'll admit I had planned to see for myself that there was a woman on the throne, that I thought I could use you to my own ends, fucking you senseless while doing it. It's not easy to override centuries of ingrained behavior, and I had no fucking clue you were my mate." He started to pace around us and flapped his hands wildly as he spoke. "But putting yourself at risk like this is insane. I believe in you, Ashera, I do, however this is almost too much to ask of me. I am going against everything I was taught to believe in, everything that has shaped not only myself, but my kingdom and its people, to be with you, and this feels like you're just shoving all of that in my fucking face."

I opened my mouth, ready to respond when Ambrose jumped in. "Caspian and I come from a very similar background. We were both raised to view humans as nothing more than cattle to be bought and sold for whatever reason we decided. We were also raised to see women as subservient to men. They had a higher standing than slaves, absolutely, but they certainly weren't thought of as equals." He ran his hand through his hair. "While I don't see you as less than, not anymore, I still have trouble seeing humans as anything other than slaves and women as equals instead of inferiors. It's only been a few days, little queen. We cannot change such fundamental parts of ourselves overnight."

I sighed and started to twist the bands on my bicep. "I'm not asking you to change immediately." I paused. "Okay, maybe I am, and I can admit that's unreasonable." I let out a frustrated sigh as I met each of their gazes. "It just feels like you don't believe I can take care of myself, let alone an entire kingdom. I've had to fight every step of the way, more so with Caspian and Ambrose."

"How about Caspian and Ambrose agree to continue doing their best to fight against their old prejudices, while you teach us all what it truly means to have a woman lead a kingdom? In return, you'll need to be patient with all of us. We're fighting instincts that demand we basically cart you off to the nearest cave and never let another see you." Jacobi, my rock, and apparently the mediator of our group, made a damn fine point.

"I can do that," I agreed. "But I need to give this plan a shot tonight. We need to try to get into the resistance. If we can capture even one of them alive, it will be worth it."

None of them looked as though they wanted to agree, but they all nodded their heads anyway.

"Adjusting to one another isn't going to be easy, and we certainly don't have time to hide ourselves away the way other mates usually do. We're going to need to take care of the resistance, and then figure out how this whole thing is going to work among several different rulers. Ambrose and Caspian are next in line for their thrones, and I can imagine that their fathers won't be very pleased that we've mated, let alone that a woman has insisted on change and they've agreed. I suppose taking everything one step at a time is best." I looked around again. *Fuck, I love these men. I don't always need to like that I love them, but fuck me, I do.* "Can we all agree to talk about things as they arise? And you certainly don't have to come to me about every issue, but you can discuss amongst yourselves too. We're all connected through the mate bond, it's not just a one-sided thing with each of you. I'm sure you can feel that."

"We can," Malachi agreed, and the others nodded. "And I think we can all agree that what you're suggesting is more than fair. Keeping clear lines of communication between all of us is a necessity to make sure we don't end up killing each other."

We all chuckled at that, because it was true, so very true.

~

Ambrose

Ashera had been right to cuss us out—not that I cared to admit it. It wasn't like I had wanted to get slapped in the face and forced to acknowledge how I'd planned to use her prior to meeting her, but being called out was a necessary evil because I did need to face the music. Not just about my failed seduction attempt, but about everything. It was the only way for all of us to grow stronger.

I understood why she'd said what she had. We had been trying to control her without realizing what we'd been doing. At least, I hadn't really realized what I'd been doing. All I had been focused on was my little mate. Keeping her safe. Keeping her happy. Keeping her well fucked. I hadn't taken the time to consider the broader implications of how I'd been acting or thinking, nor had I realized I'd brought my initial mentality into our mate bond. To own. To possess.

And now I felt like a giant dick, because I had been a giant dick.

I could tell the others felt the same way, even Jacobi who had literally done everything right. We'd all been overbearing cavemen. I wasn't exactly sorry, but I needed to figure out how to go about that better. Balance. That was what we needed. We needed to find balance.

We dropped our conversation after Malachi's truce and headed into the Beltane festival. The four of us had spread out so we could keep an eye on our mate without being too hands-on. We wanted the resistance—if they were even here—to assume that we had been lulled into a false sense of security, or that we were cocky. Regardless of what happened, the latter was probably true.

The courtyard was decorated with fresh flowers, and there

was food and drink everywhere. A few children had even woven delicate flowers into Ashera's hair along her circlet. What struck me the most was the way Ashera interacted with her people, both demon and human alike. No one seemed to be beneath her attention, and everyone who stopped her became her sole focus. I'd known from the moment I met her that she was unique. She had a way of looking at someone as though they were the only damn person on the planet. It made you feel things. It made *me* feel things. Things I hadn't realized I was even capable of feeling. Things I was afraid to put a name to.

I'd never seen so many happy people in one place, never witnessed a kingdom love a ruler the way Shaytan loved Ashera. Masas ruled through fear and control, but this... this was different.

I'd originally agreed to free Masas' slaves for the wrong reasons. I'd wanted to own her, and the only way I could even get close to doing that was to agree to free our slaves. I'd had every intention of seeing my end of things through, regardless of why I'd made the agreement. Once I gave my word, that was it.

But now...

Now I wanted Masas to have what Shaytan had. I wanted to be a king that would make her proud. I wanted us to stand shoulder to shoulder as equals.

Fuck. I was going soft, but I honestly didn't care. So long as she was with me, I didn't give a fuck how "soft" I got. As far as I was concerned, she made me a better man, made me strive to be worthy of her every fucking day. After I'd failed her so spectacularly by allowing her to get kidnapped, I realized I didn't want the cold life I'd once led, especially knowing it had been my people who had taken her.

I glanced over at the others as they moved around, keeping mostly out of sight. They were all just as sucker punched as I was. All of us were completely lost to this amazing woman. I doubted Caspian would admit to it, but the other two would. Jacobi seemed ready to walk into Malak with Ashera by his side and present her as his queen, as his equal. Malachi didn't have a kingdom of his own, but that didn't mean he wasn't just as willing to show her off. Frankly, I wanted to do the same. I wanted fanfare as I presented Masas with its future queen.

The fae fucker would take a while to settle in. He was far more stubborn and opinionated than I was. More stuck in his ways. Yes, he'd agreed to free Juniya's slaves and had seen the light when it came to Ashera, but he was in no way happy about it. He'd caved, but I worried about his behavior and whether or not he'd truly keep his word to Ashera.

Trying to fight the mate bond was pointless. So was trying to avoid the fact that she was completely and utterly right about all of it. Women. Slaves. The way things are done in the kingdoms.

So. Fucking. Right.

I was only angry that I hadn't thought of it first.

The night droned on with nothing of particular interest happening. Ashera, even when seemingly alone, wasn't approached by anyone threatening. She'd even given a wonderful speech about new life and new beginnings, and nothing had happened. I wasn't sure whether to be suspicious or relieved.

The celebration was drawing to a close, and most people had already gone home for the night. Ashera had stayed to make sure those too inebriated to stand were escorted home, and servants were starting to clean up. I was eager to head back to our rooms and worship our queen. We made it out of this celebration with no fuss—thank the gods.

We all gathered in the throne room. It was quiet and peaceful in here for once, the five of us the room's only occupants.

"I can't really say I'm disappointed." Ashera's tone was low, almost as though she didn't want to break the silence around us.

"We'll have other chances to lure them out," Jacobi assured her. "What happened with the vampires was a significant loss, even if there weren't many of them compared to their overall numbers."

"I'm just disappointed I didn't get to kill anyone," Caspian grumbled. Ashera simply rolled her eyes at him. "Everyone is lucky they didn't touch you. I would have taken their hands."

"Okay, princess." Ashera shook her head, looking both amused and exasperated.

"Finally!" I threw my hands up. "Finally, I am no longer the princess."

"Oh, you are." My eyes narrowed on my delicious little mate. "But he's just as bad as you are."

"Am not," we both retorted before glaring at one another. How dare she say we're even remotely similar?

Ashera threw her head back and laughed. The sound had all of us enthralled and hard as a rock. She rarely laughed like that, and it was always the most beautiful sound and sight. Gods, I wanted to listen to her laugh every day.

Jacobi slid up behind our queen, his hands expertly massaging her wings. She let out a husky moan and practically turned into a puddle of desire at the angel's feet. Malachi moved in front of her, his fingers twisting and pinching her nipples through the fabric of her dress. Her back arched to give them both better access to her body.

"It's been a long day for our queen," Jacobi rumbled. "I think she needs to be taken care of."

"Mmm," Malachi hummed in agreement. "Pampered."

Caspian and I were beside them in an instant, our growls of approval echoing throughout the room.

"It just so happens that I have a little something that will help us." Malachi unraveled his belt, which wasn't actually a belt but links of delicate chains.

We're going to tie the little queen up. Fuck me. I might just bust right here.

Jacobi led Ashera behind the throne, and Malachi chained her so that she was standing with her front pressed against the back of the chair. We watched as he ripped her beautiful dress away from her body, tearing it to shreds. Ashera lifted her lust-filled gaze, her glowing green eyes settling on me. She parted her lips as she panted lightly, her body giving away just how turned on she was by all of this.

Perfect.

"You will each take turns pleasuring your queen. You will not stop until she has had her fill of you, is that understood?" Malachi glared at each of us until we nodded our understanding. Ashera's low moan told us she approved of this plan.

Jacobi went first, kneeling between Ashera's legs. He slapped her ass until she spread her thighs and adjusted herself so her ass was out and uptilted. Diving between her legs like a man possessed, the angel king devoured our little succubus queen. Her cries of pleasure drove the rest of us wild.

Just when it seemed like Ashera was about to fall off the edge, Jacobi eased back, and a whimper of protest filtered through the room as Ashera's ass followed him. He chuckled before slapping her ass a few more times. For having been known as the virgin king before her, Jacobi learned quickly.

"Soon, love. I want to build up your release until you can't walk." In a flash, he was naked and pressed against her back, her body arching against his in an attempt to feel him along any inch of her skin. She released her pheromones in an attempt to coax the large angel to do her bidding but he merely chuckled.

The feathered fuck didn't slide his cock into our queen's tight little pussy. Instead, he brought one hand up to brutally play with her nipples and drifted the other down to stroke her clit. Ashera cried out, and her head fell back against Jacobi's chest, her hips twitching with each stroke. I could tell by her breathing that she was close again. I dropped my pants, allowing my cock to spring free from its torturous confines.

The fucker stopped... again. I was both amused and frustrated. I wanted to get my hands on her, damn it, and I was sure if she hadn't been chained to the throne, she would have throttled the angel king with his dick. I'd happily watch that.

"Jacobi," Ashera warned. Never mind. I didn't want to be on the receiving end of that tone. That tone suggested pain, torture, murder, and maybe a resurrection just so she could do it all over again. For the time being, I was happy to keep my dick to myself.

"It's okay, love." Jacobi chuckled. He ran his cock along her dripping pussy, and all of us groaned. If he didn't fuck her soon, I would.

Ashera pushed her ass back at the exact moment Jacobi slammed his hips forward. She cried out as he buried himself to the hilt. Her shout of ecstasy had me fisting my dick and jerking off to the brutal pace the angel set.

The pounding rhythm of flesh against flesh echoed loudly in the room, punctuated only by our mate's moans and Jacobi's grunts. My little queen's scream as she came had those of us who weren't buried balls deep inside her groaning. Jacobi roared his release alongside her.

"Next," Ashera demanded—sassy little thing. This earned one last slap to her already pink cheeks before Jacobi moved away. A dark chuckle rumbled through me.

Malachi gestured for Caspian to step forward. The fae didn't tease her the way Jacobi had. Instead, he plunged deep, causing the little queen to squeak, and then he set about fucking her raw. She didn't last long before she was coming again, Caspian right there with her. I was surprised he hadn't lasted longer. Then again, that pussy could strangle a dick.

Dick Slayer was an appropriate nickname for our mate.

I held my hand out for Malachi to go next. I wanted my little queen last. I wanted her so spent that the only thing she'd be able to do was just feel my dick and take all the pleasure I could give her.

Malachi took his time with Ashera, his thrusts slow but damn hard. Each time he bottomed out, Ashera's breath caught in her lungs. Her legs started to shake as she chanted his name over and over again.

"That's right, Sher. Grip my cock with that sweet pussy. Harder," Mal gritted out as he slowly dragged his cock out of her. "Just like that. Such a good little slut." He slammed into her once again.

Ashera's head fell forward, and her breasts jiggled with each desperate thrust of Mal's hips. She'd be ripe for me, only able to take what I gave her. Good. My cock hardened to the point of pain as I watched them.

Both the succubi and the incubi started to feed off the lust in the room. It was a heady feeling and my fangs dropped at just the thought of feeding off my little queen's blood while she fed. Her blood gave me more power than I could have ever imagined. I wasn't sure if it was because she was my mate or because she was just that powerful, but either way, I felt like a fucking god whenever I sipped from her veins.

Ashera's sob of pleasure as she came had me shaking out of my blood-filled thoughts. Malachi's hips jerked against hers as he came moments later. He stayed like that, letting her just pulse around him, her entire body shaking from her release. *Gods, she is perfect.*

Mal gently released her hips, and she slumped a bit, not quite able to stand on her own anymore. Her chest heaved as she sucked in air, making her breasts sway enticingly. I moved to stand directly behind her, studying her closely. Her skin glowed brighter than ever, a clear indication that she'd been well fed. Her wings were tucked tightly to her body, but they quivered as pleasure continued to flood her. Her pert little ass twitched as I stared, and my mouth watered at the sight.

I'd be fucking that tight little hole again... later. Right now, I needed to get my cock into that perfect pussy of hers and my fangs into her neck. I needed to fuck and feed. Preferably at the same time.

"Are you ready for one last ride, little queen?" My voice came out huskier than I'd intended, and she shivered at the sound.

"Please," she whispered.

"Please what, little queen?" I wanted to hear her say it.

"I need your cock, Ambrose." She arched her hips back in invitation. She always left me feeling so damn humble whenever she submitted to any of us in bed. This mighty queen who had literally slain her way to the top was trusting us to take care of her.

That was all I needed. I slid smoothly into her and groaned loudly when she immediately clamped down around my painfully throbbing cock. I reached for her breasts as my body curved around hers, working my way between her wings so I could nuzzle her neck. Her breath hitched, and she pulsed around me again.

I wanted to see if I could make her come without moving. I set to work tweaking her hard nipples and nibbling on her neck. She murmured my name, her pussy continuing to pulse around me. I abandoned a nipple and dropped my hand to her clit. I kept my strokes light and teasing, but it didn't matter to her, she was already so overstimulated. She came with a soft cry of my name, and I smirked against her neck. Going last had its benefits.

I started to move, setting a slow but steady rhythm. I didn't stop playing with her nipple or her clit. Her orgasm never stopped, and she just continued to strangle my damn cock. *Fuck, it feels amazing. She feels amazing.*

Just as I got to the edge myself, I leisurely sank my fangs into her neck. She screamed to the heavens and came so hard I was briefly worried she might actually cut my dick off with her pussy. But fuck me, what a way to go that would be. I groaned against her skin as I fed from her.

When I was finished, I gently eased myself out of her and undid her chains. Caspian was there to catch her before she slumped to the floor. He cradled her protectively in his arms as his gaze roamed her body to assure himself she was fine.

"Come on, Dick Slayer, let's get you cleaned up and in bed." I was mildly surprised at how caring he'd become. He was still the bigger asshole, but I couldn't deny he cared about our little queen, which was good. I might have wanted to kill the fucker, but that would have hurt Ashera, and none of us wanted to do that. I had no doubt he'd continue to fight being a part of this, *us*, but he'd never allow anyone to hurt our mate. I was certain of that.

14

ASHERA

I awoke to fresh morning air blowing in through the open window. The sky was still gray with dawn, streaked with the bruised purple color of early spring. For the first time in recent memory, I felt content. I was surrounded by love and the hope that maybe I could make a difference. I was only one person, but now I had four mates by my side. I also had a kingdom of people who believed in my dreams, and a generation of humans who were able to live freely for the first time.

Change was in the air, heavy on the breeze. I could practically taste it on my tongue as I lay in bed, staring at the odd color of the sky. Ambrose was curled tightly against my back, leaving no room to breathe between our bodies. Jacobi had his arm across my chest and his leg hooked over my hip. Malachi had left while it was still dark out—an issue with a guard. He had pressed a kiss to my forehead and slipped out before I could fully wake up. And Caspian... I sighed quietly so as to not disturb the two men still snoring gently. Caspian was Caspian. He had accepted the bond with me, but he was still struggling to accept his place with the other men. Since Beltane, I had convinced him to share our bed once or twice, but he usually preferred to keep to his chambers. I couldn't imagine he was getting much sleep that way, but he was so fucking stubborn that once he made up his mind on something, there was no convincing him otherwise.

He'd see logic eventually. I would just have to wait him out. Caspian wasn't the only stubborn one in this relationship, and he would find that out the hard way.

My inner torment had woken my empathetic angel king, and Jacobi brushed his hand lightly across my cheek before propping himself up on his other elbow. "What's troubling you, love?"

I gave him a gentle smile, pressing his hand against my lips for a kiss. "Just thinking of Caspian."

Ambrose groaned behind me, and I could feel the hard length of his cock grind against me as he awoke. "Don't worry about Princess Prick. He'll get over himself eventually."

"I don't believe you get to use that nickname, *Princess* Ambrose." Mal stood in the doorway, looking every inch the delicious incubus warrior he was, smirking at the vampire next to me.

He walked toward me, dripping with sensuality, and for a brief moment, I thanked whatever gods listening that he was mine. Mal sat on the end of the bed, meeting my gaze.

"Come to bed," I whispered, suddenly desperate for touch. My mates' touch. I was certain nothing could put this fire out inside of me. Ambrose groaned again, and Jacobi dragged his hand back down to my nipple. I felt powerful, seductive, and deliciously female.

Mal pursed his lips, and the three of us froze, waiting to hear what he would say next. "Unfortunately, I'm here on business. You need to get up. All of you. One of my men reported whispers of an attack today in Cresta City, and while I would normally just chalk it up to post-Beltane excitement..." He trailed off, but I was already out of bed, pulling on the first clothes I could grab.

"But with the resistance, we need to check out any and all rumors," I finished for him, quickly weaving my hair into a tight braid. Jacobi and Ambrose were already starting to dress.

"Exactly." Mal's voice gave nothing away, but I had learned a long time ago not to trust his calm aura. The city could be burning around him, and he would look no worse for wear than he would if he was at dinner. "Where's Caspian?"

"In his chambers." The reply came from Ambrose, already in trousers, shirtless as usual. He kissed my neck, sending electric waves of arousal through my body, but those would have to wait. "I'll get him. I'll meet you at the entrance shortly."

Mal gave him a brisk nod. "Perfect." He tugged my hand and pulled me through the door, Jacobi trailing after us.

"Does this happen often? Security warnings, I mean," Jacobi asked, buckling his pants as he walked.

"Around Beltane, sure," Malachi responded. "Young folk getting overly excited or getting into their parent's stash of alcohol. Things escalate quickly and get blown out of proportion, but it's always better to be safe than sorry."

I realized that Jacobi, for all his brute strength and sheer size, probably hadn't seen much fighting in the peaceful kingdom of Malak. The angels were a passive bunch, fighting was rare, and war was unheard of. Usually in battles between kingdoms, they would remain neutral, offering aid and assistance to both sides, so for him to walk into a potential battle for me struck a chord within me. I stopped and turned on my heel to face the angel king. "You don't have to come, you know. You could stay back and keep an eye on the castle."

Mal tilted his head from side to side. "Not the worst idea in the world, to keep someone behind."

"No." Jacobi's response was gruff and more intense than I had heard from him before. His bright gaze met mine, and I found myself unable to look away. "I will not stay behind and merely wait for word to be sent back. This may be a minor scuffle, but I will stand by your side. All of yours." He gave Mal a serious look, and Mal nodded.

Okay. Understood.

"I didn't mean anything by it," I whispered to him as we walked, reaching out to hold his hand.

Jacobi took my hand, squeezing it tightly. "I know, but I won't have you and the others going off into any kind of danger while I sit back and twiddle my thumbs. I will protect you and our life together. I knew what it meant to mate with you."

My heart stuttered, warming at the intensity of Jacobi's words and his love for me. I was truly lucky. As we turned the corner, Ambrose and Caspian appeared out of the other hall. Ambrose fell into line with Jacobi, the two of them whispering as they walked. They had grown closer over the time they had spent together, even though "feathered douche" and "blood sucking prick" were still common insults for each other. Men. I turned to Caspian, who looked more disheveled than his usual put together self. Ambrose must have rushed him out the door.

He greeted me with a wry smile. "Dick Slayer. Some wake-up call this morning."

I shrugged, raising a brow at him. "Could have been avoided if you'd sleep in the same room as me."

Caspian rolled his eyes. "And share a bed with the vampire asshole?"

I opened my mouth to speak but then shook my head. It wasn't worth it. When he was ready, he'd come.

"Where is this city we're headed to anyway?" Caspian inquired. "How are we getting there?"

Ambrose laughed loudly. "You're in for a real treat, princess."

Mal elbowed Ambrose. "What the hell did we just talk

about?" He turned to Caspian. "It's a couple hours north of here."

Confusion raced across Caspian's face. "So how are we getting there in time then?"

This time it was my turn to laugh. "We fly."

Caspian's expression shifted to one of pure horror. "You've got to be fucking kidding me."

~

Caspian

I COULDN'T FUCKING BELIEVE I was being held by the king of fucking angels. The same king I watched plow my mate while I was held back. I tamped down a growl and side-eyed Bat Fuck and the blood sucker.

Assholes.

Dick Slayer's ass looks fantastic from this angle though. I quickly shook my head at my wayward thoughts.

I was aware she felt hurt that I wouldn't share her little love nest, but her little harem had made damn sure I knew my fucking place—at the bottom of the fucking food chain.

Cocksuckers.

That was only part of the issue though. While I'd been more than willing to fuck her as she'd been chained to her throne with the others, the thought of sharing her still ruffled my feathers. Not to mention all the changes in my kingdom and life I'd agreed to. I didn't regret it, but it was a lot to process.

With the mate bond now in place, I knew Ashera was damn worth it. I just wasn't sure that I was. I wasn't sure I could really change. I wasn't sure I really wanted to change. But I did want to change... for Ashera... right? I wanted to be a good mate...

I have no idea how this is going to work. I groaned at the realization that this mate thing was going to be a lot fucking harder than I had initially hoped. I'd imagined that if I ever took a mate, she'd be subservient, quiet, happy to make me happy, and ready to fall into place in my kingdom at my side. Ashera was the antithesis of those things. Sometimes she was happy to play submissive in bed, but we all knew who was in charge around here, and it was the blonde beauty with the golden circlet. Dammit. How had I gotten myself into this mess? Life would have been so much fucking easier if I had just sent my sentry to Shaytan like I had wanted. But then I would never have gotten to taste Ashera, and that would have been a true pity. *Fuck.* I was getting as sappy as fucking Ambrose. Next thing I knew, I'd be walking around shirtless like a true prick.

I shook my head to rid myself of all my thoughts that were going nowhere as Jacobi dropped lower, the ground almost close enough to touch. We were here—wherever here was. From what I remembered, Shaytan was a lot less built-up than Juniya.

We landed on a large hill just outside of Cresta City. Surprisingly, it was roughly the size of the capital. I hadn't been aware Shaytan had other cities this size. It had been far too long since I last visited, that much was obvious. Well, that was going to change, especially since we still had to work out where the hell we were all going to reside. Just another problem to solve. *Fuck.* Nothing was going to be fucking easy, was it?

Everything appeared quiet as we stared down at the buildings and people. I glanced over at Dick Slayer. For her sake, I very much wished the threat of unrest here was just that, a threat.

"Let's work in pairs to scout the city." Malachi glanced at all of us. "We'll meet in the city center in an hour or if anything happens. Jacobi and Caspian, you two are together, and then Ashera and Ambrose. I'm going to go meet up with a few of the city guards."

I fought the urge to argue. There really wasn't time, but I wanted to be with my mate. Fuck that blood sucker prick. I glared over at him. Why did he get to search the city with her, be close to her? What was wrong with me?

"Put a fucking shirt on, you annoying prick," I grumbled. Ambrose shot me a smug smirk. My hands clenched into fists as I attempted to refrain from throat punching him.

"Down, you two." Ashera sounded annoyed with us, which had me wincing. I needed to grow the fuck up, if only for her sake. I unclenched my fists, attempting to shift my face into something neutral. It didn't feel right.

"Gods, I can't believe the little queen fucked you with a face like that," Ambrose taunted.

Fuck's sake. I clenched my fists again, ready to put this prick in his place.

"Ambrose!" Okay, now Ashera was definitely pissed. "You two need to work out whatever is bothering you, but you can fucking deal with that later. Right now, we need to make sure the people here are safe. Your petty fight is at the bottom of my priority list."

Fuck. She was right, as usual. I'd learn one day. Hopefully. But looking at Ambrose, who was still grinning at me from behind Ashera's back, made me doubt myself.

Jacobi clapped me on the shoulder, and I stepped away from his touch. "Come on, man. We should head down." He turned to Malachi. "Caspian and I will take the east side."

Malachi gave him a brief nod before turning to face Ashera, and I could see why, between the two of them, they were able to take down Shaytan. Both were already in soldier mode, their faces set in grim masks as they surveyed the land. Ashera's dress was not one designed for fighting, but I knew that wouldn't hold her back. From what I had seen, nothing held back the Queen of Shaytan.

≈

Ambrose

As ASHERA and I made our way through a narrow alley, I thought back to the first image of Cresta City. It had been quite a while since I'd seen it, and the changes were drastic.

"This was where they brought me after slaughtering my parents." My mate's voice was soft. "They leveled the village we lived in looking for me. Once they found me... nothing is left now." *Fuck.*

"The old lord here took me in. Since I wasn't human, I wasn't a slave, but they didn't know my lineage either, so that left me with few options."

My stomach churned. I was well aware of what those options consisted of, especially for a female.

Ashera glanced over at me, and I was surprised her eyes weren't haunted by the memories of her past. My love for her burst through my chest, pride swelling alongside it. My little queen was a warrior through and through. I was one lucky asshole.

She stopped about halfway down the alley, leaning against one of the walls with her head tipped back to look at the sky. "I met Mal here. I'd been given some leeway, enough to come into the city proper on my own. I thought it was a good idea to run." She let out a humorless chuckle, and I settled myself next to her, my body turned to face hers. "I quite literally ran into him. He convinced me to stay, then he helped me kill the lord here and start a life, but it wasn't enough."

No. I didn't imagine it ever could be. Not after everything she'd been through. She'd gotten out, but that wasn't enough. She needed to get everyone out. Gods, I was just now realizing how damn brave she'd been. Still was.

I closed the gap between us, turning her face to mine. I studied her for a moment before leaning down to capture her lips. Gods, I'd been such an arrogant prick when I'd first arrived here. Guilt gnawed at me when I thought back to how I'd treated her, what I'd thought of her.

My lips became frantic against hers, and I grasped her hips to pull her flush against me. Her soft moan had my dick hardening to the point of pain. I knew we were here for a reason, but I needed to be buried in her. Now.

"Hard and fast, little queen. We don't have much time."

"Yes," she mewled, already raising the bottom of her dress.

I undid my pants and lifted her so her legs could wrap around me. Without a second thought, I slid myself home, both of us moaning.

"You always feel so fucking tight, little queen." I set a fast pace, needing both of us to hurtle off the edge as quickly as possible.

As though she sensed my need, she buried her hands in my hair before she started chanting, "I love you," over and over again. My fangs dropped as I moved my hand down her body to find her clit. I sank my teeth into her neck, and both of us came as soon as I started to pull her blood from her veins. I saw fucking stars. *Fucking. Stars.*

This succubus was *every-fucking-thing.*

15

ASHERA

Ambrose and I made our way out of the alley hand-in-hand. My mates surprised me more and more every day. Jacobi, my sweet angel king, had turned into a sex fiend, and I couldn't lie, I loved it. Malachi was now showing me a completely different side of himself. He was feisty and possessive, dominating. It was perfect. Even Caspian had started to change, only for me, but it was there, and it meant the world to me. But it was Ambrose's transformation that was probably the most drastic. He'd come across as an overly dramatic asshole, yet he was truly anything but. He loved me with his entire being, and he was so damn proud to show it off. I squeezed his hand.

An explosion rocked the square we were entering, sending us flying back into the alley. My head cracked against the ground, and my ears rang as I tried to blink smoke and debris out of my eyes. Dizziness disoriented me as the sound of screams echoed around the square.

Another blast. More screaming.

Taking a fortifying breath, I pushed myself up. Ambrose was just getting to his feet, his eyes focused on me. His mouth was moving, but I couldn't hear him. It would take a while for my ears to heal. Fuck.

I watched his mouth intently. "We need to get the people out of the square."

Yes. Right.

With a nod, we both took off out of the alley, and the sight that greeted me ripped my heart from my chest. Bodies were scattered around the square, some hardly recognizable, and limbs littered the area. The odor of blood was so strong it even overpowered the scent of smoke from the explosions. My ears finally stopped ringing only to be replaced with the sounds of screaming, people running, and fighting. Gods, what the hell was happening?

"Ashera!" Ambrose shouted to gain my attention. "There!" He pointed to the opposite side of the square where a group of people dressed in black cloaks stood. Some cast magic while others took off after the civilians.

"You're faster than I am, Ambrose. You need to get the others!"

"Like fuck am I leaving you here alone." He stalked over to me, but I was already on the move.

"Just do as I say," I snapped. In a flash, I grabbed hold of a robed figure who had taken off after a little girl, and the hood fell back to reveal a male vampire. I gripped him tightly as I snarled before ripping out his throat with my bare hands. I took a moment to relish the feel of his blood splattering across my face. These resistance fuckers were going down.

"Ambrose, find Malachi. Tell him he needs to sound the alarm. The people will know what to do. Until then, we need to hold them off and get an idea of exactly where these assholes are. I doubt this is the only spot in the city they've attacked." I turned to search his face. I could see that he didn't want to leave me, but I wasn't about to give him a choice. My people depended on him not being a fucking princess right now.

"Fine, but I swear, if anything happens to you, I am going to turn your ass red. Do you understand me?" I could feel his anger and concern barreling down the bond. I nodded, and he narrowed his eyes on me before taking off in a blur.

A glint caught my eye. Those bastards were streaming this to all the other kingdoms just as they had my torture. They wanted to play? Fine. Game on.

With a deep inhale, I launched myself at the group attacking the square.

~

Malachi

I FUCKING KNEW those assholes would try something again. They hadn't been successful when kidnapping Ashera, and they wouldn't rest until they'd made an example of her. Only this time, there were more than just vampires involved. This was a widespread, coordinated attack on Cresta City, and I could smell fae and witch magic all over the damn place.

I hacked at the enemies around me with a singular focus that seemed to alarm them. These idiots had no idea who they were dealing with. I wasn't just a top general, I'd been the best assassin in Shaytan's history before receiving the rank of general from Ashera. I killed with a silent blade, taking down rebel after rebel without so much as blinking.

Once I finished with the group closest to me, I took a moment to survey the scene around me, trying to determine my next target.

"My lord." A soldier ran up to me. "There are reports coming in from all over the city."

"I figured as much." A rush of air rustled my hair as Ambrose slammed to a stop next to me. I tied the strands back tighter, not wanting them to get in the way. "What the fuck are you doing here? Where's Ashera?"

"She told me to find you and have you set off the alarm. Now do that so I can get back to her," he snapped with a glare.

If Ashera wanted me to sound the alarm and evacuate the city, that meant she wasn't going to fuck around with the resistance. She would be sending a message of her own, and I could get behind that.

"Do it and make sure you grab one of the attackers so we can question them later," I ordered the soldier, who bowed and ran off. "Now let's get back to our queen."

Ambrose nodded and raced off. I took to the skies and allowed the mate bond to pull me to Ashera. I was landing as the alarm started to blare. Once it started, the people knew that they had minutes to flee the city before all hell broke loose. We just needed to hold the resistance off until then.

Jacobi and Caspian came running into the square moments after I landed, and we all looked to Ashera. She stood in the center of the square, bathed head to toe in blood, her wings spread wide as anger radiated off her. She was glorious.

She stalked over to us, her hips swaying and her eyes heated. Sher always loved a good fight followed by a solid fuck. We were going to get very lucky when this was all over.

"I'm going to give you all two minutes to get as many people out of the city as you can by whatever means necessary. Most of them are already out, but check for anyone who needs help. Then, get to the hill we arrived on." Ashera's voice was laced with desire as she dragged her gaze over each one of us. "I want you all to watch what I do to them, especially you." Her eyes narrowed on Caspian.

Caspian growled at her before taking off, the rest of us following suit. Ashera was right, most of the citizens had already fled the city. I was able to get three more people out, and the resistance members were now setting fires to the buildings. Our time expired, so we congregated back on the hill.

Ashera stood there in all her glory, her head flung back, back arched, and wings wide. She looked like a goddess of war ready for vengeance and hungry for blood. It made me rock-hard.

"Things might get a little shaky." She threw a grin over her shoulder at us before returning her focus to the city.

The ground rumbled and a low roar filled the air. Clenching her hands by her sides, Ashera threw her fists above her head, creating a wall of earth around the city. The resistance was stuck. I adjusted my dick as it throbbed in response to her power. Sher being a badass would always do it for me.

With a deep breath, Ashera slowly lowered her hands as she ... *Holy. Fuck.*

The streets were flooding with lava. I could hear the screams from here and smell the scent of molten earth as it slowly overtook the city.

I glanced over and saw all eyes were on our queen. Jacobi was watching her like a lion watched its prey. I smirked. He and I would be pouncing on her as soon as she was finished with her magic. Caspian stared at her in stunned awe, as though he was truly seeing her for the first time, while Ambrose had a combination of admiration and sheer lust written across his face, almost like he couldn't quite believe Ashera was real. *Same, man. Same.*

My eyes moved back to Ashera. Her body was shaking slightly as she continued to wield such powerful forces. I knew she was strong, I knew she was capable of this, and it put my dick in absolute agony to see her in action. When she was finished, she would need to feed. Deeply.

With a sweep of her hands out to her sides, the lava in the city cooled. Fires still raged in some buildings, but she'd ensured that the lava hadn't caught anything else aflame. She'd also made sure that the buildings were all still standing. Once complete, she sunk the earthen wall back into the ground in an amazing show of magical prowess.

She was finished. Those that had come to sack the city were hopefully dead, except for the single person my soldier had taken earlier. Ashera had set out to send a message, and she damn well succeeded.

Jacobi and I were on her in an instant, the other two still too stunned to move. Jacobi ripped the bloody dress off of her before dropping to his knees in front of her. I positioned myself behind her and lifted her lithe form so her legs rested on Jacobi's shoulders. Sher's upper body rested against my chest as I wrapped my arms around her so I could pinch and tease her nipples. The angel king buried his head between her lush, delicious thighs before her head fell back against my shoulder.

Her eyes fluttered closed, and a moan escaped her lips. "Make sure you're feeding, Sher," I murmured against her ear, causing her to shiver. Moments later, I felt her feeding off the sexual energy Jacobi and I were creating. Good. She was bound to be exhausted.

I continued to play with her nipples as Jacobi devoured her sweet little pussy. Her hips started to buck, and her breath came in short little pants. She was getting close.

"Do you like the way your once virginal angel king eats your tight little pussy, my queen? Do you enjoy seeing him on his knees as he services you?" She moaned in response. "Do you like knowing that you've corrupted him?"

"Gods, yes." Her voice was breathy and hitched. "I need more."

Jacobi locked eyes with me as he slid two fingers into her dripping core, moving his mouth to attack her clit, and she started to grind her hips on his face. One of Ashera's hands tangled in Jacobi's hair as the other tangled in mine.

"That's it, Sher. Fuck the angel king's face. Come all over it,"

I growled to her. She screamed as she came, crying out both of our names.

We didn't give her a moment to catch her breath, moving her so she straddled Jacobi's waist. He surged into her dripping pussy, while I used the blood to lubricate her ass before sliding my cock slowly into her. She clenched down, and I had to grit my teeth as pleasure flooded my body.

"My love, you were amazing." Jacobi's praise had Ashera's face lighting up as bright as the damn sun. I used that moment to slide in completely, all three of us moaning.

I could feel Jacobi's cock pressing against mine. *Shit.* Ashera was tiny.

"Move," she demanded as she once again rested her head against my shoulder.

"Yes, my queen." I chuckled.

With a brief nod to the angel king, I gripped Ashera's hips and started to move her along our cocks. Jacobi covered one of her nipples with his mouth and trailed his fingers to her clit.

"Harder." Demanding little thing. But I complied, lifting her hips only to slam them back down on both of us.

We groaned as our little mate cried out her pleasure to the heavens. Each time I slammed her onto my cock, I had to fight not to come, not until she was ready. But fuck me, it wasn't easy. She was still feeding off us, her pheromones drifting on the breeze. It felt like I couldn't get enough of her, couldn't get close enough.

Jacobi and I started moving in time with the rise and fall of Ashera's hips, both of us too caught up in our mate to think straight. She was screaming our names now, chanting them like a prayer, and professing her love for any who bothered to over-hear us.

That was what did it. Ashera shouting out that she loved us had me coming so hard I damn near passed out. I felt her clench around us as she found her own release, dragging Jacobi over the blissful edge with her.

Panting, I gently slid her off our cocks, and we all groaned when she was free. I placed her on her feet, adjusting my pants and taking off my shirt to tug it over her now naked body. Her dress had been ruined, not that any of us minded, and my shirt was long enough to keep her covered. We needed to go through the city, make sure the buildings were actually empty, and start putting out the fires, and none of us wanted her walking around the city naked.

"What the fuck did I just watch?" Caspian demanded.

"You just watched me get fucked to the heavens, Caspian." Ashera shot a broad grin at him over her shoulder. "I didn't think we were hiding anything."

"Not that," he growled, gesturing to the city with a dramatic flair of his arm.

"I flooded the city with lava." My mate turned to face the fae prick.

"How the hell were you able to do that?" He stomped over to her. Since she was so short, he towered above her, her head hardly reaching his sternum. "That kind of elemental magic..."

"I've always been able to do magic like this if I'm well fed." Ashera shrugged. "It got the job done, didn't it?"

Caspian glowered down at her, but she just shook her head. "We don't have time for this. Why don't you get all pissy later? We have people who need to be soothed, tended to, and relocated."

He reluctantly nodded, storming off into the city ahead of us.

I shrugged, gesturing after the fae, and one by one we trailed behind him. We had a lot of ground to cover and a lot of people to check on.

Good thing there were five of us now.

16

AMBROSE

I wasn't sure what I had expected when we went into Cresta City. Maybe scope out the city a bit, meet some new people, and possibly get a low-key riot under control caused by some out of control youth excited about Beltane.

What I wasn't expecting was a whole fucking battle, and for the city to be under attack from my fucking people. *Vampires. Again.* I also wasn't anticipating Ashera using fucking elemental magic like a fae. This was a fucking disaster. We needed to get to the bottom of this resistance and fast, before any more innocent lives were lost.

Innocent lives? Who the hell was I? The little queen was turning me into a godsdamn pussy, caring about people's feelings and their lives, but seeing Ashera interact with her people on Beltane changed something in me. Freedom was no longer just Ashera's or Shaytan's cause. It was our cause, and I was prepared to fight for that.

Speaking of my little queen, she had been fucking glorious. I had thought it was a turn-on when I witnessed her punish those traitors in her courtyard, but seeing her in action like that had been something else entirely. My cock was already hardening in my pants again as I pictured her laying waste to the enemies who had tried to destroy Cresta.

Ashera stood at the edge of the city with Malachi's shirt blowing around her knees in the hot winds of the fire. The delicate bones of her face were striking in the dying daylight, emphasized by the red gold of the blaze still burning around us. My golden queen looked like she was on fire.

She appeared determined but sad, and I was ready to go to war to punish every single person who had put that look on her face. I would slaughter every last vampire if they so deserved it. They weren't my people anymore. I was sure some of them would side with me, with freedom, and I would gladly welcome them with open arms. But those who sought to destroy the world Ashera had dreamed of for so long and then built with blood and love? They could burn in the flames of my golden queen.

We had split up to search the city, put out fires, and find places for citizens to stay, the others parting regretfully from our queen. I wouldn't be parted from her though. I reached out to Ashera, clasping her finely boned hand in my own much larger one. Did this delicate hand really spill all that blood? My touch woke Ashera from whatever stupor she had been in, and she gave me a sad smile before tossing her hair over her shoulder. Ashera pulled away from my touch, stepping toward a group of people who were slowly making their way back into the city, huddled together for comfort. I didn't know where this woman had come from, but one thing was certain—she was born to be a queen.

"My friends, do not mourn what you've lost today. We will rebuild our city stronger and better than before." Ashera's voice was not loud, but I was certain every single person looking up at her could hear every word she spoke. Covered in dirt and ash, it was hard to identify who was a demon and who was a human. Both had been affected by the attack on their city and were looking to their queen for support. "Do not go to bed and fear for your lives or the lives of your children. I made a vow when I became your queen, and I intend to keep that promise. Sleep easy, because I will eliminate any threat to our happiness. These rebels think we are weak because we do not have slaves. They think they can walk into our city and control us like puppets. But they are wrong." I watched the faces in the growing crowd as they looked up to Ashera, revering every word she spoke.

Jacobi appeared out of the shadows and stepped up to my side, obviously not having gotten far in his search before he turned back. "What did I miss?" he whispered, looking around my shoulder at Ashera.

I tipped my head so I could speak to him without taking my eyes off my little queen. "Just watch. Isn't she fucking beautiful?"

Ashera shot a glare at us, and we immediately shut up. She snapped her attention back to the townspeople. "They are wrong for thinking we are weak because we refuse to own another's freedom, but we will show them how feeble they are. They build their palaces and their castles on a pyramid of cards. They are fragile. Remove one of their carefully placed cards, and the whole thing will come toppling down. Now is not the time to back down or show fear. Now is the time to rise up and gather our strength for the days to come. Send word to your families in Masas. Tell them not to be afraid. Tell them we will protect them."

The small crowd roared with approval for their queen. They loved her, and I could understand why. I loved her. We all did, even Caspian, that ungrateful little prick. Speaking of, where was the asshole? I hadn't seen him since just after Ashera had flooded the city with lava. *Fuck.*

I turned toward Jacobi as Ashera walked into the crowd to reassure her people. Mal was nowhere to be found either, but I was certain the incubus could handle himself. "Have you seen Caspian?" I muttered.

Jacobi's eyes widened. "No. You don't think..."

"Fuck, I hope not." My chest tightened painfully at the thought of anything being wrong with Caspian. Not because I cared about the fae fuck, but because I knew it would tear Ashera to pieces if he had gotten hurt somewhere searching the city. "We need to find him, and quietly, before Ashera finds out."

"Before Ashera finds out what?" *Fuck.* Ashera stood in front of me with her hands on her luscious hips and an expectant look on her face.

I groaned, running my hands through my hair. "Caspian. He possibly—maybe—he's—"

Ashera did not look impressed. "Spit it out, Ambrose."

"Caspian's missing," Jacobi responded for me. Because of course he did. King Perfect.

"Are you sure he's not with Mal? He went to scope out some of the buildings on the west side for survivors." Even as she spoke, I could hear the doubt lacing her words.

Jacobi shook his head. "I saw Mal before I joined you guys. He was alone. We both assumed Caspian was here with you two."

Ashera closed her eyes, groaning. "You've got to be fucking kidding me. This is not what I needed today." Her eyes sprang open, and she pointed at each of us. "This is what's going to happen. You two are going to stick close to me, no wandering off. We're going to scour every fucking inch of this city until we find Caspian."

"What about Mal?" I asked.

"What about him?" Ashera was already moving away from the city center, leaving the two of us to trail after her like lost puppies.

"Shouldn't we wait around for him?" My little queen was focused on the task at hand, not paying attention to me.

Ashera scoffed, dismissing me with a wave of her hand. "Mal's a big boy. He can handle himself. Caspian on the other hand..." She trailed off, but I knew what she meant. Caspian came from a kingdom where, like Jacobi, he hadn't experienced a lot of war. His family ruled with absolute control and power, and there were no disputes against their leadership. The fae fuck wandering around in a battle zone at night... well, there couldn't be a lot of good outcomes to that scenario. We'd have to hope for the best and prepare for the worst.

Fucking fae.

~

Ashera

OF COURSE CASPIAN had to be the one who was fucking missing. The other guys could handle themselves, even Ambrose. For as much as Jacobi and Malachi liked to mock Ambrose and call him a princess, I knew he thrived on violence. He just hid it better. But I saw it when I was kidnapped. Sometimes when he fucked me, I got a taste of it. It was there, so a warzone would be nothing to him. But fucking Caspian? We just had to hope that he was trapped somewhere and not being held hostage for being a fae in Shaytan. That wouldn't end well for him.

And the other possibility... I wouldn't even give space inside my mind to contemplate that. We'd find him, figure out who was behind all of this, and go the hell home. End of story. I threw my shoulders back, Jacobi and Ambrose trailing behind me as we left the city center. He couldn't have gone far. He had been with Jacobi when the fight broke out, and I had seen him throughout the battle. I couldn't remember, though, the last time I had seen my fae mate since returning to the city. We had split up after the battle, and I had stupidly assumed he was with Mal. Stress started to creep through my body—fear that maybe we wouldn't find him. Or maybe we would, beaten and bloody, lying in the street.

No. I needed to focus. Thinking like that wouldn't help anything. The only thing that would help Caspian was a clear head. He was going to be fine.

We wandered the city, calling Caspian's name. Our bond was so new that I couldn't use it to pinpoint his location. The fighting had done some damage, and the chaos in the streets wasn't helping our search. Thankfully, even though I was out of practice, I had managed to control the elements so that the lava only minorly damaged the buildings. Most of the families who lived here would be able to move back in tonight, and those whose homes were hit by the explosions or the fires could room with neighbors until we could send in help to repair and rebuild. This was a good city, and the people here were friendly —grateful was a better word for it. They looked out for one another.

I would just have to hope like hell that someone was looking out for Caspian. Surely, he couldn't have been that pissed when I used my elemental powers. Yeah, I probably should have told him about it ahead of time, but then I would have missed out on that delicious look of surprise. It never got old. I would explain it all to him if we found him. When we found him.

"Caspian! For fuck's sake, where are you?" I screamed, my voice echoing off the buildings of a mostly empty street. This part of the city had been hit the worst by the bombs, and it still smelled like a bonfire.

Jacobi put a gentle hand on my arm, and I felt his influence over my emotions, warm and soothing. "It's going to be okay, love. We'll find him."

I nodded, trying to keep a strong face, which was ridiculous, because both of these men could read my emotions without trying. "Caspian!"

Then I felt it. A tug down the mate bond. I whipped my head around, and Ambrose nodded. He felt it too. Caspian was close by. *Alive.*

"This way!" I ran into the building across the street from us. It was still intact, just a bit charred, and dark inside, but Caspian was inside, I knew it.

"Would you fucking wait, little queen? You don't know what's in there!" Ambrose's annoyed voice followed me into the building as I started throwing open random doors, hoping to see my fae prince inside one of the empty rooms.

"My mate is in there. I really don't need Princess Ambrose on my back right now," I snapped, opening a door leading down into an even darker basement. The pull was there again. Caspian was down there, I was sure of it.

Jacobi threw his arm out before I could take a step down. "Let me go first at least, please."

I rolled my eyes. "Fine. But let's go. He might be hurt."

Ambrose scoffed over my shoulder as we walked single file down the stairs. "Maybe his pride is hurt. But that's about it."

"Fuck off, Ambrose." I had no patience for him right now. Whatever this pissing contest was between Caspian and him needed to be worked out, and fast. Ambrose muttered behind me, but I was focused on getting down the stairs and making sure Caspian was okay.

Jacobi was at the bottom of the stairs, unmoving. I pushed past him, waiting for my eyes to adjust to the darkness of the basement. "What the hell are you waiting for?"

"Love, don't..." But it was too late. I had already spotted Caspian across the room, chained to a wooden frame.

"Caspian!" I ran over to him, checking his chained body for any injuries. Besides the gag in his mouth, he seemed to be relatively unharmed, so why hadn't he freed himself from the chains? I tugged the gag out of his mouth, and he gasped for air.

"Ashera. Trap. Behind..."

I whirled around. From the shadows, a lone cloaked figure rushed me. I crouched in a defensive stance, prepared to take him on. This asshole didn't stand a chance. Before he could reach me, however, Ambrose was behind him, efficiently snapping the man's neck. My vampire mate spat on the body and kicked it out of the way. "Fucking prick."

I smiled at him, feeling slightly less pissed off than I had been a moment ago. "Help me get these chains off Caspian." I touched one of the chains and snatched my hand away. It fucking burned. "What the fuck?"

Caspian nodded, groaning as one of the chains slipped onto the bare skin of his neck. "They're enchanted. It's why I couldn't use my power to get them off."

"These are stronger than the ones they used to kidnap me. Fuck. Okay." I could figure this out. No problem. I was debating another lava attack when Jacobi came up behind me and pulled me away from Caspian's side.

"Let me." I gave him an uneasy look but stepped back. Ambrose pulled me against his chest, and we watched Jacobi approach the chains.

Caspian eyed him warily. "You really think you can handle these?"

"Just keep quiet, or I'll leave you there." Jacobi ripped the bottom of his shirt into a long strip before wrapping it around his hands several times. "Should be fine," he muttered.

"Should be?" My voice was sharp, and Ambrose squeezed me tighter.

Jacobi looked back at me over his shoulder. "It'll be fine. Do you want Caspian free or not?"

I sighed in reluctant acceptance, watching Jacobi move closer and closer to the enchanted chains. He reached out with a wrapped hand and... touched the chains without any difficulties. I took a deep breath, watching Jacobi unwind the rest of the chains. "Enchanted items usually can't harm angels. Pure and all. How do you think we got you out of those chains?" I hadn't really considered that, as dazed as I had been when they found me.

"Are you still considered pure?" Caspian asked as he sat up, rubbing his wrists. Jacobi tossed the chains into the corner with a loud clank. "But, uh... thanks."

I pushed Ambrose's arms off me and ran over to Caspian. "Are you okay? What the hell happened?"

Caspian pressed a hard kiss to my lips. "That witch caught me in one of the buildings I was searching. Fucking trapped me with those goddamn chains before I had a minute to think. I'm sure they were hoping to catch you off guard once you found me. Although, that didn't exactly go to plan." He shot Ambrose a quick glance, but he simply shrugged.

"I'm just glad you're okay. Fuck. Don't do that again." I pressed my forehead to Caspian's. He felt weak. "Those chains drained you. Take some of my energy."

He kissed me again before whispering against my lips. "I'm okay, Dick Slayer. Just happy you're here now."

"Mmm..." I moaned from his touch, grateful to be near my mate once again, but a kiss wasn't enough. I needed to feel our bodies touch in every way possible, desperate to know he was actually okay.

Caspian's voice was a low chuckle against my collarbone as he kissed his way down my neck. "Are you sure I'm the one who needs to feed?"

"Yes," I murmured. "Now shut up and kiss me."

Caspian didn't need to be told twice, kissing me hard as he dropped his hand under the oversized shirt I wore. He slid his fingers between my legs, groaning when he realized how wet I was. My control on my pheromones slipped, and I heard my other two mates growling behind me. They wouldn't interrupt Caspian though. Not now. Later... later, all bets were off.

I pushed some of my energy into him where our skin touched. He needed the extra dose, and I knew that the stubborn fae wouldn't properly feed until we were home. He didn't want to appear weak.

"I want you to scream my name, Dick Slayer. I want this whole fucking city to know who's making you come."

I heard Caspian undoing his pants underneath me, and then he fit his thick cock right at the entrance to my soaking wet pussy. He sank into me, inch by inch, so that I could feel every bit of him stretching me in the most delicious way. "Caspian, fuck."

I sat up to straddle him better, feeling him moving even deeper. I rolled my hips, desperate for more friction. Caspian held my hips and forced me to move in time with him. What would I have done without him? He was grouchy and irritable and downright stubborn, but he was a part of me, no different than any of the others, and I needed to reassure my soul that he was still here with me. Our pace increased, and Caspian forced me down on his cock in his usual demanding fashion. He wouldn't hear any complaints from me.

"Scream, Ashera. Tell the world whom you belong to." He groaned, and I arched my back, diving into the pleasure. I was so fucking close. "Scream."

I couldn't hold back any longer. I screamed Caspian's name as I shattered around him. He continued thrusting into me, calling out my name as he found his release.

Caspian tossed his head back onto the bench he lay on. "Ashera, you're going to be the fucking death of me."

I climbed off him, straightening my shirt. "Are you telling me you can't keep up with my sex drive?"

He ran his hand through his icy blond hair, making it stand up in tufts. "I meant this whole fucking mate thing. I thought I was dying. I mean, like I actually thought I was going to die, but I felt like I was dying when I couldn't call out to you."

My chest tightened painfully at his words. I knew exactly what he meant, but the fact that he was acknowledging it... that was a step in the right direction.

"Join the club, prick," Ambrose grumbled behind me, and I rolled my eyes. First step, making sure Caspian was actually okay and fed. Next step, getting these two to stop their pissing match.

"Come on, Caspian. We should find Mal." I offered the fae my hand, and he got to his feet, brushing invisible dirt off his clothes. Even after being captured, his clothes were still impeccable. Ridiculous.

We walked up the stairs the same way we had come down, only this time I was hand-in-hand with Caspian. A comfortable silence surrounded us, the calm before the storm. We all knew what was coming and the battle we faced, but right now, I could only feel grateful that we had all made it out of this alive.

The four of us had just made our way back out into the street when Mal landed in front of us. He wore a look of utter confusion as he took in Caspian's beat-up face, Jacobi's wrapped hands, and the unmistakable aura of sexual energy in the air. "What did I miss?"

Caspian groaned, pulling me tightly against his chest again like it was the most natural thing in the world. "It's a long fucking story. Can we go home first, before you interrogate me?"

Home. Caspian had called it home. And that sounded pretty damn good right about now.

17

ASHERA

Once we'd settled everyone in the city, we'd made our way back to the palace. I hadn't let Caspian out of my sight the entire time. I couldn't. While I'd assured myself he was physically fine when I found him, I was still shaken. Our bond was so new, and knowing that I'd almost lost it... I shuddered.

"Dick Slayer?" We were all in my large shower, standing under the spray and attempting to wash the day from our bodies. Caspian slid his arms around me from behind and rested his head on my shoulder.

I placed my hands on his and looked at my other mates. I couldn't lose them. I wouldn't. I would burn the whole fucking world for them. My grip on Caspian's hands tightened slightly. I wasn't fighting the resistance just for my people, I was fighting them for my mates too.

"Talk to us, Sher," Malachi rumbled, dipping his head so our eyes were level. "We can feel all your emotions churning in you."

I sighed and tipped my head back against Caspian's chest. "I'll kill them all. They hurt Caspian."

Caspian stiffened behind me, his hold tautening around me. "Let's not forget they hurt you too, Dick Slayer."

I scoffed. "I don't give a fuck about that." I spun in his arms so I could stare into his eyes. "You're *mine*. They need to learn what happens when they fuck with those I love."

A predatory gleam flashed in Caspian's gaze as he stilled against me, and a low growl rumbled from his chest. "You love me?"

"Of course I do, you idiot. You're an asshole, but you're still mine." My tone was firm, leaving no room for argument.

Caspian slammed his lips against mine, his hands coming to tangle in my hair as he ground his hips against me, then he pulled back just enough to whisper against my lips. "I'm going to fuck this up, but you're my fucking mate, and I won't let anyone change that." His lips crashed onto mine again.

"Fuck," Ambrose muttered behind us. "The rest of you walked around hard as a rock all day too, right?"

I pulled back from Caspian and giggled. All three of my other mates voiced their confirmation of Ambrose's assumption. I knew their... issue had nothing to do with the fact that I was a succubus and everything to do with the fact that we were mates. Gods knew I walked around wet all the time now.

"I think we should move to the bedroom," Jacobi chimed in. "As much as shower sex appeals to me, I think five of us slipping around in here is asking for someone to get hurt."

The others chuckled, and I let out another giggle. He was right, shower sex with the four of them would be a bit too much. That was when it hit me. My lips parted in surprise as I turned to stare at my angel. He was suggesting the five of us have sex together. I shouldn't be surprised, considering Mal had fucked him while he fucked me, but that had been my idea.

"I can feel how turned on our little mate is by the thought of all of us fucking her at once." Malachi released a low growl, causing the other three to release rumbling growls of their own. "Tell us what you want, my queen."

My gaze met his as images of all of us sliding against one another played in my mind. My chest rose and fell sharply the more I thought about it.

"Come on, little queen. We know you're thinking about it. Tell us how you want us." Ambrose moved closer to me, sliding his fingers against one of my nipples. I moaned.

"Dick Slayer, you know we wouldn't deny you. Just tell us." Caspian nipped my neck, and I shuddered.

My mouth worked, but I was too overwhelmed to form any words. Ambrose continued to play with my nipples as Caspian's fingers moved to my clit. He didn't touch it, merely circled around it in a manner that made me want to scream. I threaded my fingers in Ambrose's hair and fisted it.

"Bed." It wasn't eloquent, but at least I got it out. Fingers were removed from my body, causing me to whimper, and my mates chuckled.

"To bed it is." Malachi swooped in and picked me up. I let out a startled squeal which only caused them to chuckle louder. He tossed me onto the bed as they moved to surround me, two standing on either side of my too small bed. "Tell us, Sher."

I looked them over as each one took their cock in hand before giving themselves a few quick pumps. My legs fell open as I propped myself up on my elbows.

"I want Caspian to eat me out," I decided, "while I suck on Malachi." My gaze slid to Ambrose and Jacobi. "I want you two to touch each other as you see fit."

Low, hungry growls met my request before all four of my mates burst into action. Caspian flipped me onto my hands and knees in front of him, spreading my legs wide at the edge of the bed. Malachi slid under me so his cock was in the perfect spot for me to bend my head and wrap my lips around his hard length. Ambrose and Jacobi stood on the other side of the bed, sizing each other up.

I felt my pussy clench at the thought of them wrestling like Malachi and Jacobi had. The thought of their hard bodies coming together as they battled for dominance was such a damn turn-on. I was so caught up staring at my vampire and angel, I didn't sense my fae move until I felt him slowly lick from one end of my slit to the other.

I shuddered with a groan. He began to lazily tease me with his mouth, clearly in no hurry to make me come on his face. Mal lifted his hips in invitation, and my gaze dropped to him to see a wide smirk spread across his features.

He grasped the back of my neck possessively. "I suggest you wrap those pretty lips around my cock, my queen. I can't come down your throat unless you do."

Caspian purred, "Our mate certainly loves dirty talk," before he continued with his lazy exploration.

"*Now*, Sher," Mal demanded. "Before I make you do it and you miss out on watching your other mates play with each other."

My breath hitched as another shudder ran through me. Caspian was still swiping lazy licks against my clit with an occasional dip into my pussy, and I did *not* want to miss out on how things played out between Jacobi and Ambrose. My mouth lowered until I sucked the head of Mal's cock between my lips, eliciting a deep groan from his chest.

Ambrose leaned over and fished around in my nightstand. He pulled out the bottle of lube we always kept on hand and waved it at the angel king, a sly grin spreading across his face. Jacobi tensed and scowled, his body shifting into a fighting stance. He'd already lost the dominance dance to Malachi, so I doubted he wanted to lose to the princess.

Caspian slowly slid a finger into my pussy, pushing down on my G-spot as he started applying more pressure against my clit with his tongue. My hips bucked back against him of their own accord, and I sucked harder on Malachi. His fist tightened against the back of my neck as he bucked his hips up, trying to get me to take more of him. I resisted, shooting him a sultry look before returning my gaze to my vampire and my angel.

Suddenly, Ambrose threw the bottle of lube at Jacobi, surprising the king who reached out to try to catch it. While he was distracted, Ambrose tackled him to the floor, his legs on either side of Jacobi's body and both of his fists on his chest. The angel king appeared to be effectively pinned. At least for now.

"Listen, you feathered fuck." Jacobi growled at Ambrose's insult. "I'm going to call a truce because I want to tease our lovely little queen over there." Jacobi turned his head to lock eyes with me. That was when I rocked forward, sliding Malachi's cock entirely down my throat and swallowing around him.

"Holy fucking shit," Mal moaned, arching his back, and his eyes fluttering closed.

Jacobi returned his attention to the vampire pinning him to the floor with a brow raised in question. Ambrose turned to smirk at me, and I knew whatever he had planned, I was going to love and hate it.

"I suggest we blow each other at the same time."

I whimpered around Mal and thrust my hips back against Caspian. The fae chuckled. "I suggest you do it. She's soaked at just the thought, and she's clenching so hard around one of my fingers right now."

I started to rock my hips gently against Caspian's face and finger, allowing the motion to slide my mouth along Malachi's cock, making sure to swallow each time he bottomed out.

My two mates on the floor shared a wicked grin and a nod before Ambrose repositioned himself. I watched, completely enthralled, as they wrapped their lips around the other's cock.

Ambrose went—pun intended—balls to the walls and roughly thrust his hips against Jacobi's mouth, choking the angel king with his dick.

"Whatever the fuck you just did, do it again," Caspian growled as he slid a second finger into me.

Jacobi decided it was his turn and thrust up into Ambrose's mouth, but Ambrose was already ahead of him, and he met the king's hips with his face. *Fuck me.* Ambrose didn't have a gag reflex either.

I came.

Screaming around Mal's cock, I exploded. Malachi groaned roughly, holding my head down against him, while Caspian sped up his fingers, drinking me down as he attacked my clit with his tongue.

Jacobi and Ambrose both set a harsh pace for the other, and it was all I could focus on. I sucked Mal harder, and he ripped my mouth from his cock before he could come. Caspian moved away from my core, leaving me feeling cold and empty. Jacobi and Ambrose broke apart before either of them finished, then Mal and Jacobi switched places.

Jacobi spread himself across my bed so his legs, bent at the knee, hung over the side, and he held the lube bottle in his hand. He squirted some into his palm and worked it over himself as Caspian moved me above him.

"I'm going to fuck your ass again, my love." I shuddered. Together, my fae and angel positioned me so I was facing away from Jacobi before sliding me slowly down his cock. Caspian stood between Jacobi's spread legs, pumping his hard dick as he watched me adjust to my angel king.

"I'm not going to be gentle, Dick Slayer," he rumbled. I smiled up at him.

His hand closed around my throat, effectively holding me in place as he stepped closer, slamming his cock into me. My head flung back as I cried out, and Jacobi took my hips to keep me steady as the two men locked eyes.

"Make it hard and fast, angel," the fae growled. Jacobi chuckled and did as instructed.

His grip on my hips would probably leave marks, but I didn't care. All I could think about was how they both roughly thrust up each time Jacobi slammed my hips down. I leaned back slightly, placing my hands on either side of my king. Malachi and Ambrose appeared on either side of me, each sucking a nipple into their mouth, while Ambrose trailed a hand down so he could play with my clit.

My brain short-circuited. The sound of flesh slapping together filled the room as I was repeatedly slammed down onto my mates' cocks, and both men's groans were peppered into the mix. I could feel Malachi feeding off the energy in the room, and I decided to do the same. Releasing my pheromones as well, I watched as all four of my mates became rougher and touched me harder. *Yes.*

"I'm going to fill up this pretty little pussy, Dick Slayer." Caspian's low growl had my eyes fluttering open and meeting his. I hadn't even realized I'd closed them. "I want to watch our seed drip out of you." I clenched around him, causing him to moan. "That's it. That's a good queen. Grip my dick just like that."

I clenched around him again, and this time, both he and Jacobi moaned. Malachi leaned into my ear at the same time Ambrose's fangs sank into the skin around my nipple, whispering, "Be a good little queen and come around your mates."

Pleasure unlike anything I'd ever felt before flooded every cell of my being. My mouth dropped open in a silent scream as wave after wave of ecstasy rocked my body. Jacobi and Caspian joined me, roaring out my name as they came, their hips jerking against mine. My arms gave out as I came down from my high, and Caspian and Jacobi held me up and assisted me off of them before gently placing me on the bed.

My chest heaved as I tried to pull much needed oxygen into my lungs. Malachi moved to settle me on top of him, my face tucking into his neck, and Ambrose slid behind me, licking and nipping his way up my back.

Feeling Malachi's breath against my ear had my nipples tightening painfully. "We let you come all over your other mates, so now you're going to work our cocks like a good slut." I pushed myself up, plastering my back against Ambrose's chest, and nodded. I was so drunk off all the sexual energy in the room he could literally ask for anything and I would do it.

Ambrose released a dark chuckle, and both men helped guide me down Mal's cock before Ambrose slid into me as well. I felt so damn full. They started to gently rock against me, Mal's fingers now working my nipples as Ambrose ran his fangs over every square inch of my skin he could reach.

"Whose little slut are you?" Malachi demanded as my mates started to thrust faster and harder. "Whose cocks do you crave?"

I moaned, unsure I could form the words, but Malachi pinched my nipples hard, and I jolted, liking the bite of pain amongst the sea of pleasure. I almost didn't want to answer him to see if he would do it again.

"Yours," I murmured.

"That's right," he confirmed. "Ours."

"Our little queen only submits to us." Ambrose nicked the skin on my shoulder, and I clenched around them. "She likes it when we use her. Fuck her raw. Mark her." He chuckled when I nodded.

"Now clench tighter around our cocks, my queen. Make us come inside of you." Malachi pinched my nipples again.

One of Ambrose's hands wrapped around my waist, and he began to rub my clit. I could feel myself almost painfully clenching down on both of them as I rocketed toward oblivion again.

"What. A. Good. Girl." Each word gritted out of Mal's mouth was punctuated with a thrust.

Ambrose once again sank his fangs into me, and I ascended into pleasure as we came together, all of us crying out. Then, everything went dark.

When I came to, Jacobi was washing between my legs with a damp cloth, a smug smile spreading across his handsome face. I blinked and then turned my head to find my other mates were once again in the bathroom, cleaning themselves off.

"We weren't sure how long you'd be out," Jacobi said with that damn smirk still in place. "And we didn't want to wake you up after you'd fed that much. Malachi said that you sort of overate."

I groaned. That was putting it mildly. I could practically feel myself bursting at the seams. But damn if it didn't feel fantastic.

∾

Malachi

I STOOD RIGIDLY in front of Ashera, every fiber of my being attuned to her and her safety. The resistance was getting bolder. We figured they'd have more than just vampires in their midst, and we'd gotten confirmation of that during the attack on Cresta City, but we needed more information, so we were now in the dungeons, staring down the single prisoner we'd allowed to live—for now.

I could feel the tension radiating off the other males. We didn't want our mate anywhere near this asshole, but we didn't have any other choice. We needed information, and we were going to get it. I didn't care what I had to do.

The vampire looked at each of us with wild, frantic eyes. He knew he was fucked. At least he wasn't stupid like the last bunch we'd dealt with. I glanced at Ambrose. "Do you mind if I take him? I know he technically falls under your jurisdiction..."

Ambrose propped himself casually against the wall opposite the cell, his arms folded across his chest in a way that highlighted his mating mark. "Be my guest, Mal. His name is Johan."

I heard one of the others pull Ashera back to the wall, but I didn't bother looking behind me. My gaze had once again zeroed in on the vampire locked in one of our smallest cells. I rested my forearm against the bars so I could lean in close.

"Why don't you make this easy for yourself?" I asked. "Tell us everything you know about the resistance. Then I'll make sure that you die nice and quick. How does that sound?"

The vampire's eyes narrowed, and a look of stubborn determination crossed his face. Thank fuck. He was going to make this fun. I fought to suppress a pleased grin.

"Just as those who took that slut of yours said nothing, I, too, will say nothing." I raised a brow at him. The way he spoke suggested he was of noble birth, which would explain how Ambrose knew his name.

"Now, Johan." I sighed. "You really should reconsider. Remember, your little group tortured our mate, and frankly, we won't hesitate to do everything you did to her and more. Personally, I would love to spend a few days locked down here with you." I shot a look over my shoulder. "What about you three?"

Ashera, wearing a pleased and slightly sadistic grin on her face, was leaning against both Jacobi and Caspian as they stood behind her, each with an arm wrapped possessively and protectively around her. All three of her other mates rumbled their agreement. I allowed a broad grin to stretch across my features as I turned back to the vampire.

He spat in my face.

Ambrose tsked, shaking his head, while Jacobi and Caspian

chuckled. I grabbed the end of my shirt to wipe my face. My gaze narrowed, and the vampire went pale.

"Now, Johan, that wasn't very nice," I chastised. "But since you insist on doing this the hard way..."

I straightened and turned to nod in Caspian's direction. With a tilt of his head, the iron bars of the cell wrapped tightly around the vampire's wrists and ankles before shoving him flush against the stone wall behind him. He let out a small yelp of surprise, and his eyes darted around in panic, but there was no one here to save him, no one who gave a fuck whether he lived or died. I would have liked to see him ripped into tiny little pieces.

I sauntered into the cell while the others remained outside. Johan was breathing in quick, uneven pants, clearly panicking about being restrained. The fact that my expression screamed he was in for a world of pain surely didn't help either.

"Now, why don't we get started, hmm?" I smiled at him as I flashed a dagger in his face—my skinning dagger. I kept it sharp enough that I was able to slice off thin layers of skin with ease.

I decided to start with a small section of his arm. In a flash, a rectangular portion of his bicep plopped in a bloody heap on the floor. The vampire screamed.

"Anytime you want to give us answers..."

"T-There a-are me-members every... everywhere," Johan gritted out after I'd sliced another section of skin off his other bicep.

"Well, we figured that much. Come on, give us something more than that," I scoffed. "Maybe you need a little more incentive." I cut the vampire's pants from his body, and he started pleading with me to stop.

"Did you know that this blade is sharp enough to cut small sections off a dick?" I asked, my gaze locked on the panicked vampire's eyes. "I can slowly remove piece by piece until you tell me what you fucking know."

I could see the indecision on Johan's face. His nostrils flared as his wide, frantic eyes focused on the blade as it moved ever closer to his cock. He opened his mouth but quickly closed it, shaking his head.

"Too bad." The edge of my blade dug into the sensitive tip of his cock, and the scream he released would haunt a lesser man.

"Y-Your father! Your father!" Johan screamed, his eyes open and pinned on Ambrose. My hand stilled, leaving the blade buried in the flesh of this pathetic creature's dick. "H-He has been the one to lead the vampires. We have moved on his order."

I turned my head to glance at Ambrose. He'd gone unnaturally still, and his eyes started to glow a bright ruby red. A low vicious snarl built in the vampire prince's chest as he stalked into the cell to stand beside me. "My father," he spat, "is too sick and out of his fucking mind to lead something this elaborate."

Johan started to laugh, and the crazed sound told us Ambrose was very much mistaken. "Your father is healthy, strong," he sneered at Ambrose, "and a far better leader than you will ever be. You're weak, siding with that slut. You would have us give up our blood slaves and kneel to her pussy."

Ambrose lifted a brow as a sneer of his own crossed his features. "The only people who will get on their knees for that pussy are the four of us. Everyone else only needs to bow before her. It's really not that hard."

While the vampire was distracted by Ambrose, I sliced the tip of his cock off. He really needed to stop calling my mate names. He didn't mean it with love and affection like I did, turning the slur on its head. She was our slut, and no one else's. *My* little slut. I shook my head free of my thoughts as the vampire screeched.

"Do you have anything else to add?" I slid the dagger along what was left of the now useless lump of flesh between his legs.

"The other kingdoms will make her kneel before them. They will make her suck their cocks and beg for them to fuck her. She will be nothing more than a sex slave to the whims of the other kings." Surprisingly, he didn't stutter through that. There was an expression of pure hatred on his face as he looked at Ashera. "They will break your pussy over and over again, and there is nothing you can do to stop it."

He went limp as a fresh spray of blood spattered my face. I looked down to find that his still beating heart was in my hand. I couldn't say I was sorry. I turned to look at Sher. Jacobi and Caspian had her sandwiched between them, both of them murmuring soothing words in her ears. Her eyes were locked on Ambrose and me, and I hadn't seen this expression on her face since the end of our rebellion.

Ambrose stalked out of the cell, running a hand through his hair. "There is no fucking way my father is leading those vampires. When I left to come here, he could hardly get out of bed."

Ashera stepped forward and placed her hands on his chest. "Why don't we go find out what's really going on?"

"Little queen, if we go to Masas, I'm not sure how welcome you'll be." He sounded tortured at the thought of his people being less than welcoming to Ashera. He'd come a long way from the vampire he'd been when he first arrived. It surprised me how much he'd embraced Ashera's views, and her, so quickly.

"We'll all be there to keep her safe," Caspian cut in. "She's right. We need to find out the truth."

I looked at the fae in shock. He was always the one shouting about never putting Ashera in danger. "I'm surprised you want to go," I stated frankly.

He glowered at me. "I don't like the idea of Dick Slayer in

danger, but I've also acknowledged that she's safer if she's with all of us. So if we're going to go, all of us are going."

Ashera beamed at him, and I just rolled my eyes.

Jacobi studied us for a minute. "I agree with Ashera and Caspian. It's best to get straight answers, which means going right to the source."

I nodded, grinning when Ambrose let out a loud groan. "Fine. We'll go. But if I go rabid, it is not my fault," he grumbled. Ashera giggled and pressed a light kiss to his cheek.

"Let's go pack and plan. It's going to take us a while to get to Masas."

Ambrose nodded in agreement.

"Sher, I would suggest wearing your battle leathers. Although packing a few dresses for easy access is also a good call." I waggled my brows at her.

She rolled her eyes at me. "I can't believe you're thinking with your cock right now."

"When the hell aren't we thinking with our cocks?" Ambrose asked. "You breathe, and our cocks are hard, so you might as well just accept it."

"I suppose I shouldn't complain. I'm a succubus getting fucked by four men, so I'm living the dream." She laughed as she walked out of the dungeon, the four of us following her.

18

CASPIAN

Somehow, without my knowledge or consent, I had managed to find my place with this ragtag group of supposed royals, although they weren't exactly royals to my standards. Jacobi was the worst example of a chaste king I had ever seen, Mal and Ashera had no royal blood to speak of, and Ambrose... well, he was Ambrose. Enough said. Despite the hazing they had put me through when I first arrived in Shaytan, they cared about me. When that asshole witch had taken me captive, it wasn't just Ashera that stormed to my rescue, it was the whole godsdamn crew. *Is this what a family felt like?* I wouldn't know. Juniya wasn't exactly known for being the warmest of kingdoms, but we got shit done.

Ashera and the men were annoying as hell, but they were growing on me, which was why I needed to do everything in my power to end this rebellion against Dick Slayer's reign, even if it meant tagging along to Masas to confront Ambrose's father. This was one family reunion I did not need to see. Yet here I was, once again clasped in the angel king's arms as we made our way to the vampire kingdom. *Fuck.* The things I would do for this woman. After we sorted out all this rebellion shit, though, we were going to have a serious conversation about our mode of transportation. This whole being cradled in the arms of a king was damaging to my carefully cultivated reputation.

I glanced over at Ashera as she flew gracefully, glittering against the bright blue sky. She was worth it. Worth it all. I still wanted to understand more about how she was able to control the elements the way she had in Cresta, but there hadn't been a moment to breathe since we had returned home. Still, I was desperate to know how the succubus queen was able to use the magic of the fae. What was I missing? With that thought, Jacobi dropped lower, and the large castle of Masas came into view. Shaytan's palace was dramatic and stunning, but the castle Ambrose had grown up in was something else. Black stone stacked on top of black stone, creating a building that was imposing and eerily beautiful. Honestly, it was no wonder Ambrose was the way he was after being raised in a place like this. I'd never fucking tell him that though.

Jacobi landed smoothly, and I brushed off my clothes. It wouldn't do to appear rumpled in front of my closest allies. *Ex-closest allies.* I couldn't exactly be friendly with the kingdom in charge of attempting to kill my mate and end her rule. Until Ambrose could do whatever he had planned for his father, and hopefully take control of Masas, they were our enemies. We would need to tread carefully while we were here.

Ashera landed last, straightening out her dress. The lace was a dark navy today, just shy of black, but the slight hue of color sent a message to the royals of Masas, for whom black was the daily uniform. She wasn't one of them, and she wasn't about to conform. Ashera caught me staring and gave me a smile and a wink. I hid my smile, nodding back. We could handle whatever the vampire pricks had to throw at us. Together.

Ashera walked over to Mal and Ambrose, staring seriously at her vampire mate. "You need to keep a level head while we're here, Ambrose, especially around your father. We need to be able to keep the element of surprise, which means you can't fly off the handle."

Ambrose glared at our queen. From what I had seen, their relationship was definitely a test of wills, but he was borderline obsessed with Ashera, and she him. "I'm not that stupid."

"I never said you were stupid." She turned her back on him, beginning to walk into the courtyard surrounded by a thick, ornate fence. "I just know you have a tendency to get... carried away."

A growl escaped me as Ambrose snaked out his hand and forced the little queen to face him chest to chest. "Listen here, little queen. You're in Masas now, which means you answer to me. Keep that in mind before I have to discipline you in front of the entire court."

My dick hardened as I imagined Ambrose bringing Ashera to heel as the cold vampires of Masas looked on. Maybe that wouldn't be the worst thing in the world.

Ashera merely rolled her eyes, pulling away from Ambrose's grip. "I answer to no one. Keep that in mind before you try to control me." With that, she turned and made her way inside the courtyard before Ambrose could snatch her back again.

Ambrose lingered before falling in line with me as we walked behind our queen. He was muttering something about turning Ashera's ass red. I stopped mid-step, grabbed Ambrose by the arm, and yanked him back to me as the others continued through the winding courtyard. "What the fuck is your problem?" I snarled.

He looked offended, curling his upper lip in a sneer. "I don't have a problem, fae fuck."

Asshole. "Yes, you do. You've been in a fucking mood since we left this morning, and I'm not about to see you screw up the entire plan because you're pissed off."

He scoffed, his eyes narrowing to slits. "Fuck you. I have not been in a fucking mood, you prick." I reminded myself that breaking his nose would probably upset Ashera, so instead, I raised a brow in question as I stared at him. For once, I chose not to respond to his bait, choosing to wait him out. I wasn't about to let him go after our mate until he stopped being a complete asshole.

A slight twitch of his left eye and a muttered curse were signs that I'd succeeded. "I've basically been ruling Masas for years, you know that." I nodded. I was well aware of the fact that Ambrose's father had taken a back seat in recent years, leaving his only son to take care of the kingdom. "I just... I can't believe that he would plan all of this behind my back. We had heard rumors since the beginning about Ashera taking over Shaytan, so why wouldn't he tell me about his plan to throw her off the throne? Am I such a worthless son that he'll let me pretend to run the kingdom while he plays puppet master behind my back?" Ambrose paused, taking in a deep breath, as if he realized he had said too much, but for the first time, I didn't mind his rambling. If I had to guess, it probably had to do with the fact that I was helping Ashera by not letting Ambrose go and take his irritation out on her.

I canted my head. "So show your father who the real puppet master is then."

Ambrose folded his arms across his bare chest, frowning. "What do you mean?"

"I mean, take this opportunity to control your father. Show him who's actually in charge. Pretend like nothing has changed and play him like a game of chess."

I watched Ambrose tip his head side to side, rolling his lip between his teeth. This facet of the vampire prince—the doubtful, unsure side—was one I was certain few people got to see. "That could work."

"Obviously. I wouldn't give you a poor piece of advice."

"Yeah." Ambrose narrowed his eyes on me. "We never had

this conversation." He turned and started toward the entrance, where Ashera and the other two were waiting for us.

"You've got it," I muttered. Even though I didn't want to acknowledge it, something had shifted between Ambrose and me. Seeing him vulnerable, I realized there was more to him than just the cold-hearted vampire prince.

But then again, maybe not.

Ambrose

I COULDN'T BELIEVE I had just spilled my fucking guts to the fae prick. What the hell was wrong with me? I had to admit, however, that I felt better as I walked up to Ashera, who was waiting with Jacobi and Mal. Ashera looked fucking regal, draped in a dark blue dress. She was going to stir shit up at court today, and I was fully on board with that. Fuck all these assholes who had sat by and watched as my father plotted behind my back.

No. I wasn't going to think like that. I was going to walk in there and act like everything was completely normal, feeding my father everything he wanted to hear. I would be pulling the strings behind the scenes, and he would be clueless. *Serves him right.*

Ashera reached for my hand. "You good?"

I squeezed it tightly. "Yeah. Let's just get this over with so I can spill some blood."

"You're an animal," Jacobi muttered, falling into step behind us.

"You should watch who you're calling an animal," I countered. "You forget I see you when you're fucking Ashera's ass. Fucking brute."

Ashera laughed, but I could feel her sexual energy flooding

her aura. She liked knowing we watched each other fuck. *Dirty girl.* "I feel like the time you spend watching Jacobi could be better spent elsewhere."

I leaned over and licked Ashera's neck up to her ear, relishing the moan she gave me in return. "And I feel you should be spending this time better preparing yourself to meet my father."

Ashera leaned into my shoulder, pouting. "You're a killjoy."

How anyone found the strength to deny a succubus what they wanted, I'd never know. It physically pained me whenever I had to say no, which was why it never happened, but on our way to meet my father, who happened to want said succubus dead? It probably wasn't the best idea.

"I'll make it up to you later," I whispered, enjoying the way her body arched against me with my words.

"Save some for the rest of us, princess," Mal grumbled behind me. I had completely forgotten he was there, but he was definitely feeling the effects of Ashera's desire. We would all have to be dead not to be impacted by our succubus.

We had finally reached the oversized black doors, heavy and ornate. Gods, I hated this place, I hated what it stood for, and I hated how it made me feel. I despised the black granite floors. I loathed the heavy wrought iron doors. I hated all of the silver decor, proudly displayed as if we had nothing to fear. If I had my way, I'd burn it all to the fucking ground. Maybe I would after we killed my father. I would bet all this black stone would look much better as ashes around my feet. Maybe I would even fuck my pretty little queen on top of the burned ruins of my past. That would definitely make me feel better. Out with the old, in with the new. With a smile on my face, I turned to the others.

The four of them stood in a semi-circle, waiting for me to speak. Caspian grimaced at me. "Hate to break it to you, princess, but your smile is creepy as fuck."

My grin dropped. "Don't call me princess, prick." Any residual warmth I was feeling for the fae fuck was gone in a moment.

Mal rolled his eyes. "Can we get this over with, please? We can have a dick measuring contest later. Besides, your smile did look pretty terrifying."

"For fuck's sake." I was ready to fight someone, irritation bubbling in my blood, but I glanced at Ashera. A warning was scrawled across the little queen's delicate face, so I shoved my annoyance deep down. *I am the fucking puppet master.* "Okay, look. My father is a paranoid man. He's got his personal collection of guards, as well as Silas, a giant jackass who follows him around at all times. The guards will be no match for the four of us, but Silas... he's a different story. I don't know what freakshow my father picked him up at, but he's a tough bastard. If you want to take down my father, then you'll have to get to Silas first. That's why the element of surprise will be our friend when we confront the court."

They all nodded, and Ashera raised an eyebrow, looking every inch the menacing warrior I knew her to be. "Leave Silas to me."

I knew there would be no arguing with her, so I just shrugged. "Fine. His left side is his weak side. Keep that in mind." I ran my tongue over my elongated fangs, thirsty for blood. "My father is mine."

With that, I turned and opened the doors, strolling into the castle like I owned the place—which I would, soon enough, and then I'd fucking burn it to the ground.

I led us down the hall, toward my father's study where he was sure to be at this hour. The corridors were lined with copper lanterns, casting an eerie green glow as we walked. When we passed one of his many butlers, he froze. I wasn't sure if he was surprised I was home or by my choice of companions.

"Um... sir! Hello! We didn't expect you home for another

week," he stammered. I didn't know this one's name, but he was young, so his loyalty to my father would be less firm. Perfect.

I glared at him, perfecting the imposing mask I wore at home. "Yes, plans change. I'm sure you aren't kept up-to-date on every matter in my life. Where is my father?"

The young butler looked terrified, and I felt bad for a moment, but then I remembered who was relying on me. Ashera. Mal. Jacobi. The slaves. Fuck, even Caspian. So I glared harder, baring my fangs. The butler struggled to speak. "Well, sir, he's not home at the moment."

I closed my eyes, rubbing my hand against my forehead. "And where the fuck is he?"

"He's... He's away sir. He's away. He should be home tomorrow." The butler looked ready to piss himself.

My eyes sprang open, laser focused on the young vampire. "You are utterly useless. How did you even manage to get a job in the palace?" I sighed heavily. "Well, my companions will need rooms to spend the night until my father arrives home. Take them to our finest guest chambers. I assume my bedroom is ready for me?"

"Yes. Yes, sir." The pathetic creature was practically shaking where he stood.

"Good." I turned to Ashera. "I have some business to deal with. Follow this worthless maggot to your rooms, and I'll come find you later."

I could see confusion in Ashera's emerald gaze, and I knew I'd have some explaining to do once we were alone, but I needed to play this part. If we tipped off anyone here, it could get back to my father before we could get to him. No one here would know what Ashera looked like, which worked in my favor. As far as the young butler was aware, these were merely my traveling companions. Odd ones, sure, but no one would dare comment on that fact except for my father.

Eventually, Ashera nodded. "Very well."

Mal gave me a brief nod, and they followed the butler down the hall. I turned the other way. I didn't actually have anything I needed to deal with. I just needed to be alone for a minute and think about what Caspian and I had spoken about. I just felt like such a fucking fraud. For years I thought I had been in charge of everything having to do with Masas and its people, and instead my supposedly sick and disabled father was laughing about me behind my back.

I roamed the dark halls, the servants staying out of my way. I shoved my hands into the pockets of my trousers. I wasn't sure what this feeling was. Shame? Embarrassment? Ridiculous. I was Ambrose, Prince of Masas. I didn't waste time on those lesser feelings. I should be focused on the problems that lay ahead.

My wandering had brought me to the throne room, the heavy black throne central in the large space. Dark tapestries detailing my family's rise to power hung behind it. The copper lanterns were in here as well, the green glow causing the walls and throne to glitter. I hated this room. It was so ostentatious and over the top, filled with the spoils of war. The ceremonial sword sat next to the throne, and I pulled it out, feeling its weight in my hands. Its size made it worthless for fighting, but it made an excellent addition to the whole ambiance for the King of Masas.

How many times had I sat on that throne, doing my father's bidding, all the while thinking it was my own decision? That would be the first thing I would burn. I ran the sword over the smooth iron, enjoying the scraping sound it made. I could imagine it melting, dripping onto the cold marble floors, when nothing remained of my father's rule except for a puddle where his throne used to sit. I tossed the sword across the room where it hit an ornate vase, shattering it to pieces. Well, that looked a little better.

Amid my destruction, a hand grasped my shoulder, and I bared my teeth, growling. Who dared to touch me?

"I wanted to make sure you were okay." Ashera's voice found its way to my ears, low and melodic. She was soothing to my soul, and every muscle in my body instantly relaxed.

I touched her hand lightly but didn't turn around. "I'm fine. I thought you were supposed to be in your chambers."

Ashera slid her arms around my waist and rested her head against my back. "I thought you realized by now that I don't like being told what to do."

I sighed heavily. "All I wanted growing up was to rule Masas. I dreamed about sitting on this throne and watching people cower in front of me." I looked up to the tapestries, stories I was once so proud of.

"And now?" Ashera's voice was a low whisper, but I had no trouble hearing her.

"Now I imagine that everything in this castle would look better as a pile of ash. I used to think it stood for power. Control. Respect. But this?" I pushed away from my little queen's touch, tugging at the tapestry with the family coat of arms. "This is nothing but the symbol of corruption." I ripped down one of the large tapestries with a swift tug.

"Ambrose," Ashera warned.

"No, little queen. You need to hear me out." I faced a tapestry depicting a fierce vampire with a small human cowering at their feet. "This isn't respect. This is greed." Another sharp pull, and the fabric lay in a pile at my feet.

I moved over to the next tapestry, but Ashera circled her small arms around me. "Ambrose. Stop. This won't help anything."

I closed my eyes, taking a deep breath. "No. But it feels damn good."

She pressed her soft mouth against my ear. "I know something else that feels damn good with a little less collateral damage." Ashera slid her hand down my stomach, and I was instantly hard.

"What the fuck is going on? What happened to keeping a low profile?"

I groaned at the interruption, turning to see Mal standing in the doorway. Of course it had to be him. I watched him take in the destruction around the room—the shattered vase, the tapestries lying in piles at our feet. "Did no one fucking listen to me when I told them to go to their rooms?"

Mal strode closer. "I did, but your guest rooms are comparable to Shaytan's prison cells, so I thought I'd look for some better entertainment."

I scoffed. "That guest room is probably the nicest thing you've ever been inside."

Malachi tipped his head, his eyes devouring every inch of our mate, as he joined us behind the throne. "I can think of nicer."

The room was heavy with the pheromones the two of them were releasing, and it was a welcome distraction from the swirling emotions inside me. I turned, pressing my hand against the back of Ashera's neck and forcing her closer. "I think you were going to show me something else that feels good, little queen."

"Mmm..." Ashera tilted her head back, her green eyes filled with lust and mischief. "What did you have in mind?"

"I can help with that," Mal rumbled, stroking the soft skin underneath the thin strap of Ashera's dress. She leaned back, allowing Mal to slip the straps down her shoulders, exposing her perfect breasts before the fabric caught at her hips. I couldn't help myself and bent my head to gently bite one of her perfect nipples. Ashera groaned, and the unmistakable scent of her desire filled my senses. Gods, she was so easy to please. To want.

"The things I want to do to you, my little queen." I traced

my fangs, then my tongue, around her breast, while Mal continued to run his hands down her body. "You'd let me, wouldn't you? You'd let me fuck you in ways I've only dreamed about in my darkest moments."

Her bright green gaze met my own. "I don't care what you do to me as long as you're touching me."

I smirked at Ashera, pressing my fangs harder into her soft flesh, just enough to observe a pearl of blood bloom from the bite. She moaned, and I watched her chest rise and fall with each breath. "You're such a good little queen," I purred, dragging the tip of my finger down her chest. Goosebumps trailed behind my touch. "I love watching you take both of us. Do you like that? When we fill you completely?"

Ashera's eyes fluttered closed. I couldn't see what Mal was doing to her underneath her pretty dress, but I could imagine. Mal met my gaze over Ashera's shoulder, his eyes dark with desire. The stupid fuck had probably scented Ashera halfway across the castle and tracked us down. Whatever. I'd share, but only because my little queen enjoyed as many hands on her as possible.

I dropped to my knees in front of my mate, pulling the light lace of her dress down over her hips before watching it pool on the floor at her feet. With her exposed and bare, I could see Mal teasing Ashera's clit with his finger. I pushed the incubus's hand away, replacing his touch with my tongue before Ashera could complain.

Gods, she was like the sweetest wine, and the most addictive drug wrapped into one perfect package. I lapped at her delicious core, looking up to watch her arch her back into Mal's embrace. Ashera reached her hand around to stroke Malachi's hard cock, and my own twitched painfully as I imagined her soft touch on me. Later. First, I needed Ashera to come on my tongue so I could taste her as she gave me everything.

She was absolutely drenched and close to orgasm as I licked

and sucked, her legs trembling beneath her. I pulled away, lightly touching the corner of my fangs against her clit. "Come for me, little queen." I pressed my lips against her, sucking hard, and Ashera cried out, yielding to her release.

I met Mal's gaze again as he rocked his erection against her hand. An unspoken question rose between us, and I nodded. I took the blissed-out Ashera and led her to the throne—the very symbol of my family's corrupt legacy that I was about to taint even further. I peeled my trousers off and sat down with my little queen standing in front of me. I grabbed her by her slim hips, pulled her to me, and sank her down onto my waiting cock. I moaned, feeling at home and in control once more. Finding peace I never knew was possible wrapped in her tight, hot pussy, I thrust slowly. "Gods, little queen. Your pussy doesn't want to let me go." I groaned, running my hand over her ass and sliding the wetness everywhere to make sure she was ready for Mal. "Now you're going to be a good little queen and let the incubus fuck your ass." Mal stepped up behind Ashera, who was already moaning and crying out my name as she rode my cock.

Another rush of their combined pheromones flooded the air as I held Ashera still while Mal ran his cock through her wetness. Ashera pressed her face against my neck, moaning in pleasure as Mal worked his way inside her tight ass. Fuck, she felt so damn full and ready to explode. I loved fucking my little queen, my mate, and I was beginning to realize I didn't mind sharing these moments with her at all. If anything, it heightened my senses, making the experiences even more enjoyable, if that was at all possible.

"Fuck," Mal groaned, thrusting in time with my own urgent movements. "Make her come, princess. Do it now."

I was edging closer and closer myself, so I ran my fangs down Ashera's neck as we continued to fuck her together. "You heard him, little queen. Come." I bit into her soft skin, relishing the delicious taste of her blood saturating my senses as she screamed her release. As she shattered, Mal roared out his release behind her, and I wasn't far behind as I fed and fucked. I could already feel Ashera feeding off the sexual energy in the room as we came down from our high, collapsing onto one another.

Eventually, I would need to get these two back to my room, but I was comfortable as I lounged with Ashera and Mal on the artificial pile of my family's legacy. Fuck it all anyway. It meant nothing anymore. The only thing that mattered was the future we would build together.

Preferably while my father watched on from a puddle of his own blood.

19

MALACHI

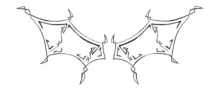

I was just returning home from an assignment. Dust and dirt clung to just about every inch of my body as I strode through the main market of my home city. Cresta wasn't as large as the capital, but it was an important trading city, which meant that the king was often here if he wasn't at the palace. This was fortunate for me, because I didn't need to leave the home I'd built to get close to the asshole.

A small, lithe body slammed into me, stumbling a bit before she landed on the road. I winced. That had to hurt. Holding out my hand, I studied the young succubus before me.

She was stunning. She had glimmering golden skin, soft blonde hair, and curves that would give a man a damn heart attack. Her golden wings shimmered in the light, and her black horns provided a stunning contrast to the bright strands of her hair. It was her bright green eyes, though, with a fire burning bright within them that shocked me to my core.

"Gods," she fumed. "What are you made out of? Stones?" She pushed her hair back and glared up at my hand, her eyes telling me she didn't trust that hand one bit.

Climbing slowly to her feet, not even bothering to touch my hand, she crossed her arms over her chest, which only served to push her ample *tits up in a mouthwatering display. Her foot started tapping on the ground, and she cocked her head slightly.*

"Well?"

Gods, that voice was made for sex. I wanted to know what it sounded like when I was balls deep inside her. "Hmm?" *I blinked at her.*

"Aren't you going to apologize for basically running me over?" *she demanded.*

"I'm... sorry..." *I was pretty sure she was the one that had run into me.* "You should probably pay more attention to where you're going. What had you in such a rush anyway?"

A beautiful blush reddened her cheeks and crept down her neck. Her lips tightened into a thin line. I wasn't going to get anything out of her it seemed. At least not without some smooth talking.

"I'm not the one who should be paying attention, you giant oaf." *I had to fight the smirk that wanted to crawl over my face. She was adorable and sexy as fuck when she was angry. I wanted to pin her up against one of the buildings and fuck her senseless.*

"Look," *I tried again,* "why don't I buy you a drink? As a proper apology?" *Her eyes narrowed as she raked her gaze over my body.*

"I have a mate," *she warned.*

"That's nice." *And wasn't an issue. Plenty of demons and other species took multiple mates.*

Wait... Why was I even thinking along those lines? I ran my hand through my hair and sighed. There was no way I could entertain the thought of having a mate. She'd be fun, but that was all she could ever be.

"Fine. But I want food too."

I didn't bother to hide my grin this time. "Completely understandable." *I swept my arm out.* "I'll also let you pick the establishment."

"Such a gentleman," *she scoffed.*

When we were seated in a small pub I hadn't even known existed, I studied the succubus in front of me once more. "I apologize for knocking you over. My name is Malachi."

"Ashera." *She seemed a bit more relaxed now.* "I suppose I should *offer you an apology as well. I'm sorry for running into you even though you took up the entire damn road and didn't seem to care if there were people around you."*

I threw my head back and laughed. Gods, I liked her. She grinned at me, and I felt my dick twitch. Hell, I wanted to bend her over, smack her ass, and then spend a few hours slamming into her pussy. I clearly needed to get laid.

"I've never seen you before," I commented. "I've lived here since I was young. I thought I knew most people in this city."

"I live on the estate." That got my attention. She lived with Lord Pyper. Lord Pyper was one of the closest confidants of the king. I eyed her in a completely different light now. I might be able to use her to get close to the dick who currently ruled Shaytan. Excitement buzzed in my veins.

I was part of a small group of rebels who wanted to overthrow the current king. Having slaves was one thing, but treating the rest of the demons no better wasn't something many of us tolerated well. The current royal family had been in power for far too long, and it was time things changed. I'd been working as an assassin in the royal army in an attempt to work my way up the ranks and gain access to him. He was a slippery fucker.

"How long have you been there?"

"Pretty much my entire life." My eyes narrowed at that statement. Was she related to Pyper? She didn't look anything like him, but that didn't rule out a blood connection, she could simply look like her mother. "I..." She stopped herself.

"You?" Curious now, I leaned closer to her.

She looked up as her order was placed in front of her. I didn't bother to acknowledge what was set before me. Ashera took the large cup and drained half its contents. Impressive.

"This is my first time out of the estate," she admitted softly. As though afraid she'd already said too much, she began to shovel food into her mouth as fast as she could.

Something about her tugged at me. I placed a hand over the one that tightly gripped her glass. "I know you don't know me," I murmured, "but I won't betray you. I swear it."

~

I WOKE from the memory to a predawn sky. Ashera had her head on my chest. It wasn't unusual for me to wake before she did, but I didn't have meetings to attend, so I didn't need to wake her up. I could simply... be. It was something I hadn't been able to do since Ashera took the throne. Hell, even well before she had taken it, if I was being honest with myself.

Ambrose was curled against Ashera's other side. I'm sure the other two wouldn't be too pleased we'd left them in the guest chambers. Watching the two of them sleep warmed something in me. Nothing about this situation was pleasant, but we'd at least been able to provide some form of comfort to the vampire prince last night. We were all connected by the mate bond. It wasn't just a one-way connection to Ashera—the four of us were bound to each other too. I knew it would take some time for Ambrose and Caspian to adjust to it. More so Caspian, I suspected.

It was hard to believe everything that had happened since I'd met Sher. I'd known that day after I'd bought her a meal that she was my mate. I knew she had Visa, but I had so desperately wanted a place in her bed too. It became clear fairly quickly that my desire would have to wait, and when Visa died... I hadn't been able to bring myself to say anything about the bond between us. I'd only been able to help her get vengeance.

Ashera stretched, plastering herself against me while also shoving her ass against Ambrose's cock. I chuckled. By now she was well aware of what that would do to us. Shifting so I could press a kiss to her head, I heard the door to the room open as Jacobi and Caspian came in, both of them glowering at the sight of us in bed without them.

"What the fuck?" Caspian growled as he glared down at us. "Why didn't you come get us?"

Ashera cracked open an eye before groaning softly. "It's too early for your temper tantrums, Cas."

Jacobi simply climbed into bed beside me, reaching over so he could take Ashera's hand in his. She beamed at the angel and wiggled away from Ambrose, who was, amazingly, still asleep, and over me so she could cuddle into Jacobi's side. Caspian's scowl deepened.

"There I was with my thumb up my ass," he began, only to have Ashera cut him off.

"Now why would you do that when there is an excellent array of dicks to shove up there?" She turned to look at him, effectively making her the small spoon to Jacobi's big spoon. "I'm sure someone would have been more than happy to fuck the attitude right out of you."

That actually shut the fae up. I was mildly impressed and so damn proud. I pressed another quick kiss to her head, earning me a pleased smile. I grinned back.

"How about you stop bitching and just get in the bed, you fucker?" Ambrose growled before burying his head in the pillow again.

Caspian huffed, glaring at all of us before slowly climbing into bed next to the vampire. He lay there stiffly on his back with his arms across his chest. Ashera wasn't having any of that. She wormed her way across all of us until her head was on Caspian's chest and her feet were resting on Jacobi, allowing each of us to touch her. "This isn't comfortable, but I'm hoping all of you will just shut up so I can get a few more hours of sleep since I'm now touching each of you."

Caspian grumbled a bit at that, but then everything was silent.

～

Jacobi

AFTER LOUNGING in bed for a few more hours to allow Ashera to get more rest, we were all gathered in the throne room. Ashera told us what happened yesterday, but you couldn't tell by looking at it now. Everything had been cleaned.

A servant scuttled into the room, bowing furiously at Ambrose. His asshole vampire mask was back on in force as he glared down at the quivering man.

"When is my father supposed to return?" I could hear the violence in his tone. I didn't blame him, not after everything we'd learned.

"H-He... That i-is..." The servant stuttered, clearly not wanting to deliver his message.

"He's not returning today," I surmised. The servant cast me a quick, grateful glance before wincing when Ambrose swore loudly. I could feel the fury as it wove its way through the vampire, at least until our mate wrapped her arms around him and rested her head against his chest.

"When the hell is he supposed to be getting back then?" Ambrose demanded while clutching Ashera close.

"He... He said he would be away for an undetermined amount of time."

"Where the hell is he?" I could feel Ambrose's rage boiling up again.

"I-I'm unsure." The servant cowered at the promise of death that shined in Ambrose's eyes.

I sighed, deciding to intervene. "I suggest we travel back to Shaytan, Prince Ambrose, we have much to discuss."

Ashera sent me a soft smile of gratitude. Ambrose scowled at the servant for a moment longer before giving a terse nod. "Fine. But I want word as soon as he returns, am I clear?" His tone made it obvious that if he didn't receive word immediately, it wouldn't just be this particular servant who lost his life.

"Y-Yes, sir." The servant bowed and ran out of the room when Ambrose dismissed him.

"Let's get back to the palace. We can plan from there." Ashera pressed a gentle kiss against Ambrose's neck. A new tension flooded the vampire, and I had to bite back a laugh. Our mate had the wonderful ability to turn our minds from anything to her soft body in the blink of an eye.

When we eventually made it back to the palace in Shaytan, Ashera excused herself when a servant asked for her attention, so I drew the others to me.

"I suggest we send out spies we trust to track down your father, Ambrose." All three nodded. "I've also been doing some reading..."

"What sort of reading?" Malachi arched a brow at me. They had no idea where I was going with this.

I swallowed my nerves. "I would like to try something with all of you and Ashera." I had their entire attention now. They practically vibrated with curiosity, so I told them my plan. Dark, devious grins spread across their faces when I finished.

"I know where to get what we need." Malachi took off, and the other two chuckled.

"He shouldn't be long," Caspian murmured. No, I didn't suppose he'd take too long to get what we needed.

Ashera returned, looking curiously at us. "What's going on?"

"Nothing, love. Why don't we head back to the bedchamber? You can change." She looked at me suspiciously before nodding her head slowly. I placed my hand on the small of her back, and Caspian and Ambrose fell into step on either side of us.

I could feel their excitement bubbling up with each step we took. We'd never surprised our sexy little mate before, and we certainly hadn't tried anything like this previously.

"Would you be willing to lend me that book you were referencing?" Ambrose asked with a sly smirk.

"Book?" Ashera questioned, looking between us. Her eyes narrowed, and I could feel curiosity and suspicion raging within her.

"Our angel king has been taking advantage of the library here at the palace. He mentioned he'd recently read something rather interesting, and I'd like to read it myself." The vampire's eye glittered with amusement.

"Oh?" Ashera looked up at me. We'd made it to the doors of our rooms and paused just outside. "I admit that I haven't been able to start in on any of the books in the way I would like since ascending to the throne."

"You have an interesting selection," I replied, narrowing my eyes on the now chuckling blood sucker.

Malachi came running up to us at that moment, and Caspian reached over to open the doors so we could all make our way into the bedchamber. Mal clutched a bag and smiled at all of us as he sauntered over to the bed.

"What's in the bag?" Ashera's voice was laced with suspicion again.

"Come here." Malachi placed his hand next to him on the bed, then he released his own pheromones into the air, causing the succubus queen to moan in need. His weren't as effective on the rest of us, it seemed, as Ashera's were.

Entranced by the scent he was releasing, Ashera made her way over to the incubus, sitting delicately on the bed beside him. With movements too fast for me to track, Malachi had Ashera blindfolded with her arms pinned down on the bed above her. A wicked grin spread across his face, one that mirrored my own.

Trying to tug her hands out of Malachi's grip, Ashera squirmed on the sheets. "What's going on?"

Caspian and Ambrose, both naked, moved to stand on either side of the bed. All three of my love's other mates turned to look at me. I'd started this, so it seemed that I was the one now running the show.

"You trust us, don't you, my love?" I asked as I moved onto the bed.

"Of course I do." Her reply came so swiftly and sure, I could feel a deeper desire rage through the four of us. *Damn, but we're lucky.*

I pressed my finger against her mouth, and she instantly sucked on it, swirling her tongue teasingly around the digit. I groaned. "Then you're going to be good and let us have our fun."

Her breath hitched, and she nodded, my finger still in her mouth. My eyes trailed down her body, taking in her dress before I reached up and ripped it away. She gasped, her back arching off the bed. Caspian leaned in and removed the remaining fabric.

"You're not going to know who is touching you. Whose cock you have inside you," I rumbled.

"We'll see about that," she chuckled, but I only grinned at the others.

I quickly removed my clothes, getting off the bed as I did so. I nodded to Malachi, who quickly tied Ashera's hands together before tethering her to the bed. She tugged on the ropes, experimenting to see how far she could reach. He hadn't given her much slack. Mal quickly divested himself of his clothing so we all stood naked around the bed, eyeing our lovely mate as she lay before us.

We didn't want her to know when we were going to touch her. We simply wanted her to feel. My dick jerked at the thought. The longer we went without touching her, the more she squirmed. We all watched as her breasts swayed enticingly with each movement of her body. Gods, she was stunning. I would happily give up my kingdom to remain by her side.

With a nod to Caspian and Ambrose, they slid their hands

slowly, gently up Ashera's legs. She gasped, instantly stilling under their touch. Their hands roamed the inside of her thighs, just grazing over her core before unhurriedly moving back down her legs.

When they reached her ankles again, they both gripped one delicious joint and spread her open for us. Ashera bit her lip in excited expectation, but we all stilled, once again remaining motionless and making her wait for our touch. Malachi and I kneeled at the end of the bed, not close enough to touch her, but close enough so we could easily slide between those lush thighs whenever we pleased.

Malachi waited a moment longer before he settled his face between her thighs, blowing gently on her already soaked pussy. She let out a soft squeak and tried to arch her hips off the bed, but the mates holding her legs placed their other hand firmly on her thighs to keep her in place. Malachi chuckled as she once again attempted to tug her hands free.

"Fucking touch me," Ashera snarled, which had us all chuckling.

"We'll touch you when we want, my love," I growled. For this one moment, I was king in this bedroom. We were going to take her the way I wanted, and she was going to love every fucking second of it.

Ashera let out a frustrated snarl but stopped tugging on the rope. We all released pleased rumbles. We knew she hadn't given in that easily, biding her time until she could pounce, but we weren't going to let her. We catered to our queen's every need, she was our entire world and our reason for existing, but she needed to hand over control occasionally—we were about to show her that.

Mal lurched forward when I gently tapped his thigh, latching his mouth onto Ashera's clit and sliding two fingers roughly into her pussy. She flung her head back as she cried out. Mal didn't hold back. He was almost vicious in his approach, which completely contradicted how Caspian and Ambrose had touched her.

Unlike how we usually operated, none of us were going to talk to her from here on out. A smirk crossed my face as I watched her thrash against the bed. It was almost as though she was trying to get away from the sensations Malachi was making her feel, but the fae and the vampire wouldn't let her.

"Gods!" she screamed as she came. Malachi didn't stop, didn't let her come down from her high. He was relentless, demanding she come around his fingers again.

I switched places with Caspian, nodding for him to replace Malachi. Ashera bit her lip to keep herself from crying out as she continued to come for Mal. The fae and incubus moved seamlessly into place. Caspian gave her pussy a quick lick that had her shuddering before he levered himself up and slammed into her.

I could see the fae struggling not to make a sound as he started to pound into her. With a look at Ambrose, we pulled her legs wider apart while Mal tipped her hips slightly.

She came again with a scream to the gods. Caspian came soon after, his hips roughly jerking against hers.

We all stepped away from the bed, and Ashera's breath stuttered out of her as she once again pulled at her bonds.

"What the fuck was that?" she demanded as she continued to tug in vain.

None of us answered. I shot Ambrose a look, and he grinned in response, moving quickly between Ashera's spread thighs. With vampiric speed, he thrust all the way into her. She moaned and tried to wrap her legs around Ambrose's hips, but Mal and Caspian held her legs once again.

Ambrose moved so just the tip of his cock was quickly thrusting in and out of Ashera's tight pussy. She whimpered and tried to shift her hips to take more of him, but he continued to tease her, only fully pushing into her as he came, keeping his hips flush against hers.

"Fucking tease!" she yelled. We chuckled again.

Mal and I closed in on her as the other two eased back. I lifted her so Malachi could slide onto the bed on his back, then I flipped her so she was straddling the incubus. I leaned over to grab the bottle of lube from the nightstand.

Ashera was surprisingly still and quiet as we got ready. I looked over at Ambrose and Caspian, gesturing for them to get on either side of us and play with her body. They happily complied. Locking eyes with Mal, I lowered Ashera so that we entered her at the same time, both of us sliding in to the hilt.

She let out a ragged moan, her voice hoarse from screaming. We paused for a long moment before the four of us burst into action. Malachi thrust vigorously under Ashera, while I did the same behind her. Caspian and Ambrose pinched her nipples and caressed any other skin they could get their hands on.

Ashera clenched down on Malachi and me, and we both bit back groans. She was always so damn tight and fucking perfect. I nodded, and we upped our pace. Ashera couldn't hold back her cries as we continued to slam into her body, unable to get enough of her.

She came twice more before Malachi and I finally found our own releases. Mal kept his hips pressed against hers while my hips jerked against her tight ass. We all slipped away from her, leaving her on her back on the bed. We quickly cleaned ourselves before I sent Caspian into the bathroom to get a bath started for our mate.

I leaned over Ashera and removed the blindfold first, and she blinked as her eyes adjusted to the light. Her skin glowed, and there was the beginning of a very satisfied grin tugging at her lips. Pressing a kiss to her forehead, I quickly untied her from the bed, gently massaging her arms to ensure proper circulation returned to the limbs.

I could hear the other three males sliding into the giant tub that would thankfully hold all of us as I picked Ashera up off the bed. Settled in the hot scented water, Ashera groaned softly and tilted her head back against the rim of the tub.

"You are all more than welcome to do that again," she stated in a husky whisper. "Anytime."

I grinned and shook my head while the others chuckled. "Believe it or not, birdbrain was the one who came up with the plan." I shot Ambrose a glare. "He'd read it in a book." His lips twitched when I punched him in the arm.

"Please feel free to explore any other ideas from this book." My queen threw me a quick grin. "I'm more than happy to explore any sexual fantasy you may have."

Fuck. I was sure I wasn't the only one who was hard again.

20

ASHERA

I was struggling to wrap my head around the idea that it wasn't just me anymore. Mal and I had been a team since that fateful day he nearly ran me over in Cresta like the dick he was back then. We'd had each other's backs, celebrated wins, and mourned losses together, but this was different. My skin was marked with the love and respect of these strong men, and theirs was marked with mine—a crown, something I had thought honored my rule. But I was beginning to realize that it meant something more. That crown was our legacy, something that we would build together on the blood and bones of lesser men.

I looked at myself in the mirror as I wove my long hair into a tight braid. I didn't look different, besides my mates' marks on my body, but I felt different. More solid. Centered. Tethered to the earth. I had always been confident in my own strength. If I worked hard enough, I could achieve whatever I put my mind to, whether that was winning a game or taking a throne.

After I lost Visa, I distanced myself from any kind of relationship that would be more than purely sexual. I'd assumed another mate would make me weak and put a target on my back. It was easier to keep my blinders up and focus on the task at hand. Killing the enemy. Taking the throne. Winning over the other territories. But then, one by one, these men had weaseled their way into my life. Into my heart.

I rubbed my wrists, even though no trace remained of the time we had spent in bed last night. All of us, together. For the first time, it felt like we had all belonged to one another. It felt right.

Like hell was I going to let anyone, even another king, take any of that happiness away from me. Satisfied with my braid, I donned the fighting leathers that hung in the corner of my room. I hated the leathers as much as I loved them. They had always felt like armor, but wearing them meant war was near. There would be no dresses right now, no frothy chiffons and heavy silks. Not until we found Ambrose's father and put this resistance to rest. Not until my people, all my people, were safe. I sighed, strapping the soft leather onto my body.

Jacobi's blond head poked through the doorway. "Are you alright, my love?"

I needed to be more careful about the energy I was putting out into the world, especially when Jacobi was around. The empath picked up on the slightest nuances of my emotions. I shouldn't complain, it was wonderful to be noticed, but I didn't want to cause my mates any concern over my constant worries. I was a queen, for fuck's sake, and I was going to act like one. I tossed my shoulders back as I stood, pressing a quick kiss to Jacobi's cheek. "I'll be fine. Where are the others?"

Jacobi pressed his lips together, and I knew he wanted to push the subject, but he wouldn't. Some things were better left unspoken. "They're in your study, waiting for us."

I nodded. "Then let's not keep them waiting any longer, shall we?"

I grabbed Jacobi's hand, and we walked in a comfortable silence down the hall. Our relationship had been like this since the first moment I'd laid eyes on him—easy, simple. I honestly couldn't have asked for more than this gentle angel king.

And yet, somehow, I wound up with three others, each one just as perfectly suited to me as my empathetic angel. The gods knew what they were doing when they selected our mates, filling gaps in our souls and hearts with what we needed most. For whatever reason, the five of us needed each other. Though the reason didn't truly matter.

I entered my study without knocking, and I found my three other mates huddled around a large map spread out on my desk. Their faces were tight, and it was obvious Jacobi and I had walked into an argument. They looked up at us, and I tapped my finger on my lips. "Don't tell me. Mal had a dream about Caspian last night, and Ambrose is jealous that it wasn't about him."

Mal and Caspian gave me sour looks, but Ambrose just laughed. He was sitting in *my* chair and had the audacity to pat his lap. "Come sit, little queen. Some female energy might sway these two pricks to my side."

"I think I'd like to know what the sides are before I decide." Regardless, I went and sat on Ambrose's lap, leaning back against his hard chest.

Malachi looked down at me and licked his lips. "Gods, Sher, I love it when you wear your fighting leathers."

I sighed, not wanting to get into my mixed emotions about what the outfit meant for me. Instead, I turned my attention to the large map in front of me. It was a map of Dunya. "What are we deciding on?"

Caspian groaned. "Well, Dick Slayer, Bat Fuck here wants to start the search for Ambrose's father in Shaytan. I told him that was a stupid idea. Runner up for stupid ideas is Ambrose's idea to search the hinterlands of Masas, where his father apparently has strong allies." Caspian acknowledged each of these ideas with a forceful jab at their respective locations on the map.

I nodded. Jacobi remained quiet, still standing in the doorway. He would go along with whatever we decided, I knew that, so it was deciphering which of these strong opinions would be the best. "And you, Caspian?" I carefully kept my tone neutral. "Where do you think we should begin the hunt? Juniya?"

Caspian's beautiful hazel gaze met my own as he shook his head. "No. I think we should start here." He pressed a finger into the bottom of the map—Qamar.

I sucked in a quiet breath. I had met the King of Qamar once fa very long time ago. It was a meeting I didn't want to remember, and also why I had been grateful that the king didn't show up when I invited delegates from each of the kingdoms. It was one thing to invite him to my land, but showing up at his doorstep was definitely asking for trouble.

Caspian continued, "King Tomas has long time allies in Qamar, and it's no secret that King Vaughn disapproved of you taking the throne. If I had to guess where he was, I'd say he was recouping his resistance losses there. They lost a lot of men in Cresta City, and Juniya doesn't have a large army, but Qamar does."

I rested my head on Ambrose's shoulder, weighing up the options. Qamar made sense. But if it wasn't one-hundred-percent certain, I didn't want to go barging into their capital, demanding another royal's head. I doubted Tomas was in Shaytan, our humble land was beneath his presence, but the hinterlands... that idea had merit. "We return to Masas and search the hinterlands. Ambrose is right. His father wouldn't want to go that far, especially if he still has allies on the inside."

Caspian glared at me. "I really think Qamar is the more realistic option."

"And I said we were going to search the hinterlands." Gods, he was stubborn.

"Ashera, I just think you should—"

"Caspian," Jacobi warned from the door, always the peace-keeper. I offered him a grateful smile.

Caspian turned his annoyed gaze onto Jacobi. "You know, you could throw your own vote into the mix instead of just playing Ashera's guard dog."

"Caspian!" My voice was loud and sharp, and I could see the fae was taken aback. "If you must know, King Vaughn is the worst kind of slave owner. I met him once a long time ago when I traveled with Lord Pyper to Zvezda. He treats his dogs better than his field slaves, and even those are treated better than the young females in his care."

I felt sick to my stomach, remembering accidentally running into a slave clawing through the garbage after our dinner while Vaughn's dogs had eaten beside him, feasting on the finest cuts of meat. As a servant, King Vaughn wouldn't remember me, and for that I was grateful. I certainly remembered him though. I hadn't seen King Vaughn's daughter during my time there, so I could only hope she was cared for appropriately, but I couldn't be sure. "Anyways, Caspian, you're right too. Zvezda has a large army, and I'd rather not provoke their wrath unless absolutely necessary. Are we clear?"

Caspian glowered at me, obviously pissed.

"Are we fucking clear?" I repeated.

"Crystal," Caspian spat before turning on his heel and leaving the room.

~

Caspian

I was pissed, but what else was new? I had stormed the corridors for some time after leaving Ashera's study, glaring at any of the guards or servants who had dared to look my way. Everything I saw irritated me further. The soft golden walls reminded me of my mate's brilliant wings that fluttered so angrily when she argued against me. So I walked the halls, unable to force myself to go back into the study and face Ashera and the other men, until Jacobi found me and told me we were making preparations to leave for the hinterlands and led me to Ashera's bedroom. I wanted to argue about checking out Zvezda for Tomas, but Ashera had her reasons for not wanting to go there without due cause, and I had to respect that, even if I was fairly certain that hiding another king who wanted to see her dead was enough cause. But who was I to talk? I was just her mate, after all. What did my opinion fucking matter?

Mal turned to glare at me, and I realized I must have spoken aloud. No matter. It wasn't like I had done a good job of hiding my feelings up until this point. So here we were again, getting ready to travel back to Masas on a wild goose chase because there was no way Ambrose's father was sticking around there, especially since I was certain word of our visit and swift departure had probably reached his ears.

This time, Ashera wouldn't put on her dark dresses—so subtly rebellious. Today, she wore the leathers of a warrior, and they fit her like a second skin. I thought back to the first time I had thought we were putting her in danger and how concerned I had been for her safety. I still feared for my little mate, but I was more confident in her ability to handle herself. The woman had pulled fucking lava out of the ground, for fuck's sake, all while keeping damage to the city minimal. I don't remember ever seeing my father have control over the elements like that, and my family was renowned for our magic.

I wouldn't be at all surprised if there was royalty in her blood somewhere down the line. To have that kind of strength and control... it was practically unheard of. *And she is mine.*

Unfortunately, it meant my control over my stubborn mate was also slim. Unless...

Ashera had her back to me as she spoke to Jacobi—the

feathered prick who had stood by and not chosen a team when push came to shove. I had to admit, her fighting clothes were a turn-on, something I wasn't expecting after years of the excessively dressed women of the Juniya court. Being attracted to Ashera was easy. Seducing her to get my way without being seduced myself was a different story altogether.

I stepped closer so my chest pressed against Ashera's back. I felt her relax into my touch, her ass grinding into my already hard cock. *Fuck.*

"I'm still mad at you, Caspian," she said, not turning around.

Her body spoke otherwise. I bit the soft skin under her ear, licking away the sting. "Let me make it up to you," I murmured, making eye contact with the angel king over her shoulder. He gave me a dubious look, probably knowing exactly what my plan was. I shrugged, returning to kissing Ashera's perfectly golden skin. I pulled the top part of her leathers down her shoulders, leaving her breasts bare to the room. I could hear the low growls of her other mates, but this was my moment. "I'll even give you a choice. Do you want me to fuck your tight little ass or your perfect pussy?" At this point, I didn't care which part of her I got to fuck, as long as I was inside of her.

Ashera moaned, grinding against me again. Gods, this woman was something else. I would never get enough of her.

Mal and Ambrose stalked closer to our small group, sensing Ashera's desire, which none of us ever wanted to miss out on. We were falling into an easy rhythm in our lovemaking, sharing becoming more natural by the day, and our mate enjoyed having all our attention on her.

Malachi pressed up against Ashera's bare side, tugging her braid back and exposing her throat for the vampire to bite the opposite side. Jacobi was already stepping forward, shoving the leathers I was so fond of to the ground. The incubus pulled her braid again. "Your mate asked you a question, Sher. I suggest you don't make him ask it again," he said, his voice husky with need.

"Or what?" she teased.

Mal tweaked her nipple hard. "Don't play this game."

Her moan went right to my cock, all of us touching her in some way as she writhed. Jacobi knelt in front of her, licking her already drenched core. "My ass," she gasped finally. "Fuck my ass, Caspian."

I chuckled, shoving my pants off my hips. A moment later, Ambrose was handing me lube. "You're such a dirty girl, Dick Slayer. But your other mates will be lonely if I'm the only one inside you."

Jacobi was still eating Ashera out like she was his last meal, and I ran my hand down between her legs, mixing her own wetness with the lube around her ass. She cried out as Jacobi moved faster and Mal bent to suck her nipple into his mouth. "Don't let her come," I commanded. "The only time she's coming is around my cock." I could feel her body desperately trying to cave to her release, her legs trembling as they struggled to hold her up.

"Please," she begged. "Please, Caspian."

I ran my dick between the cheeks of her ass, toying with her as she arched into me. "I would just feel so guilty if I was enjoying myself and they just got to watch."

"Fuck," she cried. "Fuck! Mal and Ambrose can fuck each other."

I laughed, imagining the demon and the vampire wrestling for control, and Jacobi joined in. "Oh, this is gonna be good," he muttered.

I bent Ashera over. "While we wait for the entertainment, you can be a good little mate and suck off the angel king." Jacobi stood, and Ashera eagerly put her lips around the angel king's dick. I was sure his moan could be heard in the next kingdom over. I tossed the lube over to Mal who was trapped in a standoff with Ambrose. I could already see how this was going to go.

"Are you watching, Dick Slayer?" I asked, pulling her braid back to make sure she could see her alpha mates wrestling for dominance. Gods, she was beautiful, her mouth full of another's cock, her pussy dripping wet for mine. I couldn't wait another second. I eased my way inside her ass, moaning at the tight fit. Ashera didn't waste a minute before she slammed her ass against my hips, forcing me to move at a desperate pace while the angel fucked her mouth. When I looked up, Mal had Ambrose in some kind of weird headlock. *Serves the prick right.* "Who do you think will fuck who, little mate?"

She loved watching us fuck one another, and the sudden release of pheromones in the air told me that now was no different. I slowed my pace, and Jacobi did the same, wanting her to see who would win the fight for dominance. When I looked up, Mal was flat on the floor with a naked, grinning Ambrose ready to slide his lubed cock into the incubus's ass. Well... I couldn't say I had been expecting that. As Ambrose slid home, both men cried out in pleasure, the same feeling reverberating through Ashera. With all of us content, we began to move as one. Jacobi and I moved in unison, fucking our perfect queen, our mate, together. Ambrose was fucking the incubus like a professional, and Mal moaned underneath him, enthralled by the spell of the room.

"Fuck," I muttered. "I want you to come with me, Dick Slayer." I looked up at Jacobi. "All of you." By some unspoken agreement, we all picked up our pace, and a symphony of moans filled the room as we found our release one by one. I finished last, the contentment of watching others in pleasure fueling some kind of primal need within me as I pistoned my hips into Ashera's ass, trembling as I came down from an exquisite high.

Mal and Ambrose collapsed together on the floor,

attempting to catch their breath, and Jacobi had fallen back on the bed, our eyes already closed.

I pulled out of Ashera and sat down on the floor with her on top of me. She rested her head against my shoulder, and I ran my fingers through her hair. "So, Dick Slayer," I whispered, hoping to catch her in the right moment of postcoital bliss.

She didn't open her eyes. "So, Caspian."

"I thought maybe we could reopen the discussion of where we would search first for Ambrose's father."

Ashera opened one eye, craning her neck to look at me. "Did you honestly just fuck me in hopes of getting your way?"

I shrugged. "Did you not enjoy it?"

She closed her eyes again and settled against my chest. "I did."

"So..."

"I enjoyed the sex, Caspian. But we're still going to Masas. I'm a fucking succubus, did you really think you could seduce me like that?"

Fuck. Ashera - 1, Caspian - 0.

21

ASHERA

W as I surprised Caspian had tried to seduce me into getting his way? No. Not at all. I was actually more shocked he hadn't tried to pull something like that sooner. But at the end of the day, this was my call, and there was no way I was going to haul ass into Qamar without definite proof. That was a surefire way to end up on the chopping block—or in the middle of *another* war.

No, thank you. Not today. I didn't feel like fighting my way out of a kingdom of shifters. Their army was second to none, even compared to my elite team of assassins. And King Vaughn... yeah, he was another story altogether. One day, his time would come, and I would be happy to serve him every ounce of justice he deserved, but I wasn't going to put my mates in danger for a hunch.

If we needed to infiltrate Qamar, I wanted to do it in a way so Vaughn would be none the wiser. I also didn't want to leave any stone unturned when it came to this resistance, especially not after what they did to Caspian. He was a complete pain in the ass, but he was *my* pain in the ass.

I watched the land below us as we flew to the Masas hinterlands. Everything looked so damn calm and peaceful. So quiet. I wished that was actually the case. I'd known when I decided to start my rebellion that if I took the crown there would be problems. I hadn't realized the lengths the dissenters would go to, nor had I realized just how strongly the other kingdoms would protest.

I glanced over at Ambrose and Caspian, both held by my other winged mates. I loved them, I'd never deny that, but there was a small part of me that ached because they'd come here to use me. I wasn't fooled into thinking the best of them when I'd sent the invitations, but knowing they're my mates... it stung deeper than I wanted to admit.

Knowing that Caspian had tried to seduce me to get his way showed he didn't truly understand or respect me, which wasn't fair of me to say. I hadn't exactly gone out of my way to ensure he had a smooth transition into our group, but he hadn't actually tried either. Ambrose now knew better than to attempt to use sex to change my mind, but Caspian... He'd said he wanted the mate bond, but I wasn't exactly sure he really understood what he'd signed up for.

Jacobi's gaze cut to mine, concern etched into his handsome features. I gave him a small smile and a quick shake of my head. I knew he could sense the turmoil I was feeling, but I didn't want him to say anything to the others. He and I could talk about it later. We needed to present a united front right now. He frowned, clearly unhappy about not being able to discuss what was going on in my head.

He and Ambrose had been the two biggest surprises in my life. Yes, Ambrose had come with the express intent of using me to get what he wanted, but seeing how much he'd changed so quickly made my heart pound. He gave his all to our bond. He was still prickly and dramatic, but it was clear that I was his first concern. And Jacobi, the celibate angel king. Gods, who would have thought that he would end up the mate of a succubus. He also devoted himself to the bond. Frankly, it humbled me. These two men had changed so much for me. My eyes watered a bit. I wasn't sure I deserved any of my mates.

I'd done a lot of unsavory things to get the crown. I'd killed so many people, I'd lost count. I'd used not just my blades, but my body as well. Would the three who hadn't been with me during the rebellion understand why I'd done things the way I had?

I just realized that we were so focused on finding the resistance and securing safety that we hadn't really sat down to get to know each other's pasts. I hadn't even told them about Visa. I wasn't sure if Mal ever mentioned her either. I made the decision to sit down and discuss the rebellion and my past with my mates as soon as we got back from the hinterlands, no matter what we found there.

When we touched down, Ambrose strode forward, his keen gaze taking in everything around us. We'd agreed before we left that we'd let Ambrose take the lead once we got here since he knew the area best. Although the hinterlands did border on Jacobi's kingdom, Malak, the angel king had never really had any interest in scouting this area. It wasn't exactly populated.

"There's a network of caves that burrow pretty deep underground. The entrances are well hidden." Ambrose glanced back at us. "I'm not exactly sure what we'll find in there, especially not after the botched attempt to kidnap and kill Ashera."

I stepped forward and laced my fingers with his, gently squeezing his hand in a show of support. "Whatever we find, we'll deal with it."

He studied me for a moment before giving me a curt nod. This was hard for him. I wanted to disembowel his father for using my strong, loyal vampire the way he had. If we needed to raze the kingdom of Masas, we would. I'd end the world for Ambrose. For any of my mates.

Ambrose led us to a series of rocky ledges and pointed down

the side of the cliff face. "The easiest way to get into the cave system is down here."

"Fucking great," Caspian muttered. "We need to fly again."

"At least we've got people with wings," Malachi growled in response. "Otherwise, you'd need to climb down there. We can leave you to do that if you want."

Caspian huffed and crossed his arms over his broad chest. "Flying is fine."

I rolled my eyes. Sometimes I just wanted to smack him.

We floated down to a cave entrance. It was just big enough to fit my mates, all of whom were giants compared to me. If it got any shorter, they would have to stoop. The silence was unsettling.

"Come on." Ambrose grabbed my hand again and led us farther into the cave. "There's a large cavern not far from this entrance."

As we got closer to the cavern, we could hear the sounds of a large group of people. We paused to listen. My muscles tensed when I heard someone talk about taking over Shaytan. These vampires were certainly part of the resistance, but would we find Ambrose's father so we could cut the head off the snake?

"There's a few hundred in the cavern." Ambrose turned to look at the four of us behind him. "We might be able to hear more if we hang out here."

Caspian went to open his mouth, but footsteps from behind had all of us stiffening. *Fuck.* My gaze went to each of my mates. We were going to need to fight our way out of here.

"We stick together as much as possible." My tone didn't leave room for arguments. "We all get out, is that clear?"

Jaws ticked and eyes narrowed, but they all nodded.

I grabbed the daggers from my thighs just as the first vampire rounded the bend and spotted us. His eyes went wide, and then more poured in behind him. For a moment, there was nothing but silence before those in the tunnel all started yelling to those in the cavern. They knew exactly who we were.

Ambrose and I braced ourselves for the attack from the cavern as the others started to take out the ones that had come up behind us. We didn't have much room to maneuver in the tunnels, and the task would be much harder for my mates. They were all big men. I also couldn't use too much elemental magic down here, or I risked hurting them or collapsing the tunnels on top of us. Caspian seemed to realize that as well, since he'd taken out the sword he had attached to his hip.

A hand lashed out, grabbed me by the arm, and dragged me partially into the cavern, starting to cut me off from my men. My heart raced at the thought of being separated from them. It would make escape that much harder.

"Ashera!" Ambrose's bellow shook the walls of the tunnel, and the four parts of my soul pushed into the cavern after me. They all wore identical looks of violent determination.

I wanted to shout at them to get back into the damn tunnel. If they came too much farther into the cavern, we wouldn't be able to make our way back, and I needed to focus on the crowd of vampires around me. I continued to slash as quickly as I could, and now that I was out in the open a little more and away from my mates, I pulled on the elements and allowed fire to spin around both daggers. My main goal now was to get back to them so we could all make it out.

The harder I fought, the farther away I got from my men. They were starting to separate too. *Shit.* I pushed harder, trying to make it to Ambrose who was the closest to me.

"Witch!" Caspian's roar had all of us turning to look at him. The blood drained from my face. The dead were now pouring into the cavern from different tunnels. Witches used souls and the dead to feed their powers. There weren't just vampires here.

"We've got shifters too!" Malachi yelled.

We were quickly running out of options.

"Get back together!" I screamed. I could possibly bring most of the cavern down around us without crushing us, but I couldn't do it if we were all scattered.

After what felt like hours of hacking at our enemies, we were finally starting to close in on each other. We had a small chance of making it out of this. I began to pull on the earth around us and the cavern started to shake.

"Stop her!" someone shouted above the sounds of battle.

We were in a loose circle, and my mates all stiffened as the group renewed their attacks. That should have been my sign to be more alert, but I was too focused on bringing the majority of this cavern down around us without getting my mates killed.

A scream tore from my throat as my gaze fell to my chest. A spear made from souls had emerged through my left breast. Time seemed to slow as my mates all turned their heads in my direction, horror written on all their faces. The metallic tang of blood was thick in my mouth, and my knees wobbled. I needed to finish this before I lost too much blood. The spear had missed my heart, but only just.

With my legs shaking and my hands unsteady, I dug deep and ripped as much of the cavern down around us as I could. A small hole ripped open above us, and that was all my mates needed to get out. I'd saved them. Relief flooded me.

A warm hand closed around my wrist, and I was lifted into the air as fire roared below us. My eyes fluttered, and my vision became blurry. I coughed and could feel the blood fly out of my mouth.

"Fuck," an angry voice cursed. "We need to get her to a healer! She used too much damn magic controlling that fucking collapse. She isn't healing."

"It's hard to heal from a soul wound. They don't just hurt the flesh," another chimed in. "The soul weapon will drain magic from the injured. They sucked out as much as they could before she closed us off."

I wasn't sure how long I floated in and out of consciousness, but I was eventually placed on something soft as voices yelled for help. My breaths were shallow, and I could hear the gurgle of blood with each inhale. I wanted to stay awake for as long as possible, but my world quickly faded to black.

~

Malachi

WE MADE it to a small hut on the border of Masas where a few of Ambrose's most trusted men were stationed. My mate was dying. I could feel the bond getting weaker in my chest. I looked at Ashera's other mates and could see that they were just as panicked as I was. A healer hurried into the room, blanching at the sight of our queen on the bed. She was covered in blood —her own fucking blood—and looked so damn pale. Her lips were slightly blue. The healer placed her hand over Ashera's chest, and a soft light shone on the wound.

"She may not make it." The healer's voice was soft, and we all snarled. "I'm doing all I can, but this wound was made by a soul weapon. I can feel it. She doesn't have enough magic to assist in the healing process."

"What if she fed?" Jacobi asked, his face and tone frantic.

The healer shook her head. "She can't feed if she doesn't wake up."

As the healer continued to work, the gaping wound on Ashera's chest shrank. I wanted to believe that was a good sign, but I knew there was a lot of internal damage. The healer would attempt to stop her from bleeding out before repairing anything else, but it might not be enough. Especially if Ashera couldn't feed.

"What the fuck was that down there?" Caspian raged at Ambrose. He shoved the vampire before aggressively getting in his face. The last thing we needed was to start infighting. I knew the fae was dealing with his panic by picking a fight, but he needed to get a better handle on himself.

"That was apparently a gathering spot for the resistance." I could hear the frustration, fear, and rage in the vampire's voice. He didn't lift his hands to retaliate against the fae asshole, however.

One of Ambrose's men rushed into the room. "My lord! I have word of your father."

All four of us stilled, our gazes narrowed on the man before us.

"Well?" Ambrose snapped.

"He was spotted in Qamar."

That set Caspian off. He launched a punch at Ambrose's face, nailing the vampire right in the nose. Caspian followed up with a kick before Jacobi and I could step in.

"She's going to die because of you fuckers!" the fae screamed. "I fucking told you we needed to go to Qamar, but none of you fucking listened, and now she's dying."

He started to struggle against Jacobi.

"I'm going to kill all of you!"

A gasp from the healer had our heads turning in her direction just as Ashera jackknifed on the bed. I saw a flash of red and a glint of fangs before she latched herself onto the healer's neck. *What the fuck?*

We all stood there in shock for a minute before launching into action. Jacobi clutched the healer as Caspian, Ambrose, and I ripped an incredibly strong Ashera away from the poor woman. She turned to look at us with glowing, ruby-red eyes, and blood dripped from her mouth. She snarled and lunged at us. Ambrose stepped into her, and she attached herself to his neck. Her fangs violently tore into his flesh, but he didn't move, didn't flinch, just let her maul him before guzzling his blood.

Jacobi rushed the healer out of the room, coming to stand beside me as we watched Ashera drink from Ambrose.

"How the hell is she showing vampiric traits?" Jacobi whispered to me.

"I have no clue," I murmured. "But if it's saving her life, who the fuck cares."

"She's going to need more than just my blood," Ambrose slurred. "One of you get ready to take my place."

Shit. She'd already drained him? How the hell was that possible? Caspian moved in as Ambrose detached Ashera from his neck. She seemed more alert now, which was good. She didn't instantly launch herself at Caspian, instead, she blinked and looked around. Her eyes were still a glowing ruby red, but they weren't crazed with hunger any longer—at least they weren't until she turned her attention to her fae mate.

She inhaled deeply before she struck. Caspian let out a low moan. "Is it supposed to feel this fucking good?" His hips jerked with each pull she took.

"Yes. It's a mate thing." Ambrose was on his back at the foot of the bed. "I bet she'll make you bust in your pants."

Caspian didn't seem to mind the thought of that. In fact, none of us seemed to mind the thought of Ashera making us come in our pants. The fae gently brought his arms around our queen and tugged her flush against him as his hips continued to grind against her. If his breathing was anything to go by, he was getting close.

Ashera ripped her mouth away from Caspian's neck, then she licked her lips as she eyed the prince in front of her. The hunger in her gaze was for more than just blood now. She pulled Caspian's mouth to hers with a snarl that had all of us hard as fucking rocks. Ambrose was back up beside Jacobi and me as we watched our queen take her fill of her fae.

"Feeding is usually tied very closely with sex," Ambrose explained. "She was too wounded to do anything with me. But if I'm right, she's going to fuck his brains out while she feeds off him." He glanced at us. "And then she'll move on to us."

"Can she really hold that much blood?" Jacobi asked as he watched Ashera move at an alarming speed to push Caspian down on the bed before straddling him. "If she feeds normally as well during sex..."

The implications were a little frightening. Just how powerful was our little mate? That was a question for another time. We were all too enraptured with her to think too much more about it.

Ashera ripped off what remained of her leathers before destroying Caspian's clothes. Her gaze snapped to us as she growled, "Take off your clothes. I want you all ready."

We groaned and obeyed.

She slid her wet pussy along Caspian's cock, and the fae moaned and flexed his hips in an attempt to push into her wet heat. She denied him. His hands gripped her hips as she dug her nails into his chest.

"She's not entirely in control," Ambrose warned. Ashera didn't bother to correct him.

In a move too fast for any of us to track, Ashera wrapped her hand around Caspian's throat. It didn't look like she was trying to choke him, merely subduing him. Forcing him to submit.

"Listen here, fae," she growled as she slid his cock into her and then leaned down so their lips were almost touching. "You are done playing games with me."

All of us stiffened, and shock slackened Caspian's face. Jacobi's brow furrowed as he watched them. "She felt... extremely upset, sad, and almost despondent on the flight to the caves. This must have been what she'd been thinking about."

Caspian's gaze flicked to us, his eyes dark and unreadable before he returned his attention to our mate. His face softened as he studied her with an intensity that had all of us shifting slightly in our spots.

"No. More. Games." Each word was punctuated with a thrust of her hips. "I am your mate." Her voice broke a little, and the three of us not inside her growled slightly at the hurt in her voice. "I am not a toy."

I was going to rearrange Caspian's fucking face.

The asshole didn't say anything, just stared up at her like the idiot he clearly was. I slapped my hand out against Ambrose's chest to keep him still. The three of us were ready to pounce on the fae, but with Ashera currently on top of him, I didn't want any of us moving just yet.

Caspian flipped her over and raised her hands above her head. He started to thrust slowly in and out of Ashera as he continued to stare into her once again glittering green eyes. My mate's breath hitched.

"You are *mine*," he snarled before kissing her. "I will share you with your other mates, but you are mine. *My mate*." Ashera moaned and arched into him. "No more games, little mate."

Ashera came with a muffled cry, and Caspian found his release a moment later, letting out a low groan.

"I promise, Dick Slayer."

Gods, that smile. It lit up the entire damn universe and had my heart bursting.

"Mal," Caspian called me before heading into the bathroom.

I slid onto the bed next to her, dragging her on top of me. "I am yours to do with as you wish, my queen." Her eyes switched between her normal green hue and the burning ruby red.

She shifted and slid me into her warm, wet pussy until our hips were flush together. Her nails dug into my chest as she swirled her hips, my own arching up under her. My hands went to her taut nipples, kneading the flesh before rolling them between my fingers.

When I was inside my mate, nothing else mattered. Everything centered around her. Everything. The way she smelled. The way her breath hitched when my cock hit just the right spot inside her. The little whimper she made right before she came. The feel of her pussy clenching around my cock. All of it.

Ashera's head tipped back as she continued to ride me. I could feel her pussy fluttering as she approached the edge. My hips met hers with each downward thrust. Her little pants and moans drove me insane.

"Come on my cock," I demanded, and like the sweet little slut she was, she clenched around me and screamed my name.

I flipped her over onto her hands and knees. She let out a surprised squeak and thrust her hips back against mine as I slid into her with a groan. I grabbed her hair and yanked her so her back was flush against my chest, and then I wrapped my hand around her throat in a tight, possessive grip.

"Angel king," I barked, "get over here and lick our queen's tight pussy while I fuck her."

Caspian had come back from the bathroom and was now sitting on the edge of the bed, watching us with hungry eyes, while Ambrose stroked his cock in time with my thrusts. Jacobi moved so he could press his tongue against Ashera's clit. Her head fell back against my shoulder as she cried out.

She clenched around me again, and I had to grit my teeth to prevent myself from coming too soon. "Caspian, get over here and play with her nipples." He scrambled over, sucking one into his mouth while his hand started to pinch and flick the other tight peak.

I moved the hand around her throat, so my wrist pressed against her mouth. "Feed, Sher. Feed both ways."

Instantly, I felt the tug of her power as she fed off the sex in the room. Her lips pressed a brief kiss to my wrist before she sank her fangs into my skin.

"Fuck." I thrust up harder, the feel of her drinking from me pushing me even closer to the edge.

With each pull, it felt like she was sucking on my cock, trying desperately to drain all the come from my body. Her pussy clenched down as she screamed around my wrist. It was all I needed to detonate inside her, roaring my release.

Jacobi took her hips and positioned himself under her, gesturing for Ambrose to take her ass as he thrust up into her soaked pussy. She'd let go of my wrist and was now licking the angel king's neck as if it were her favorite treat.

Ambrose grabbed the bottle of lube we always kept on hand, prepping her before sliding into her with a single thrust. She cried out, trying to push her hips back against both men, but Jacobi prevented it. I leaned in with a small dagger and sliced open the angel's chest, and Ashera instantly latched onto the wound. Jacobi groaned, his hips pushing against her almost violently in his need to reach that edge.

"Come on now, little queen," Ambrose taunted. "Finish us both off fast."

He slapped her ass. Once. Twice. Three times. She exploded. Her pleasure was a near palpable thing that we all greedily drank in. The two mates inside her came with her, both of them cursing at how tight she was.

When Ashera flopped onto the bed beside Jacobi, she had a drunken look on her face and a lazy smile stretched across her lips. Her craving for blood sated for the time being.

"Don't think we're done, Dick Slayer." Caspian pressed a kiss against her stomach. "We'll let you rest before we take you again. You almost fucking died. That's unacceptable. We're going to reassure ourselves multiple times tonight that you're alive and well."

I couldn't argue with the fucker about that.

22

JACOBI

I still wasn't sure what I had seen back at the healer's home, but Ashera was alive, and for that, I would thank every single god around. Twice, if they'd let me. We convinced the healer not to speak of our visit—with a handsome payment— and now the five of us were traveling to my home.

Malak.

When I'd first met Ashera and imagined introducing her to my people, I expected to walk inside my palace gates with my head held high, proud of the beautiful succubus I had been blessed with. Our return to Malak would not be like that though. A quick discussion amongst the five of us led us to the realization that it was safer for Ashera if the resistance believed her to be dead after the fight in the cavern. If anyone had escaped, all they would have seen was us mourning our dying mate. And if no one escaped, it was just as well.

We had flown out of the mountains, stopping just short of the border and traveling the rest of the way to Malak on foot. Luckily the borders out this way were mostly farm- land, and the wheat had already been sown for harvesting later in the summer. I glanced over my shoulder. Ashera was just behind me. She was draped in a heavy black cloak that the healer had so generously offered her, the hood pulled up so her face was even deeper in shadow than the dark of the night around us. The healer had also provided clothes for Caspian to replace those Ashera had shredded. When she caught me looking, she gave me a bright, easy smile. I wasn't sure if it was the blood or the sex or a combination of the two, but Ashera was absolutely radiating power.

What the hell was she? I had never seen a succubus act the way she did or have control over the elements she had demonstrated, let alone drink blood. I grabbed her hand, pulling her up to walk at my side. I might not be able to parade down the main street with her by my side, but at the very least, I could introduce her to her new kingdom.

"What are they growing?" Ashera asked, her voice quiet as she studied the fields we traveled through.

"Wheat. It's small right now, but it's one of the hardiest crops we grow." I used our joined hand to point out the light in the distance, illuminating the cool white stone of the castle. "That's my home. I grew up there."

"You did?" Ashera sounded surprised. Then she shook her head. "I mean, I guess I knew your father had been king, but I just didn't picture you growing up in the castle."

I smiled down at her. "Well, believe it. My mother and my older sister still live there with me."

Ashera stopped in her tracks, shock splashed across her features. "Older sister?"

"Yes. Her name is Eva. Gods, we used to get into the biggest messes growing up. The housemaids would chase us around and..." I trailed off, noticing Ashera's uncomfortable emotions. "What's wrong, love?"

"If she's older, why isn't she queen?" Her softly asked question held barely contained rage.

Ambrose scoffed in the darkness behind us. "Here we fucking go."

There was a quiet scuffle in the dark as someone, probably Malachi, punched Ambrose. I looked down at Ashera, blinking. "Well, um. You see..." I had no idea how to answer her without pissing her off.

Ashera glared at me. "Malak doesn't believe in queens." *Fuck.* What was she going to think of me?

"We didn't," I corrected, "but I have a feeling things are going to change around here."

She nodded, moving forward once again, and I breathed out a sigh of relief. "What's Eva like?"

I smiled, imagining my excitable sister in the same room as the queen who had changed the world as we knew it. I was also grateful for the topic change. "I think you'll love her."

"Are you fucking kidding me?" Ambrose muttered. "I was tortured for days about my beliefs prior to mating with Ashera, and the feathered fuck gets off with a smile?"

"Because he isn't opposed to change, you moron," Malachi growled at him. "He never once thought Ashera shouldn't be on the throne. He also instantly realized the hypocrisy and didn't try to excuse or ignore it. You, on the other hand, were nothing but an insufferable dick for days."

I chuckled. Mal had a point, but then again, so did Ambrose. I hadn't thought of my sister, of the implications that I was king and she couldn't rule before discussing it with Ashera. Malak was willing to welcome a queen in another kingdom but hadn't wanted to have one of their own. I'd have to change that. If Ashera and I had a daughter...

I stopped dead. Ashera tugged gently on my hand before turning to look at me in surprise. I hadn't thought about children with my little mate until this moment. It wasn't safe to do so now, but the thought of her round with our child was surprisingly welcome—surprisingly arousing—regardless of who had actually fathered the child, though I'm sure we would all fight for that privilege.

"What is it?" she inquired as she studied my face.

"Nothing." I shook my head, smiling and tugging her along. I had a feeling that if I were to voice my thoughts, Ashera and the others would lose their minds.

It was a conversation for another day. Right now, we had to focus on keeping Ashera and her kingdom safe. I could feel Ashera's desperation for answers about my thoughts, but she was cut off before she could speak.

"Who goes there?" a brusque voice called across the dark field.

The others behind me all froze. "It's okay. It's my king's guard," I reassured them before stepping forward into the dim light of the moon. "It's me, Jacobi."

The closest of the two guards stepped forward, his defensive posture relaxing as he realized I wasn't a trespasser. "Sir! We heard news out of Shaytan that..." He trailed off before shaking his head. "Your mother has been worried sick."

I ran a hand through my hair, my wings tensing in frustration. "I know. I need to ask a favor of you. I shouldn't, because it involves dishonesty, but I must. We need to get into the castle unseen. No one can know that we're here. Not even my mother."

The guard closest to me froze in alarm. These men had protected my father when I was just a boy, and now they protected me. They cherished me as if I was their own son. But dishonesty was something Malak didn't abide by. The guard behind him was younger, newer to the squad, and he saluted me. "We'll do it, sir. The south wing should be empty this time of night."

I breathed out a sigh of relief. "Thank you. I wouldn't ask you unless there was no other way." I waved Ashera and the other men closer, and together we followed the guards to the castle. The young guard had been correct, and the south wing was all but deserted. We made it to my chambers with only one minor incident with a young maid stepping out of her room. Ambrose's quick reflexes ensured we were all hidden in the shadows as she passed by, unaware of our presence.

I turned to the two guards at the door. "I am forever in your debt for your help tonight. Please, tell no one that we're here. We'll be gone before anyone is the wiser."

The young guard paused. "What do we tell your mother if she finds out?"

"Tell her I'll be home as soon as I can. I just have to take care of a few things first." My mother worried too much, but this time it was justified.

The older guard gave me a knowing look. "And if you don't return?"

I closed my eyes for a minute, remembering how I felt when Ashera was being ripped from me in the hinterlands. "I'll return."

At this point, it was the only option. I would never allow Ashera to feel any of us fading as the bond grew cold within her.

Ambrose

I HAD to give the feathered fuck props. His chambers were much nicer than I had expected them to be. For some reason, I expected the virgin king to live in a monastery, dressing in brown rags, sleeping on concrete slabs, and eating Gruel for breakfast—that sort of thing. But the rooms were bright and colorful, a reflection of the waters they bordered.

I knew not every king in Malak was celibate. Jacobi took the crown after his father died, and he had a sister, so clearly his father didn't have the same hang-ups about purity as his son. Jacobi had taken a vow of chastity when he ascended the throne, and then he had broken that promise. Surely whispers of his mating with Ashera had wound their way back to Malak, yet his guards accepted him home with welcome arms. The asshole got away with everything, even with Ashera.

Speaking of, the little queen sidled up next to me, her hair damp from the bath she had just taken. We had all been disgusting from the cave-in in the hinterlands and Ashera's demonstration at the healer's. I could still feel the rush as she drained my blood, each eager suck of her sinful mouth sending waves of desire through my body. She looked much better now. Healthier. Stronger.

"Stop pouting," she whispered, pressing her lips against my ear and biting my earlobe lightly. Jacobi's guards had returned a few minutes after they left, providing clean clothes for all of us.

I whipped her onto my lap, pressing my own fangs into her supple neck as I spoke. "I'll tell you what, little queen. I'll stop pouting if you let me drain you the way you drained me. Watching your eyes flutter back in your head..." Ashera moaned loudly, her back arching so her neck was pressed harder against my teeth.

"Can both of you control yourselves for five minutes? I know you want to suck each other dry and all that shit, but we have a territory to invade," Malachi snapped at us.

Ashera laughed and turned in my lap. I glared at the grumpy former assassin over her shoulder, wrapping my arms around her waist. "Rich, coming from the incubus who can barely keep it in his pants for a full meal."

Mal shook his head, sending water droplets in all directions from his wet locks. "Let's focus, for fuck's sake. Sher, when was the last time you went to Qamar?"

She shivered as I ran my tongue up and down her neck, watching the demon as I did so. He wouldn't try to stop me physically, at least not while Ashera was on me, so I was safe. "Ambrose, let me focus. I went with Lord Pyper over a hundred years ago. It's been a long time, so I doubt anything is the same as when I was there."

Mal sighed as he pinched the bridge of his nose. "Anyone else? I've never been inside their borders, so I'm going in blind. Ambrose?"

I shook my head, sneering, "My father didn't trust me to meet with King Vaughn. At least now I understand why."

"I was there a couple months ago." We all turned to stare at Caspian in disbelief. He raised his hands in defense. "I had to sort out our trade agreement, same as I was doing in Shaytan."

"And you didn't think you should tell me this important bit of information?" Ashera's voice was sharp, and I was glad I was behind her and not receiving the brunt of that tone. For once, I was on his side. I completely understood why Caspian hadn't announced his visit to Qamar earlier. In Shaytan, we would have seen it as an act of betrayal, and then when Ashera was injured... well, that wasn't exactly the time to plan a coup in another country.

Caspian gave her a disbelieving look. "It wasn't exactly like I went there to spy on the goings-on of King Vaughn. We had dinner. We signed an agreement. End of visit. Also, when did you want me to tell you this, little mate? When you were busy dying in my arms? Or maybe while you were fucking me?" His voice dropped low. "I love you. It wasn't important at the time, but it's important now."

Ashera huffed, reassured with the profession of love, and settled back against me. "Fine. But you owe me."

Caspian leaned forward, raising a brow. "I can think of one or two ways to pay my debt."

I could feel the moment Ashera found herself aroused. *Fuck.* I wanted to be balls deep inside of her tight little pussy, listening to her scream my name. I grabbed her hips, grinding her into my already rock-hard cock.

Mal groaned, but not out of pleasure. "Children, can we please focus on the task at hand? Work first, play later." He turned to Caspian. "What border did you cross on?"

Caspian did not look pleased with the turn of events, his hazel eyes burning with need. "About ten miles south of here, the Malak-Qamar border."

"Guards?"

The fae shrugged, getting off the couch and coming to kneel between my and Ashera's legs. "A few. Two, maybe three. Not too many in the farmlands. I think most of their forces are guarding the more volatile borders." He pushed Ashera's dress up and over her knees, causing the little queen to vibrate with anticipation before he paused and turned back to look at Mal. "We traveled through the night and crossed at daybreak. They change shifts just after dawn. We passed the new guards as we made our way to the palace."

Mal nodded. "I guess you're not useless after all. Listen closely, this is what we're going to do." The four of us were quiet, listening to the demon describe the plan in detail. It was tricky, but doable. He turned to Jacobi. "What time is it?"

"Just after midnight."

Mal nodded once more. "We leave here in two hours, ready or not. But now, since we have some time to kill..." The assassin mask he wore dropped away, exposing the dark desire lurking beneath. Instead of making his way over to us, he turned and strode into the bathroom. *What the hell?* Ashera wiggled on my lap, and I groaned as she rubbed against my cock.

"Fuck, little queen. Let me at least get out of these pants," I muttered.

Jacobi also came closer, tugging at the loose belt of silk he wore around his waist. "You're going to have to be quiet, love. Very quiet. It could blow this plan if anyone else knew we were here." He stopped and glared at each of us. "That goes for all of you too. You will be silent."

As if in protest, Ashera let out a soft cry as Caspian finally found his way to her core, obviously trying to make amends rather quickly.

"Love." Jacobi hooked two fingers under Ashera's chin to get her to look at him. Caspian never stopped as he devoured our queen's delicious pussy, and Ashera whimpered, arching her hips against the fae's face. *Lucky bastard.* "I told you that you need to be quiet. Do you trust me?"

She nodded eagerly, and he dropped her face, using the silk belt to loosely gag the little queen.

"Can you breathe?"

She nodded again.

"Good. Caspian, make her come."

Caspian didn't need to be told twice, never moving his face from between Ashera's legs as he tore her skirt off her body. I nipped and kissed her neck, holding her down so Caspian could do as he wished. She was panting heavily through her nose, but Jacobi's gag had done its job, and the most our normally noisy queen could muster were quiet whimpers.

Her body was tense, and she was getting close as Caspian licked and sucked her drenched folds. I loosened one of my hands and ripped off her top to tweak her nipple. "Come on your fae's tongue, little queen," I commanded. Ashera came. Hard. Her whimpers turned into low groans, her body trembling on my lap. "Good girl," I whispered, kissing her hair as Caspian lapped up her release.

Caspian pushed his pants off before falling back on the floor and tugging Ashera down with him. "I believe I owe you more than one, Dick Slayer." He pulled Ashera onto his cock, sliding into her almost tenderly. I knew that wouldn't last. Still gagged, Ashera moaned low, her entire body shuddering as he entered her.

I watched Ashera ride the fae while I stroked my cock. As if he could hear what I was thinking, Caspian spoke up. "Dick Slayer, do you want one of your mates to fuck your ass?"

Ashera nodded desperately, but before I could make a move, Jacobi was there, stark naked and already easing inside her. Fuck, I was going to burst. This was too much. Where was Malachi anyway? *Fuck it.*

I strode over to Ashera, her breasts swaying with Caspian's and Jacobi's thrusts. I ripped the gag off her mouth, her gaze showing her surprise as she stared up at me.

"You don't need a gag in your mouth if it's full of my cock."

My little queen eagerly opened her mouth, waiting for me to feed her my dick. Her lush lips wrapped around my cock, sucking and licking as the other two fucked her below. Gods, no matter which hole I was fucking her in, it felt like heaven. All of us being together like this wasn't awkward anymore. It just added to the dense aura of desire that enveloped all of us as we moaned softly and moved together as one.

Ashera looked up at me. Her gaze was dark with pleasure, and I could feel her riding closer and closer to the edge. "Where the fuck is Mal?" I groaned. It wasn't like him to miss this, even if we had interrupted his little speech earlier.

"Here." The demon's hard, warm body pressed up behind me, his breath heavy against my neck. "I'm not impressed that you took advantage of me the other night, and I'm ready to return the favor, especially seeing as Sher is otherwise occupied." He must have found something in the bathroom to lube himself up, because I could feel his slick cock sliding between my ass cheeks. "Now be a good little princess, and let your queen watch me fuck you."

I knew I had to be quiet. I knew I shouldn't make a sound. But between Ashera's lust-filled gaze, her low moan vibrating around my cock, and Malachi pushing his way into my ass, the sensations were wreaking havoc in my brain. I parted my lips to curse as I bottomed out in Ashera's mouth, and the incubus bottomed out inside of me, but before I could, Mal slapped his hand over my mouth. "Don't make a fucking sound, vamp," he growled. He took his hand away, and if Ashera hadn't been doing something crazy with her tongue, I would have ripped his throat out. Instead, I gave myself over to the pleasure.

Caspian's thrusts were growing more frantic. "She's close," he grunted.

"Fuck, little queen," I murmured, fisting my hands into her hair as Malachi slammed into me again. "Do you see what you do to me? What you do to all of us?"

She tightened her lips around my cock, arching her back as she came, with Caspian following soon after. Jacobi was still thrusting away like the beast he'd become, forcing Ashera's mouth to pump me harder and faster. She looked up at me, and I saw the sexual vixen and the powerful queen she was, and I came hard in her mouth while Mal still pumped in and out behind me.

"Fuck," Mal muttered, thrusting one more time before he fell apart inside me.

Ashera released me, giving me a playful smile. "Jacobi," she whispered, and like a charm, he sighed and shattered.

We moved apart, catching our breath. I could feel Ashera and Malachi feeding off the energy in the room. I had no idea how Ashera still had space left inside of her to feed, but who was I to tell her any differently?

What the little queen wanted, she got.

23

ASHERA

B y the time we made it back out of the castle, we were all
fed, dressed, and armed with new weapons Jacobi had
snuck out of the guards' stash. Weapons weren't something the
King of Malak typically had on his person, but all the guards
were armed, so we were able to make do. We were headed into
enemy territory now, and it was better to be safe than sorry.

We had decided to cross the border on foot to maintain the
element of surprise. It would take us a bit longer, but it was
worth it. I cast a quick glance at each one of my mates, a tug of
fear pulling at my heart as I remembered that I'd almost left
them.

I knew all too well the pain of feeling a mate die. I never
wanted to put these men through that. My gaze locked with
Caspian's, and I could feel his relief that I was okay mingled
with another emotion I didn't know how to classify. That was
when I realized that the tug of fear I'd felt wasn't my own... it
was theirs, and it wasn't coming through the mate bond. I felt
the bond through my entire body, but this was all in my head. It
was an understanding instead of a feeling.

"Jacobi." My breath left me in a rush, and all four of my

mates paused to look over at me. "I... I can feel everyone's emotions."

Shock flashed across their faces, and I could feel it rushing through them, followed closely by excitement, wonder, curiosity, and a hint of panic. I cocked my head at the last one, trying to figure out who it was coming from. My gaze flicked between Malachi and Jacobi, sensing they were both feeling that panic. Not for themselves, I realized, but for me.

"What?" I asked, staring them down.

"You can control elements better than any fae." Caspian scoffed a bit, but Jacobi ignored him. I still had to explain that to him. "You have your own succubus powers, which are far more potent than any other. You've also started drinking blood."

"You're exhibiting the powers of the other races, Sher," Malachi pointed out. The chilly fingers of dread tingled down my spine. "We can all do basic magic, and we all feed that magic in our own unique ways, but you're something else entirely."

"That can't be possible," I argued, but we all knew I was lying. My gaze now darted between all four of the men around me. I was... different. Panic welled within me. My breathing grew shallow, and soon my lungs screamed for more air.

"Hey," Ambrose murmured as he stalked up to me and placed his hands on my cheeks. My gaze narrowed on him. "Regardless of what's going on, you're our mate." He pressed a gentle kiss to my lips. "Once we get rid of the resistance, we'll figure out what's going on. You're not hurt because of these changes. You're strong."

I nodded, tears pooling in my eyes when the other three crowded around me to touch and kiss where they could. My breathing returned to normal. I allowed myself a moment to be scared before shoring myself up, using my bonds with my mates to center and ground me. Ambrose was right. The changes weren't hurting me in any way, at least not yet. We had more important things to worry about.

I kissed each one of the men around me before we started off again. After that, I knew it was time to talk about Visa, about my rebellion, my past. All of it.

"I had a mate before all of you." Silence greeted my poorly planned statement. I could feel some shock and curiosity through my newly discovered angelic powers. "Her name was Visa." There was more shock over the knowledge that my former mate had been a female, and I took a deep breath. "She was killed because of me."

"That's bullshit, Sher, and you fucking know it," Malachi spat. "She was just as involved in the rebellion as we were."

"And who started that fucking rebellion, Mal?" I exploded before taking a deep breath and lowering my voice again. "That's not the point. I felt Visa die, so I know what you just went through, and I don't want to put you through that again."

"Dick Slayer," Caspian began in a soothing tone that surprised me. "I'm assuming that's the dragon you hide under your war marks?" I nodded. "As much as I hate to say this, we're all aware that our lives are on the line right now. Yours in particular. We'll do everything we can to make sure that you're safe and protected, but there is always a risk."

The others growled, not liking the thought of me in danger, but at least they were acknowledging that I wasn't about to sit any of this out. And I knew, or some part of me knew, that they could very well end up in a position similar to the one I'd just found myself in. I couldn't bring myself to actually say the words in connection with them. I knew they would protect me with their lives. I would do the exact same.

I sent a small smile to Caspian. Taking a bracing breath, I continued, "I was found near the void by humans when I was just a baby. They found me in the forest that surrounded our village. My mother couldn't have children, and even though they were well aware that taking me in would be a death sentence, they did it anyway.

"I was still a child when Lord Pyper found out about me. I'm still not sure how. But he had his men destroy that entire village of slaves to find me. When I ran out of our burning house, I found my father beheaded and my mother being raped and stabbed." All the men around me were silent, and their fury slammed through me. Caspian and Ambrose also felt horrified. "I was sixteen the first time Pyper tried to force himself on me. Thankfully my succubus powers were potent even then, and I was able to make him finish before he even got far enough to actually touch me. But I was his ward, and I was to do whatever he wanted of me."

I tilted my head up to study the stars as I walked. "I met Malachi on my first ever outing from his estate. Pyper had allowed me out for being good and entertaining him and his guests." More fury lashed at me from the men around me. "I never forgot that he was the reason my parents were dead. I never once looked at a human as anything other than family, an equal. I was already planning to murder Pyper when I met Mal."

I grin over at him as I pause. "He also had the fantastic idea to assassinate the incubus lord. By then, I was already mated to Visa, but Pyper didn't care. After all, I was mated to a *female*, I was still under his thumb, and he assumed he could pawn me off as another consort for the king. He thought he could sell us as a package deal. After all, what male doesn't want two women for the price of one?" My laugh was hollow.

"Mal, Visa, and I started planning for something much larger. I'd learned through Malachi that many of the citizens of Shaytan, including the army, felt the same way I did about humans and the nobility. Many had even found mates among the humans and had to hide their bond."

"So you started a rebellion." Caspian sounded awed. "You

didn't do it as a political power play. You did it out of love." I thought that fact shocked him the most.

"Fuck, little queen." Ambrose ran a hand through his thick hair. "You were essentially treated as a slave and then rose to become a queen."

"She was never a slave." The deep, masculine rumble had us all whirling to find the source of the voice. He was tall, much taller than even Malachi, with glowing bright blue eyes and a shock of white-blond hair. His skin was a beautiful shade that was somewhere between Caspian's black as night tone and Mal's dark olive. I'd never seen another man that looked quite like him. He appeared to have some features from all the species mixed into his appearance—the pointed ears of the fae, a hint of fang from the vamps, angelic wings that were a stunning shade of heather gray, and horns like a demon. I was curious to know if he could shift or if he had the magical tattoos of the witches.

My mates stepped in front of me, but the stranger just threw his head back and laughed. "Don't worry. I have no intention of harming the sweet goddess. She's far too important."

"Who the hell are you?" Caspian snarled. Despite being prickly to begin with, he felt the most protective right now—he was the closest to exploding all over this stranger. I needed to figure out how to adjust to feeling all these emotions and get a handle on them before they overwhelmed me.

"Just someone who has an interest in seeing the sweet goddess behind you succeed, but she was never born with the blood of slaves. In fact, she comes from the most royal bloodline of them all."

What the fuck did that mean? I stood on tiptoe so I could study the stranger as he spoke. Something tugged at me, but I couldn't be sure what it was. Before I got the chance to ask any questions, he just... vanished.

"Someone want to try to tell me who the fuck that was?" I

asked as I continued to stare at the spot where the mystery man had been standing.

"What the fuck was he going on about?" Malachi grumbled.

They all turned to look at me as though I had all the answers, which was hysterical. I shrugged, glanced around to make sure he was actually gone, and then gestured for all of us to continue on. We were close to crossing the border, and we couldn't delay.

~

Caspian

WE SUCCESSFULLY SNUCK INTO QAMAR, and I had a shocking sense of pride swell within me at the thought that my information helped my mate. I was quickly understanding that seeing her almost die was, quite possibly, the worst thing I'd ever gone through. And she'd been right. No more fucking games. I needed to get my head out of my ass.

Ambrose had already shown the entire group that he would be true to his word. He'd free the Masas slaves and change everything. I wasn't a fool, I knew they all expected me to say whatever had been necessary to get into Ashera's pants and then not stick to my word, and they hadn't exactly been wrong. As much as I was loath to admit it, they'd been right. I'd still assumed I could use Ashera to get what I wanted. I'd thought I'd be able to tame her in some way and still hold complete autonomy.

I'd been a fucking idiot.

That was not how any of this mate business worked. Ashera and I should compromise on things that were important to both of us. Frankly, while Juniya hadn't known anything but slavery, I'd seen how Dick Slayer had been able to make the change in Shaytan, and I knew that my own kingdom could make that same transition. I couldn't use her, and the fact that I thought I could left a sour taste on my tongue.

I had every intention of changing the way things were between myself and my mighty dick slayer. Fuck, if she asked for my kingdom on a silver platter, I'd kill my father and give it to her. I'd even give my life for the fanged fuck walking next to me, which told me just how much the succubus queen leading us meant to me.

The freak who had shown up a few hours back had me wondering more about Ashera's powers. He appeared to be a perfect blend of all the species, which was extremely strange. He also claimed that she came from the most royal bloodline. There was no way she could have come from a royal bloodline. The former king of Shaytan wouldn't have run the risk of bastards, and there were no other royals in that country, at least none that I knew of. That would have to wait. We couldn't focus on finding answers *and* taking down the resistance, as much as it irritated me to admit.

A soft touch to my hand had me blinking in surprise before I turned my gaze to my mate. I was often shocked that so much power was contained in such a small package. She was a bit shorter than most of the other succubi and nowhere near as tall as any of us, but there was no doubt that she was the strongest of us.

"Everything okay?" She was still wearing that damn cloak. I knew we needed to keep her presence a secret, but I hated the fact that I couldn't look at her properly.

"Everything's fine. I was just thinking." I gave her a small smile. "We're probably going to need to stop somewhere before we get to the capital. We'll all need to rest up, feed, and find food."

She giggled quietly. "Feed and find food." Her eyes met mine from the shadow of the hood. "You're right. We shouldn't go storming in after having walked all this way. We need to make sure we're at the top of our game."

"When I was here last, there was a small, abandoned cottage around here. If it's still empty, I think we should stop there for a bit." I glanced around at the others, and they nodded their agreement.

I led us to where I'd seen the cottage, and thankfully it was still empty. It was a bit dusty, but it would allow us to rest a bit before we hit the outskirts of the capital. We'd packed some food and water, so we dug into our packs to pull out our supplies. I helped Ashera shuck off the cloak. The windows were covered in such a thick layer of dust that if anyone happened upon us, they wouldn't know who she was if they looked in.

Ashera grabbed my hand and tugged me into an empty room I assumed was a bedroom at one point and closed the door. I raised a brow in question as she turned to face me.

"I wanted to talk about what I said before I drank your blood." Her voice was soft, an indication that she didn't want the others to overhear our conversation. "I realize that was an intense moment."

"Dick Slayer." I sighed, tucking a strand of hair behind her ear. "That moment put a lot of things into perspective for me. You were right."

Her lips twitched slightly as she stared up at me. "How much did that hurt to admit?"

I chuckled and placed a light kiss on her lips. "You were right, Ashera. And I know that my word probably means shit right now, but I want you to know that while I'm still going to be an asshole, I'm your asshole. I won't be a complete dick to you anymore."

Her laugh brightened the room around us and made me smile like an idiot. "I love you, Caspian. Thank you for wanting this to work."

"I'm sorry I gave you any other impression, Dick Slayer."

She stood on her tiptoes and wrapped her arms around my neck. "Now what do you say to a quickie before going back out there?"

I hadn't had her alone yet. Every time I'd been inside my mate, her other mates had been around, so the thought of having her to myself for a small moment excited me. I stripped us in record time before pushing her back against the wall. I lifted her up so her thighs rested on my shoulders. She said a quickie, but I needed the taste of her on my tongue. I needed her to come unraveled in my mouth before I dived into her tight, wet pussy.

I ran my tongue up her slit, and she tangled her hands in my hair. I met her gaze as I started to suck on her clit and groaned when she tugged on my hair. Her head fell back against the wall. I slid two fingers into her pussy and crooked them just enough to rub against her G-spot with each tug of my lips.

Ashera's breathing and her pussy fluttering around my fingers told me she was close. I could feel her feeding off the sexual energy we were creating, Mal too if the extra tug was anything to go by. With one last pull on her clit, my little dick slayer exploded. She screamed my name as her pussy clamped down on my fingers.

In a flash, I readjusted our position so her legs were around my waist, then I pressed into her.

"Caspian." Ashera's plea was breathy, and her eyes were filled with heat.

"Don't worry, my queen. I'm going to give you my cock." She moaned as I rubbed against her.

I took her lips at the same time I thrust to the hilt inside her, capturing her whimper with my mouth. Aware we didn't have much time, I set a rough pace. I made sure to angle my hips in such a way that I rubbed against her clit with each thrust. Her nails dug into my shoulders, and her moans soon filled the space around us.

"Come on my cock, Dick Slayer." My command was harsh as I fought the urge to come, not wanting to finish before she did.

Ashera's breath hitched right before she came. Her sweet pussy clenched so tightly around my dick I couldn't do anything but follow her into oblivion.

"I love you, Ashera." She shuddered against me as I kissed her, trying to pour everything I felt for this amazing woman into that one sentence.

A loud banging against the door had us breaking our kiss. I growled low, displeased with being interrupted. Ashera grinned at me, pressed a light kiss to my lips, and then wiggled until I let her slide to the floor.

"If you two are done, the rest of us also need to feed." Ambrose, that fucker. I might be willing to give my life for him now, but I wouldn't hesitate to throat punch him into next fucking week.

24

ASHERA

We waited until the sun set before venturing out. We were close to the outskirts of Qamar's capital city, so it didn't take us long to make it to the city center. The palace was enormous, much larger than the palace in Shaytan, which was a waste, really. Who the hell needed that much space? I actually wanted to downsize at some point in the near future, but hadn't been able to bring myself to do it simply because the palace now employed so many humans.

"*That's* the palace?" Malachi scoffed. "I'm assuming the king is compensating for something."

I snickered beneath my hood. I'd been careful to make sure that it fully covered my face and had put my glamor back in place to ensure that the hood concealed everything. My mates had also pulled on cloaks in an effort to blend in. I'm sure if anyone realized who they were, there would be quite a bit of suspicion, not to mention panic and hostility. They were fairly well known—in name at least.

"I may have... dallied... when I was here last." Caspian shot me a look of panic. "So I know a way to get in that should hopefully keep us from getting noticed."

I raised a brow, and then realized he couldn't see my expression. "Dallied, huh?" He winced. "Caspian, I'm well aware every one of you, save Jacobi, had lovers before me. Though, if we ever come across one of them, I can't promise I won't torture her before killing her as slowly as possible."

That had the three of them fidgeting slightly. Jacobi looked extremely smug. My angel wasn't physically pure anymore, and I couldn't help but feel a bit smug for being the only woman he'd ever been inside. They were mine. I'd cut a bitch for looking at them the wrong way.

"Lead the way, fae." Ambrose swept his arm out for Caspian to take the lead. Jacobi moved closer to my side and took my hand in his. "We'll need to hit the guest rooms first. I'd rather get my father out of the way as soon as possible."

We all agreed to that plan back at the cottage, but I could tell Ambrose was anxious about the confrontation with his father. I doubted my vampire was worried about killing him. He seemed more than ready to see his father put in the ground. But I knew that this wouldn't be easy—regardless of whether Ambrose wanted him dead or not. The man had lied to him, but he was still Ambrose's father.

None of us would take the kill from him. It was his right to go after his father. We'd support Ambrose in any way he needed, but he'd have to be the one to end things. As for the King of Qamar... Vaughn was fair game.

"If we kill the king," I started, keeping my voice low as we closed in on the palace, "do we replace him with another shifter? One that shares our ideals? Or is this a hostile takeover sort of thing, and I become Queen of Qamar too?"

A thoughtful silence followed my inquiry. At least none of them questioned whether they'd become King of Qamar. Admittedly, they *all* would if I became queen. I refused to have them be labeled as my consorts. They were my kings, I just hadn't told them yet. My hood hid my smirk. I'd commissioned a new crown for myself as well as one for each of them. I'd planned to give the crowns to them once we'd found Ambrose's father. Now it would have to wait until we got back from Qamar.

"I think we'll need to figure that out after." Malachi shrugged. "We can make a decision at the moment if we need to."

Caspian gestured for us to hush. We stood in front of a rock wall. He pressed his hand to a stone and a door swung open into a dark passage. Someone had clearly fucked someone he wasn't supposed to if he knew about this entrance. We followed my fae into the passage, and it dumped us out into a dimly lit hallway.

"These are the guest quarters," Caspian whispered. "I would assume that your father is in the room at the end of the hall. It's their best room."

We quietly made our way down the hall, making sure to keep a close eye out for any guards or slaves who might be in the area. It was oddly quiet. I'd be worried about a trap if everyone didn't think I was already dead. My mates grew tenser the closer we got to the room, most likely feeling the same way I did.

A sudden explosion of yelling had us all freezing in place. It came from the floor below us. We remained still as the cacophony of a battle greeted our ears. Glancing at each other, we slowly moved back toward the stairs. If there was an issue within the palace, it was reasonable to assume that guards would be sent up to secure guests. We would need to take care of them if that happened.

A bloody slave came barreling up the stairs, and horror was written on every inch of her face. When she spotted us, she paused.

"Shh," I whispered. "It's okay. We won't hurt you."

"They're t-trying to kill the king." Her voice trembled, and she clutched her hands tightly together in front of her.

We looked at each other again. Someone was trying to kill the King of Qamar? Had we stumbled in on a coup?

"Can one of you show her out? We want to keep the humans and other servants who aren't fighting safe." Jacobi nodded and gently led the woman to the passage we'd exited earlier. Once he was back with our group, I pointed to the stairwell. "Let's head downstairs. Ambrose, I know you wanted to deal with your father first, but he might be down there helping, and it's best if we know what we're dealing with right now."

I could see the indecision on his face, but he nodded, and we headed downstairs. The resonance of the battle raged louder down here, coming from the end of a long elaborate hallway. We slowly made our way toward the sounds, keeping a wary eye out for more slaves, servants, or soldiers. Thankfully, we only ran into a few more traumatized slaves. We sent them toward the passage and continued on.

"They're fighting in the throne room," Caspian murmured. I nodded and crept closer to the partially opened door.

I peeked inside, and my eyes widened at what I saw. A female shifter was fighting against Vaughn while a large group battled around them. It was clear that the king's forces were outnumbered, but with the way they fought, they had a clear advantage. A broad, tan mountain of a man—clearly on the female's side—was battling against three opponents. He carried a large broadsword and, like my damn vampire, was shirtless. *What the hell is with men and not wanting to wear shirts?*

I felt the tug almost immediately and shock flashed through me. Jacobi spun to face me, and his eyes held just as much surprise as I felt. The female and the large male... this tug was the same thing I'd felt for the four men with me. *What the fuck is going on? Two more mates?*

I shook my head, we didn't have time to think about that right now. It answered at least one question—we'd be helping them take out the king and his men. Jacobi murmured a few things to my other mates, most likely telling them what I'd felt as I continued to stare for a moment longer.

The female shifter was stunning, with skin nearly as dark as Caspian's which was currently soaked in the blood of those she fought. She was slender, taller than me, but the way she handled her sword betrayed her strength and power. This shifter had been training for this moment. She spun, her long braids whipping around, and I caught a glimpse of her face. Resolute. Determined. I knew that face.

Turning to face my mates, I took a deep breath. "We're going to help them."

They all nodded. Oddly, none of them looked irritated or angry that I had two new mates in there. They appeared eager to bust down this door and kill a few assholes. I was sure they'd give the newcomers a hard time after the fight was over. The only two who hadn't gone through any sort of hazing were Jacobi and Malachi.

I slid my cloak off my shoulders and pulled my daggers from their holsters on my thighs. My mates did the same. With a nod, I kicked the door open and calmly strode into the battle.

Everyone in the room paused for a heartbeat, all of them turning to glare at us. The king roared his fury when our eyes caught. He'd clearly thought I was dead. *Man, word travels fast.* I smirked over at him and blew him a kiss, then I lopped the head off one of his soldiers all while maintaining eye contact. I could feel his rage spinning out of control through my new gift. Good, I hoped that made him sloppy.

The battle kicked back into high gear as my mates and I started shredding through the king's forces. The female fighting the king felt surprised at our entrance but thrilled that we'd sided with her. The large male had taken one glance at me, probably gotten a raging boner judging by the heavy lust he felt, and gone right back to killing as many as he could.

Props for killing a bunch of dudes while also fighting a raging hard-on.

I pulled from the lanterns to lace my blades with fire as I continued to hack away at any soldier unfortunate enough to get near me. I didn't want to use too much of my elemental powers here out of fear that something similar to the cavern collapse would happen, but having flaming daggers helped keep my opponents at a good distance. My gaze sought out my mates to ensure that they were holding their own. I didn't question their battle skills, but after my near-death experience, I wasn't about to just assume things were fine, especially if Ambrose's father was here.

Speaking of the fanged asshole, I didn't see any vampires. Were they still up in their suite? Why wouldn't he come down to help defend his ally? Then again, he'd been a coward and hadn't faced us during either of our visits to Masas. There was no way that he wouldn't know we headed there. For a vampire associated with the resistance, he certainly didn't seem invested in fighting the battles he created.

IT TOOK us a while to finish off the king's soldiers since more arrived the longer the battle played out. The female who had been battling Vaughn had him subdued, letting the giant male hold onto him. All of us now stood around them in a circle, the female and I standing side by side.

"I'm Ashera, by the way," I introduced myself with a smile.

She beamed back at me, her responding smile stunning. "Oh, I know who you are. You're actually the reason I decided to start my own rebellion." That was... extremely flattering. "I'm Winta, and the one holding the former king is my general, Thorne."

"He's a traitor, that's what he is!" Vaughn screamed as he

started to struggle in Thorne's grasp. Thorne just held him tighter, rolled his eyes, and shoved a torn piece of cloth into the shifter's mouth to shut him up. I gave him a grin, openly admiring his muscular, shirtless form. He was as tall as Malachi, without an ounce of body fat in sight. His dark hair was cropped close to his skull, and when I met his gaze—his eyes a rich, chocolate brown—he gave me a wink. Ambrose's annoyance at my admiration was palpable, and I had no idea how Jacobi put up with the constant barrage of emotions.

"I'd been a general under him. My men and I had been planning our own rebellion when we met Winta and her people, so we decided to team up." The similarities between their rebellion and my own weren't lost on me. It warmed me knowing that so many wanted change. It meant there was hope for all of us.

"How do you want to handle him?" I asked, not bothering to spare the defeated king any more attention.

"Well, he certainly can't live." I nodded. "But I'm not sure if I want to perform a public execution or not. We decided to attack tonight because Masas' king was also here, but he left earlier." Winta's gaze flicked to Ambrose. He looked furious that his father had fled yet again.

"Oh, I'm sorry. I didn't introduce my mates." I introduced the four males who held my heart, each of them offering a smile.

"I heard rumors that you'd acquired quite the powerful and influential harem. We hadn't been sure if they were actually mates or if you'd agreed to be with them for political gain." That often happened with royalty, but I had no interest in it myself. "You do realize I'm your mate too, yes?" The casual way Winta dropped that little bomb had me staring at her in shock.

"I am too," Thorne rumbled, and a wicked grin spread across his face. His eyes roamed down my body before he shot me another playful wink. I could practically hear Ambrose's outrage in my mind.

"And yet we hadn't felt the mating pull to each other," Winta mused, looking at Thorne. I wanted to laugh. We needed to decide what we were going to do with Qamar's deposed king, but here we were talking about mating bonds.

"The little queen is well aware of who you are to her, and while we were happy to help you out, don't think touching her will be easy," Ambrose growled.

"We haven't decided if you're worthy enough to be her mates," Caspian sneered.

I rubbed my temples and let out a heavy sigh. Really? The two of them were going to drive me insane. They were teaming up against the two newcomers. I wanted to punch both of them. Thorne and Winta just laughed.

"Shifters aren't like the rest of you idiots. We feel the mate bond instantly. We also don't let our mates slip through our fingers." Winta glared over at my vampire and fae. "So you're just going to have to deal with us. We aren't going anywhere." Thorne nodded his agreement.

Gods, her spunk reminded me so much of Visa. Which, surprisingly, didn't hurt the way it normally did. Instead, it warmed me, wrapping around me like a comforting hug. I beamed. I thought I felt complete before, but these two made me realize I was so very wrong.

"As much as I'm sure we'd all love to discuss getting Ashera naked, we should really figure out what to do with the trash," Malachi stated, gesturing to the glaring Vaughn at Thorne's feet.

"I didn't kill Shaytan's king in public," I confessed, "but by the time I reached the palace, it was no surprise to anyone what was happening. How popular was your uprising?"

"Not quite as popular as yours, but we kept our plan quiet. If he'd gotten wind of what we were doing, things would have gone downhill quickly," Winta explained. "Shifters have to listen to their alpha. We can get around it when we need to, but we didn't want him knowing what was happening and then start picking our people off. We were highly selective about who we told."

That made sense, given what I knew about shifters. They weren't loyal to their king, per se. They really had no other choice. Their animal natures demanded a hierarchy be observed, but that made knowing who to trust extremely difficult.

"Then you should execute him publicly once the sun rises." Malachi, always my tactical thinker, knew how to make a damn statement. "We want the people to know that there's a new ruler in town and that the old ways aren't going to be tolerated."

Thorne's wicked grin returned. "I like that one." I wasn't surprised. "He's right, Winta."

"Okay. We'll do that then, but I want to introduce you all as co-rulers." That had shock sliding through all of us. "We're Ashera's mates, regardless of your little temper tantrum. We'll let the people of Qamar know that we're allied with and ruling alongside Shaytan's queen."

"Malak has plans to do the same." Jacobi seemed pleased that he'd been the first to decide that we were to merge our kingdoms and rule together.

"Masas will be doing the same once I kill my sperm donor." Not to be outdone, Ambrose puffed out his chest to clearly display his mate mark.

"Juniya as well." Caspian stepped up next to Ambrose and mimicked the vampire's pose. *What the hell is happening with the two of them right now?*

Then, reality slammed home. This would not look good to Sahira. They were the only kingdom that wasn't aligned with Shaytan in this manner.

"We should hold off on saying any of that," I argued. "Sahira never met with me, and I'd really rather we didn't piss off the witches who fight with the dead and use soul weapons. At least not right now. Once we get the resistance taken care of, then we can approach Sahira and let them know what we're planning, and we mean them no ill will."

"Fine," Winta reluctantly agreed. "I'll say that we're allied with Shaytan for the time being. Thorne and I will be joint rulers of Qamar until we are able to announce our plans."

"What resistance?" Thorne asked, his gaze fixed on me. Whatever his animal was flashed in his eyes, and waves of violent protectiveness rammed into me. Winta wasn't kidding. Shifters felt the mate bond *immediately*.

"As I'm sure you're well aware, there are some who don't like the way I do things. They're fighting to keep the old ways alive. We actually came here in search of Ambrose's father. He's the leader or at least *a* leader." I shrugged. "We went to find him in Masas, but we found a resistance base instead. That's when we decided to come here, knowing he was here recently."

"That's why the rumors of you being dead spread." Winta looked at me appraisingly. "Well done. Should we keep your wellbeing a secret?"

"Let's keep the fact that I'm alive a secret. Introduce Malachi as the King of Shaytan." Malachi's surprise slithered around me, so I turned to grin at him. "I planned a little surprise for all of you. You are all going to be announced as Kings of Shaytan. I even had new crowns made for us. Looks like I'll have to add two more."

All four of my mates stared at me blankly for a minute— their emotions surprisingly absent. Thorne and Winta didn't seem surprised by this news, and their happiness radiated off them.

"We'll discuss this later," Caspian growled with a finger pointed at me. I shrugged and nodded.

"Okay. We kill this useless piece of shit at dawn, then

announce that Malachi is the new King of Shaytan and that we're allied with him." Winta nodded. "We're also going to announce an all-out war against the resistance."

Gods, I loved this woman already.

AFTER WE SECURED Vaughn somewhere he wouldn't be able to escape, my mates and I—minus Thorne and Winta—headed to one of the guest suites to rest. We only had a few more hours until dawn. I'd remain in our room, hidden from the public, while my mates made an appearance at the execution. All of them.

Pride swelled in my chest as I looked at the four males before me. I'd never been prouder to call them my mates. I knew they needed some time to get used to the idea of not just adding one new mate, but two, another female at that. We were all connected. Our souls were forever intertwined. I'd give them the time they needed to come to terms with everything. I didn't want any discontent between us, though I'm sure Winta and Thorne didn't want to wait.

"Dick Slayer." Caspian broke the silence. "We're going to have one hell of a long talk after the execution, and not just about the resistance."

"Fuck, little queen." Ambrose ran a hand through his hair. "You're making us all Kings of Shaytan?"

"We've been talking about merging all of the kingdoms, so it made sense." I didn't see the issue, and getting a read on their emotions right now was difficult. My gift was too new, and we were all emotionally and physically drained.

"We can talk about this later," Malachi growled. "We need to show our queen how much we appreciate her generous offer and then get some rest."

Being the subject of their intense attention always left me

all tingly and aching with need. They each had a way of making me feel like the only person in existence when they looked at me like this, and all I could see during these moments was them.

With surprisingly reverent hands, Mal removed my clothes while the others stripped themselves. He stepped back and then shed his own clothes, watching me with hungry eyes the entire time. Hands grabbed my wrists, pulling them behind my back and securing them with a swatch of silk. I turned my head and found Jacobi, my precious angel, looking at me with desire darkening his sapphire gaze and a wicked smirk spread across his luscious lips.

"Since this is going to be all about thanking our stunning queen, we need to make sure she feels everything we do to her." Fuck, his low rumble went straight to my clit. The others chuckled as they moved closer. Thanks to my new gift and my innate gift as a succubus, I was drowning in their lust.

I shifted slightly in an attempt to ease the tension between my legs. Just feeling how much they each loved me and wanted me had me painfully aroused. How on earth did Jacobi deal with this all the time? I'd have to ask him to teach me to block it out.

That thought flew into the wind as my angel's arms wrapped around me so his fingers could play with my nipples. Caspian and Ambrose each lifted one of my legs, spreading my thighs so Mal could step between them. My pussy was right in line with his face. I shuddered and leaned back against Jacobi.

Mal slowly circled my clit with one of his fingers, being careful not to actually touch it. He gently blew on the little bundle of nerves, and the incubus was damn lucky my hands were tied behind my back. I wanted so badly to tightly grip his hair and pull him to me. Malachi's eyes rose to meet mine, and he gave me a knowing grin as he continued to tease me.

"I swear to the gods, Malachi. If you do not stop teasing me,

I am going to end you." Chuckles filled with masculine pride met my threat, and I released a growl. I'd end them all if they kept this up.

"As my little queen demands," Mal replied. He slid his finger into my pussy, and I cried out in relief.

I wasn't given a chance to bask in the sensation before he closed his lips around my clit. I moaned and started to grind my hips against his face. He instantly pulled back, and I groaned at the loss.

"Bring her over here." Mal crawled onto the bed so his head was close to the side, but there was still a bit of room over his head. "Put her over my face. One of you can fuck her ass while I eat her pussy, and one of you can fuck her mouth." I clenched at his words, feeling so damn empty. I needed them to fill me now. "Whoever doesn't get a turn now has time to plan all of the things he wants to do to our little slut."

Why the hell do I love it when he calls me a slut? It always turns me on.

Jacobi placed me over Mal's face then stepped back. Caspian moved in behind me as Ambrose positioned himself in front of me. My once pure angel king was up to something. There was a gleam in his eyes that gave him away, and I was eager to experience whatever caused that gleam. I wasn't given the opportunity to think about it further, however, because Malachi tightly gripped my hips and yanked me down so my pussy was pressed flush against his mouth. He didn't waste any time devouring me.

Caspian pushed me forward, holding onto my bound hands to keep me steady. He then slid his lubed cock into my ass at the exact same moment Malachi sucked hard on my clit. I moaned, which gave Ambrose the opportunity to slide his cock between my lips. It was too much, and I came against Mal's mouth, humming around Ambrose's cock.

All three men let out pleased growls as they continued to move against me in unison. Caspian kept me stable by holding onto my bindings, and Ambrose tangled his hands in my hair as he started to pound into my mouth. Malachi and I both fed off the sexual energy in the room. I couldn't very well let a good meal go to waste.

As I felt another orgasm coming, Caspian and Ambrose picked up their pace simultaneously, trying to meet their own release as close to mine as possible. They were both surprisingly quiet, sticking to moans or groans of pleasure instead of their usual sexual banter. That didn't detract from how fucking amazing they felt though. Quite the opposite. Their silence forced me to focus on the pleasure that seared through my veins.

With a muffled cry, I came again. Ambrose rammed his dick down my throat, and I swallowed around him until he came with a quiet moan. Caspian cursed behind me, his hips now jerking against me as he emptied himself in my ass. They righted me on Mal's face and then moved away from me.

Jacobi slid in front of me, running a gentle and loving hand down my cheek. His eyes blazed bright with need as we stared at each other. His gaze then focused on Malachi behind my shoulder.

"You're going to take her from behind. I want her to suck on me before I come all over her gorgeous tits." My nostrils flared with my heavy inhale, and my eyes widened slightly. He'd been so damn shy and pure not too long ago. I felt more turned on than ever knowing that I'd shown this powerful king the pleasures of sex.

Mal shimmied out from under me and moved so he could grip my hips with both of his large hands. He slid into me with one powerful thrust and then remained still. Jacobi stood against the side of the bed, and Mal positioned me as Caspian had. He pushed me forward so my mouth was level with the angel king's cock while holding me steady by my bindings.

Jacobi once again ran a loving hand down my cheek before

he tightly gripped my hair and slowly slid his cock into my mouth until he hit the back of my throat. I swallowed around him, and he groaned. I glanced up to see him staring at Mal before giving the incubus a nod.

They started to move inside me, my body swaying from one mate to the next. I closed my eyes against the bliss. They weren't rushing, but they weren't going slow either. They set an easy pace that would undoubtedly lead me to an amazing orgasm. Mal growled low in his throat and dug his hands into my hips. I would have bruises later, but it was absolutely worth it.

"Play with her clit and make her come," Jacobi commanded. Malachi was more than happy to obey and slid a hand around me so he could press it against my already oversensitive clit.

That was all it took to make me shatter. My pussy clenched around Mal's cock, causing him to curse as he came as well. Jacobi, true to his word, quickly pulled out of my mouth as Malachi lifted me so my angel could come all over my breasts. Once he was finished, he gestured to Mal to turn me around.

My hands were freed, and I spun so they could all see me as I trailed a finger through the mess on my chest and then stuck that finger into my mouth with a moan. All four of them groaned as though they were in agony. I just smirked at them before sauntering into the attached bathroom for a shower, reveling in the sound of their scrambling footsteps behind me.

25

ASHERA

I watched out of the window of our rooms as my mates, all six of them, led the former King of Qamar onto a balcony that faced the city. Word of the battle in the throne room had been strategically leaked by those in the rebellion to draw a crowd this morning.

"People of Qamar," Winta began, her voice magically enhanced so everyone could hear her. "Last night, I challenged a corrupt ruler and won. I challenged our way of life and won. I challenged how we viewed women and slaves and won. I fought against a tyrant and won." A low rumble started within the crowd as people began to eagerly whisper amongst themselves.

"As I'm sure you're all aware, Shaytan had herself a remarkable queen. One who saw the need for equality and fought for it. I, too, have seen the need for equality. I, too, have fought for it. And I will bring you into a new era. One without slaves. One without women in fear of what a male might do to them.

"This morning, you will witness the death of oppression and the birth of freedom. The general and I will rule Qamar together as equals, and we are formally offering our pledge of allegiance to the kingdom of Shaytan and her new king." The muttering started to grow louder as the people realized that the rumors of my death were true. At least as Winta had led them to believe.

Winta nodded to Thorne. In a move so quick I had a hard time following, Thorne sliced the head off Vaughn's shoulders. A few shouts of protest rang out from within the crowd, but they were mostly silent now. Their shock hit me like a punch to the face.

"As I'm sure some of you know, there has been a resistance building against Queen Ashera's reign, just as I'm sure there will be resistance against our reign here in Qamar. I want those who would join and fight for such a resistance to know this—we will not allow you to win. The death of Queen Ashera has only fueled our resolve to eradicate you from history.

"We will find you. We will not spare you or show you any mercy. You will not be given a chance to comply with our new regime. You will all burn." Well, hot damn. Winta was so much like Visa it was almost frightening. It was little wonder now that she was also meant to be my mate.

Malachi stepped forward, commanding and sinister. Gods, how I loved him.

"Shaytan lost her beloved queen, but make no mistake, I will continue her work. I will continue to fight for justice and equality in all the kingdoms. Her vision will live on through me and the three males who stand behind me—her mates. We will not allow those who murdered our mate to continue to spread their poison."

And I thought I was proud of them last night. I felt tears welling in my eyes as my heart practically burst with my love and pride. We still had a lot of work ahead of us, but I knew that with the seven of us together, there was nothing we couldn't accomplish.

"As a demonstration of our commitment," Mal continued, "this symbol of oppression and tyranny will be burned to the ground." He gestured to the palace. We agreed early this morning that I was going to burn this hideous thing to ash. We already had a route picked out for me that would allow me to exit without being seen so I could join them at Thorne's home.

Those gathered glanced around nervously. I could tell a few in the crowd would run off to the resistance, but the majority of those in attendance supported the changes being made. Their main concern seemed to be centered around the fire, but Caspian would contain it to just the palace as I slipped away.

I took one last look at the room around me before I flipped up my hood. I placed my hand on the bed, a few chairs, and on the doorframe as I walked out of the room. All of them burst into raging infernos the instant my hand made contact. I continued to drag my hand along the wall of the hallway as I made my way back to the passage we'd snuck in here through. Soon, the entire hallway was blazing furiously.

A feeling of righteousness settled within me as I made my way back outside the palace and then to Thorne's home. We were going to burn the resistance just as Winta had claimed.

IT FELT as though it took years for the palace to burn to the ground. In reality, it only took a few hours thanks to the magical fires I'd lit. My mates had all stayed to ensure the fire remained contained to only the palace, and to meet with and talk to some of the people of Qamar.

They were finally back, and I couldn't wait to get my hands all over them. I wanted them all separately tonight. We had dinner together—all seven of us—before Winta and Thorne excused themselves. It tore me up a bit that they couldn't be included, but my four established mates hadn't had time to properly process things, and I wouldn't take on new mates until they felt comfortable.

I ushered them into the room Thorne had designated for us, then I looked at them all before speaking.

"I want to take you all individually tonight." They grinned, more than willing to oblige me.

"Jacobi, Caspian, Ambrose, and then Malachi." They cocked their heads, possibly trying to determine why I'd picked that specific order. Then, with a shrug, Jacobi started to take off his clothes. I did the same, and the others left the room.

He picked me up and threw me onto the bed. I giggled as I bounced a bit. It appeared that my more dominant angel was in a playful mood tonight.

His large cock stood at attention, and I was already so wet I didn't need foreplay. I just wanted to feel them all inside me. I didn't want to wait for it, so I used my enhanced strength to flip Jacobi onto his back before straddling him. My hands steadied me as they rested on his chest. He grabbed his cock and lined it up with my aching pussy, and I slid down his shaft until our hips touched. We both groaned in pleasure.

I gazed deeply into his eyes, not wanting to break the connection as I continued to move. I angled my body in a way that allowed me to grind my clit against him, and my pussy fluttered around him with each downward movement. He brought his hands up and started to play with my nipples. I wanted nothing more than to toss my head back and lose myself in the ecstasy that coursed through every fiber of my being, but I was determined to keep watching him.

Jacobi's jaw clenched as I started to move a bit faster. He was trying to hold off his orgasm until I came, which just made me clench harder around him as I kept moving. His eyes fluttered, and he groaned. I beamed at him.

His grip on my nipples tightened and the small bit of pain mixed with the intense pleasure had me crying out his name. I was so damn close.

"Come around my cock, my love," he rumbled. "I want to feel your sweet pussy milk my cock."

My breath hitched, and I found myself nodding. He removed a hand from my nipple so it could press against my clit, and after a few more thrusts, I was launched into oblivion.

"Just like that." Jacobi thrust his hips against mine a few more times before he followed me. He groaned through his orgasm, his hips jerking under me. When we were finished, I leaned down to press my lips to his. He kissed me as though I was the most precious thing in the world, and thanks to my new gift, I could tell that I *was* the most precious thing in the world to him.

We untangled ourselves, and Jacobi moved to the attached bathroom. I heard the shower turn on as I grinned over at Caspian, who was already naked and approaching the bed. My fae prince had come a long way in such a short amount of time. I was aware that change was difficult for him. He was very much a man who liked to stick to the way he'd always done things, and he certainly didn't like being told how to do anything.

I collapsed onto my back and held my arms out to him. Caspian's eyes shone with both love and desire. I honestly hoped that he never stopped looking at me that way. That look was everything.

He came down on top of me, and I instantly wrapped my arms and legs around him. He chuckled as he bent to press a light kiss first to my forehead and then to my lips. I let out a wistful sigh.

"I need you, Caspian," I mumbled against his lips. He smiled at me, and I couldn't help but smile back.

He groaned, sliding into my pussy with an easy thrust. "And I you, Dick Slayer. Always. Forever. Until the end of time." Each word was punctuated by Caspian moving deeper inside of me. He pushed my knees up to my chest, and I cried out softly, no longer sure where I ended and he began. We moved as one, his pleasure blending into my own.

I gasped, my already sensitive body riding the edge of ecstasy once more. "No more games, Caspian."

His stunning hazel eyes locked onto mine. "Never."

We came at the same time, screaming each other's names to the heavens. This had to be what true bliss felt like—connecting to another soul. Caspian and I shared everything, the good and the bad. He gave me a brief kiss on my forehead. "Next time, I'll make you beg for me, Dick Slayer," he whispered against my ear. I shuddered. I knew he would, and I also knew I would love it.

Caspian pulled himself off the bed. "Princess, get the fuck in here and bed your queen!" he yelled, and I laughed. Ambrose was not going to be amused.

Sure enough, Ambrose strode in with a pissy look on his face. "I told you, you can't fucking call me that, you fae fuck!" He turned around to see me waiting on the bed for him, and his demeanor immediately changed. A predatory smile took over his features, and he tore his pants off as he stalked closer. "Little queen, you look absolutely delicious."

I smiled back at my vampire prince, biting my lip as I stared at the hard cock between his legs. "You'll have to taste me and find out."

"Oh, I plan to." He grabbed my ankles and pulled me to the end of the bed. "But first, you're going to get on your hands and knees for me."

I moaned, already desperate for his cock. I positioned myself on my hands and knees, arching my ass into his hips. "Please."

Ambrose dragged his hand down my spine, my skin tingling wherever he touched, then he slid his heavy cock between my wet folds.

"Who am I to say no to my little queen?" Before I could

respond, he slammed deep inside me, both of us crying out. "Hard and fast, Ashera. Just the way you like it."

I did like it like that. Ambrose enjoyed teasing and tormenting and getting his way, but I also knew he would do anything in his power to please me and to keep me safe, including making me orgasm so hard that I would see stars. Like now, for example, as he thrust desperately into me, using his fingers to play with my clit.

I was so fucking close, arching my back and meeting him thrust for thrust. Release was tingling in my toes and spreading through my veins, and once Ambrose called out my name, I followed suit, shattering into a million pieces.

"Alright, princess, time to let a real man take a turn." Malachi's voice rang out behind me, and then where Ambrose's warm body had been, there was nothing.

I was flipped in the air and placed on my back on the bed, looking up into my assassin's handsome face. Ambrose was muttering, and I heard him storming off into the bathroom.

I leaned up, giving Malachi a light kiss. "Mal."

"Sher, you made me wait until the end."

I shrugged. "Figured you could handle it."

He grunted, forcing my wrists above my head with one of his hands. "You figured wrong. I was desperate listening to them all pleasure you and knowing you wanted us to take turns. I'm not a patient man, Ashera." He dipped his head and scraped his teeth along my neck.

I moaned, arching my body up against his. "Then I guess you need to practice."

I could feel the broad head of his cock nudging against my folds, still slick with the release of my other mates and damp with my own desire. "For a queen, you can be such a brat sometimes."

"And for a king you—" I couldn't finish my sentence,

because Mal slid to the hilt inside of me. He always stretched me in the most delicious way. "What was that for?"

Malachi moved lazily, still pinning my arms above my head. "Call me a king again." His voice was deep and husky with desire.

I grinned, moving my hips in time with his. "You like being called a king?"

"I only want to be *your* king."

I was so drunk on pleasure, my body flooded with the emotions of all my mates. I knew it wouldn't take long for me to come again, but I didn't want to do so without Malachi—my rock, my anchor. I clenched around him, enjoying his haggard moan. "Of course, my king."

Mal roared, his gentle pace no longer slow and easy, but urgent and harsh. I wanted to squeeze him close and run my nails down his back, but he was in control.

"Come for me, my queen," he gritted out.

I did, filled with his release and the heavenly feeling of being at peace, listening to my mate call my name. He finally released my wrists, fell to my side, and curled up against me.

I trailed my finger down his arm. "So, king, eh?"

"Fuck off, Sher," he muttered.

I gently cupped his face in my hands, rubbing my thumbs along his cheeks. "I saved you for last because you're my rock, Malachi. You anchor me and keep me grounded. *You're* the reason I made it through Visa's death, not the rebellion. *You*. I've loved you for centuries."

He stilled under my hands, and his eyes shone with the burst of emotion I felt coming from him—searing love, dedication, pride, and humility. This demon, once the greatest assassin in all Shaytan, a general, and now a king, was humbled by my words. Tears burned the back of my eyes as we continued to stare at each other.

"You're the only thing I've ever wanted for myself, Ashera.

The only thing that has ever mattered more than anything else in this world. It killed me to be near you every day and not have you. You. Are. Everything." Mal leaned down to press a tender kiss to my lips. He pulled back, a mischievous glint in his eyes. "Well... being king matters more."

I laughed loudly. "Should we get cleaned up with the others?"

"In a minute." We were quiet for a couple moments, enjoying the silence between us. With the five of us—now seven—there weren't a lot of one-on-one moments. "Well?"

"Well what?" I asked.

"Well, did you get everything you wanted? I know I did."

Mal was right. I had gotten everything I could have ever hoped for and more while lying awake dreaming during those sleepless nights at Lord Pyper's. I was blessed with my freedom, my mates, and the strength to help free others. The resistance didn't fucking stand a chance, and I felt so peaceful with that realization. I gave Mal an easy smile and shook my head.

"This is more than I ever could have imagined. Sometimes I think I'm still dreaming, but you know what?"

"What?" Mal mumbled sleepily, nuzzling into my neck. My other mates stepped out of the bathroom, one by one, joining us in the bed.

Calm. Content. Peace. "If this is a dream, I don't think I want to wake up."

ABOUT BETH:

Beth is a loving wife and mother—both of the human and fur variety--best friend, enemy, *that* coworker, work wife, hero, all around sarcastic badass, and self-proclaimed Queen of Smut. She advocates to get rid of the stigma around mental health—having CPTSD, anxiety, depression, and panic. She advocates for the understanding of ADHD in girls and women, having ADHD herself, and she wasn't diagnosed until she was thirty. When she isn't writing, she's playing with her young son, getting sassy with her husband, reading with the cats, roughhousing with the doggo, or sleeping for days. She loves to hear from fans and makes an effort to answer any messages sent her way and like any posts she's tagged in.

- Instagram: @authorelizabethbrown
- Twitter: @authorelizabet3
- TikTok: RomanceAuthorBethBrown
- Facebook Group: Beth's Resurrected Queens
- Subscribe to my website: authorelizabethbrown.com
  (I blog, provide a twice weekly newsletter, and post **extras** from all my series!)

- Feel free to shoot me an email: authorelizabethbrown@gmail.com

ABOUT TORRI:

Torri has always loved control. Her mind was blown when she discovered she could control entire worlds through story writing. Throw some steamy romance in there, and it was pretty close to perfection. Torri loves dark heroes who ride off into the sunset on their motorcycles, fierce heroines who can fend for themselves, and a sprinkle of the paranormal to keep things interesting. When she's not creating alternate realities, you can find her managing her three-ring circus of kids and animals.

- Instagram: @torriheat
- Twitter: @torriheat
- TikTok: @torriheat
- Facebook Group: Heat's Hotties
- Subscribe to my newsletter over at www.torriheat.com
- Feel free to shoot me an email at torriheat@gmail.com

OTHER BOOKS BY BETH:

Discovery of a Queen (The Resurrection of Queens, Book 1) — Now available on all platforms!

Vengeance of a Queen (The Resurrection of Queens, Book 2) — July 1, 2021

OTHER BOOKS BY TORRI:

Nyctophilia (Darkling, Book 1) — Ebook Available now!

Caligo (Darkling, Book 2) — Ebook Available now!

The Ruins (Watcher, Book 1) — Ebook Available now!

Nighted (Darkling, Book 3) — June, 2021

OTHER BOOKS BY BETH AND TORRI:

Book 2 in the Freedom's Harem series will be coming out some time in 2021! (We haven't officially picked a title or a date for release, but if you follow us on any of our social media platforms, we'll keep you updated!)